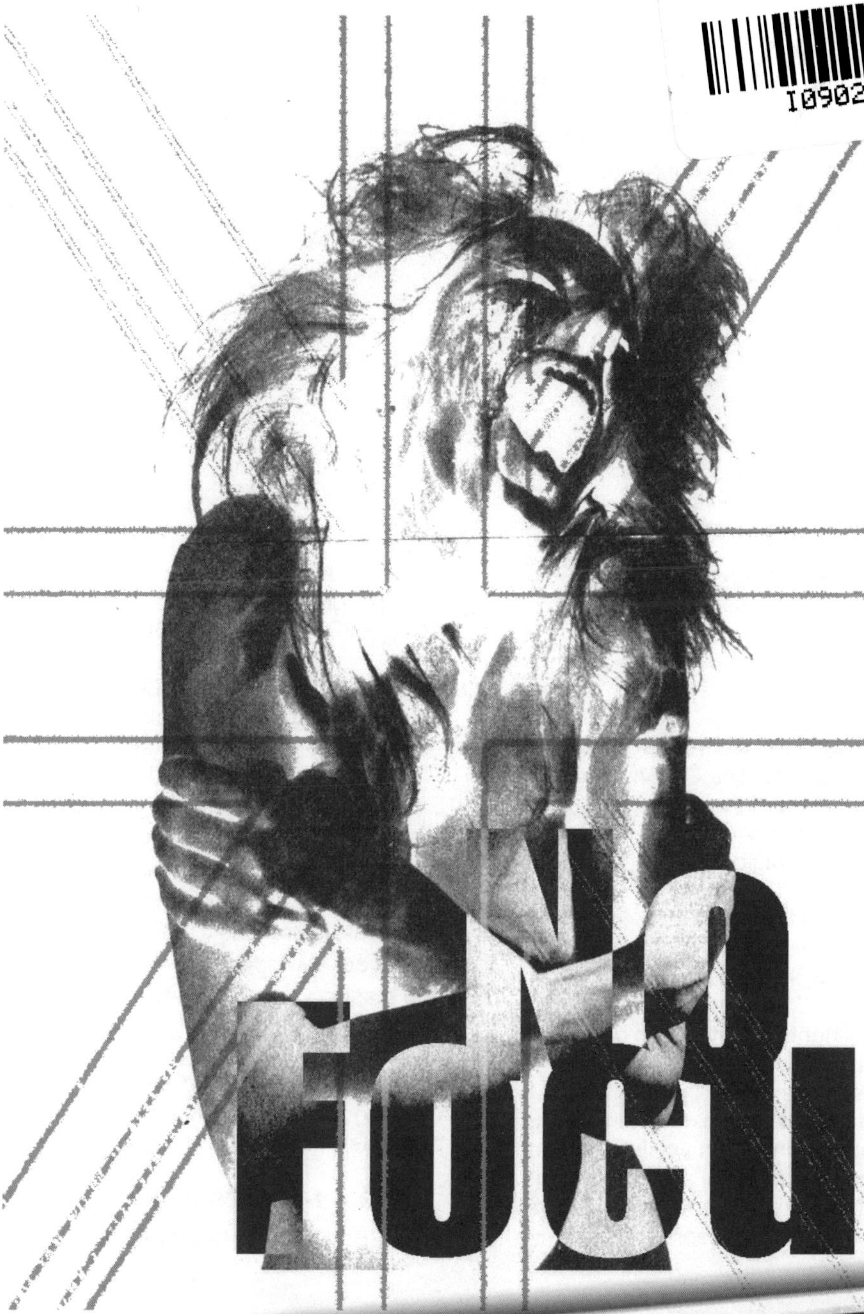

No Focus

Chris Barber & Jack Sargeant

"onetwothreefour!"

headpress

A Headpress Book
Published in 2006

Headpress
Suite 306, The Colourworks
2a Abbot Street
London, E8 3DP
United Kingdom

[**tel**] 0845 330 1844
[**email**] nofocus@headpress.com
[**web**] headpress.com

No Focus

Book design & cover: Hannah Bennison
Cover image: Sex Pistols
Title page image courtesy Richard Kern

Grateful acknowledgement is made to the respective studios, artists and distributors.

British Library CIP Data
A catalogue record for this book is available from the British Library

ISBN **1-900486-59-8**
EAN/ISBN13 **9781900486590**

Contents

Acknowledgements

Thanks to David Kerekes for his support and enthusiasm, and to Hannah Bennison for her design and editing; contributing authors and comrades, Stephen, David, Gavin, Neil, Tessa, Richard, Lance and Mark, each of whom wrote their superb contributions free of any payment (the great book'n'roll swindle!); Tony Ratcliff for technical assistance; Will at the Screen on the Green, Islington; Jill at BFI press/publicity; Ruby Ray for permission to use her previously unpublished photographs; Richard Kern, Lee Oliver for help in sourcing films and visual materials; Mark Bennett and Julian Weaver for technical support. Finally, our gratitude to Grant Pettitt for his support.

Chris Barber: Special thanks to my partner Gavin Mitchell, for help and support throughout; co-writer/editor Jack, without whose assistance this book could not have been 'filmed.'

Jack Sargeant: Special thanks to Roslyn for her love and help, Monte Cazazza, Michael Spann and Andrew Leavold for their insights.

"One. Two. Three, Four."

Punk was (and perhaps is) wildly schizophrenic. To even speak of punk is in someway nonsense. Like all radical culture punk was a savage rupture, tearing into and through dominant mainstream culture. But like its precursors — the romantics, Dada, surrealism, the beats — punk tore into culture without setting any new rules, beyond savagely challenging convention. And afterwards it remained centre stage:

> ...what looks like a possible rebirth of true rebel music, hope in its eventual victory over the bland products professional pop stars have been feeding us. May the punks set this rat infested industry on fire. It sure could use a little brightness [1]

Punk was part of a continuum of radical artistic rebellion and of self-expression; it did not emerge fully formed from the ether, rather it had roots in sixties garage punk, glam rock, and the rebellious rock of The MC5 and The Stooges. Despite this it was also a breaking away from previous subcultures. Punk's most radical gesture was the realisation of the do-it-yourself mentality of learning a handful of chords and forming a band, or running a record label, or producing a fanzine. The massive explosion of independent record labels and publications throughout the eighties was the praxis of this aesthetic.

If you believe the pop-mythology it was simple: there was before punk and there was after punk. And nothing was the same again. But even as it hit the media, following the Sex Pistols' now mythic appearance on the *Today* programme, the tabloids stamping and shouting their disgust damning "The Filth And The Fury," it was over. Yet conversely it had not even started, the media shock and rage inadvertently inspiring discontented suburban kids across the western world. The initial personalities and bands, most of whom never embraced the limits imposed by the name punk, moved on artistically and musically, but teenagers across the globe whose only knowledge of the form came from rumours, half truths, and outright lies spun via the dominant media were galvanized.

Punk embraced disparate contradictions. While proponents valued individuality, independence and rebellion, its most recognisable manifestation to the general public was the Sex Pistols, considered (clearly inaccurately) by some at least, as nothing but a quasi-manufactured boy band complete with svengali manager, rather than as the garage band they were. Its earliest (unwitting) icons wore cheap thrift-store clothes because they were poor; its followers brought designer bondage trousers and mass produced T-shirts declaiming rejection.

Punk was somehow sexless, as John Lydon observed: "By the time you're twenty you think — yawn — just another squelch session."[2] Yet its American antecedents were utterly queer, lapping up and affirming joyful sexual deviance, for example the S&M *mise en scene* of the Velvet Underground, the predatory raw sexual power of The Stooges, the sleaze and drag of the New York Dolls, and the demand to "fuck me or fuck off" of Wayne County and the Electric Chairs. In marked contrast punk's stage-diving shaven headed hardcore descendents were often absurdly macho, fired up in the mosh-pit like marines on basic training, a literal manifestation of the homosocial.

Punk claimed bored nihilism, for example Richard Hell and the Voidoids' Blank Generation, Destroy All Monsters' Bored, and the Sex Pistols' Pretty Vacant, but groups spun through various radical political perspectives (from both ends of the spectrum). Anarchism became a statement of personal abjection and social rejection for those such as G G Allen, and a reawakening of notions of libertarian pacifism for Crass.

Punk was presented by the tabloid media as ignorant pogoing and gobbing stupidity, but it was embedded within avant-garde traditions ranging from poetry to bubblegum pop. Its most exciting proponents mixed radical aesthetic and philosophical ideas with stripped down re-workings of rock (see: Television, the Voidoids, The Saints, The Fall, This Heat, PiL), its most musically accessible groups became by default pop music (see: The Ramones, the Sex Pistols, Blondie).

To many, punk was a return to 'authentic' rock'n'roll, free of the excesses of seventies prog and pomp rock exemplified by Deep Purple and Yes. But while Suicide's version of punk embraced the raw Elvis yelps and pelvic thrusts of rock'n'roll, it mixed these with wild synth sounds and electronic rhythms: a sonic palette antithetical to previous rock incarnations.

Conversely, by the early eighties, hardcore — save for a handful of bands — was reduced to a blur of generic thrash, its followers steadfast in their refusal to consider anything beyond the rigid form. In its earliest incarnation punk advocated libertarian individualism, bands as diverse as Pere Ubu and the Germs were both in some way viewed as punk, but both had a unique style and embraced personal expression and musical experimentation. While some visionaries, such as DNA, Butthole Surfers, The Birthday Party, Sonic Youth and Black Flag, followed their own radical visions, by the early eighties punk had also given birth to some absurdly conformist uniformed tribes, largely becoming dumbed down and eventually reduced to a caricature of itself.

Punk cinema is a construction of various films that fulfil a collective notion of punk because of their themes, subjects, stripped back gritty style, and because of their attitude. Some of the films included here, such as *The Decline of Western Civilization* (1981) or *Jubilee* (1978), are clearly punk because they were made by those from within the subculture who appreciated how best to depict their interests and lives. Other films come from within the punk and post-punk underground; radical visions that share with punk a sense of urgency, rage, nihilism, radicalism and subversion.

Others such as *Meantime* (1983) or *Scum* (1977) are punk because of their sense of rotting urban aesthetics and political outrage. The inclusion of some films may superficially appear as strange, but *Taxi Driver* (1976) and *The Driller Killer* (1979) are punk films because they share a visceral sense of disgust at the swollen and bloated seventies, stripping back the gloss to reveal the shit beneath. It is hardly a surprise that these films found an audience amongst punks, or that *Taxi Driver*'s Travis Bickle's bloody gun-toting visage became an iconographic image on numerous T-shirts.

Then there's exploitation. The moment that the first tabloid editor rolled his eyes, clicked his tongue in mock outrage at punk antics and wrote the first headline it became apparent that there was money to be made from punks. Punksploitation and juvenile delinquency movies are some of the most popular manifestations of punk culture.

In *No Focus* punk cinema emerges across genres, forms and styles — like punk it knows no limits, like punk it may be contradictory, and like punk all the contributors and their subjects reflect personal interpretations of the questions raised by the notion of punk and film.

Jack Sargeant, Brighton, Halloween 2005

Notes

1 Claude Bessy aka Claude Kickboy Bessy, 'So This Is War, Eh?' *Slash*, no. 1, July, 1977, quoted in Marc Spitz and Brendan Mullen, *We Got The Neutron Bomb: The Untold Story of LA Punk*, Three Rivers Press: NY, 2001, p.81.

2 Jon Savage, *England's Dreaming: Sex Pistols and Punk Rock*, Faber & Faber: London, p.189.

Politics

Chris Barber

Punk cinema – like punk rock, is ANTI-GENRE!

Journalists in the mainstream music press first applied the term 'punk rock' as a music category in 1976. It did not strictly define a shared style, but served as a catchall category for a diverse cornucopia of new bands that burst onto the rock music scene that year. The label was applied to angry agit-prop rock bands like the Sex Pistols and The Clash, pub rock R&B outfits like the Tom Robinson Band, rock'n'roll revivalists like Eddie and the Hot Rods, and noise experimentalists like Throbbing

Gristle; numerous other musical influences included glam rock, heavy metal, psychedelic, pop and reggae. What all the new generation of groups had in common was that none of them fitted neatly into established music-market categories.

Dick Hebdidge says it better in *Subculture*:

> A new style was being generated combining elements drawn from a whole range of heterogeneous youth styles... Strands from David Bowie and glitter-rock were woven together with elements from American proto-punk (The Ramones, The Heartbreakers, Iggy Pop, Richard Hell), from that faction within London pub-rock (The 101-ers, The Gorillas, etc.) inspired by the mod subculture of the sixties, from the Canvey Island forties revival and the Southend R&B bands (Dr Feelgood, Lew Lewis, etc.), from northern soul, and from reggae. Not surprisingly, the resulting mix was somewhat unstable: all these elements threatened to separate and return to their original sources. Glam rock contributed narcissism, nihilism and gender confusion. American punk offered minimalist aesthetic: the cult of the street and a penchant for self-laceration. Northern soul brought its subterranean tradition of fast, jerky rhythms, solo dance styles and amphetamines; reggae its exotic and dangerous aura of forbidden identity, its conscience, its dread and its cool. Native rhythm'n'blues reinforced the brashness and the speed of Northern soul, took rock back to its basics and contributed a highly developed sense of iconoclasm, a thoroughly British persona and an extremely selective appropriation of the rock'n'roll heritage. [1]

The system of modern music genres was a marketing device developed by record multi-nationals to maximise sales, by telling consumers what sound they were buying. Since the rock/pop boom a decade or so earlier record sales had become big business. To gain maximum advantage of the recently emerged youth-with-disposable-income market, record companies seized control of the music business; via controlling what was played on the airwaves. Performing artists were tied to contracts and the supergroups were invented (like Genesis and Yes) — their status guaranteed by promotional saturation, limiting consumer choice and offering mass-produced musical products... You swallowed this shit so here's more of the same!

The first rule of punk genre is there is NO punk genre... Punk sub genre movies, like punk rock, defy audience expectations! This book is not establishing punk cinema as a new (sub) genre. It is a perambulation of the concerns shared by a diverse range of films, which pre-figured, were contemporaneous with, are inspired by, or exhibit the influence of punk rock.

Punk rock is egalitarian, encouraging you to engage in production — your creative expression, as well as consumption; now a blurred duality. No more professional artistic maestros or star performers to be worshipped... Anyone can have a go! Amateurs, fans and spectators can make a noise too. Or fashion your own sartorial look, clothes, outfits, garments via cheap home-designer, do-it-yourself creativity (safety-pins, zips, tears, bondage-straps, leather and rubber fetish gear).

Many punk films owe a huge debt to Surrealism and Dada, sharing similar cultural targets for their attacks: the culture industry, social hypocrisy, public complacency, audience complicity, and organised religion, class… Punk cinema also frequently employs tactics from avant-garde theatre to attack the audience, in particular Brechtian agit-prop and Situationist street theatre.

Another especially persistent target for punk movies, based on an awareness of how censorship has long been one of the most powerful weapons deployed by the state, politicians, the church and the military establishment, was how citizens were controlled through propaganda and morality. Because art and cinema are realms of representation that do not physically hurt anyone, extensive censorial interference in these areas over many years is something every competent filmmaker is aware of. While mainstream filmmakers tend to conform to prevailing censorship (to ensure certification), punk movies repeatedly confront and challenge censorship, attempting to force back the boundaries. Derek Jarman, Julian Temple, Paul Cox, Penelope Spheeris, Don Letts, Bruce la Bruce… Are there any punk auteurs or is the director OUT OF CONTROL?

After WWII, a new movie-literate generation flocked to the movies. American films dominated even the European market, but alternative approaches to film production were evolving which did not fit comfortably into Hollywood genres. In particular, Italy's Neo-Realist cinema offered films casting ordinary working class people (instead of professional actors), depicting their lives in poverty during the post-war depression, with political didacticism. Depressingly real and challenging to audiences, they relied essentially on the director's artistic vision.

The status and influence of the film critic was also growing as more sophisticated audiences, now accustomed to cinema and offered a wider choice of films, scanned the popular media for reviews. Auteur theory was developed by a group of film aficionados and critics in France. Their love of cinema covered all expressions, from Hollywood mainstream to European art films. Borrowing and adapting from critical approaches to literature, the director is regarded as an author or artist, organising his technicians, actors etc. to create his vision on celluloid. The co-operative efforts of film production are ignored, instead the director's intentions are seen as paramount. The director becomes the individual responsible for the film's successes or failings.

In a sense, with increasing consumer awareness and product sophistication, Auteurism became the latest genre — a more specialised marketing category by which ad-men (or critics) could flog more movies to discerning consumers. Now the category was not based on linking plot themes shared by movies arranged to meet audience expectations. Instead, Auteurism followed market strategies pertaining to the publishing trade, putting an individual in the spotlight, in this instance the floor manager or top on-set technician — the director. This maximised bums-on-seats by selling to two consumer groups, genres for the mass market and auteurs for discerning professionals: John Ford's westerns, comedies by Howard Hawkes etc… But when market demand for Cowboys and Indians slumped (due to elasticity of price demand, over production and market saturation) Ford could manufacture social dramas based on best-selling novels (like *The Grapes of Wrath* or *How Green Was My Valley*). Add the John Ford reliability logo to the product, alongside a box-office star (like Henry Fonda) and you got another bestseller! Here was the director as star, a new hero/logo, less vulgar than the star-sell, so appealing to wealthier, middle class consumers.

Critics kept themselves busy by pointing out recurrent themes in a director's output, psychoanalytic sub-texts, shot continuity, progressive craftsmanship, stylised nuances, and so on. All amounting to the creative genius of each particular director.

Punk cinema challenges and opposes this systematic approach.

Feature film production is a co-operative or group process. With few exceptions, a director relies on skilled writers, actors, editors, cameramen, sound engineers, wardrobe and set designers, lighting technicians, stuntmen and so on to produce the final cut. Further, continuous directorial improvement, from one film to the next, is a blatantly silly notion. And the innate creative genius of the artist — be he painter, musician or director, is a dumb myth which ignores commitment, hard work, experience, financial capability and technical skill.

There are also significant, one-off punk influenced movies, made early in the careers of directors, who later achieved both critical acclaim and box-office appeal, like Mike Leigh's *Meantime*, Steven Frears with *My Beautiful Laundrette* (1985), even *Death Warmed Up* (1985). Each of these films was made within a more conventional production framework, still very alternative to Hollywood and allowing a large degree of directorial control, more akin to the European art movie tradition.

Then there is the independently produced exploitation film (like *Breaking Glass,* 1980) largely intent on making producers a quick profit from youth trends, but usually only demanding directors keep productions on schedule and within a limited budget. Until the late 1980s this low-budget, quick production tradition got very little critical attention, but actually enabled a plethora of fabulous, cult-orientated films to be made (sadly *Breaking Glass* is not a good example, but *Suburbia* [1984] is).

Finally, like every other cultural expression once its commercial viability has been established, punk influence was represented in Hollywood blockbusters — initiated by *Blade Runner* (1982) — courtesy set design, make-up and costumes.

If punk movies do not fit neatly into a genre and these filmmakers are not auteurs in the established sense, how should we view them? Further, all of these filmmakers subsequently directed features exhibiting no traces of punk (thereby excluding auteur analysis), so how can the relationship between punk and filmmaker be explored?

For the purposes of this book and with the help of you, the reader, two loosely applied punk approaches are proposed: catalyst and attitude.

Catalyst This is a very punkified and unrigorous interpretation of an extremely rigorous critical model, Cine-Auteurism, espoused by the filmmaker and critic, Peter Wollen (without his approval).

Effectively, punk subculture as a whole and its expression in cinema are viewed as catalysts which inspire particular filmmakers towards a related mode of production, or incorporate relevant themes in some of their movies. Simultaneously, some filmmakers (especially those named in this chapter and involved with punk from its inauguration) are also catalysts whose approach to film production or concerns with content, can be regarded as contributing to — or defining — punk subculture. By each serving as a catalyst, it enables a mutual exchange of ideas and concepts, between filmmaker and his/her productions, and their evolving socio-cultural milieu. Hardcore punk cinema is defined by the spaces where these two catalysts overlap, an interactive process. This method allows distinctions to be made between modes of production and concerns of content. It recognises the creative development of punk itself, its artistic sources and cinematic sources, and the directions it mutated in (like the post-industrial). Further, it lets punk films be coherently reviewed, whether as individual productions, groups sharing thematic concerns, or defined via artistic integrity.

Attitude If punk rock is anti-music and punk cinema is anti-genre, punk subculture cannot be explained as a coherent/unified movement. Some saw it as fashion — just a passing fad. For others it was an alternative lifestyle; the vanguard of a sweeping cultural revolution. As the anger and spontaneity abated a couple of years after it swept throughout urban Britain, and the counter reaction set in (with the election of Thatcher's Conservative government in 1979), punk appeared to be a transient pose. But as the punk generation matured, a slow, quiet cultural revolution had indeed taken place. Perhaps not in the way young punk rockers had envisaged, but nevertheless monumental in the way its influence has infused and transformed almost every aspect of life in Britain. And mercifully there's no going back.

What punk inspired was ATTITUDE — sensibility. A generation of angry and intelligent citizens who were and are prepared to say NO to governments, bosses, the police, the establishment, parents… the state apparatus in all its authoritarian guises. Although aspirations have been lowered, many ambiguously expressed objectives have been surpassed or become irrelevant with the passage of time. And the attitude remains, silent but belligerent; if not opposing then at least exposing every expression of hypocrisy, corruption, injustice, and the lies and propaganda spewed out by arrogant, self-inflated rulers.

Notes

1 Dick Hebdidge, *Subculture: the Meaning of Style*, London: Methuen & Co, 1979. p 25–26.

25 Years On: Julien Temple and

The Great Rock 'n' Roll Swindle

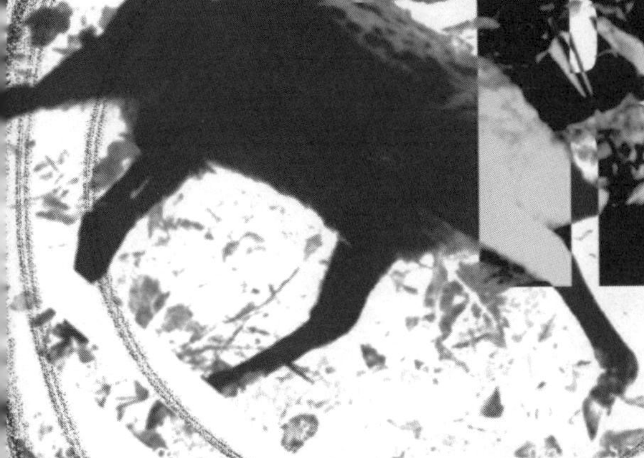

David McGillivray

In 1980 the American trade

paper, *Variety*, famously hailed *The Great Rock'n'Roll Swindle* (1980), directed by the unknown Julien Temple, as "the *Citizen Kane* (1941) of rock'n'roll pictures". The conceit of comparing a new masterpiece to the film that is regularly voted the best ever made has been much imitated. Thus *Café Flesh* (1982) was the *Citizen Kane* of porn, *Moulin Rouge* (2001) was the *Citizen Kane* of musicals. Last year, Jack Black told a *Guardian* reporter that his next film, *The Pick of Destiny* (2006), will be another "*Citizen Kane* of rock movies." But predicting a legend is a risky business. What if the next generation doesn't see it your way? Twenty-five years down the line, is *The Great Rock'n'Roll Swindle* still a masterpiece?

Until recently this question has been difficult to answer. Because of arguments over ownership of the Sex Pistols' name, the film has been unavailable. Director Julien Temple is also a hard man to find. "He never returned my calls," complained a journalist who interviewed him for the magazine *American Film* in 1989. Nowadays Julien doesn't reply to e-mails. But in January of this year, weeks before this book was due to go to press, there was a turn of events. With hostilities at an end, it was announced that *Swindle* would be re-released on DVD. Then, out of the blue, I got a response from Julien. He was due in London to do the film's director's commentary and willing to talk to me afterwards. We met at the Groucho Club. "I used to hate this place," Julien told me, "but you mellow with age."

Julien could only spare me an hour and there was a lot of ground to cover. When I first saw *Swindle* at its press show in 1980, I agreed with the *Variety* verdict. But I didn't understand the film. Contemporary reviews and articles were no help. We had all been battered almost senseless by Julien's genius and nobody asked any questions. But now I wanted to know what the Cambridge Rapist, the Gordon Riots and Martin Bormann had to do with the Sex Pistols. I was like Steve Jones in the film, probing Malcolm McLaren's secret affairs.

Julien's life sounds incredible from the day he was born. His parents apperently named him after "St Julien," a brand of tobacco his mother smoked in her pipe? He adds that he would have preferred to be called Wat. "I like the questioning nature of the name," he says, "although I do admire Wat Tyler a lot." (Tyler led the Peasants' Revolt of 1381.) Julien studied architecture and history at Cambridge but then saw Godard's *Le Mépris* (1963), a film about film-making, and was inspired to apply for a place at the National Film School. It was 1976. He was taking "a *lot* of acid" (he told the *Sunday Express* in 1986) and affecting a Byronic look. He won his place at the NFS, "I think because they thought I was gay," he claims.

In the summer of 1976 Julien was in Rotherhithe, east London, when he heard what turned out to be the Sex Pistols playing in a warehouse. The music changed his life and he became a punk. "I can remember missing buses because I couldn't run in my bondage trousers," he told the *Sunday Times* in 1989. The story often told is that Julien and fellow students began filming Pistols gigs with a camera 'borrowed' from the film school: "We put it back every morning," he informed. He remembers that producer David Puttnam visited the school and asked the students for film ideas. Coincidentally somebody else suggested a documentary about this new punk group called the Sex Pistols. Puttnam scoffed, "This film will never be made," which Julien thought was funny because "We were making it!"

Julien soon came up against the Pistols' manager, Malcolm McLaren, who wouldn't allow any unauthorised film of the band. (In the mid seventies a big new chart act was still expected to follow a hit with a feature film, and McLaren was already looking for Hollywood finance.) Julien had to start smuggling the camera into venues. He was caught and thrown out of the celebrated 100 Club gig. But gradually Julien won McLaren around. "I suppose he thought, well, they're kids with energy, they've got a free camera, why not?" Julien says. "We filmed the

Pistols until the autumn of 1977." This material became the shorts *Sex Pistols No. 1* (premiered at the Screen on the Green in Islington, north London), *Jubilee Riverboat* a.k.a. *Sex Pistols No. 2*, and *The Sex Pistols in Stockholm*. For some reason the latter two films are credited to John Tiberi, the Pistols' roadie. But they were made by Julien. "Tiberi couldn't direct traffic," says Pistols' historian Alan Parker.

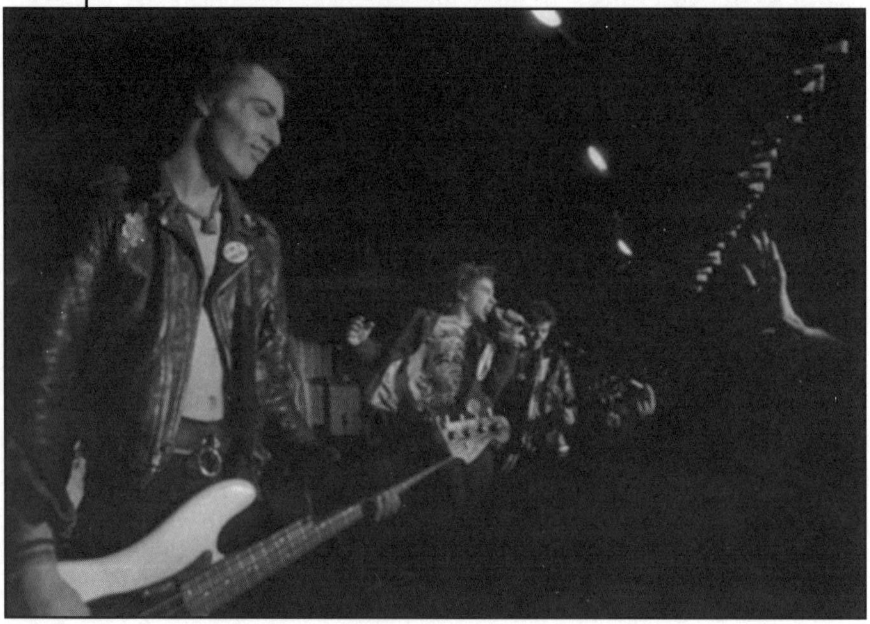

Shortly after the Grundy fiasco (December 1, 1976) and the Pistols' first hit, Anarchy In The UK, McLaren did a deal with Warner Brothers and Twentieth Century Fox for a Pistols feature film, budgeted at £200,000, to be directed by American softcore porn mogul Russ Meyer, renowned for his love of big breasts. McLaren admired Meyer's *Beyond the Valley of the Dolls* (1970) and reputedly wanted something along the same lines, but much stronger. (There is a reference in *Swindle* to "a script so disgusting it couldn't possibly be made.") An early treatment, *Anarchy in the UK*, written by McLaren himself, features the Gordon Riots, which were to be shot in sets from the musical *Oliver!*, at the time still standing at Shepperton Studios. Other writers McLaren auditioned included Johnny Speight (*Till Death Us Do Part*) and Graham Chapman (*Monty Python*).

The first person to make an attempt at a screenplay was probably Dutch writer-director René Daalder, who in 1974 had written *Hollywood Tower* for Meyer. It was never filmed, but before coming to London Daalder had completed a splatter movie, *Massacre at Central High* (1976). At least one website claims that Sid Vicious' performance of My Way, which is in *Swindle*, originates in Daalder's script. It's unlikely (read on). Daalder was then replaced by another of Meyer's writers,

Roger Ebert. Ebert was "locked in a flat in Primrose Hill" and eventually came up with the screenplay of *Who Killed Bambi?* — the source of one of the most confusing elements of *Swindle*: the Mick Jagger-style rock star (James Aubrey) who is murdered by McLaren but turns up later in the plot to watchVicious sing My Way.

Julien, who worked as an assistant to Meyer, was one of many who knew that *Who Killed Bambi?* would never be completed. Meyer knew little about punk and the more he saw, the less he liked. "The flat-chestedness was anathema to him," Julien says. Nevertheless Meyer began auditions. One of the people he saw was Alan Jones (formerly an assistant in McLaren's shop Sex and currently a film critic and authority on Dario Argento). Alan remembers McLaren saying to Meyer, "This is Alan. I want him to play one of the queers" (a reference to the gay group, The Blow Waves, who raped Paul Cook). Alan read something from the script, but was interrupted by Meyer, who left the room to have sex with his girlfriend, stripper Kitten Natividad. Both Johnny Rotten and Sid Vicious opposed McLaren's choice of Meyer, and Rotten showed his displeasure by turning up to an audition disguised as a hippy.

The filming of *Who Killed Bambi?* was suspended by McLaren after two days. Meyer referred to McLaren as "Hitler." Furious that he had no control over Meyer, McLaren sacked him. The only sequence filmed involved James Aubrey, strongman Dave Prowse (the body but not the voice of Darth Vader) and a little girl. Notoriously, a deer was killed for real. Julien remembers Meyer being "quite friendly" and was amused by him. "When he said, 'Action!', it was like he was back in the Korean war," he recalls. He implied in another interview that the deer was killed by Meyer. Meyer threatened to sue until Julien apologised. "I despise Mr Temple," stormed Meyer after Julien had replaced him as director, "He's a treacherous, no good, son of a bitch."

Undeterred, McLaren sent for another American soft porn director, Jonathan Kaplan, who had made *Student Teachers* (1973) and *Night Call Nurses* (1972). (In 1988 Kaplan directed Jodie Foster in *The Accused*.) The plan was to start again, with a new script about a Woodstock-type festival, but minus the peace and love. Kaplan brought a writer to London and he too was set up in a flat, this time near Baker Street. After a while he began having hallucinations. He was a junkie. The project was abandoned and McLaren turned to the director often referred to as Britain's Russ Meyer — Pete Walker. Walker had graduated from soft porn to four horror films written by me. But we had fallen out and so he asked my friend, Michael Armstrong, the man who wrote *The Sex Thief* (1973) and *Eskimo Nell* (1975), to pen yet another new script for the Pistols. This was *A Star Is Dead*, a riposte to *A Star Is Born* (1954). It was an appropriate vehicle — the Pistols are exploited by a film company — but it required all four Pistols to give performances of which three would have been incapable and one (Rotten) would have refused. As it turned out, none of them was required to do anything. In January 1978, two weeks after Armstrong had delivered his first draft, the Pistols broke up in the wake of an infamous American tour. Rotten returned to the UK, reverted to his real name, John Lydon, formed Public Image Ltd., and announced that he would have no further dealings with McLaren.

At this point, most producers would have thrown in the towel. But McLaren didn't. He was determined to see his Sex Pistols movie on the screen and, as he could think of no more porn directors, he offered the project to the man who had been around from the beginning — Julien Temple. Together Julien and McLaren wrote yet another treatment, this time a quasi-documentary charting the Pistols' rise and fall, but suggesting, fancifully, that everything had been engineered by McLaren as a ruse to make money. The new project comprised Julien's short films; animation representing well-known incidents that had not been recorded (the Pistols vomiting at an airport and wrecking an hotel room); TV programmes Julien had filmed from the TV screen; and new footage, some of it inspired by *Who Killed Bambi?,* much of it influenced by Julien's film studies. Julien also wanted to copy Orson Welles' new film, *F For Fake* (1974), in which Welles cheekily presented fiction as fact. Jeremy Thomas, who had been involved in *Who Killed Bambi?*, remained on board as executive producer and, claims Julien, influenced the comic tone of the film. (Jeremy is the son of Ralph Thomas, director of the *Doctor* series and other saucy British comedies.)

These factors explain why the film that was finally completed — *The Great Rock'n'Roll Swindle* — looks the way it does. It was so successful that many people probably believe that it's a historical document. But as Julien told the *Daily Telegraph* in 1999, "It was meant to be a joke on many levels, to puncture the way people put them [the Pistols] on a pedestal. I think in the end Malcolm really did believe that he had done what we were spoofing in the film. It became his reality."

The Great Rock'n'Roll Swindle begins with a figure in a bondage mask, who says that he is Malcolm McLaren and that he wants to tell us about his greatest success: punk rock. The remainder of the film is divided into ten chapters or "lessons," supposedly a primer on how to fool the public while making money.

Lesson 1, "How to Manufacture Your Group," is introduced by dwarf Helen Wellington-Lloyd (as Helen of Troy). McLaren declares that it is essential that the members of the group hate each other and can't play. He introduces Steve Jones (a former "cat burglar"), Paul Cook ("a typical lout"), Johnny Rotten (whose name was inspired by his "green teeth") and Sid Vicious (to ensure an "unpredictable bloody mess"). Julien's re-creation of the Gordon Riots, in which Lord George Gordon's mob of 50,000 protesters ruled London for five days as a protest against Catholic emancipation, establishes the concept of "anarchy in the UK." Julien's spurious audition for a replacement for Rotten, filmed in 1978, attracted a layabout named Edward Tudor-Pole, who claimed to be descended from Henry VIII. During a break for lunch, Julien noticed Eddie with a cigarette held between the sole and the upper of his worn-out shoe. He kicked his foot, releasing the fag, which he caught in his mouth. Purely on the strength of this trick, Julien offered Eddie a role in *Swindle*. He appears at the end as a kiosk attendant at a grindhouse, the Classic Moulin, and sings Who Killed Bambi? (Subsequently he became a character actor. He was also in *Sid and Nancy*.)

Lesson 2, "Establish the Name," features the Pistols performing Anarchy In The UK on the TV show *So It Goes* (as recorded by Julien).

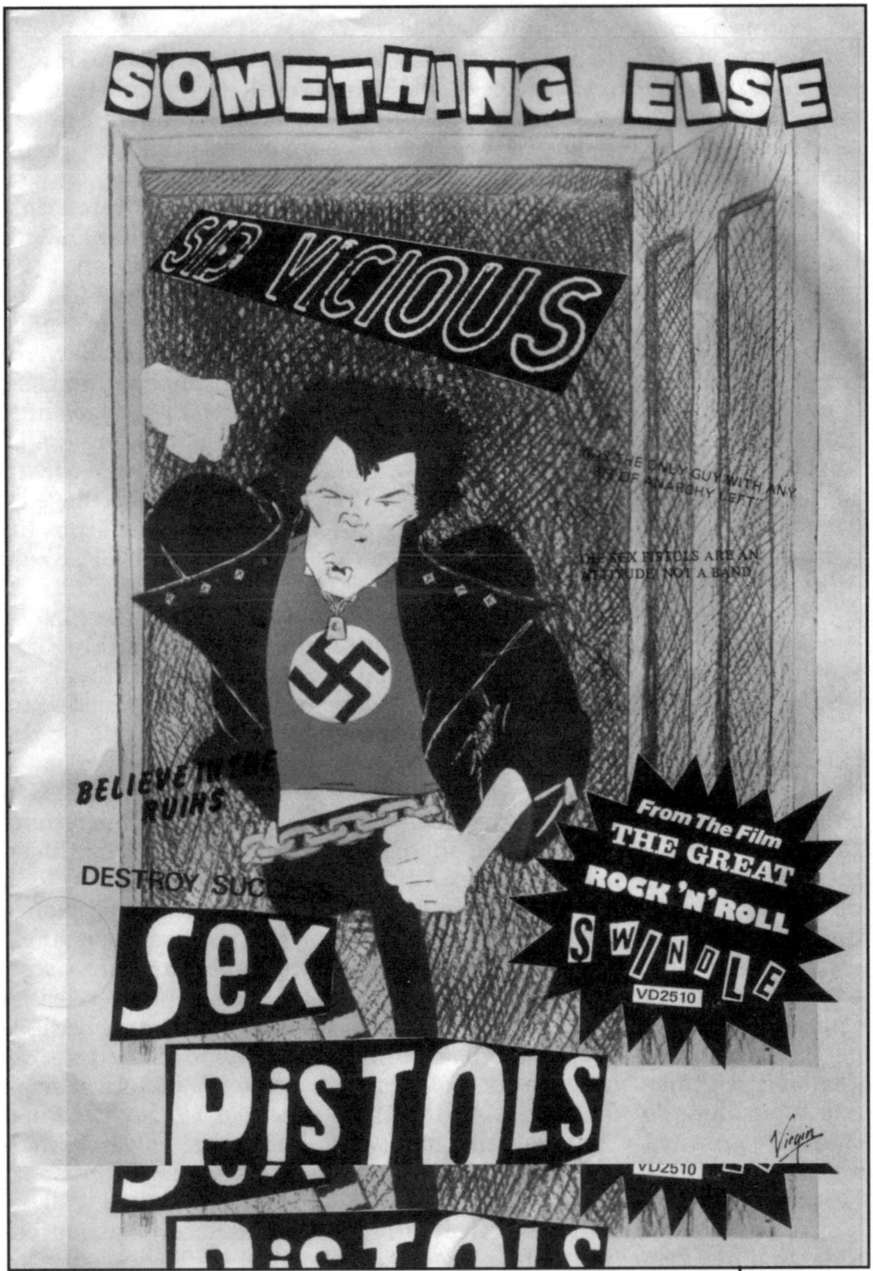

Above and p24: ads from *Zig Zag*, Mar 1979

Steve Jones then makes his first appearance as a private eye, prowling Soho as he tries to discover what McLaren has done with the money he earned from the Pistols. After passing various shady establishments, Jones breaks into the office of McLaren's company, Glitterbest. (Glitterbest was in fact financing *Swindle* with royalties earned from the Pistols' records on Virgin.)

Lesson 3, "How to Sell," includes interviews with real-life A&R men Dave Dee, Doug D'Arcy and Nick Mobbs, who recall early Pistols gigs. "I went back two or three times," says Dee, "to make sure they were as bad as I thought they were the first time." McLaren reveals that the Pistols signed to EMI, which released Anarchy In The UK.

One of the longest chapters, Lesson 4, "Do Not Play," represents the first six months of 1977, a time when everyone was talking about the Pistols, but nobody could see them perform. The Bill Grundy TV interview is re-created (Thames TV refused McLaren the rights to the original broadcast) and this incident inspires the *Daily Mirror*'s "The Filth and the Fury" headline. The Greater London Council's Bernard Brook-Partridge, who was in charge of licensing public premises, splutters that the Pistols' music is "nauseating, disgusting, degrading, ghastly, sleazy, prurient, voyeuristic and generally nauseating [*sic*]." Christians in Caerphilly demonstrate against a Pistols concert. We learn that EMI cancelled the Pistols' contract, but that McLaren allegedly pocketed £50,000. At a party thrown by A&M Records Jones drops his pants and shits on a gold record awarded for the Pistols' first LP, *Never Mind the Bollocks Here's the Sex Pistols.*

Lesson 5, "Get Off the Label," shows A&M picking up the Pistols' contract (for a further £50,000) with a signing outside Buckingham Palace. (The Pistols never recorded for A&M and signed finally to Virgin. Because Virgin was indirectly financing *Swindle* and ended up distributing it, this is not mentioned. Subsequent sequences refer to the fictitious Mamie Records.)

Lesson 6, "Tourist Attraction," shows the Pistols performing God Save The Queen on a boat on the Thames. Vicious then sings Something Else in a promo shot by Julien in the spring of 1978. It was filmed in a squat off the Edgware Road, where there just happened to be a motorcycle. Vicious wanted to ride it. So he did. His girlfriend, Nancy Spungen, can be seen watching him. (The song was released as a single after Vicious' death the following year.) Jones then goes to King's Cross, where he finds the "Cambridge Rapist Hotel." (The rapist terrorised Cambridge women in 1975. McLaren was obsessed with him because he believed that he bought the leather mask he used for his attacks at Sex. Julien thinks that, even if he didn't, he probably bought it from Sex's supplier. To McLaren, the rapist was a threat to the state and therefore grist to the anti-establishment mill. Feminists, however, were not convinced. The rapist was revealed to be a man named Peter Cook. He died in prison in 2004.)

In various rooms in the hotel, Jones finds Mamie Records executives indulging in various vices and perversions. Steve Jones has (simulated) sex with a girl and sings Lonely Boy. Then Vicious, still on his motorcycle, sings C'Mon Everybody (his second posthumous single).

Lesson 7, "Cultivate Hatred," and Lesson 8, "Diversify," concern *Who Killed Bambi?* and therefore involve the rock star played by James Aubrey. In *Who Killed Bambi?* he was to have been murdered by the Pistols. But in *Swindle,* he's strangled by McLaren, who then escapes in drag. McLaren reveals that Warner Brothers paid him £200,000 for a film that was never made.

Lesson 9, "Take Civilisation to the Barbarians," is the record of the final American tour. At the Longhorn Ballroom, Dallas, the Pistols taunt the redneck audience; one punter remarks: "As far as I'm concerned, they're not worth killing." At the Pistols' last gig, at the Winterland, San Francisco, Rotten sings Iggy Pop's No Fun, after which the scene fades out with Rotten's famous quote: "Ha! Ha! Ever get the feeling you've been cheated?" At a disused airfield (Julien's dig at our noble wartime spirit), McLaren gives a press conference, then escapes, never to be seen again.

Lesson 10, just entitled "Who Killed Bambi?," is a somewhat desperate attempt to round everything off. Much of this chapter was improvised and apparently nobody knew quite how the film was going to end. There are three intercut sequences: Jones and Cook in Rio de Janeiro, Vicious in Paris, and Jones and Cook in the Classic Moulin, watching the film we have just watched, which is called, strangely, *Who Killed Bambi?*

Of the Brazilian footage, Julien admits, "It was insane. It didn't make much sense." It came about because of an incident, which occurred after the Pistols split in 1978, in which a failed attempt was made to kidnap Great Train Robber Ronnie Biggs from his home in Rio and bring him back to the UK to stand trial. McLaren saw the newspaper stories and said, "Let's use him." Because Brazil was one of the reputed hideouts of Nazis, Julien devised a crazy plot about Martin Bormann's plan to use punk to take over the world. An American TV actor, James Jeter, was flown in to play Bormann.

"We thought that Biggs was going to be this bandito," explains Julien. "But no. He said, 'Crime is strictly for mugs.' It's the weakest bit of the whole film." Julien tried to make something out of nothing. Cook and Jones are shown arriving at Biggs' house. They're greeted by a little boy, Biggs' son, Michael, who grew up to battle ceaselessly but unsuccessfully with the British government for his father's pardon. Biggs sings Belsen Vos A Gassa in a recording studio. Bormann arrives, flits through the Carnaval, then directs Cook, Jones and Biggs, exercising naked on the beach. Jones has (unsimulated) sex with a hooker. It doesn't add up to much.

The behind-the-scenes story to the Rio sojourn sounds like a better plot. At a press conference, Julien maintained that Martin Bormann was going to replace Rotten in the Pistols. He remembers a headline reading "Son of Shirley Temple in Brazil." When Steve Jones crashed a hired car, Malcolm McLaren went through the windscreen, and spent the remainder of the trip covered in bandages.

The Parisian sequence with Vicious is mostly inspired by the *nouvelle vague*. It begins with Vicious buying a gun, then a cake, which he squashes into a prostitute's face. "It was a Godard moment with a Sex Pistols twist," Julien explains. The climax, Vicious on stage singing My Way, probably contains *Swindle*'s most famous imagery. It's not surprising, therefore, that others want to take credit for it. But it sounds to me as though it was devised by Julien: "I wanted Sid to sing Je Ne Regrette Rien. But there was no way that was going to happen. Then

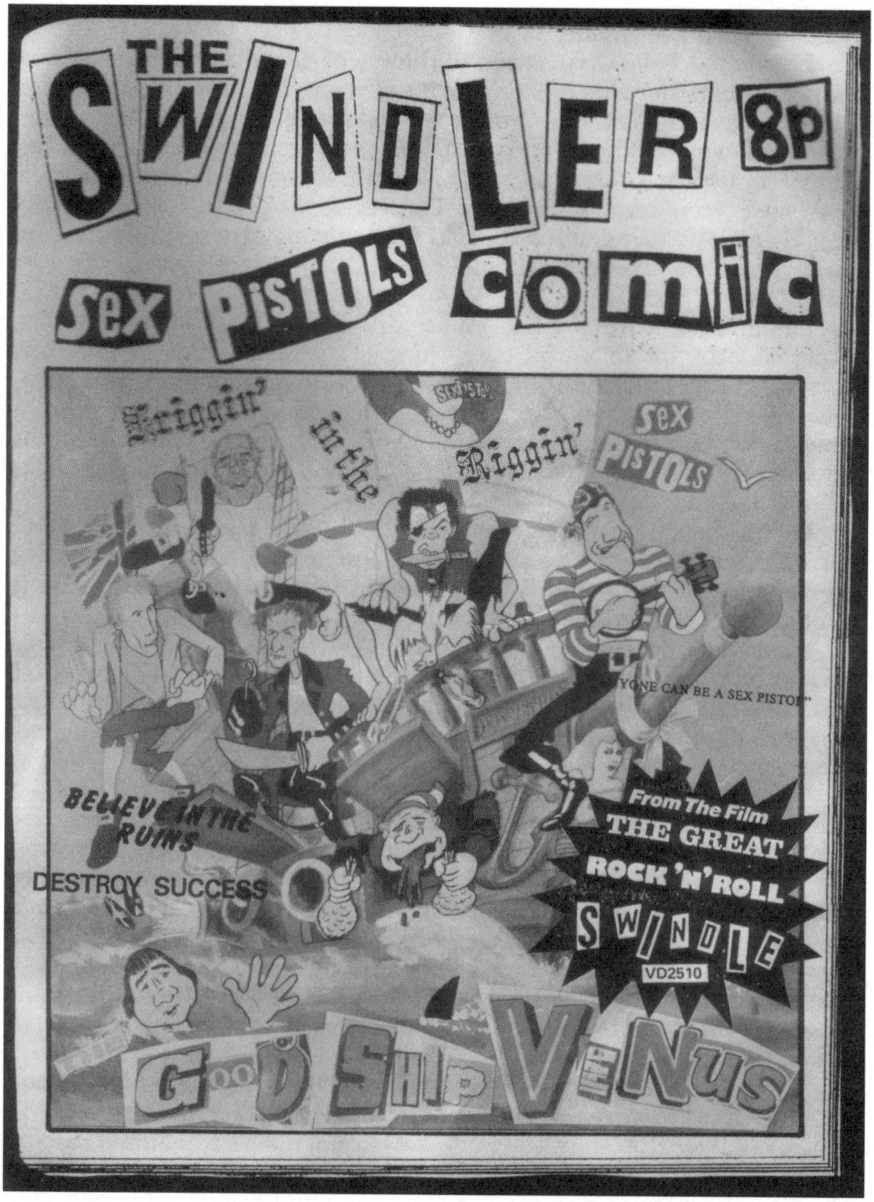

this French guy from the record company said, 'We own the rights to My Way. Why don't you use that?'" Vicious agreed, but wanted to sing it like The Ramones and change the words. "We fought over every line," says Julien. But eventually "I'll say it clear" was altered to "I'm not a queer" and "I chewed it up" became "I shot it up."

Vicious' audience (filmed in the Screen on the Green) includes James Aubrey and Vicious' real-life mother, Anne Beverley, who cries, "I can't believe it's my son up there!" Vicious then takes out the gun he bought and shoots everyone dead. It's virtually the end.

At the Classic Moulin, people arrive for a screening of *Who Killed Bambi?* In the cinema foyer, Eddie Tudor-Pole sings the title song, which he wrote with Vivienne Westwood. Sitting with Steve Jones in the audience are porn star Mary Millington, ageing juvenile Jess Conrad, and *Carry On* actress Liz Fraser. Why such an ill-assorted bunch? Because these low-rent, show-bizzy types were everything the Pistols weren't (and because they were cheap). The usherette is played by seventy-seven year old Irene Handl whom Julien loved. Also a writer, Handl habitually re-wrote her dialogue, and *Swindle* was no exception. "Oh, shut up, Tadpole," she says to Eddie, "You'll give yourself a conniption fit." This was virtually Handl's catch-phrase. She used it again and again, in films and on radio and TV. "She was a bright spark," says Julien. "She had no problem with the Sex Pistols."

The audience watch a newsreel, which announces that Rotten has been fired from the Pistols (not true) and that Cook and Jones have gone to Brazil. He leaves with Millington, but she returns and has (simulated) sex with Jones. "Oi, Sex Pistol!" shouts Handl. "Pack it in, will you?" Jones replies, "What you fuckin' want, you cunt?" Later, Eddie learns from TV that Vicious has been arrested for the murder of Nancy Spungen. Jones and Millington leave the cinema.

The end titles are part of a pirate ship cartoon accompanied on the soundtrack by Jones singing Friggin' In The Riggin'; Lydon is seen jumping ship only to be eaten by a shark called Virgin. The ship sinks. The final montage, imposed by the British Board of Film Censors (as a warning to youngsters to stay away from punk rock?), shows newspaper headlines screaming "SID VICIOUS DEAD".

The legend persists that, by the time *Swindle* opened at the London Pavilion in the spring of 1980 ("At last! The film you thought you'd never have to see!"), punk was dead. But it wasn't. Post-punk groups like Blondie and Dexy's Midnight Runners were at the top of the charts, and The Clash and The Damned continued to have hits almost throughout the eighties. Consequently there was a huge amount of interest in a film about the most famous British punk band of them all. Julien fanned the flames of curiosity by railing, "It was aimed against the... alternative Mafia who run *Time Out*, the British Film Institute and what is supposed to be hip, left, liberal, smug London. I hope they don't like it. I don't think they will. I think they'll think it's a pile of shit."

Julien was wrong. It wasn't only *Variety* who loved the film. *Time Out* called *Swindle* "one of the most imaginatively amoral and ambiguously violent strips of celluloid since Buñuel and Dalí once shared an idea." Even the *Daily Express* conceded, "Though distasteful, the film is never boring." None other than Jean-Luc Godard wrote somewhere that "*The Great Rock'n'Roll Swindle* is the future of film-making." (Julien comments, "Some time later I was at a film festival in Italy and I saw Godard in a café. I thought I'd say hello. I went up to him and said, 'Monsieur Godard, I'm Julien Temple.' He said, 'Fuck off.' It was perfect.") A week after its release, *Swindle* was number three in the box office top ten, an extraordinary achievement for such an experimental, multi-layered film. Julien was the man of the moment, the most talked-about new film director since… well, Welles?

Looking back twenty-five years, it's tempting to see that *Citizen Kane* accolade as a self-fulfilling prophecy. Like Welles, Julien "started at the top and worked down" (the quote is Welles' own). Julien didn't make another major feature film for seven years. In the meantime he directed music videos, albeit superior ones (Undercover Of The Night for the Rolling Stones, Jazzin' For Blue Jean for David Bowie). He worked for TV, "messing around with reality" (*F For Fake* style again) in a documentary called *It's All True* (1993). (The title was a *hommage* to Welles, and Welles himself appeared in it.) Then Don McPherson, who had reviewed *Swindle* for *Time Out*, approached Julien with the idea of making a film of Colin McInnes' cult novel *Absolute Beginners* (1986). For me, writing in *Films and Filming*, it was "British film-making at its most exhilarating, and worth all the *Gandhis* and *Chariots of Fire* put together." But for almost everyone else it was crap. "The reviews were like acid thrown in your face," Julien complained. The film cost $10 million, but made less than $1 million from its UK release.

After a generally non-productive, ten-year sojourn in Hollywood, the nadir of which was an action adventure called *Bullet* (1996), which went straight to video here, Julien slunk back to the UK and, after two art house pictures, returned to his roots with *The Filth and the Fury* (2000), another film about the Pistols, but this time one in which the "lads" (now the old men) had their say. "I owed the Pistols a different type of film," Julien says. The sight of Lydon getting tearful about McLaren's responsibility for Vicious' death showed how far we'd come from the anarchic seventies. The Grundy interview was included in full. The clip cost £40,000 ("a tenth of the film's budget"). Julien also emphasised the Pistols' music-hall and end-of-the-pier forebears by including footage of British comics like Ken Dodd and Benny Hill. Julien claims that Lydon loved these juxtapositions. He likes to think that it was *The Filth and the Fury* that encouraged Lydon to reinvent himself as a jungle celebrity and natural history "expert."

Perhaps *The Filth and the Fury*'s biggest coup was a 'new' interview with Sid Vicious. Where had this material been hiding all these years? Is there still more to come? Rumours persist about hours of unseen footage from *Swindle*. Does it exist? "It might be mouldering on a shelf somewhere," Julien replies cagily. Where? "That would be telling." Why won't you tell me? "I don't want to. I've answered every other question." My sixty minutes are up. After bumming two fags off a Groucho waiter, Julien gets up to greet a female friend. "Did you get enough?" she asks me. "I've *had* enough," snaps Julien and sweeps out of the club, leaving me with his £22.95 bar bill. Is this as 'perfect' a valediction as Godard's? Given that 'punk'd' has come to mean, in the TV show of that name, hoodwinked, yes.

P.S. *The Great Rock'n'Roll Swindle* is still a masterpiece.

The Filth and the Fury

... Sid And Nancy... Alex Cox directs...

Chris Barber

Punk Rock took-off during the long,

hot summer of 1976 when the Sex Pistols headlined the Punk Rock Festival at the 100 Club, supported by their rambunctious and dedicated Bromley (fan) contingent. (Other performers included Siouxsie and the Banshees, The Clash, The Damned, and Vibrators.) Julie Burchill and Tony Parsons waxed polemical about Pistols gigs in the *NME* (*New Musical Express*). Clothes designer Vivienne Westwood kitted out the Pistols, and punk rockers, on the King's Road. An anarchic new fashion was developing, based on an irreverent collage of personalised trash-aesthetic, pop art, and fetish/bondage gear from Soho — sartorial DIY!

Artist Jamie Reid provided their cut up, proto-Situationist, advertising and marketing graphics, with posters and record packaging. Managed by Malcolm McLaren, the Sex Pistols signed to EMI, releasing Anarchy In The UK and appearing on Bill Grundy's *Today* Thames TV programme. Taunted and insulted by drunken Grundy, Rotten swears profusely into the camera, shocking housewives and pompous pensioners. The tabloids have a field day, vehemently bombasting the band with sensational, vitriolic headlines. Deluged by complaints from the public and record-pressers, EMI terminate the band's contract with a grand pay-off. After briefly signing to A&M Records, McLaren negotiates another pay-off. At live venues around the country, the Pistols fail to turn up or are pulled off amidst chaos and protest. Finally, the Sex Pistols sign up with Richard Branson's Virgin Records. It's 1977 and Britain celebrates the Queen's Silver Jubilee with dreary street parties, dumb flag waving and stupid hats. The Pistols release their second single, God Save The Queen. Despite being banned by the BBC, it reaches number one in the pop chart. The band organises and plays on a Thames boat party trip, but the police accost it, making arrests.

Two more singles follow — Pretty Vacant and Holidays In The Sun. All the singles are included on their album — *Never Mind the Bollocks, Here's the Sex Pistols*. In 1978, the Pistols fly to the US, on tour. Their reception is mixed: punk was fundamentally alien to American culture and could only be grasped as a pop/fashion. Yet shock, outrage and violence beset the eight-show tour: fights break out between performers and audience; Vicious outrages spectators in Texas by slashing himself and bleeding. Worse problems are brewing inside the band: McLaren isn't paying them, Vicious has a heroin habit, Rotten and McLaren aren't getting along, nor are Rotten and Vicious (once close buddies). At their final gig in San Francisco, Rotten announces, "Ever get the feeling you've been cheated?" and pisses off. Jones and Cook fly to Brazil, to record with Ronnie Biggs, the exiled Great Train Robber. Sid Vicious records a solo cover version of (Sinatra's) My Way and bids farewell.

In October 1978, nine months after the band split up, Vicious is arrested in his room at New York's Chelsea Hotel and charged with murder. The corpse of his hooker-junkie girlfriend Nancy Spungen is discovered, slashed up, under the bathroom sink. McLaren bails Sid for $50,000, but the guitarist dies from a heroin overdose on February 2, 1979. There's No Future, in England's Dreaming!

Born in London in 1953, Julian Temple is a director and screenwriter, who graduated from the National Film School. A punk filmmaker from the start, he attached himself to the Sex Pistols entourage, complete with Super-8 and video cameras, at the outset of their career. This enabled him to accumulate a unique movie archive of the band. He stuck with them until they broke up and remains a personal friend of the surviving members.

His first completed feature film is the 1980 Sex Pistols movie, *The Great Rock'n'Roll Swindle* (originally to have been directed by sexploitation master Russ Meyer). But it wasn't until 2000 that he was able to complete this project with the punk cine masterpiece *The Filth and the Fury*.

The Great Rock & Roll Swindle

In 1987, Temple wrote and directed a short film for *Aria*, a feature consisting of short movies by several different art movie directors, including Derek Jarman, Jean Luc Godard and Robert Altman. His other films include *Absolute Beginners*, *Earth Girls Are Easy* (1989), *Bullet* (remake) and *Pandemonium* (2000). The latter title, produced by BBC Films, is a fascinating and beautiful film about the fraught relationship between the eighteenth century poets Coleridge and Wordsworth, much of it filmed in the punk style of Jarman. Temple also directed *Vigo*, a film based on the movies of the French filmmaker, Jean Vigo.

Between features, Temple has won notoriety for his music videos and he also makes commercials.

The Filth and the Fury (2000)

> The Sex Pistols story as it really was. It's the band's chance to set the record straight... People have exaggerated and blown up the Sex Pistols into something they never were... The truth is far more shocking and far more interesting. ***John Lydon (Johnny Rotten)***

The Filth and the Fury is a documentary feature film, consisting of raw and previously unreleased material, re-mixes of archive footage and recent interviews. It charts the story of the Sex Pistols — perhaps the most important rock group ever — and the punk phenomenon, against the backdrop of 1970s, strife-ridden England, divided by class conflict, hypocrisy and authoritarian anachronism. Its title comes from a pejorative *Daily Mirror* headline from 1976, heralding the media's campaign against punk. It also utilises video footage of television programmes and news archives, recorded during 1976–78.

The Cut: editing and assemblage is all-important to *The Filth and the Fury*. Temple cites Sergi Eisenstein, the great Soviet filmmaker, whose montage techniques exerted a significant influence on the film. Certainly montage, (quick) cutting between associated images, is what gives the film its unique quality. With the exception of a few live Pistols songs, and the intercutting of longer interview sections with the band, the film comprises of cut-up collages, lasting from a few seconds, up to about thirty seconds per clip.

Despite deterioration to the sound quality on some of the recently discovered material, the music used in the film has been digitally processed and re-synched, to achieve superb audio quality. The film includes complete new versions of several Pistols songs and edited versions of others. In *The Filth and the Fury*, the Sex Pistols soundtrack includes: God Save The Queen, Submission, Don't Gimme No Lip Child, What'cha Gonna Do About It, Road Runner, Substitute, Seventeen, Anarchy In The UK, Pretty Vacant, Did You No Wrong, Liar, EMI, No Feelings, I Wanna Be Me, Problems, Holidays In The Sun, Bodies, My Way, No Fun.

While Temple has cited Eisenstein's use and theory of montage, another groundbreaking Soviet silent film suggests its influence on *The Filth and the Fury*: *The Fall Of The Romanov Dynasty*, directed by Esfir

Shub in 1927. Made as a Soviet propaganda documentary, this ninety minute film is an assemblage of pre-revolution newsreel footage of Czar Nicholas II and the Russian royal family, shot between 1912 and 1917, some by the Czar's own cameramen. Prior to the Bolshevik Revolution, the newsreels were screened around Russia as pro-royalist propaganda. Shub re-edited the material, with new juxtapositions and narration/subtitles, to show the Russian aristocracy as a corrupt, decadent and out-of-touch institution on the verge of collapse, effectively creating a more honest and truthful representation than its original form.

A documentary-film must be outstanding to get cinema distribution. *The Filth and the Fury* is an absorbing movie, with tight, associational editing. Mixed mediums are carefully juxtaposed — Super-8, video, and transfer to 35mm celluloid. It feels contemporary and immediate, while encapsulating you in 1970s periodicity. Much of the material has never been publicly shown before — remarkable considering the cult interest in obscure punk footage, but down to legal disagreements over rights of ownership. This also presents a new perspective on what was considered a closed subject. Thirty years after punk exploded into British culture, much of its intelligent, anarchic radicalism had been forgotten, but it may offer a suitable alternative to today's synthetic and homogenised society. As a previously untold version of past events, depicting both negative and positive aspects with candid honesty and humour, one feels an imbalance has at last been redressed; a cutting edge retelling of a *truly* great story, for a new generation.

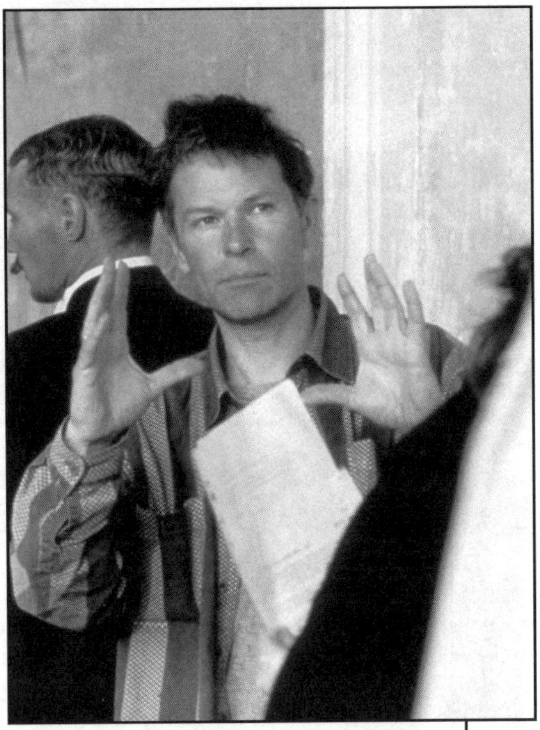

Temple directs *The Filth and the Fury*

In 1975, the film's director, Julien Temple, happened to overhear a rehearsal in a Rotherhithe warehouse by the recently formed Sex Pistols. After sneaking into the building, he was so impressed by what he heard and saw, that he found out where the band was playing and started going to all their gigs, with a camera borrowed from college. Following the Pistols soon interfered with his studies, so he dropped out of film school to stick with the group, documenting the rise and demise of the most notorious punk band, using video and

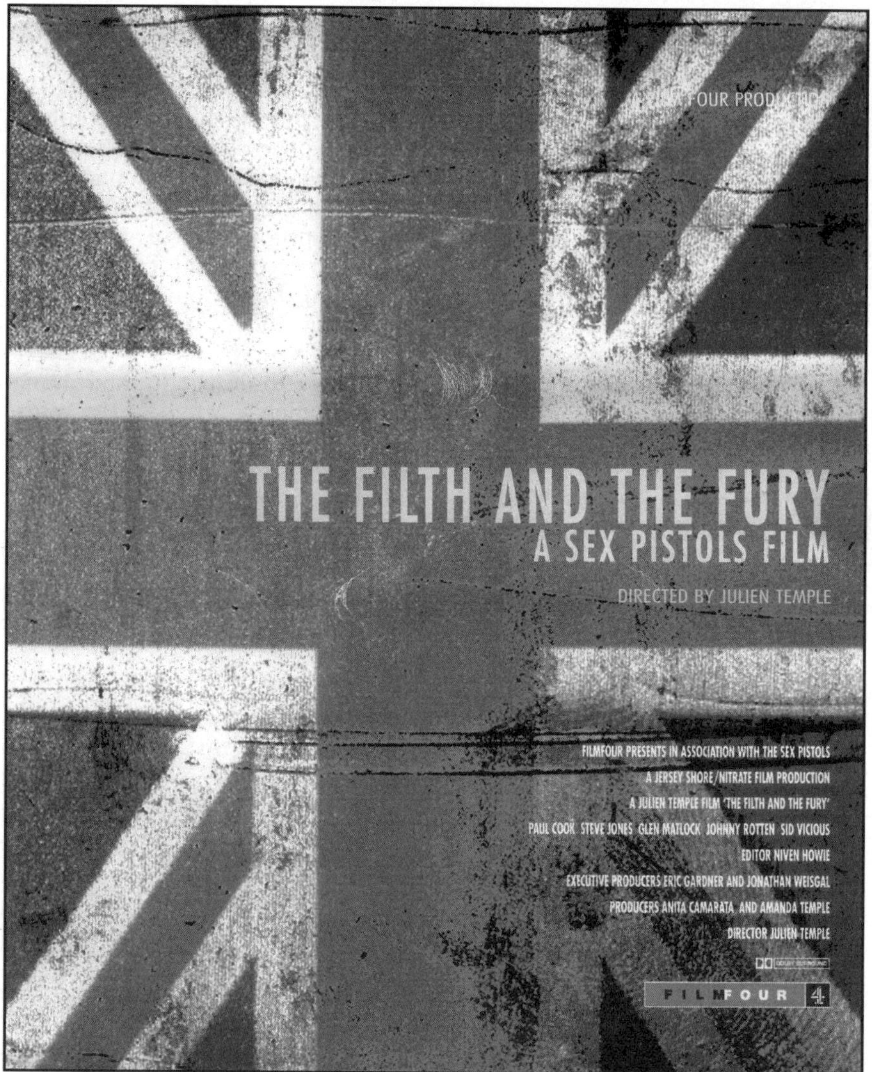

FilmFour promotion for The Filth and the Fury.

Super-8 cameras. The Sex Pistols were together for just twenty-six months. Temple's unique archive included performances, interviews and events, as they happened. Some of the material from his *Sex Pistols 1, 2* and *3* shorts, was utilised in *The Great Rock'n'Roll Swindle*, which concentrated on McLaren's version of events. Despite Temple's efforts to bring Surrealist form to *The Great Rock'n'Roll Swindle* (in homage to Luis Buñuel) it was competent, but ultimately prosaic and pretentious. More importantly, Rotten refused to participate or cooperate with the production and much of the recorded material could not be used. Eric Gardner — Lydon's manager, referred to it as, "Completely Malcolm McLaren's slanted egocentric vision." The band had no say in the production. Only after Lydon took

McLaren to the High Court in 1987, were the reams of unreleased footage rediscovered. It was alleged McLaren had not acted honourably towards the band in his role as manager. Lydon won the case, securing ownership of the Sex Pistols name and all concerned material. Lydon contacted the other band members and the estate of Sid Vicious (Sid's mum). He told them they should all own the material together.

Anita Camarata was hired to manage the interests of various parties; she says, "We discovered there was a storage facility in the Sex Pistols' name. No one knew what was in it. So I went down there to look, and found over twenty hours of Sex Pistols footage: all the old interviews and performances, from their inception to the end." Julien and Amanda Temple were asked to make a ten minute film from the footage, to see if it could get financial backing for a documentary. In 1999, FilmFour chief Paul Webster saw the sampler and immediately said FilmFour would finance the production. Further, Temple had his own stored archive of Pistols material, some of which had been used in *The Great Rock'n'Roll Swindle*, but a lot more stuff besides. Much of the material was deteriorating, but the two archives were amalgamated and everything examined and archived properly. This would make up the bulk of *The Filth and the Fury*. Unfortunately, much of the sound on the films had deteriorated beyond repair and had to be re-synched for the movie.

Concentrating on the Sex Pistols' alternative version of events, *The Filth and the Fury* tells a different story, for the first time. Essentially McLaren seems to have fallen for his own hype, as portrayed in *The Great Rock'n'Roll Swindle*, suggesting the whole phenomenon was creatively engineered by him and the Pistols were essentially a boy band. As *The Filth and the Fury* shows, that's just not true. There was a joint effort by the whole band in creating the Sex Pistols.

The film's message is provocative and challenging. While largely avoiding nostalgia and mawkishness (antithetical to punk) it suggests that in today's world of packaged lifestyles and designer conformity, the rage and indignation associated with punk is needed more than ever:

> A film of The Sex Pistols is relevant today because it's very important that people — young people especially — know their own history and should challenge what they are told and not simply accept things at face value, something I believe is happening more and more often. **Julien Temple**

The Filth and the Fury is perhaps the finest addition to punk cinema since *Jubilee* (1978).

Sid and Nancy (1986)

The actual events, which happened less than a decade prior, were extensively reported in the mass media and frequently captured live on film… Why bother making a feature film about a real, sad, sordid and brief affair between a punk rocker, a hooker groupie — and some heroin (completing the threesome)?

Following the commercial and cult punk success of *Repo Man*

(1984), his debut as a professional director, and believing more options would be open to him as a consequence, Alex Cox acted upon word he had received that Hollywood was considering making a movie about the Sid Vicious and Nancy Spungen affair. Madonna and Rupert Everett had been cast for the film.

Cox claims he was initially horrified by the prospect and the more news he heard about Hollywood's treatment of the project, the more it pissed him off. But he now considered himself a sort of vanguard of the punk movement and decided if the movie business was determined to film the Sid and Nancy story, he should make it and ensure it was authentic to history and punk. He had written a fictitious script about murder and a rock band in 1980, called *Too Kool To Die*. A few people had read it, but no offers materialised and Cox had dropped the idea. He concluded that now was the time to revivify his script as the basis for the Sid and Nancy film.

The film opens as Sid Vicious (Gary Oldman) sits staring blank-faced into space... A detective (Ed Pansullo) questions Sid in the room he shared with Nancy at New York's Chelsea Hotel; in the background a corpse is being removed by paramedics and cops. "Where did you meet

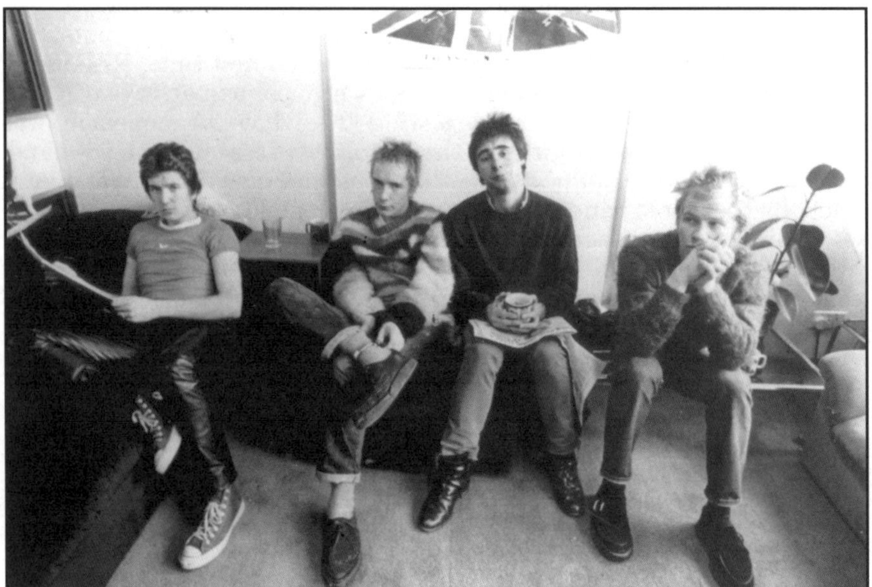

The Sex Pistols

Nancy?" "I met her at Linda's." "Who's Linda?" Flashback...

On the bathroom floor of Room 100, Chelsea Hotel, New York, on October 12, 1978, the police discovered Nancy Spungen's corpse, drenched in blood. Her boyfriend Sid Vicious was also spattered with blood, in the bedroom where he was arrested. Vicious was held for four months, awaiting trial for murder, before bail was posted (via Malcolm McLaren), securing his release. Later he would die of a heroin overdose.

Cox claims there are two reasons why he made *Sid and Nancy*: to precipitate the planned Hollywood version with Madonna and Rupert Everett, because he considered Everett to be a poor actor at that time; and because Sid was not a punk hero, but "betrayed the punk movement" and its "revolutionary ethos." By becoming a junkie, Sid "betrayed the revolutionary movement we were part of." But that doesn't mean Cox considers the movie is anti drugs, "I don't think drugs are necessarily bad, but heroin is bad... People should do what they want," but accept the consequences.

Too Kool To Die — the script Cox had written about "a Sid Vicious type... in a Vicious type band" — provided the core of *Sid and Nancy* after being rewritten by Cox and Abbe Wool. News reports covering Sid and Nancy's affair, and their deaths, were researched for the script. There were also extensive interviews with their friends and associates, including Lech Kowalski and James Spacely at the Chelsea Hotel, punks from the Bromley contingent, Sid's mother, Johnny Rotten (who notoriously hated the movie, as does Malcolm McLaren — at least that's something they agree on!), Glen Matlock (who was employed as Music Director on *Sid and Nancy*) and Nancy Spungen's mother (who had written a book about the ill-fated couple that was considered interesting but an unreliable source due to its glossing over of crucial details concerning Nancy's childhood — perhaps in order to displace any parental responsibility?).

Eric Fellner produced the movie (based on reading the script), with Zenith Productions and Embassy Home Entertainments. Margaret Matheson was Head of Production. Gary Oldman was asked to audition for Sid, based on his performance in Mike Leigh's *Meantime* after Daniel Day Lewis had been turned down. Kathy Burke got her first notable screen roll, as Brenda. Tim Roth was originally asked to audition for Johnny Rotten, but declined because he considered the movie was premature. Courtney Love (then unknown and turning up with an entourage of punk friends) was among the 500 actresses who auditioned for Nancy, but was turned down for the part because of her lack of experience. Instead she got a smaller part, as Gretchen, Nancy's friend. Despite the real Johnny Rotten's tirades against *Sid and Nancy* (in his autobiography) he agreed to cooperate pre-shooting, meeting with Drew Schofield who plays him and going out together on an eighteen hour drinking binge.

Love Kills was the working title. Cox was researching the project from about January 1985; Wool completed the second script in February, and the contract with Zenith was signed in May. The production budget was $4 million, with an allocated eleven-week shooting schedule. Filming began in late September and wound up on December 18, 1985. The first cut of the film was three hours long, but edited down the final, completed 111 minutes version was premiered at Cannes in 1986. Other notable credits include the renowned cinematographer Roger Deakins; songwriters Glen Matlock, Shane McGowen and Joe Strummer; music score composers: the Pogues, Pray For Rain and John Cale. Iggy Pop makes a cameo appearance.

When it comes to behind-the-scenes anecdotes, sourced post-production, it's inevitably problematic sorting fact from myth (particularly when punk/the Sex Pistols fall into the PR remit!). Apparently, a lot of drugs were used during production by all involved, in order to achieve a heightened sense of reality with the events being depicted (according to actor David Hayman). It's also claimed a lot of animosity developed on-set between the director and actors: Cox has been referred to as a fascist and an anarchist, who keeps actors in cages between bouts of abusing them, disrupts performances, or constantly mumbles meaningless and incomprehensible instructions. Despite making his name in this movie, Gary Oldman is loath to talk about it, because of his dislike of Cox's working methods. Martin Turner made a forty-five minute 'making of' documentary to accompany the film's release, but it's a parody — joke publicity material involving most of the film's cast.

To its credit, *Sid and Nancy* is a broadly serious portrayal of the horrors of serious drug addiction — be it heroin or alcohol — that manages to neither glamorise addiction, nor moralise by exaggerating the negative side. More importantly, it shows how quickly the negative side spins out of control when an addictive relationship between two people is part of the equation. The end is just silly: a couple of dead junkies zooming off together in a cab. Even Cox admits this now, explaining he got too involved with the characters while making the film and felt the need for a romantic ending as catharsis, when they should have been left dead in blood and vomit. Some of the portrayals of the early punk scene are also nostalgic nonsense (over-crowded gigs, choreographed pogo-ing etc).

Although many British punks asked on its release why it had made, it was far more popular in the US, where it became a cult movie. American audiences were not greatly exposed to the media sensationalism that surrounded punk in the UK, and in particular the Sex Pistols — only to the deaths of Sid and Nancy, in New York. From a sober standpoint, *Sid and Nancy* is not really that bad a movie (Johnny Rotten amusingly insisted it was made by 'evil people'), which isn't to say it's good, just somehow a pointless project from its inception.

The commercial success of the movie ensured Cox was offered several Hollywood jobs to consider, including directing *The Three Amigos* (1986)! Understandably Cox rejected this and similar offers. He wanted to do something of his own, sticking with his punk concerns, as well as channelling his adoration for spaghetti westerns. The result was his 1987 punk, comedy-western, *Straight To Hell*. This messy film was neither commercially successful nor critically acclaimed.

Cox moved straight on to his next project, *Walker* (1987). Set and shot in Nicaragua, *Walker* was overtly political, based loosely on historical events and people, including William Walker, an American renegade who supported the Nicaraguan people's revolutionary war against imperialism in the 1850s. Using contemporary anachronisms, the film's overt aim was to draw parallels with the Sandinista Marxist FSLN revolution in Nicaragua, and their protracted war against the right-wing Contras, during the 1980s. The reactionary Contras were covertly supported by the US government, to the tune of many millions of dollars, personally endorsed by President Reagan. Cox protested this in filming on location in Nicaragua and spending as many US dollars as possible. Despite his noble intentions and spirited defence of *Walker*, the film bombed big-time and Cox walked from Hollywood to land a weekly television slot, on BBC2, introducing and talking about other peoples' movies on *Moviedrome*.

It took Cox almost four years to get back into the director's chair, with a Mexican movie, *El Patrullero*, or *Highway Patrolman* (1991). Made in Spanish, it's about endemic corruption in the Mexican police. Lots of hand-held camerawork, and relatively little editing (187 cuts), add to the film's semi-documentary look.

While finishing editing on *El Patrullero*, the BBC tracked Cox down for a TV movie based on a story by Luis Borges, *Death and the Compass*. It's an enigmatic tale about murder, conspiracy and the occult, lasting fifty-five minutes. After its completion, it was decided to turn the film into a full-length feature for theatrical release in 1996. For fans of *Repo Man* who were subsequently disappointed by Cox's efforts, *Death and the Compass* (1992) could be seen as a return to form. Like a cross between *Repo Man* and a low budget attempt at Terry Gilliam's *Brazil* (1985), it's an extraordinary and appropriately enigmatic movie. The same year *The Winner* was released.

Cox then got embroiled in the drawn-out and capricious production of *Fear and Loathing in Las Vegas* (1998), based on Hunter S. Thompson's cult, anarchic, drug-binging novel. Originally he was hired to direct it, but there were so many competing production interests vying for a stake in the movie that Cox was eventually replaced as director by

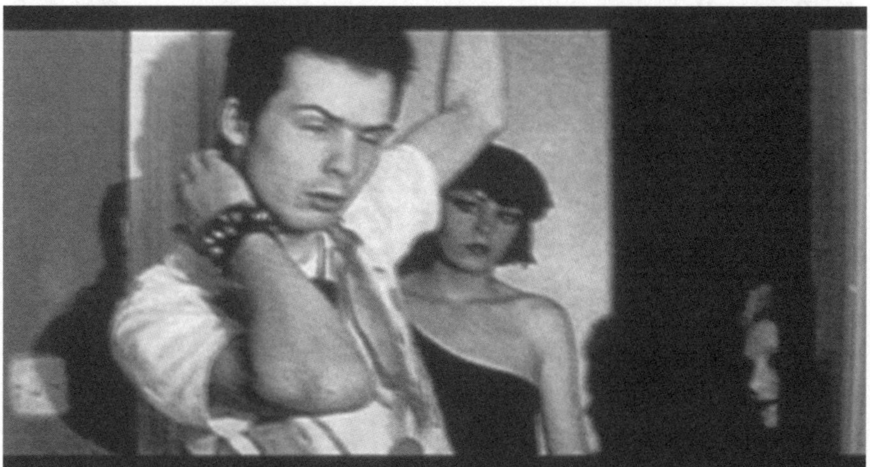

Sid, Filth and the Fury

Terry Gilliam; Cox shares the final screenplay credit (with three other writers).

In 1998, Cox directed another US feature, *Three Businessmen* (with a title song performed by Debbie Harry). Cox has one project in particular he hopes to direct some day

— a biopic on his favourite film director, the anarchist and Surrealist Luis Buñuel.

Novelty Extras

(Strictly to fill stockings and stuff Christmas crackers — No Christmas for John Quays!)

John Lydon stars alongside Harvey Keitel in the best forgotten movie, *Order of Death* aka *Copkiller* (Roberto Faenza, 1983). Set in New York, most of the film takes place in a claustrophobic apartment. Keitel plays a psychopathic cop who, for quite implausible reasons, takes in Lydon as a joint tenant/prisoner, sharing a cosy bachelor apartment. Lydon plays a crypto-anarchist who represents an untidy counterpoint to Keitel's obsessively authoritarian character. For a while, things buck up as Lydon, complete with dog collar and chain, patters around at his master's call... Which all sounds quite promising: repressed homosexuality, kinky S&M, transference and psychological intensity — something in the vein of *The Servant* (1963) or *Performance* (1971)... Sorry, afraid not. All such hopes are frustrated as the plot opts for order of the prosaic!

Steve Cook and Paul Jones star alongside Paul Simonon (of The Clash) in a band fronted by a young Ray Winstone in the film, *Ladies And Gentlemen: The Fabulous Stains*. Made in 1981, it also features Laura Dern and Diane Lane, and is directed by Lou Adler. "We don't put out!" is the rallying cry for some punk young ladies and best sums up the film's message to the audience! Apparently the movie's fan club includes the Beastie Boys and Courtney Love, which is too weird... Think B-movie to *Breaking Glass* and you'll know what to expect.

The Clash and Cinema

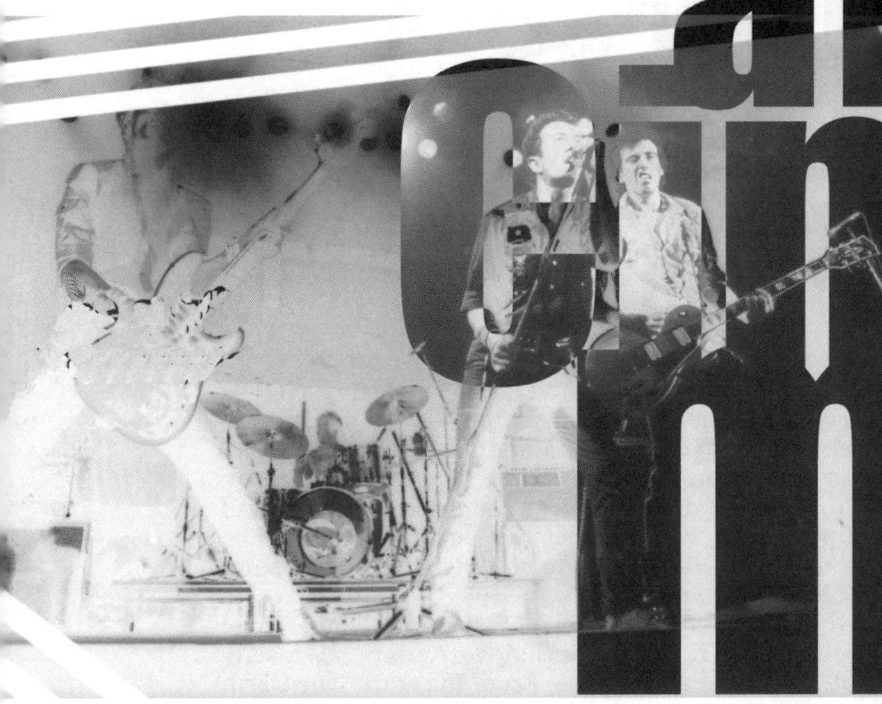

Chris Barber

The Clash formed in London in

1976, fronted by Joe Strummer on vocals and guitar, and supported by Mick Jones on vocals/guitar, Paul Simonon playing bass, and drummer Topper Headon (Nicky Chimes was an occasional substitute on drums). Their debut gig was supporting the Sex Pistols at Sheffield's Black Swann, July 4, 1976. They became the most commercially successful band to come out of punk rock, winning meteoric popularity in the US, but by then their sound had dramatically changed, abandoning punk roots for a more familiar rock sound.

Initially inspired by the Sex Pistols, The Clash were an art-school amalgam whose in-house DIY outfits included trousers abstractly splattered with paint, Jackson Pollock style. From the start, The Clash proclaimed their intent to become a great rock band, citing The Rolling Stones as another inspiration. But it was their well-rehearsed street-cred that distinguished their punk appeal. This shrewd makeover, along with their left-wing revolutionary politics, was adopted after visiting the Notting Hill Carnival in August 1976. The final day of celebrations among Britain's biggest black community erupted into a huge, violent street riot, largely provoked by heavy-handed police tactics. It equipped

Strummer and co. with first hand experience of ruthless state repression, and improvised struggle by a poor, socially disadvantaged community.

These events inspired their first single White Riot, released in 1977 after The Clash became the first punk band to sign to a major record label, CBS. Their first LP, *The Clash*, soon followed and remains perhaps the seminal punk rock album. As early as their second album, *Give 'Em Enough Rope*, The Clash sound was moving away from punk rock. With *London Calling*, they made one of the greatest and most eclectic rock albums ever. Whether The Clash completely abandoned their punk roots or pushed punk's musical eclecticism and diversity into new terrain remains a controversial issue. Their other albums include the triple LP, *Sandinista* (named after the Nicaraguan Marxist revolutionary, to whose cause the album's profit's were donated) and *Combat Rock*.

The Clash also consistently promoted reggae music, in particular Aswad, who achieved notoriety as a Clash support band, and Big Audio Dynamite, whose line up included Mick Jones.

Rude Boy (1980)

Rude Boy is a feature length docu-drama/rock musical, starring The Clash on their 1978 UK tour, and is jointly directed by David Mingay and Jack Hazan (who also produced it). Hazan had previously directed *A Bigger Splash* (1974), a feature length docu-drama, starring and about British artist David Hockney (the title borrows from one of Hockney's highly valued swimming pool paintings). Interviews with the artist, at work in his studio, are intercut with a dramatised homoerotic love story about the crumbling relationship between an ageing queen and an adolescent (the latter played by director John Slezhenger's son). A further visual strand intercuts cinematic re-creations of Hockney's swimming pool paintings. Ultimately *A Bigger Splash* is an informative, but somewhat stark, austere and dogmatic exercise in docu-realist formalism, stylistic traits that are even more pronounced (but less informative) in *Rude Boy*. Offering little pleasure to the viewer — other than some great Clash live footage — it makes the average Ken Loach film look like a Steven Spielberg movie! Yet there are conceptual elements and documentary footage in *Rude Boy* that should have inspired a far better film. So what went wrong?

The establishing shots comprise gritty footage on the streets of South London, where flag-bearing members of the fascist National Front assemble to march. Rallying to a counter demonstration are Anti-Nazi League supporters. Between them are rows of uniformed cops, linking arms and somehow appearing more thuggish than anyone else. The story follows Ray, a young, dumb punk, who quits his "career opportunity that never knocks" in a seedy Soho porn shop to become a Clash roadie, on the band's 1978 tour. Ray is consistently reckless and careless towards other people and behaves like a drunken sociopath unable even to roadie right. His inept stumbling around backstage, brawling with bouncers, turfing crew workers out of their hotel beds so he can shag his pick up girls, and mindless racist comments, gradually alienate the band and he's eventually politely sacked. He doesn't take the hint and continues to impose his antics on band and crew, provoking them to humiliate him.

There are occasional didactic political arguments between Strummer and Ray, and a brief sub-plot exposing the inherent racism of the British justice system.

The Clash live performances are intercut throughout: White Man At Hammersmith Palais, USA, Janie Jones (cut short), White Riot (at the Apollo in Glasgow), The Prisoner (in Aberdeen), Tommy Gun (Dunfermline), All The Young Punks and Stay Free (performed by Joe Strummer and Mick Jones in recording studio), Complete Control, Safe-European Home, What's My Name (at London's Music Machine), No Reason (by Joe Strummer in a rehearsal studio), and I Fought The Law (at London's Lyceum).

Other finely edited archive material includes part of Margaret Thatcher's conference speech as Conservative Party opposition leader (pre-figuring the use of her Falklands War speech a few years later in *The Ploughman's Lunch* [1983]). The film's doom-laden final minutes show Thatcher entering 10 Downing Street as Prime Minister after her first election victory.

Background to Documentary/Archive Footage

1978 was a watershed year in British politics. The legacy of the 'Winter of Discontent' continued, the country was polarised by strikes and industrial unrest, and unemployment soared. Prime Minister James Callaghan's minority Labour government teetered on the verge of collapse, abandoning its socialist manifesto, introducing increasingly draconian measures to enforce social control and appease the International Monetary Fund (IMF). A general election was eventually announced. The fascist National Front (NF) party grew rapidly, taking advantage of the situation by organising provocative marches in racially tense areas. Left wing and liberal fringe groups allied together as the Anti-Nazi League to counter demonstrate, and violent street clashes ensued in inner cities. Police were deployed in force, using ruthless tactics to protect NF marches. The Conservatives won the next election and Margaret Thatcher became Prime Minister.

Too Little, Too Late

Much of The Clash footage is well filmed, capturing the raw, live excitement of early gigs, while they were still a seminal punk act. So *Rude Boy* is a must for Clash fans. Along with some gritty documentary material, it offers an interesting picture of the changing social conditions and contradictions that created the beginning of the end of punk as a mass subculture.

The stark realism and docu-drama form suggest far greater potential than the final film achieved. *Rude Boy* appears to be attempting the extraordinary achievement of Pontecorvo in *The Battle of Algiers* (1966), hence the agit-prop cross editing between news style documentary material — people playing themselves (like Joe Strummer)

— and apparently objective and inconclusive political discourse between characters (diatribes calculated to expose real social contradictions that provoke the spectator to form his/her own conclusions). Regrettably, *Rude Boy* ultimately fails in this regard for various reasons. Firstly *The Battle of Algiers* tackles far broader issues of concern to the (French) public of its time, while *Rude Boy* deals with more obscure political fringe issues (like the relationship between politics and music) of little interest to the mainstream (British) public. Secondly Pontecorvo's masterpiece was released quickly after filming, provoking controversy and alarming the French establishment with its pertinence. By contrast, *Rude Boy* was not released until 1980, almost two years after it was filmed and into a dramatically changed socio-political landscape; it was already dated. Thirdly, *The Battle of Algiers* compiles news-style, in-camera interviews with front-line military/establishment spokesmen. *Rude Boy* only manages poorly contrived chats between musicians and youths, hardly appealing to the average worker.

The fumbling, contradictory and psychotic characterisation of Ray in *Rude Boy* presents another problem. Not only is it impossible for any reasonable viewer to identify with Ray (as is doubtless intentional), it is as difficult to empathise or find anything interesting about the character at all. Perhaps there is a hint of Jean-Luc Godard's *Le Petit Soldat* (The Little Soldier, 1962) at work here. But in *Le Petit Soldat*, the central character's contradictory and hypocritical persona is fascinating and compelling to watch, veering between jovial Mr Average citizen (your next door neighbour) and ruthless fascist terrorist (a French nationalist fighting to maintain France's imperial rule of Algiers). Where Godard skilfully adapts Brechtian theatrical devices to cinema, *Rude Boy*'s Ray fails abysmally. Ray is not a model citizen whose contradictory nature forces him to become a rogue outsider (now a well established cinematic tradition, achieved with perfection in films like *Taxi Driver*, Ray is a social outsider from the start: dumb, lazy, racist, sexist, selfish, boorish and inconsequential. He has no redeeming features, leaving the viewer perplexed as to why Strummer employs his services in the first place and why it takes the band so long to ditch him.

The Clash: Westway to the World (2000)

A well made if somewhat conventional documentary feature, charting the rise and fall of The Clash; it was completed in 2000, lasting 107 minutes and directed by punk cine maverick, Don Letts.

Covering a period from 1976 to 1982, *The Clash: Westway to the World* intercuts archive period footage from Clash gigs, behind-the-scenes tour material and general London punk scene clips, much of the footage previously unseen by the public, from the private collections of Letts and Clash members. This is cut with talking head interviews with members of The Clash, roadies and music critics, filmed shortly before the film was released. There's extensive use of voice-overs, completing a slick and tightly edited film.

Perhaps the only criticism is that all the excellent performance clips are cut or faded out, without allowing any song to be completed. This may be because Letts wants to focus the spectator's attention on other related issues raised in the narrative (recalling Godard's *Sympathy for the Devil* [1969]). And, as you would expect from a filmmaker as astute as Letts, there are a plethora of issues pertaining to punk, politics and music, worthy of consideration.

"It seems to me inspiration is perhaps instinct not intellect," comments Joe Strummer in the opening minutes. Each Clash member in turn succinctly voices their early biographical details and pre-punk interests — particularly regarding the 1960s counter-culture — while archive news footage of the Vietnam war and political demonstrations roll on screen. References are made to formative music influences such as The Rolling Stones and The New York Dolls, and early live Clash clips including Janie Jones are featured.

"Authority is a system of control..." The band talk about art school and the development of their attitude and style towards punk. Archive photo shots interpolate footage. "We were Stalinist, you had to shed all your friends," Strummer explains, moving on to the band's developing political stance, and how this DIY punk aesthetic infused their lives, music and rehearsal methods. Commentators on The Clash and punk scene include former *NME* journalist and author, Tony Parsons. "This garage band should be returned to the garage, the garage locked, and the motor left running," music critic Charles Shaar Murray said of their live debut at the Screen on the Green, Islington (supporting the Sex Pistols).

Cool urban-punk style computer graphics flash up periodically, dividing the film into chapters (another Godard device). The landmark punk fanzine, *Sniffin' Glue is* featured. Archive footage of the Notting Hill Carnival riot is shown, which significantly inspired the band. The band members recount their solidarity with the Sex Pistols on their UK tour, in the aftermath of the controversial 1976 Thames TV show *Today* fronted by Bill Grundy, by refusing to play gigs where the Pistols were banned. Due credit is also given to Don Letts who, in addition to his punk films, played a vital role in the musical development of The Clash and other punk bands, by introducing them to reggae (while resident DJ at The Roxy in Covent Garden — the first punk club). A collage of early Letts Super-8 footage includes snippets of Siouxsie Sioux and Sid Vicious. Anecdotes recall The Clash's recording contract, first album and the part played by manager Bernie Rhodes.

"Punk was getting narrower and narrower, we thought we could do any music..." The Clash defend their musical eclecticism on the *London Calling* double album. Roadie Johnnie Green talks about working Clash gigs, and photographer Pennie Smith tells how her no-focus picture became an iconic punk album cover (*London Calling*). The band's record and be damned approach to the *Sandinista* triple-LP is discussed. There's also an amusing clip of TV dance group Pan's People's performance for Bankrobber, on *Top of the Pops*, after The Clash refused to play on the show.

"Weirdo punk white guys..." Strummer recalls the baffled enthusiasm with which New York's black street rappers greeted The Clash on their first American tour. The band explain how their planned seven gigs in New

York, 1981, were over sold, causing disgruntled fans to riot outside the venue. After The Clash agreed to play enough gigs to meet demand, they were subjected to an exhausting sixteen consecutive performances.

Their massive success in the US marked the beginning of their decline. Exhaustion antagonised Topper's heroin addiction and his ability to perform. Committed to continue their tour in Hong Kong, Mick Jones became a prima donna. His performances became erratic and, despite The Clash recording the successful *Combat Rock* album, the 'chemistry' was lost. Predictably, The Clash fell apart amidst unresolved feuding and bad blood. Some sixteen years elapsed before Don Letts persuaded the entire band to cooperate in making *The Clash: Westway to the World*. Ending on a positive note, all the members apologise for their respective faults, referring candidly and fondly to their involvement with The Clash. In 2002, Letts won a Grammy Award for the film. Sadly, Joe Strummer died on December 24, 2002, aged fifty, shortly before he was due to join Letts at the award ceremony.

Clash on Broadway (1981)

Made by Don Letts in June 1981, on Super-8 and 16mm, this is an eight minute short following The Clash on tour in New York. It opens with a rapper/graffiti-artist spraying the title directly into camera. There follows a fast-moving, edited collage of live gig footage, forays into the band's hotel rooms, interviews in the back of cabs, and raw glimpses of New York's punk and rapper street life. Slow motion is sporadically employed. And smacked-up Topper moans about his ongoing argument with the makers of *Rude Boy*, who allegedly owe him cash… (Presumably he can't afford his next bag!) When not on stage, the band also enjoys bumping dodgems at a funfair.

Punk in London (1977)

A live music documentary shot mainly in London in 1977 by Wolfgang Büld, then a student in West Germany, on 16mm for German television. The two-man film crew consisted of director Büld, assisted by cinematographer Helge Weindler. When news of the British punk scene reached Germany, Büld was excited and persuaded a television channel to send him and his assistant to London for a few weeks to make a documentary.

The Clash are one of eleven punk bands captured performing live, but significantly The Clash footage is filmed in Munich, comprising a brief backstage interview and performing four songs — more than the other bands. Before an excited German crowd, The Clash render Complete Control, Hate And War, Police And Thieves, and Garageland, forming the climax of the film. Preceding bands include The Adverts performing Gary Gilmore's Eyes plus One Chord Wonders, Chelsea playing Right To Work, X-Ray Spex rendering Oh Bondage Up Yours!, The Lurkers do Shadow, The Jolt offer You're Cold and another track, The Electric Chairs singing (You Make Me) Cream In My Jeans, The Killjoys perform

It Could Be Me and At Night, Subway Sect play Ambition followed by Out of Touch, The Jam render Carnaby Street plus In The City, and The Boomtown Rats — Do The Rat.

The gig footage is intercut with an assortment of rough-cut cameo, interviews and punk related location clips, selected to capture the mood of the time. There are punk rockers wandering London's streets and pogo-ing at gigs, a visit to the Rough Trade record shop, interviews with band managers and roadies (including The Damned's roadie, Rat), and Miles Copeland (who founded the indie Step Forward record label). Two clips are particularly amusing and worth looking out for: an attempt by the filmmakers to interview Jean Jaques Burnell of The Stranglers, and a confrontation with ageing, beer-swilling teddy boys in a rock'n'roll club to offer an anti-punk counterpoint. There's also a lot of crude, rude, angry and incomprehensible punk attitude in the shape of wide-eyed comments linking punk and the Angry Brigade. Presumably unable to catch a Pistols gig within the tight shooting schedule, the film's soundtrack includes Anarchy In The UK and Pretty Vacant.

Punk aesthetics pervade the form of *Punk in London*. The editing is rough and jerky, and virtually all the camerawork is hand-held, single takes: the camera moving erratically over the action, capturing a sense of the urgency and chaos of its subject.

The live performances are of mixed interest. Some offer rare and exciting glimpses of obscure bands or early performances by later renowned groups; other performances are lacklustre, by bands best forgotten. In conjunction with the off-the-cuff interviews, the portrayal of punk subculture captured here sometimes looks naïve, disingenuous and silly. However most spur-of-the-moment documentaries attempting to record fashionable cultural phenomenon, provoke similar criticisms when reviewed decades later (try watching *Woodstock* now).

Punk in London is not a lost masterpiece of punk documentary making, but it remains an interesting, entertaining and genuinely obscure item of punk-abilia, capturing the spontaneity and raw anger of 1977 punk in London.

Straight To Hell (1987)

Purely for Clash obsessives. Punk auteur Alex Cox (yawn) stitched this little prank of a feature film together (probably in about an afternoon!) straight after *Sid and Nancy*, probably thinking he could get away with anything. Joe Strummer (as Simms) is one of its stars. The rambunctious folk-punk band, The Pogues, also stumble into it and provided much of the soundtrack. Bespectacled new waver Elvis Costello also got caught in it (as Hives), adding to its punk credits, along with Grace Jones, Dennis Hopper, Kathy Burke, Courtney Love and Jim Jarmusch. Conversely, its lead stars Sy Richardson and Dick Rude were virtually unknown… and still are. Would 'a comedy western that isn't funny' be an apt description? Cox says "It's a spaghetti western homage," but I think he's having us on. Either that or he hates spaghetti westerns!

No Fut-ure Now

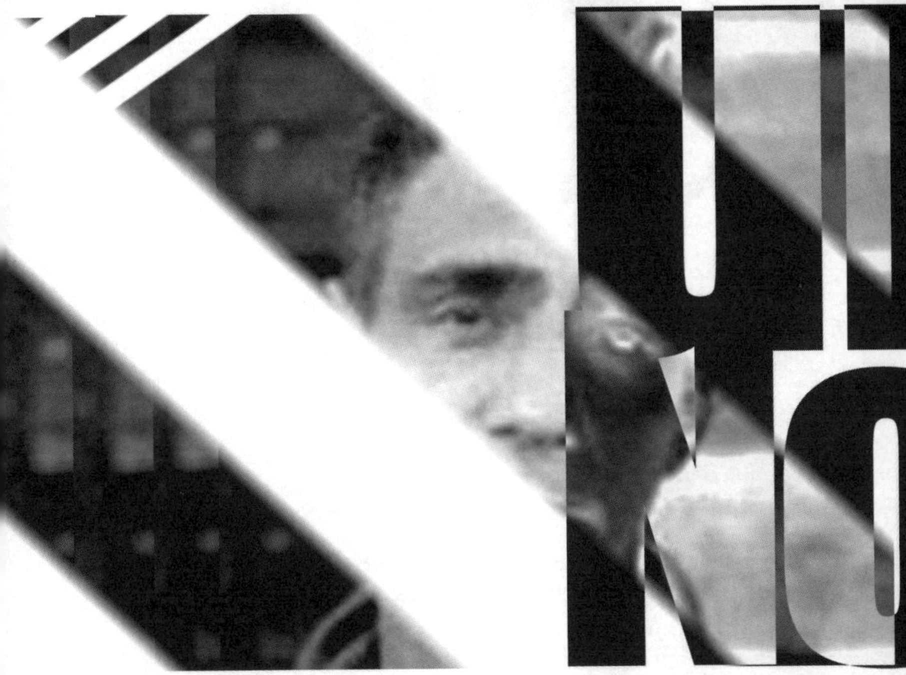

Chris Barber

"The working class think art is wank,

and the middle class think wanking is art ***Julie Burchill reviewing Jubilee for NME, 15 April 1978***

It's a laugh... that's the point everyone misses... Any other director would have done a... sensationalist sex and violence quickie ***Jordan***

With its persistent air of disillusion and warning, *Jubilee* captured the mood of punk England better than anyone could have predicted ***Jon Savage***

Jubilee set out to be prophetic. I thought punk was an understandable and very correct disgust with everything, but it wasn't focussed ***Derek Jarman***

Derek Jarman was born in Northwood, England, in 1942. His New Zealand born father was an RAF officer, providing a comfortable middle-class upbringing; his mother was a socialite with an interest in the arts and music. His father's job necessitated re-posting to new air bases every couple of years and Derek spent part of his childhood in India and Italy. Derek moved to London, alone, to study History, English and Art at King's College and soon discovered the capital's wild bohemian subculture. In 1963 he enrolled as an art student at Slade and frequented the art school's gay society, where his fellow activists included David Hockney and Patrick Proctor. At the Tate Gallery's 1967 Young Contemporaries Exhibition, Jarman's abstract work won the Peter Stuyvesant Award.

After working as a designer on the Royal Ballet production of *Jazz Calender*, Jarman opened his own exhibition at the Lisson Gallery, in 1968; he was an instant hit. Less auspiciously he designed an ill-fated ENO production of *Don Giovanni*.

Jarman began making films in 1970 using Super-8: an experimental and personal medium. His poetic and visionary home movies became a lifelong vocational project: a life recorded on celluloid. These no-budget shorts, often made with help from friends, enabled Jarman to experiment with his high-art skills and modernist sensibility in an alternative medium and significantly influenced his later feature films — *Glitterbug*, completed in 1994, is a sixty minute collage that includes some of these early films alongside other personal films. The cheap Super-8, one-man 'guerrilla' approach to filmmaking was the equivalent of amateur video/digital home movies today. His family had long been recording their travels on Super-8, providing some of the material used in *The Last of England* (1987).

Jarman got his break into feature film production when director Ken Russell hired him as set-designer for his controversial masterpiece, *The Devils* (1971). Russell encouraged innovation from his production crew, for this loose adaptation from Aldous Huxley's historical novel and John Whiting's play. Camp cavalcade, high and pop culture, political allegory, and an orgy of sex and violence, clash together in late Renaissance France. Jarman's oppressive sets combine Renaissance influences with stark modernism, remaining one of the film's most remarkable features. A year later Jarman returned to Russell's sets for *Savage Messiah*, exploring early British, modernist sculpture. Further, Russell and Jarman planned a production of *Gargantua* (by Rabelais), which was never filmed.

Sebastian (1976) was Jarman's directorial feature debut, shot in 1975. It's a personal and (for its time) shockingly homo-eroticised rendering of the martyrdom of St Sebastian: a Roman soldier, punished for converting to Christianity (around 300 AD). It is the only feature film spoken in Latin (with English subtitles) and the first British feature to show an erect penis on screen. Predictably the BBFC demanded these scenes be cut, but Jarman had carefully filmed them in the bottom section of the frame. By obscuring the lower frame image and strategically placing the subtitles for the BBFC screening, Jarman managed to sneak erections past the censor and obtain a certificate.

Living in a Chelsea flat (just off the King's Road) at the time, Jarman was immersed in punk from the start, and quick to pick up on its creative energy and poetic anger. Punk's no-budget, DIY art and fashion aesthetics, radical cynicism and avant-garde sensibility, coincided with Jarman's artistic concerns. So it's not surprising that

Jarman made the first — and arguably still the finest — punk feature film: *Jubilee* (1977).

After *Jubilee*, Jarman filmed a wonderfully unique, magical and punk adaptation of Shakespeare's *The Tempest* (1979). Over the next six years, Jarman stopped making feature films but remained prolific, completing ten short Super-8 films and publishing his first book, *Dancing Ledge,* in 1984 (originally entitled *Queerlife*). It includes a fascinating chapter on making *Jubilee*; Jarman's subsequent books include *Kicking the Pricks* (1987, aka *The Last of England*), *Modern Nature* (1991), *At Your Own Risk* (1992) and *Chroma* (1994).

In The Shadow Of The Sun (1980) is an avant-garde music video (filmed on Super-8) for proto-post-industrialist sound experimentalists, Throbbing Gristle. Replete with alchemical and magic references, it might also serve as a homage to Kenneth Anger.

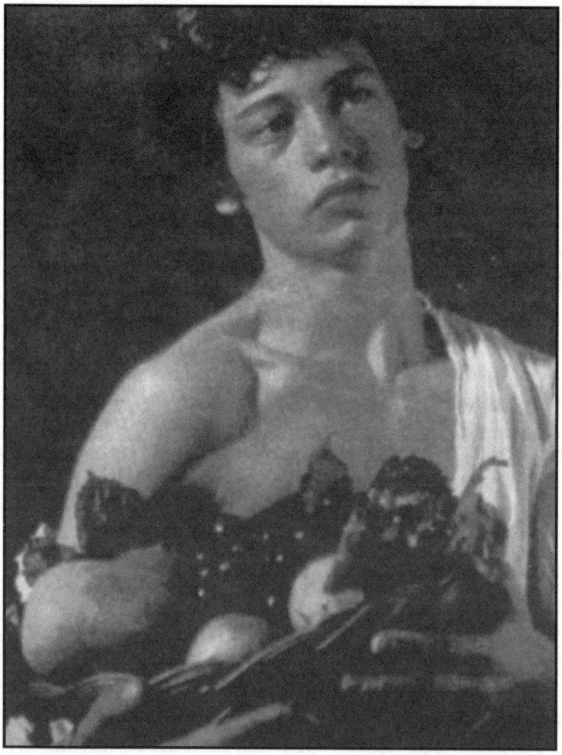

Dexter Fletcher in Derek Jarman's Caravaggio

Imagining October (1984) may be the finest and most obscure of Jarman's short movies. Boot stomping in its punk and post-industrial aesthetic concerns, a post-production diplomatic altercation between the Home Office and the Soviet Counsel prematurely curtailed the film's distribution. A reappraisal is long overdue.

In 1985, Jarman returned to directing features with *The Angelic Conversation*. His most dogmatically non-audience-friendly film to date, it continues to evoke punk formalist concerns, as well as pointing towards the emerging post-industrial underground scene.

Caravaggio followed in 1986. Partly financed by the British Film Institute (BFI), *Caravaggio* is Jarman's biggest-budgeted and most commercially accessible film. A biopic of the maverick Italian Renaissance artist and queer outsider, Nigel Terry renders an excellent performance in the title role. The film explores the relationship between the artist's life, work and partners, vividly and dramatically recreating some of the painter's famous pictures as set pieces. Filmed on location in Italy,

Jarman continues to subvert the image, subtly utilising anachronism and low key theatrical audience distancing techniques.

The Last of England is arguably Jarman's cinematic masterpiece, and final attempt to animate his punk formal aesthetic sensibility. It was followed a year later by *War Requiem*, a homage to Wilfred Owen — the WWI poet — using Benjamin Britten's choral compositions. Pretty and effortless in its overbearing pomposity, *Requiem* is perhaps Jarman's least challenging movie.

By the late 1980s, Jarman was an internationally renowned and critically acclaimed art film director. This combined with his outspoken tirades against Thatcherite politics and increasing activism in the gay liberation movement; issues which frequently explored in his films. Around this time he tested HIV positive and soon became a frontline spokesman on AIDS-related issues. He inhabited a small London flat off Charing Cross Road, but had also acquired a cottage in Dungeness, where he began to spend more time.

The Garden (1990) is an astonishing and mesmerizing feature, in which he incorporates years of cine-experimentalism into an apparently effortless kinetic visual feast. It's a concatenation of allegorical dreamscapes, floating timelessly from one strand to the next and back again like a Proustian novel. Elegant set-pieces include the aimlessly wandering Christ figure depicted as a pale criminal who's about to have the whistle blown on him; the sumptuous long table arrangement, where ageing teachers bang their canes as a young boy treads carefully over the tabletop; and the nightmarish police station, where an innocuous gay couple are victimised, humiliated and tortured, by sadistic cops wearing Santa Claus costumes.

Edward II (1991) has acquired a significant Jarman fan base, with many considering it his greatest film; some of us beg to differ. Loosely adapted from Christopher Marlowe's play, Jarman continues to revivify his fascination with esoteric English Elizabethan culture. Court intrigues, skulduggery and power-plotting are rife in the story of a queer Plantagenet monarch, assassinated by being impaled on a poker. One could argue that here Jarman's gay liberation political tirades are over-egged, cheapening its artistry.

Among friends who worked most frequently on Jarman's films are the producer James Mackay, Tilda Swinton — an eminent actress with the Royal Shakespeare Company (RSC) — and Simon Fisher Turner who provided so many of the eclectic and evocative music soundtracks.

Wittgenstein (1992). Jarman had been planning a film about the philosopher for several years before its realisation. A difficult project from the start, Jarman made an inspired choice for the scriptwriter — Oxford based Marxist literary critic, Terry Eagleton. 1960s student radical Tariq Ali joined the team as producer. The minimal stage-sets illuminated against pitch black nothingness create a stark, intense and thought-provoking back-drop to the action.

Blue (1993). Jarman's health had now deteriorated to the point that he was virtually blind when he made his last feature. His awareness of his imminent death and courage in facing it is apparent in *Blue*. The feature is one of the most remarkable and audacious films ever made: a static shot of a plain blue screen with Jarman's narrated monologue. It comprises three reels edited together of artist Yves Klein's blue canvas, filmed at the Tate Gallery. It is as mesmerising as the monologue is thought provoking.

Derek Jarman died in 1994 of AIDS-related illness.

Jubilee (1977)

The catalyst for *Jubilee* was Jarman's 1977 Super-8 short, *Jordan's Dance*, a substantial chunk of which is recycled in *Jubilee*. Set in punk London, where anarchy and violence prevails on the streets, *Jubilee* takes on board time travelling royals, punk bands, punk parties, some familiar punk faces, killer cops, casual sex, and Adolf Hitler, mixing them together with some risqué dialogue ("As a child my hero was Myra Hindley") and arresting imagery, such as Amyl, the film's "heroine," goose stepping to the British national anthem. Reverse angle shots (360° camera pans) are frequently employed by Jarman, challenging Hollywood's conventional rule that these shots confuse the audience; Jarman uses their poetic aesthetic to disrupt realist conventions.

Jarman magnifies and radicalises conventional cinematic depictions of gender, potraying (physiological differences aside) women as capable of anything men are, be it positive or negative. This is further emphasised by contrasting Elizabeth I, arguably England's most robust female ruler, with a man, Borgia Ginz.

All the bands' live performances are cut short before any song is complete (except Rule Britannia) playfully challenging the spectator's expectations and recalling Jean Luc Godard's *One Plus One/Sympathy For The Devil* (1968). The squat-like pad of the punk girl gang is similar to the Parisian Maoist student cell in *La Chinoise* (Godard, 1967). Episodic narrative, deconstructed road movie theme, post-apocalyptic futures, historical characters, revolutionary violence and destruction, and more, all suggest *Weekend*. The final beachhead and sea location echo the Mediterranean seaside location in *Pierrot Le Fou* (Godard, 1965).

The filming of Jordan's dance sequence may be partly inspired by Kenneth Anger's *Inauguration of the Pleasure Dome* (1954). Several of the characters claim to be musicians or actors within the plot; this reflects their real, out of character roles, playfully reminding the audience there's real life outside the movie: a Brechtian device.

Far from appealing to all punks, *Jubilee* split the punk movement: some loved it, others loathed it and refuted its status as a punk film. In retrospect, it's probably the finest punk film of all and much more besides. Punk was a diverse movement from the start, full of unresolved contradictions and recognising difference as a virtue — this was integral to its creative energy. What could be more punk than provoking controversy even among punks?

"No future," cry the Sex Pistols in God Save The Queen. Fundamentally, *Jubilee* presents a concept of time and change as relative and retrogressive. This complex notion is repeatedly expressed

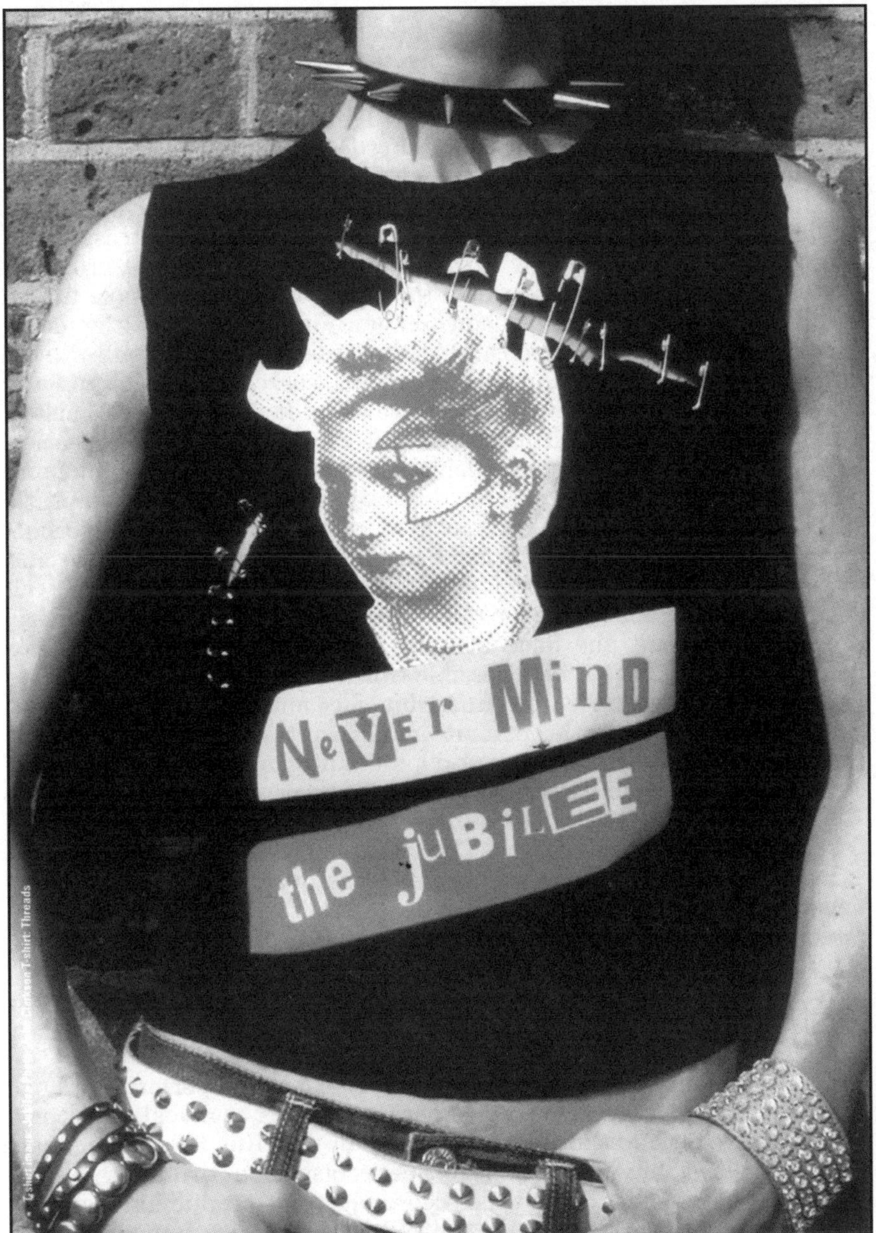

Promotional material, *Punk at The National Film Theatre*, 2002

in *Jubilee* in various innovative ways, and is frequently misunderstood by the film's critics. It blatantly contrasts with Borgia's expressed defence of 'progress,' a character who cleverly and correctly recognises progress as a capitalist ideal. If time is retrogressive, progress is a myth, arguably created by capitalist society to promote the work ethic and consumerism; it always insists there's a better future, an ideal end to achieve. But if time is retrogressive, one moment is equal to the next in a quantum universe, so there really is *no future*, because there is no end to obtain. The journey or process is the end and change is permanent — eternal. This concept is probably best expressed by the German philosopher Frederick Nietzsche, in his notion of eternal recurrence. It allows the spectator to accept the apparently contradictory, simultaneous present and possible future world depicted in *Jubilee*. Further, past or history (Elizabeth I) is both contrasted and equated with the future-now world; there is change but not progress; past worlds are no better or worse than the present or possible future worlds. Whether the Virgin Queen and her minions, or a wealthy media entrepreneur and his minions, rule the ordinary people makes little difference to most. Both exert power over us, coerce and exploit us.

Retrogressive time is not regressive time. It does not look back to the past for solace. The Elizabethan plot strand, with its Shakespearian English rants, is most widely misinterpreted as being pretentious and nostalgic for a supposed past golden age. This is an over simplistic summation, ignoring the juxtaposition of sequences and the film's overall coherence. The brief flashbacks don't show the violence and savagery of Elizabethan England, but they don't need to. It's well documented that the period was rife with power-plots and skulduggery, executions, torture, the mass slaughter of Catholics and more... We don't need to recreate it as a possible world. Further, note the Queen's lady-in-waiting: her miserable, unsmiling face and put-upon expression; she needn't say a word throughout (and doesn't) as she runs around at the behest of her boss. Her face and midget proportion says it all — the centuries of misery imposed upon the common people.

Anarchy in the UK... The punk future-now world of slaughter and destruction is not simply attacked by a reactionary Jarman. Its depiction is usually ambiguous and sometimes celebratory (but also occasionally negative). The film recognises that death and destruction are creative forces, inescapable expressions of change and becoming.

Shot from behind

In *Jubilee*, Siouxsie and the Banshees appear briefly, performing Love In A Void live on stage. But the camera pulls back to reveal that it is a videotaped television show, being watched by The Kid, the leading male character played by Adam Ant. Banshees replacement drummer, Kenny Morris, also assisted behind-the-scenes, helping production designer John Maybury create a set at Butler's Wharf with rubbish they collected from skips. The original Adam and the Ants line up play Deutscher Girls and Plastic Surgery. They had only been together two months at the time and were introduced to Jarman by their manager, Jordan. Additional punk music on the soundtrack includes Chelsea, Maneaters and Amilcar. Rule Britannia is sung by Suzi Pinns, to accompany Jordan's goose-stepping punk Britannia performance. Paranoia Paradise is performed by Wayne County as Lounge Lizard. The Slits also appear briefly as a punk street gang.

Starring Jenny Runacre as Bod/Elizabeth I, Jordan as Amyl Nitrate, Little Nell as Crabs, Toyah Wilcox as Mad, Orlando as Borgia Ginz, Ian Charleson as Angel, Hermine Demoriane as Chaos, Linda Spurrier as Viv, Karl Johnson as Sphinx, Neil Kennedy as Max, Richard O'Brian as John Dee, and David Haughton as Ariel. Filmed in London during 1977, most of the exterior wasteland footage was shot in Deptford; this really is punk Britain. Jarman said his screenplay was partly inspired by cut-ups of punk fanzines like *Sniffin' Glue*.

Jarman insisted the cast use real guns as opposed to props in the film. During one day's location shoot, Jordan and the punk girls were enacting a street firefight, when suddenly the (real) police appeared and arrested them. They tried to argue the firing pins had been removed, so the weapons couldn't fire, but the cops hadn't a clue what they were on about and nicked them anyway.

When Adam and the Ants performed Plastic Surgery for the film at London's New Victoria theatre, Adam, dressed in black bondage gear, bounces around the stage like a real lunatic. He dislocated his knee during the shoot.

Jordan was given ballet lessons from age four until she was eighteen but confessed, "*Jubilee* pushed me to the limits mentally and physically. I had to dance to points on concrete — no ballerina has that — they've got supple wooden floors. My toes bled!"

Source influences cited by Jarman and others, pertaining to *Jubilee* include: JG Ballard's cult sci-fi novel, *Crash* (itself later filmed by David Cronenberg) for wasteland-scapes and road carnage. Stanley Kubrick's film *A Clockwork Orange* (1971), and the Anthony Burgess novel on which it was based, for depictions of futuristic urban street gangs and thought provoking lingering violence. The stage and screen productions of *The Rocky Horror Picture Show* (1975), with two of its cast acting in *Jubilee*. Psychoanalyst Carl Jung's *Seven Sermons to the Dead* (Jarman also refers to psychologist Erich Fromm's *Fear of Freedom* in an interview). The *SCUM Manifesto*, a radical feminist polemic (Society for Cutting Up Men) by Valerie Solanas, has also been cited.

In his book, *Dancing Ledge*, Jarman explains events behind-the-scenes. *Jubilee*'s pre-production working title was *High Fashion*. Jarman refers to the production company as R.I.P. OFF Films, who later registered as Megalovision. Producer James Whaley raised £50,000 in Tehran. Jarman's headquarters during filming was a production studio at Butler's Wharf. Additional cast members were picked up at punk gigs. Production underway, the working title changed to *Chelsea on Ice*. The censor initially demanded five cuts from the completed film, but Jarman fought the decision, and was eventually only forced to make one cut: seven seconds from the sexual asphyxiation scene. *Jubilee* opened at the Gate Cinema in Notting Hill. The première immediately divided opinion among its punk audience: a 'strong man' fainted and a hippie lady proclaimed love, dancing in front of the audience; a group of girl motorcyclists in leathers (who stood in for the bike scene) got up declaring they were Christians and left the cinema. One of *Jubilee*'s most avowed critics was Vivienne Westwood, who produced a T-shirt declaring the film was boring.

Jarman commented on making the film:

> With *Jubilee* the progressive merging of film and my reality was complete. The source of the film was often autobiographical, the locations were the streets and warehouses in which I had lived during the previous ten years. The film was cast from among and made by friends. It was a determined and often reckless analysis of the world which surrounds us... The shooting script is a mass of Xeroxes and quick notes on scraps of paper, torn photos and messages from my collaborators, and the resulting film has something of the same quality... in *Jubilee* our world became the film... a fantasy documentary fabricated so that documentary and fictional forms are confused and coalesce.[1]

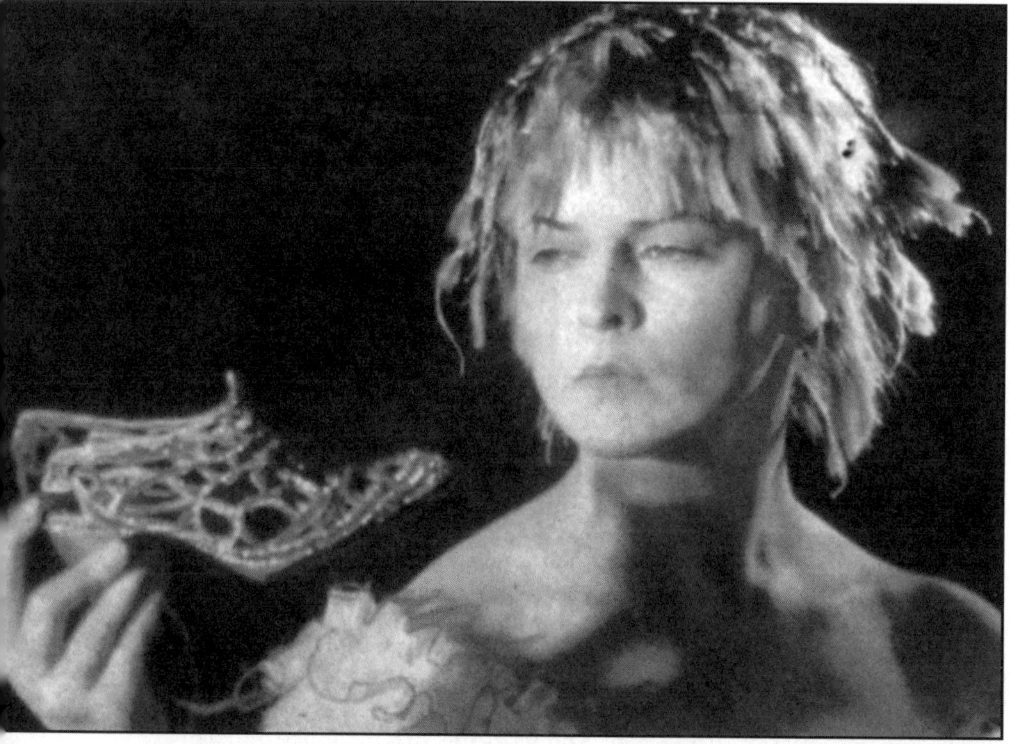

Toya Wilcox in Jarman's The Tempest

On reflection, it's probably *Jubilee*'s retrogressive depiction of time (expressed in both form and content), its amazingly well-founded prophetic qualities, and its innovative use of radical techniques, derived from 1960s European art films, which keep it looking surprisingly fresh and undated today. A controversial masterpiece of punk cinema.

SHAKESPEARE-A-POGO

How Shakespeare would have loved the cinema! ***Derek Jarman***

Derek Jarman's poetic and symbolic evocation of Elizabeth I, and scripted parody of Shakespearian English in *Jubilee*, was undoubtedly the primary complaint among the film's punk critics. But the underlying depth and significance of this historical juxtaposition was largely misunderstood. Nevertheless, Jarman certainly nurtured a deep fascination with the Elizabethan epoch, and Jacobean artistic renaissance, most enduringly expressed in the plays of Christopher Marlowe and William Shakespeare. This would become profoundly apparent in Jarman's next two feature films: a punk adaptation of Shakespeare's dreamy comic play *The Tempest* (1979), and a post-industrialist visual interpretation of the bard's collected love poems, *The Angelic Conversation* (1985).

Yet the apparently tenuous connection between Shakespeare and punk was not solely Jarman's prerogative. Sex Pistol Johnny Rotten has adumbrated at length that the distorted figure of King Richard III, as realised by Lawrence Olivier in his 1955 cinematic adaptation of Shakespeare's *Richard III*, influenced Rotten's ugly and wildly expressionist stage act. Director Julien Temple even included clips from the Olivier version in *The Filth and the Fury*.

In Jarman's punk *The Tempest* he was not specifically trying to make it punk. Nor was he avoiding punk influence. The final result is achieved because of the coincidence of DIY aesthetics, attitudes and innovative methods shared by Jarman and sections of the punk movement, together with its time and place, and the resources available to Jarman after *Jubilee*. Toyah Wilcox as Miranda exhibits the most obvious punk manifestations in her remarkable performance, for which her slight natural lisp was considered an asset; Wilcox was a child of the punk generation, following up her screen debut as Mad in Jarman's *Jubilee*. (Between *Jubilee* and *The Tempest*, Wilcox was cast in *The Corn Is Green* and *Quadrophenia*, both 1978.) She also had a modestly successful music career by presenting herself as a pop-punk performer; her live performance of Danced, at London's Lyceum, was filmed for Derek Burbidge's *Urgh! A Music War* (1980). The other inescapable punk influences are in *mise en scene*: set design, wardrobe, hairstyles and make-up.

It is perhaps the shear eclecticism Jarman realises in *The Tempest*, which ultimately (and perhaps accidentally) creates its punk veneer. Reviewers have acknowledged the influences of Gothic horror and melodrama, Baroque painting, Hollywood pastiche, and high camp. Jarman's preoccupation with anachronism adds to this; juxtaposing a modern punk attitude with a fascination of Elizabethan and Jacobean drama. Pasolini's innocent homoeroticism is recalled; even Vincent Minnelli's influence has been cited in *The Tempest*'s "lush sense of décor and colour." Jarman himself claimed *The Wizard of Oz* (1939) as a major influence: "As Stephano, Trinculo and Caliban danced along the Bamburgh sands I realised I'd directed them as if they too were on the road to the wicked witch's castle."[2] Further, he cites Eisenstein's *Ivan the Terrible* (1944) for its magical interior design. Jarman's literary sources included the renaissance magi — Dee, Cornelius Agrippa, Bruno, Fludd and Paracelsus, in conjunction with Carl Jung.

Yet *The Tempest* contrasts radically with *Jubilee*. While *Jubilee* is a celebration of Thanatos, *The Tempest* is equally defiant in its commitment to Eros. Part of Jarman's legacy as an artist was his acknowledgement that there is both good and bad, on each side; both are necessary and it is up to the artist to explore the attributes pertaining to each, seeking a balance where each can hold the other in check. He recognised this as an endless pursuit, because the balance is always transient.

Regarding the film's interpretation of Shakespeare's work, *The Tempest* is again controversial. Interestingly, while the film was widely attacked by highbrow film critics for trivialising Shakespeare, many Shakespeare scholars rushed to the film's defence, claiming it was closer to the spirit of Shakespeare than almost any other movie. Whatever Jarman's approach to Shakespeare's *The Tempest*, it is certainly unconventional, idiosyncratic, innovative and perhaps, therefore, punk.

When he came to filming *The Tempest*, Jarman "needed an island of the mind, that opened mysteriously like Chinese boxes: an abstract landscape..."[3] The budget was £150,000, and he was determined to create a magical ambience, without a hint of realism; wrapping the surface to dazzle the spectator. In November 1978, Jarman took out his scissors and cut up the play for the third time. By choosing a dream-like film format, he felt he could take liberties with the text, cutting away most of the obsolete comedy. Jarman's *Tempest* stands out from other productions as it upholds a fresh and modern aesthetic, exuding sensuality, sex and youth. As the medium is film and not theatre, Jarman has more scope to create magical effect and has instilled his version with a cool, surreal, timelessness.

Notes

1 Derek Jarman, *Dancing Ledge*, London: Quartet Books, 1984, p.176–177.

2 Ibid, p.41.

3 Ibid, p.186

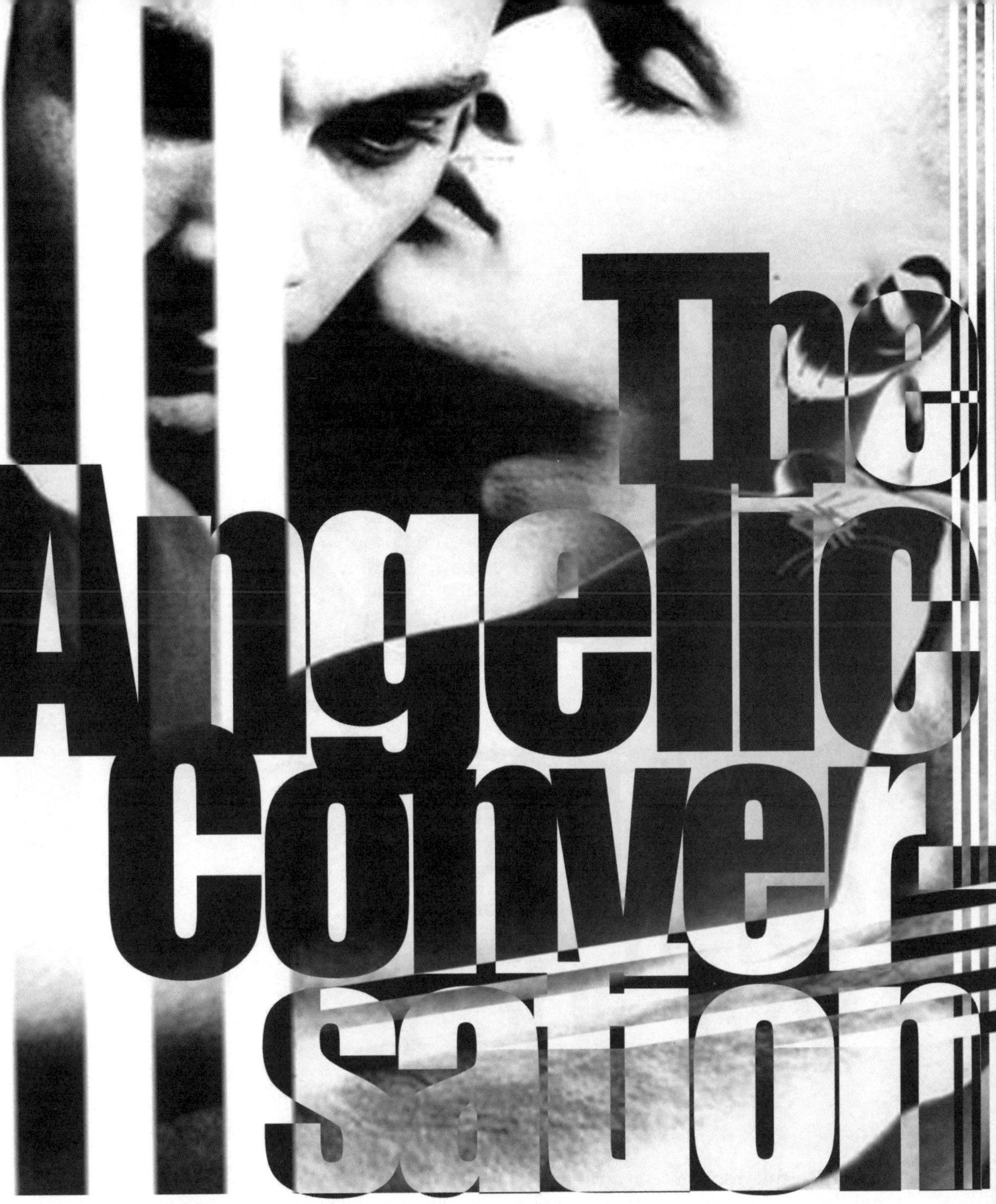

Stephen Thrower

Those who dream are co-authors of the world

Heraclitus, The Last of England

When punk rock music grabbed the headlines in 1976, it felt for a while as if some sort of cultural meltdown was imminent. However, big business soon reasserted its control of the culture industry. Punks proved susceptible to the blandishments of money and fame, like anyone else, and signing to a major label became the norm. Whilst it was undoubtedly very funny to see EMI and A&M hand over cash to the Sex Pistols, only to squirm out of their own contracts when media attention blew up — and the band threw up — in their faces, the true legacy of punk took place away from the tabloid glare courted by Malcolm McLaren. The closest thing to a real revolution was happening at a smaller level: demystification of the production and distribution process — a devolution of the recording industry that was essential not only for punk and post-punk, but also for the acid-house and drum'n'bass music cycles of the late eighties and early nineties. Bands such as The Desperate Bicycles, Alternative TV and Crass set up their own record labels, producing their own low cost singles and bypassing the major labels. Marxist post-structuralist clever dicks Scritti Politti included a meticulous breakdown of the costs for their first single on the cover itself. A small London record shop in Notting Hill — previously a haunt for those seeking obscure psychedelia, US garage band trash and dub reggae imports — offered to distribute many of these one-off labels, turning Rough Trade into a record label and distribution outlet for the weird and wilder shores of late seventies music. It was the birth of the independent music scene in Great Britain (later known, in its debased form, as the 'indie' market), and its influence extended far beyond the antics of a few high profile bad boys.

Most of the 'famous' punk rockers chose to sign with major labels. The never-very-hip Stranglers went straight to United Artists, The Clash, with sublime irony, to CBS in January 1977 for a reputed £100,000. Siouxsie and the Banshees, the last major punks to secure a recording contract (graffiti adorning parts of London through 1977 screamed "Why don't you sign the Banshees?"), could easily have gone to a small independent label or released their own singles. Instead they spent eighteen precious months waiting for the big boys to offer them a comfy chair in major-label heaven (they eventually signed to Polydor, home of the Rubettes).

The value of releases such as the first Buzzcocks single, the self-financed Spiral Scratch, can't be overestimated. The band went on to sign with United Artists, but the practical example of that landmark record eclipses the disappointment of their shift to the majors. The same freedom by example was initiated in publishing, when Mark Perry started the fanzine *Sniffin' Glue* to cover the developing punk music scene ("Punk died the day The Clash signed to CBS,"[1] he announced).

Neither independent records nor independent magazines were invented by the punks — sixties psychedelic and garage rock scenes in America had their self-produced records and the despised 'lazy' hippies printed many a cheaply Xeroxed magazine. Not every self-produced record was a revelation (The Desperate Bicycles were, frankly, shit), and not every corporate whore was a fool (Poly Styrene, of EMI acquisitions X-Ray Spex, skewered the punk-by-numbers crowd with the line, "Did you do it for fame, did you do it in a fit, did you do it before you read about it?"[2]). But the independent culture, able to bypass the demands and expectations of the conventional rock world, offered a freedom to experiment and participate without being part of an exploitative corporate machine. You had to wonder about the character of those who signed up for the big money...

There were few who saw the coming absorption of the 'revolution' as clearly as Derek Jarman (I'd include Mark E. Smith, Genesis P. Orridge and Mark Perry). *Jubilee*, Derek's take on punk, was a withering satire but from 1984 onwards he set out to explore real alternatives, applying the critique he'd used on punk to his own cinema, changing his working methods and lighting a beacon of independence for others. Whilst film production is rarely as independent as music, due to higher costs, Derek's work in video and Super-8 suggested how filmmakers could enjoy similar experimental freedoms to those of the independent musicians of the punk and post-punk era.

In 1984 Derek set about cataloguing his stockpile of Super-8 film material, which had grown considerably since his early experiments of the 1970s. The occasion for this was a retrospective of his feature films and an exhibition of his paintings at London's Institute of Contemporary Arts (ICA). In preparation, he and his friend and producer James Mackay took the reels to the ICA, projected them on the wall of the cinema, and videoed them. One of the rolls of film was a shot of the Pantheon in Rome which Derek projected onto ICA employee Steve Radnall, transferring the result onto video.

It was this 'short film' that Derek first suggested as a possible collaboration with Coil, a band whose line-up at the time comprised Geff Rushton (aka John Balance), Peter 'Sleazy' Christopherson and myself. Derek, Geff and Sleazy already knew each other, as Sleazy's first group Throbbing Gristle had scored Derek's *In The Shadow Of The Sun* and Derek had appeared as 'Spokesman' on a promotional video for Geff and Sleazy's previous band Psychic TV. James Mackay recalls: "Derek always leaned towards Gen (Genesis P. Orridge, Sleazy's ex-colleague in Throbbing Gristle and Psychic TV) but I pushed him towards Peter. By the time that we got to the music we'd already completed *Imagining October* — shot after *Angelic* but completed before *Angelic* was finished and featuring Gen's music — so I was able to argue for balance, no pun intended."

I can't remember the original film that Derek suggested we work on — possibly I never saw it — but according to Sleazy, "It was really awful, and we said, well, we'd love to do some music for one of your films but can you do it again?" [3] I spent quite some time at Derek's London flat in Phoenix House between 1984 and 1987, and I remember there was an impulsive, slightly hectic air to some of his creative decisions, with projects mooted on the basis of an evening's wine-fuelled conversation or a page of notes scribbled in a ledger. Numerous film ideas were discussed, including a fairly well-developed sci-fi script called *Neutron*, and plans for an adaptation of Wyndham Lewis's novel *The Childermass* (the mind boggles...). The reel he originally sent to Sleazy sounds typical of these spur-of-the-moment ideas, perhaps best suited simply for screening on the wall of Derek's flat. Thankfully, Derek remained committed to working with Coil, and *The Angelic Conversation*, as it finally emerged, proved to be a strange, beautiful, and considerably more complex piece of work.

Derek had already made three feature films: *Sebastiane, Jubilee* — which incorporates Super-8 — and *The Tempest*. All three were shot in 16mm (blown up to 35mm) and utilised the basics of a conventional crew structure. But, as financing for his proposed fourth feature, *Caravaggio*, hiccupped through umpteen false dawns throughout the early 1980s, he began to regard the industry with loathing, and embraced his 'home movie' shorts as a more viable, less hopelessly compromised alternative.[4]

A retreat from intransigent opposition? As subsequent work would underline, it was more of a road to Damascus moment. When I met Derek at the time of this transformation of his ambition, I'd only seen one of his films, *Sebastiane*, which I didn't really like. We got on well together though, and as luck would have it his other two movies were playing on a double bill at London's (long lost) repertory cinema, the Scala. I was dreading I might not like them, but instead I was pleasurably surprised. I raved about *Jubilee* in particular, but Derek was very self-effacing. His best work wasn't the features, he said; the Super-8 films were far more important to him. This was before the wave of Super-8 and video artists Derek inspired — it impressed the hell out of me that an established feature film director could say that his private, almost zero-budget short films, in the cheapest possible format, were his real work and the 'big' films were the sideline. You knew he meant it too; it wasn't just a pose. If his subsequent career has its well-timed 35mm moments, careful observers can see where the locus of his art truly lies: *Caravaggio*, *Edward II* and *Wittgenstein* have their qualities, but it's *The Last of England*, *The Garden* and *Blue* where you encounter the full force of the director.

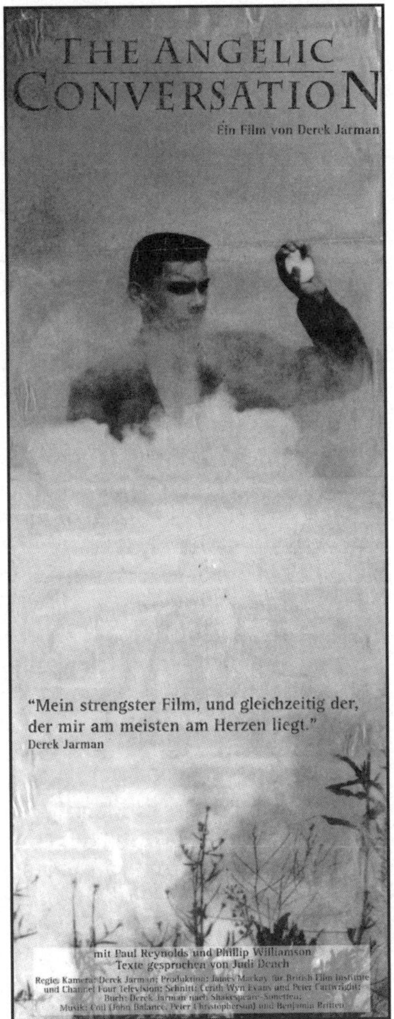

German poster for *The Angelic Cinversation*

Derek's notes before embarking on what was briefly called *Psychic Billy's Angelic Conversation*[5] (a lame pun on 'psychobillies' which thankfully never saw the light of a projector) show how important Super-8 and its 'limitations' were in his conception of the film. He writes:

> Form: The reasons for super-8 and how the medium dictates the form — e.g. non-narrative/sound rebuilt afterwards, the 'quality' of the image, the limited palette of 16mm, 35mm.[6]

The medium enters into the form of *Angelic Conversation* at every stage of its development, beginning with the shooting itself, where Derek chose to use a feature peculiar to Super-8 cameras. As he explained in his book *The Last of England*:

> On the Nizo camera there is a dial which allows one to take speeded-up film; you take single frames, if this is projected at normal speeds it goes fast. But I have projectors which go at slow speeds, so the film is restored to a near normal pace, like a series of moving slides. I refilmed the projection with an ordinary Olympus home-video camera connected to a U-matic deck. In order to get unusual colours I fiddled around with the white balance button. Sometimes I put a piece of red paper in front of it, which gives the film a greenish tint, or a piece of green paper, which would give it a reddish tint.

Producer James Mackay explains in more detail: "Derek would film at around six frames per second and then project rather slower, more like 3fps, so there was a sort of slow motion effect. He didn't project at the same speed as he shot it. There was also a shutter mechanism peculiar to the Bolex projector he used, which affected the result quite a bit." The Nizo camera allowed speeds of incredible slowness all the way up to the standard speed of 24fps. The dial was not limited to fixed increments but rotated smoothly, and the camera casing's fps markings were imprecise. Theoretically, any setting up to 24fps was possible, whereas the Bolex projector had calibrations for 3, 6, 9, 12, 18 and 24fps only. This meant that it was possible to 'tune' the Nizo against the Bolex's settings, achieving unusual visual effects.

The slowly juddering image that results is *The Angelic Conversation*'s defining characteristic. It turns the grainy, hand-held Super-8 footage into a series of textured stills, yet also manages to suggest real movement, hanging on by the skin of its teeth to cinema's illusion of motion. Derek uses the effect for all of the Super-8 material, with only the video shots in 'real' time. I use the inverted commas advisedly — we grow so acclimatised to the film's slowly clicking Super-8 that when the 25fps video kicks in it's like being woken from a dream to find oneself embroiled in some dodgy performance art piece. I'm not sure if I really ever liked the video material — the experiments with colour and re-filming which yielded such mesmerising results from Super-8 look ugly and half-cooked when applied to video. The five minute scene where Dave Baby is anointed by Paul Reynolds has a beautiful intention ("Service to others" as Derek defined it) — but for me, the mundane video quality available at the time robs the scene of visual poetry.

Of course, cynics will say that this technical malarkey is a fine way to stretch twenty-five minutes of footage out to feature length. They would have a point, and the frugal, ever-practical Derek would readily have agreed, but it's barely a third of the truth. Derek's parallel career as a painter meant that for him the results of the Super-8's gizmo were aesthetically irresistible. This technique — rarely used before 1984, except in the early films of David Cronenberg, where post-production processing achieved a vaguely similar effect on 35mm film[7] — bridges the gulf between film and photography, if not painting.

The portability of the Super-8 camera, and the lack of any need for cumbersome film crews, lends a 'private' feeling to a Super-8 shoot, and, because of the cheapness of stock and developing, Derek embarked on his new project without the need for investors, scripts, and the scrutiny that comes from hidebound financial arrangements. The 'crew', during what can loosely be called production, of *The Angelic Conversation* frequently comprised just one or two people behind the camera: Derek and second cameraman James Mackay. If you were to visit the set of even the lowliest mainstream Brit film — say, *Chariots Of Fire* (Hugh Hudson, 1981) or *Sex Lives of the Potato-Men* (Andy Humphries, 2004) — you could multiply that by at least ten, if not thirty.

Mackay not only filmed certain shots, like the lily in the pond, but also set up sequences such as Philip looking out of the window at Montecute House, and brought along the smoke and collision flares which play a major part in the film's eerie atmosphere. "There were very few people involved in the shooting, apart from a day or two in the ICA cinematheque," Mackay confirms, "In fact the two main actors were filmed separately, apart from one evening in Derek's flat. Mostly it would be Derek, myself, a driver and one of the actors."

Much of this man-economy is down to the lightweight camera and Super-8's maximal depth of field, which means that focus isn't a major problem; there's no need for tape measures and time-consuming 'blocking.' The choreography of camera and performer is freed from such restraints. Spontaneity — a sense that filming is simply an extension of a day out in the countryside with a small group of friends — means that art and life are part of the same fabric, rather than two different forces being laboriously stapled together in the meshes of film production.

The principal cast comprises two handsome young men, Paul Reynolds and Philip Williamson, who between them occupy three-quarters of the screen time. Williamson leans noticeably towards contemporary gay fashion with his very eighties flat-top haircut, but given that much of his 'action' is simply to bathe, or gaze, lovelorn, through windows or at some off-screen horizon, he acquits himself with a remarkable lack of preciousness. Reynolds, an archaeology student of Portuguese origin, is perhaps the greater find. He appears unanchored by time, a compelling screen presence who could probably have worked elsewhere in the industry had he wanted to. His high cheekbones and intense brow — two dark, converging diagonals — seem born of distant, pre-Christian times: Derek, a devotee of Pasolini, must have felt he had his Oedipus, his 'Visitor.'

Having shot various scenes at locations such as Winspit, Dancing Ledge, and Montacute House, the question now arose for Derek of how to turn the reels into a feature within the technical means at his disposal. So far, the filming itself had used thirty-one reels of Agfa Super-8, at a cost of £2.50 per roll, including processing: a total stock expenditure of just £77.50! Once the Super-8 was transferred to three-quarter inch video for colour manipulation (another inexpensive process), Derek began to cast around for money to transfer the video to 35mm film. It was at this stage that the British Film Institute (BFI) became involved,

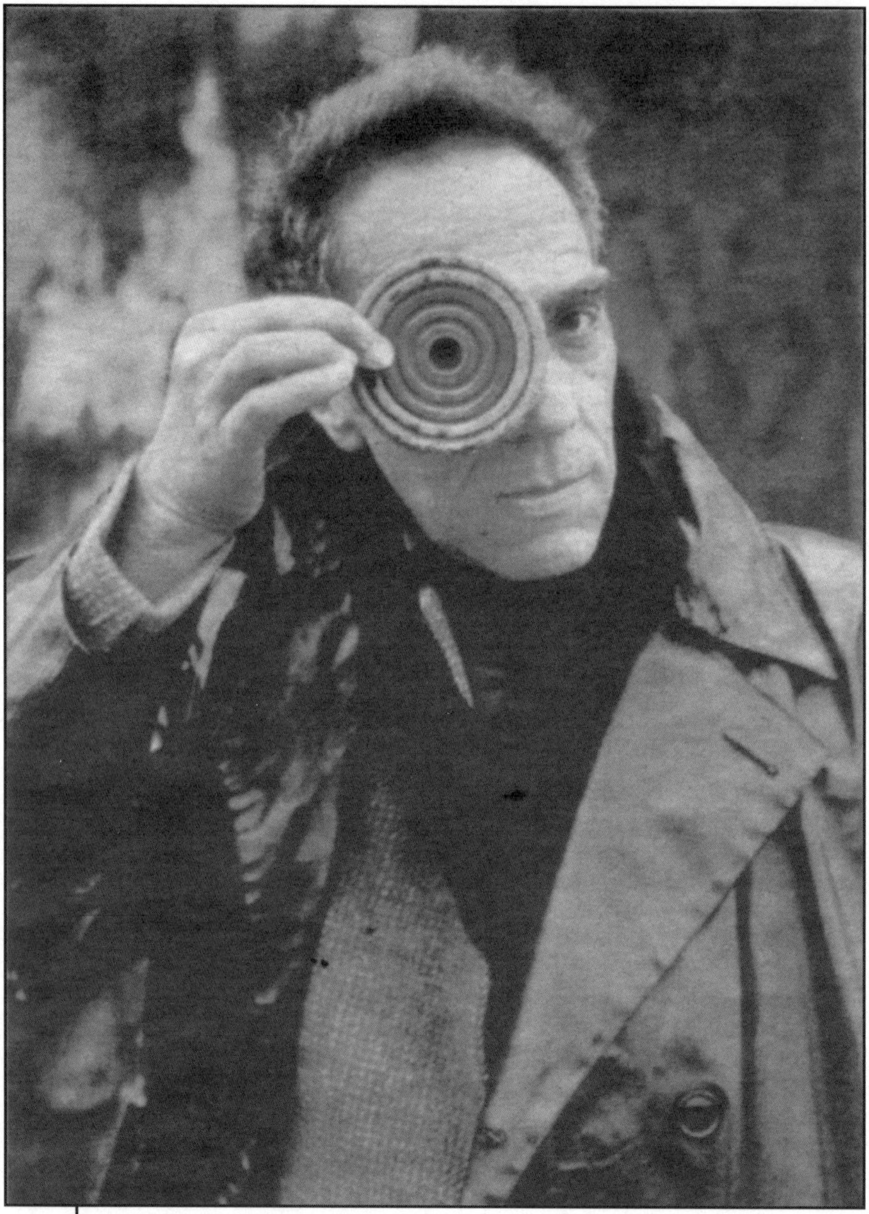

Derek Jarman

as the budgetary requirements for a transfer to high band video and from there to 35mm went beyond Derek's individual means. Even then, the eventual cost of this post-production transference was £50,000, estimated by the BFI's Peter Sainsbury as "about one-fifth of what would normally have been spent on a very low budget feature."[8]

The Angelic Conversation is sometimes criticised for the demands it makes on its audience. *The Times*, in a generally positive review, called it "An excellent short that spun out of control."[9] Certainly no pulse-pounder, the film nevertheless has a pulse, even if it's one you'd normally associate with meditation. Perhaps it should only be screened after a series of deep-breathing exercises...

In one of his most quoted mission statements, Derek coined the term "a cinema of small gestures," to describe the aesthetic he was accumulating through his Super-8 adventures; sure enough, *The Angelic Conversation* often hinges on little more than a flicker of longing on a face wreathed in shuddering fog, or the mesmeric curl of a flame. Just as with the technical relationship between the Nizo Super-8 camera and the Bolex projector, the film's reception hinges on a tuning of metabolisms between the audience and the film. If we surrender our demands for speed and pace, for narrative development, we enter another world, where a walk through a cave lit by flares becomes a journey across the fantastical terrain of a far distant planet; a place where invisible forces warp our sense of time.

Cinema that's been whittled down to entertainment precludes such drastic changes of pace. *The Angelic Conversation*'s absence of 'action' or overt narrative development in favour of a suspension of 'real time' and a step into mythic time requires not the clichéd 'suspension of disbelief' but a suspension of expectation. Half the battle obstinate viewers will have with the film is in demanding that something should happen. Such expectations erode patience and intrude on reverie. Having said that — to be fair — I do think there are a few scenes that drag, along with a tendency to return later to images already explored that can have the viewer shifting impatiently in their seat. What's not at fault though is the overall concept and the commitment to forging a new time relationship: somewhere between the early films of Andy Warhol and the intimately personal assemblages of Stan Brakhage.

The Angelic Conversation sees the beginning of Derek's experiments with soundtrack construction and a preference for sound montage and monologue in place of dialogue — a style that found its apotheosis in *Blue*. The music score blends with sound effects and atmospheric recordings of gulls shrieking, water dripping, the hiss of emergency flares. At times the music becomes indistinguishable from the effects, achieving a total sound world as vital as the images.

Derek's familiarity with Italian cinema will have suggested the way that sound and image can be constructed separately. In the Italian film industry, dialogue was, until quite recently, always dubbed on later. This originally came about because the older film cameras were very noisy to run and even noisier to move. One could either 'blimp' the camera (i.e. soundproof it with a large casing to suppress the noise of the motor, which made cameras too heavy to move with any real grace or fluidity), or shoot silent and dub the sound later. When narrative and even dialogue are removed from the picture, the freedom to build the film through separate manipulation of audio is increased. *The Angelic Conversation* breathes through its soundtrack, through the careful selection of sound effects and distribution of music cues, and of course the sonnets, as read by Judi Dench.

James Mackay recalls how the sonnets came to be included:

We filmed in the summer of 1984 and didn't really have much of a plan. At about the same time, Derek had discovered that Peter Greenaway had been commissioned by Channel Four to make Dante's Divine Comedy as a series of short films (cantos). This really got Derek wound up[10] and he launched an offensive with a demand that Channel Four commission him to make a series of short films from Shakespeare's sonnets. This was a distinct project from *Angelic Conversation* and it wasn't until that autumn that the idea of combining the two into a single project manifested itself. It also helped Derek out of the narrative conundrum that he had struggled to solve during the editing — how do you impose a plot on a series of random image sequences? [11] But the film was edited before the sonnets were added. Having a female voice was Derek's way of trying to make the film more acceptable for straight, not so much audiences, as funders, critics etc. Why Dench? Well, our first choice was not available so we made do. Anyway, Derek's first choice was Derek. Let's just say that the sonnets are a lot harder to read than you might think.

The music

On a personal note, I have to say that, listening back, about half of what we gave to Derek must rank as some of the weakest music we ever did in Coil — if Derek had asked us to start again, just as we asked him to shoot something else in place of the Rome footage, I think he would have been perfectly justified! In our favour is the fact that all the music, regardless of quality, does at least manage to stay *sotto voce* and avoids cluttering the soundstage (clutter would have played ruinously against the grain of the slowly flickering images). Nevertheless, there are some very poor passages where the early samplers we used are plundered for their most basic sounds, from discs issued as standard with the machine. It's one of the pitfalls of a taste for novelty that today's shiny new music toy becomes tomorrow's naff old cliché. Our use of choral samples is weakest of all, with the same simplistic note sequence played relentlessly at various pitches, with no underlying sense of progression or structure (see the album track Cave Of Roses). Far more successful is a piece (called Never on the soundtrack album) where Geff improvised an extended romantic, pastoral string melody of great beauty over an arpeggio of sampled cello. As far as I know he never rehearsed this performance, despite having only rudimentary keyboard-playing skills. He channelled his musical ideas in real time without a bum note throughout. I remember being very impressed by the spontaneity of his playing that day.

The recording session for the film soundtrack was exactly that — a recording session, maybe two days in a London studio, with the clock ticking by (just as it does, audibly, on the soundtrack itself).[12] It seems quaint today, in a world where your kid brother has a home studio in his bedroom, that we made the recording in such a formal way for a film with virtually no budget. Basically, the music had to appear from our imaginations, come what may, with minimal opportunity for re-recording. Très punk, darling. I suppose it was a fairly expensive studio, not some grotty little Brixton cave (and I've worked in my fair share of those). But the pressure was the same — make approximately sixty minutes of music in two days. Although the production now had BFI money attached, Derek could ill-afford to pay for another session if we dried up. I suppose if we hadn't completed the soundtrack he would have scored it entirely with Britten, or his friend Brian Eno (whose music was always around at Phoenix House).

The sequence where Paul and Philip wrestle, which seems to stand for the carnality that is otherwise so absent in the film, betrays perhaps the darker side of Derek's eroticism. In his sleeve notes for the soundtrack CD, Derek discusses the scene as "...a struggle to overcome dark forces of repression which lingered." Lingered where? We played samples of horses whinnying in fear or desire (the factory disc was unhelpful in establishing which). I thwacked earnestly away on kettledrums and a snare drum, in a style that was becoming de rigueur in the music of Death In June. Geff played his e-bowed Chapman Stick guitar, bumping into figures he'd already used that year on a track from *Scatology* called The Sewage Worker's Birthday Party — which made me, the drummer that day, feel less guilty about accidentally stumbling into the crude rhythm of Throbbing Gristle's Discipline (if Sleazy noticed, he said nothing). What saves the music from unadulterated bombast is its naïvetè and hesitancy, and a less than fascistic precision brought to the matching of forward and backward sounds.

Reviewers have commented on the supposed chasteness and romanticism of the love scenes, especially the one that follows, where Paul and Philip lie naked, kissing tenderly and holding hands. Derek described this as "a scene that repossesses the 'screen kiss' for homoerotic love,"[13] and if ever a single emotional gesture needed reclaiming it's the male-to-male kiss, which even today is subject to a paroxysm of disgust from most heterosexuals that far exceeds the fear of sodomy. I've known straight acquaintances who can watch gay porn without flinching but who confess to feeling 'weird' when my lover and I kiss each other in greeting...

This sweet, gentle scene, however, is obviously post-coital — the fight scene is therefore the sex scene. *The Angelic Conversation*'s reputation is of dreamy same-sex romanticism ("a homosexual version of heterosexual kitsch" as Tony Rayns once cruelly called it[14]), but when we were scoring the wrestling scene, I was struck by the image of one boy's hand pushing down on the back of the other's neck, a gesture of dominance, met with an equally gestural submission, that speaks volumes of the inescapable power dynamics of sexuality. In this idyll there still exists a shadow of aggression. It makes me laugh today to watch the film and see how this darker strain emerges, about two-thirds of the way in, as if neither Derek nor Coil could refrain for more than three-quarters of an hour from aggressive, Mars-oriented sexuality. The limpid tones of Judi Dench seem suddenly twee, a thousand miles away. (Not Shakespeare, though. The sonnets are hard in their way: they can seem almost demanding in their supplication, the ebb and flow of language conjuring images of a narrator with a passive-aggressive streak. Oh Bondage, Up Yours! is only a stanza away...). Derek was ambivalent about the 'affirmative image' strategy in the film anyway: in his book *The Last of England*, he took up the theme when quizzed about its harsher sexuality:

> Safe sex can be awfully drab if you've experienced sodomy. I'm not certain that I want comfortable sexual encounters, deep down it all seems too cosily suburban and fits too nicely — that's the right word — into the chintzy Englishness of it all... Like a lot of us I'm being good against my better instincts. At first I thought: put up affirmative images; but then I'd done that in *Sebastiane* and *The Angelic Conversation*. I don't want to be too precious and protective.

The most successful passages of music, I think, in terms of their melding with the images, are those which came from existing recordings. The first ten minutes of the film are accompanied by an augmented version of How To Destroy Angels, a 12" single that was Coil's first fully-fledged record release. Made a year earlier, before I joined the group, its whirring bullroarers, gongs and sundry metallic clangings suggest a ritual suspended out of time, which is perfectly in synch with the needs of the image. The second success is a passage from Benjamin Britten's opera *Peter Grimes*, which accompanies Philip Williamson swimming in a tidal rock pool (the ancient idyll of which is slightly undercut by the occasional glimpse of Philip's trendy black briefs[15]). The third passage to strike a perfect balance with the screen is At The Heart Of It All, a song we recorded earlier in 1984 for the Scatology album, used here in stripped down, demo form. Built around a melancholic clarinet melody that keens like a seabird's lament, and a lovely keyboard structure that doesn't intrude on the film's own rhythms, it's nevertheless dramatic enough to bring the whole journey to an end.

Is *The Angelic Conversation* an escapist entertainment for art junkies? It might seem so at a glance. I remember that Derek was reading a lot of Jung, and was passionately interested in Jungian theorist James Hillman at the time. The film's archaic, timeless aura is furthered by Derek's choice of elemental imagery, sure to have been amplified by his reading of Hillman.[16] Light shards probe like antennae from mirrors held aloft; smoke renders visible the air's movement; fire leaps and dances in unrepeatable arabesques; poured water turns to gelatinous fronds caressing the flesh, cave walls and cliffs loom, like film grain magnified through an electron microscope and turned into solid matter. *"What is your substance? Whereof are you made, that millions of strange shadows on you tend?"* The politics of archetypal psychology are dubious from the standpoint of Freud, who broke off relations with Jung because of what he perceived as Jung's mysticism. The question being, where do archetypes originate, and how can we interrogate them if they precede language? It sounds like a recipe for letting God in through the back door. And yet, recent developments in the cognitive psychology of early childhood have established recognition of forms amongst children who have yet to learn language, either written or verbal. Perhaps archetypes are about to enjoy a surge of popularity amongst scientists and their believers?

Bio-metaphysics aside, *The Angelic Conversation* most definitely addresses the outside world from which it seeks refuge. The film may be a dream but it's not born of ignorance. Agreed, the other 'characters' who emerge as the film rolls on are avatars of symbolic importance to the lovers, rather than individuals themselves. A cynic might laugh at this 'epic' journey from the narcissism of gay identity to the mutual absorption of lovers — yet behind it, the malignance of the state cajoles, spies, and spreads its poison. "There's no such thing as Society — there are individual men and women, and there are families," Margaret Thatcher pronounced later, in 1987, speaking to *Woman's Own* magazine... No room for lovers then, nor even friends, and certainly not comrades... Trying to erase in one single arrogant rhetorical gesture the possibility of opposition to the state, Thatcher and her philistine oxen are the threat that looms at the edges of *The Angelic Conversation*. It's the intolerant, supposedly non-interventionist, but in truth monstrously invasive, Thatcherite state that Derek is railing against with his shots of radars and burning cars: surveillance and social decay, with the former seeking scapegoats for the latter. Tory politics makes much of its desire to reduce the state and give 'freedom' to the individual, but such 'freedoms' as they offer are merely economic and acquisitive. Freedom to rip off, and freedom to be ripped off. Sexual freedom was never part of their agenda, nor was freedom in the arts, freedom of ideas, images, desires — these were to be controlled, denied, forbidden, with the same vehemence as a Marxist might forbid profit, privilege or private ownership. *The Angelic Conversation* is a dream snatched from a nightmare: it makes a stand against the attempt to negate the very essence and value of gay men's love, and can thus never be anything less than political.

In memory of Geff Rushton:
The Dreamer Is Still Asleep

The Angelic Conversation credits

Director: Derek Jarman. Producer: James Mackay. Original Music: Coil (John Balance, Peter Christopherson, Steven E. Thrower [Stephen Thrower]). Shakespeare's sonnets read by Judi Dench. Camera: Derek Jarman. Second Camera: James Mackay. Editors: Cerith Wyn Evans, Peter Cartwright. Sound Editors: Richard Anstead, Peter Christopherson. Sound Effects: Adrian Fogarty. Production Manager: Stuart Dolin. Production Assistant: Christopher Hughes. Titles: Sally Yeadon, Dave King. Crew: Kenneth Bolton, Steve Radnall, Alice Stepanek, Andy Wilson. Stills Photographer: Alistair Thain. Other music sources: How to Destroy Angels and At the Heart of it All by Coil. Sea Interludes from Peter Grimes by Benjamin Britten, performed by the Chorus and Orchestra of The Royal Opera House, Covent Garden, conducted by Colin Davies. Video Post-Production: Research Recordings. Video Transform: Colour Video Services. Sound: Videosonics. With thanks to: The Olympus Optical Company (UK), Research Recordings, the ICA, Andy the furniture maker, Shaun Allen, Chris Bligh, Ian Christie, Jo Comino, David Curtis, Ian Dickens, Andi Engel, Pam Engel, Alex Graham, Christopher Hobbs, Jocelyn James, Jem Leigh, Andy Powell, Peter Sainsbury, Jon Savage, Henry Stein, Anne Whitfield, John Cartwright, Peter Grey. Produced with the financial assistance of the British Film Institute. Cast: Paul Reynolds, Philip Williamson, Dave Baby, Timothy Burke, Simon Costin, Christopher Hobbs, Philip MacDonald, Toby Mott, Steve Radnall, Robert Sharp, Tony Wood

Thanks to James Mackay and Peter Christopherson for additional information.

1 *Sniffin' Glue* fanzine, 1977.
2 From the song Identity, released in 1978 but played live as early as the spring of 1977. The line quoted also has a dark, bitterly personal slant referring to self-harm and suicide: Poly was already looking beyond punk's sneering nihilism, and the encouragement it gave to acts of personal negation, towards concerns that emerged again in the song Germ-Free Adolescents.
3 Peter Christopherson aka Sleazy, quoted in David Keenan, *England's Hidden Reverse*, London: S.A.F Publishing Ltd, 2003, p.131.
4 According to James Mackay, the BFI's Colin McCabe tried to have *The Angelic Conversation* shelved because he thought it would harm the commercial chances of *Caravaggio* — ironic, considering McCabe's discussion of the work of Jean-Luc Godard, in his book, *Godard: Images, Sounds, Politics and Godard: A Portrait of the Artist at Seventy.*
5 James Mackay: "I've got the title at that time — on tape boxes and things — as *Psychobilly's Angelic Conversation.*" ST: "I found the reference to the *Psycho Billy* title in the Tony Peake biography — was it possibly called both at various times?" JM: "Undoubtedly and probably on the same day!"
6 From Jarman's notebooks, quoted in Tony Peake, *Derek Jarman*, LB and Co, 1999.
7 Cronenberg's early film, *Stereo* (1969), and his first two feature films, *Shivers* (1975) and *Rabid* (1976), feature the effect. In *Shivers* it accompanies the final succumbing of the protagonist to the parasites, and in *Rabid* it appears in the scene where Marilyn Chambers is thrown into a refuse lorry at the end of the film. A brief anecdote: I took Derek to Canada House in 1984 to see a double bill of David Cronenberg's *Scanners*, and his 1972 made-for-TV half-hour short *Secret Weapons* (for its only UK screening ever). The first film he merely smiled at but the latter — Cronenberg's "suppressed film", to quote its director — met with Derek's startled admiration. He immediately likened it to Godard and seemed impressed that a commercial horror director should have such a defiantly avant-garde streak.
8 From Jarman's notebooks, quoted in Peake, *Derek Jarman.*
9 Ibid.
10 Derek was often quite volatile, and one sure-fire way to light the blue touch-paper was to mention Peter Greenaway.
11 James Mackay: "Editing had begun with Derek and me editing — not something that I was particularly comfortable with, I had a technophobia about editing — and Cerith came in and helped sort it all out. He did so, he told me at the time, by imposing a time period on the action. So there they are at 3pm and 5pm through to midnight and 3am — you get the picture."
12 Sleazy recalls that he spent about a week on the film, as he worked on it after the recording to sort out the technicalities of placement and the merging of music with sound effects for the overall film mix.
13 Quoted from Derek's notes for *The Angelic Conversation* soundtrack CD (Threshold House), written in 1986.
14 From Jarman's notebooks, quoted in Peake, *Derek Jarman.*
15 "Philip refused to swim nude," recalls Mackay.
16 James Mackay: "At the Berlin Film Festival — we took the film there ourselves as the BFI didn't want it in — we got into the festival pavilion the night before it opened proper and took all the BFI's posters for *1919* — some film about Freud — down and made *Angelic* posters by drawing on the backs with felt tip. Derek came up with the tag line: 'before Freud there was Jung'."

Derek Jarman Directs: Imagining October and The Last of England

Post Punk Industrial Modernism

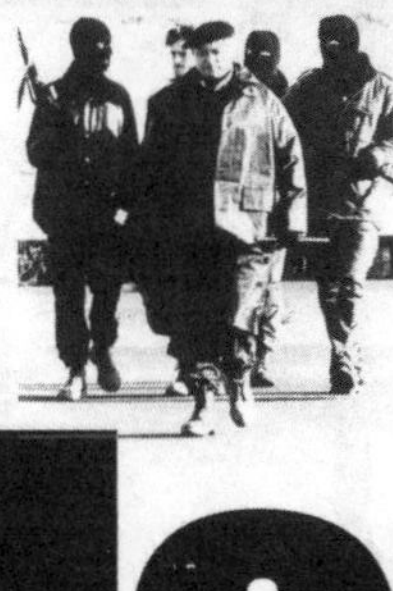

Chris Barber

On the outer reaches of music experimentation

associated with punk were Throbbing Gristle — Genesis P-Orridge, Cosey Fanni Tutti, Chris Carter and Peter Christopherson — who had already left their mark on the contemporary avant-garde art scene. Their grunge/noise experiments were influenced by concepts developed by The Futurists, an early twentieth century European abstract art movement. These artists recognised the changing role and potential of art in modern, industrial societies. While other artists of the period tried to ignore it, or attacked industrial culture through their art, The

Futurists embraced it.

Around 1909, The Futurists added music to their conceptual manifestos for avant-garde (and non-figurative) painting, sculpture and performance art. The new industrial aesthetic for music proposed radical anti-music to smash past traditions. Conventional modes of musical composition would be trashed; sounds recorded from anywhere — particularly factory machinery and roaring engines — would be collaged together, forming new paradigms of audible experience. Subsequent avant-garde movements, including Dada, Surrealism and Lettrism, developed the concept further.

Throbbing Gristle, P-Orridge and Christopherson's Psychic TV and (later) Christopherson's breakaway project Coil, like Derek Jarman (with whom they frequently worked), recognised an affinity between this avant-garde aesthetic and some aspects of punk from the late 1970s. This mutual artistic exchange inspired one of the most innovative and controversial expressions of punk subculture. Moving into the 1980s however, developed industrial societies were undergoing massive economic upheaval: along with the fragmentation of the punk movement, the critical awareness advocated by Postmodernism recognised the decline of Industrial culture and drift towards a Post Industrial epoch.

Industrialist aesthetics emphasise productive form over creative content, and there are many reasons why Industrialists embrace film as perhaps the most important mode of artistic expression. Filmmaking was a new medium that evolved concurrently with avant-garde art movements, which championed the new over the old. It necessitates the use of technology as integral to its process; filmmaking can incorporate pre-existing modes of artistic expression, painting, performance, music, sculpture and photography. It also presents new and exciting modes of formal expression.

The Post Industrial aesthetic is clarified by its analogies with the wider critical concerns of Postmodernism. Importantly, Postmodernism was never a counter movement in opposition to Modernism. Quite the contrary, Postmodernism acknowledges its most dynamic expressions are firmly rooted in Modernism and its critique represents a revision of Modernism's systematic approaches and notions of originality. Postmodernism favours methods over the systematic (locating the relevance of Nietzsche rather than Hegel) and recognises the need to revise Modernism's flawed and dated obsession with the new and original. Likewise, the Post Industrial does not discard Industrial aesthetics, but revises its systematic approach and exclusivity, revivifying its contemporary relevance and broadening its scope to embrace more populist as well as eclectic past modes of aesthetic representation.

In a sense, this demonstrates immediate affinity with Derek Jarman's aesthetic concerns and production process. In opposition to many of his critics, Jarman always maintained his films were not intentionally elitist or exclusive. Whilst he refused to patronise his audience with aesthetic compromise, he insisted all his approaches were developed from the simplest, crudest processes available; the results achieved through empirical trial and error. Further, Jarman's films utilise diverse influences, ranging from punk modernism to the Renaissance. He also stressed the primacy of the spectator's own interpretation of his films; what you see and feel is what you get!

The avant-garde artist and critic Wyndham Lewis had particular impact on Jarman's Modernist aesthetic sensibility. Canadian-born Lewis lived in Britain, but spent much time in Europe, associating with the major artists of the early twentieth century avant-garde. Lewis is a highly controversial figure and some of his sillier notions (like his anti-Semitism, paranoia of homosexuals and flirtation with Nazism) would have been deeply objectionable to Jarman. But Lewis also founded the Vorticist avant-garde movement and was a prolific commentator on developments in modern art — especially painting and literature. In his *The Enemy Within* and *Blast* polemical manifestos (which include contributions from TS Elliot and Ezra Pound) Lewis exhibits near proto-punk tendencies in his innovation, anger and determination to provoke controversy. The work of Wyndham Lewis significantly influenced Marshall McLuhan's media philosophy in the 1960s.

Jarman's early filmmaking veers between his 16/35mm, Euro-art movie-style features (like *Sebastiane* and *Jubilee*) and his Super-8, experimental 'home movies.' Whilst the results and experiences of each production process doubtless cross-pollinate his work, the radically contrasting processes involved, and Jarman's alternative agendas for each, produced two distinct bodies of work. This was inevitable: even screening the films requires two quite different set-ups. Conventional cinemas do not have Super-8 projectors, which are incapable of projecting onto a full cinemascope screen. Designed for home use, Super-8 projectors require far more intimate surroundings and closer proximity to a small screen (problems which had to be technically overcome making *The Last of England*). Jarman's earliest Super-8 films, from Studio Bankside in 1970, predate his 'professional' features and were originally screened for small groups of friends. Between 1970 and *The Next Life* in 1993, Jarman made about thirty-two such shorts, which excludes *Imagining October* (1984), *Glitterbug* (1994, a sixty minute compilation feature of excerpts from home movies 1970–1985), *Pet Shop Boys: Videography* (1991, music videos), *The Smiths: The Complete Picture* (2000, music videos) and *Depuis le jour* (1987 segment for the feature *Aria*). Some of these home movies relate to other cine projects Jarman worked on like *The Devils at the Elgin* (1974), *Sebastiane Wrap* (1975) and *Jordan's Dance* (1977), which inspired *Jubilee* and the later *Jordan's Wedding* (1981). Others relate directly to Jarman's friends, like *Andrew Logan Kisses the Glitterati* (1972), *Miss Gaby* (1972), *Ula's Fete* (1974), *Picnic at Ray's* (1975), *Gerald's Film* (1976) and *Ken's First Film* (1982). Several record personal events or projects Jarman was involved in: *A Journey to Avebury* (1971), *A Walk on Mon* (1973), *Stolen Apples for Karen Blixen* (1973), *Duggie Fields* (1974), *Sloane Square: A Room of One's Own* (aka *Removal Party*, 1981), *Pontormo* and *Punks at Santa Croce* (1982) and *Waiting For Waiting For Godot* (1983).

While all these shorts are playful and experimental, some are poetic muses with special attention being given to associative and abstract editing and the textural-effect qualities of the film, as in

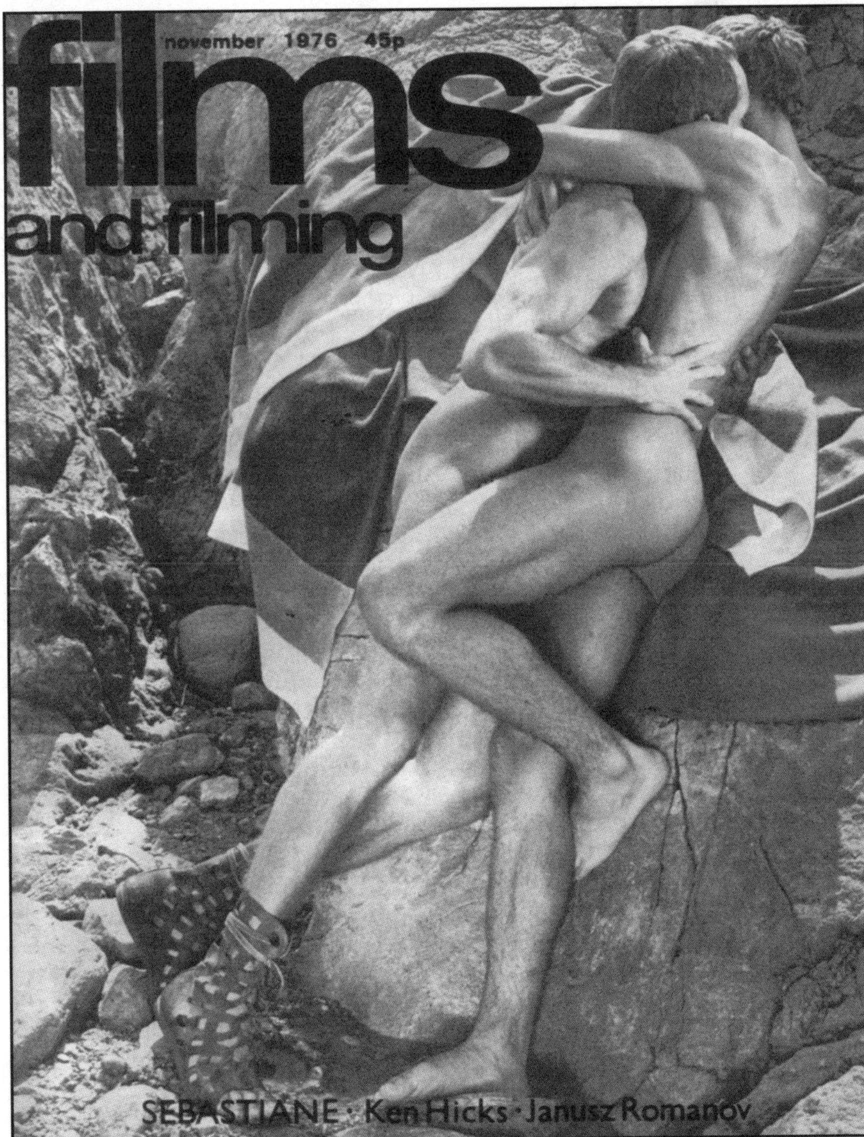

Derek Jarman in art movie style: *Sebastiane*, on the cover of *Films and Filming*, Nov 1976

Garden of Luxor (1972), *Sulpher and Art of Mirrors* (1973), *Fire Island* (1974) and *Sea of Storms* (1976); or to composition: *Art and the Pose* (1976) and *Every Woman for Herself* and *All for Art* (1977). As early as *The Pantheon* in 1978, Jarman appears to have developed a proto Post Industrial aesthetic sensibility. Recycling and reprocessing are integral concepts of Post Industrialism: in 1980 Jarman recycled material shot on Super-8 between 1972–74 (for about £100) and added an ambient soundtrack recorded by Throbbing

Gristle. *In the Shadow of the Sun* is in colour, runs for fifty-four minutes and is produced by James Mackay. The improvised soundtrack was recorded on an eight-track tape deck to a VHS video recording of the film. There is no narrative or obvious beginning or end to the film, which was premièred at the 1981 Berlin Film Festival. Also in 1981, Jarman carried the Post Industrial concepts further with a sort of abstract sequel, *TG Psychic Rally in Heaven*. In 1983, Jarman made three shorts, two being *Pirate Tape* and *B2 Tape* (aka *B2 Film*). Between filming features, Jarman took time out to produce his Post Industrialist, short home movie masterpiece *Imagining October* in 1984 (this was his last home movie until *L'Ispirazione* in 1988.)

So far as Jarman's feature films go, Post Industrialist aesthetics pound onto the big screen in *The Angelic Conversation*. But it was another couple of years before Jarman realised his epic Post Industrialist feature film, *The Last of England*. Utilising his experience from the preceding fifteen years of making experimental, Super-8 home movies, along with technical proficiency from directing feature films, Jarman synthesises the intimacy of the home movie viewing experience with the intensity of an art feature film. *The Last of England* is, internationally, the most authentic avant-garde film of its time, a tour de force; a unique and subversive viewing experience.

The film is shot on Super-8, transferred to high band and edited in video, then transferred to 35mm; filming commenced in August 1986 and took six months to complete. It also extensively recycles older, arcane material, including footage shot by Jarman's family and dating back to his childhood, some filmed 'on location' in India towards the end of the Rajah. There is innovative technical and textural experimentation with the chiaroscuro of light and shadow, colour, composition, sound and form, b&w sequences, slow motion and fast motion (all created in-camera) sequences. Montage and collage are utilised to leap back and forth in time, creating an elliptical, dream-like, allegorical aura (analogous to Marcel Proust's novels). It cost £240,000; the most expensive part of making the film was the process of blowing up the image to 35mm for cinema screens, achieving a unique vibrancy to the colour. Some of the technical innovation is inspired by music promos.

The final 35mm cut runs for eighty-eight minutes. It is filmed in London, Liverpool and New York, with 1920s footage by Harry Puttock (Derek's grandfather, on family holiday in Bexhill) and 1940s footage by Lance Jarman (Derek's father, of Wellington bombers at Lossiemouth, and New York World Trade Fair, 1939). The film features appearances by Tilda Swinton, Spencer Leigh and Spring, as well as Derek Jarman himself, with design by Christopher Hobbs, and costume design by Sandy Powell. Camerawork is by Derek Jarman, Chris Hughes, Cerith Wyn Evans, and Richard Heslop. James Mackay, Don Boyd and Yvonne Little produce; the soundtrack is by Simon Turner, with a voiceover by Nigel Terry. Many of the cast and crew comprise Jarman's personal friends and frequent contributors to his films, including James Mackay, Cerith Wyn Evans, Chris Hughes, Simon Turner, Nigel Terry, and Tilda Swinton.

In his book *Kicking the Pricks* (originally published as *The Last of*

England in 1987) Derek Jarman says:

> I improvised *The Last of England* — no script, scripts are the first restraint... I'm out to destabilise and destroy... There's no narrative, though there is a love story; it's silent... my reaction to the view from this window of a culture riddled with the death-watch beetle... The battle for a cinema which grows up and up and uses the direct experiences of the author... which stands up to the commissioning bodies and declares that experience is the basis for serious work... The Super-8 camera is free. 35mm is chained by money to the institutions. It could have been shot on 35mm, but economics have gutted the mind from that format... Later the audience will tell me what I've made. I'll find out in the question and answer sessions, I'll adopt their best guesses... The film is a documentary. I've come back with a document from somewhere far away. Everything I pointed the camera at (my fellow cameramen pointed the camera at) had meaning, it didn't matter what we filmed... All film is fiction, including the news, or, if you want to reverse it, all film is fact. My film is as factual as the news... I'm happy with it, and all its flaws... The arbitrary gesture to spoil a perfect shape. I love the moments which are out of focus.[1]

The title *Last of England* is a painting by pre-raphaelite artist Ford Madox Brown. One of the visual props is a copy of *Caravaggio's Profane Love* (painted by Christopher Hobbs) that Spring kicks around and masturbates over; Spring consistently evokes Thanatos. Jarman as the Author is the central thread holding the film together, starting at his desk in Phoenix House at night. There's a violent homoerotic sex scene, with a naked lad and a uniformed and masked soldier on a Union Jack. Spencer Leigh is dressed as a heretic for garrotting (which evokes Goya's *The Disasters of War*). There is contemporary location footage of New York filmed by Jarman. Two soldiers dance together in a yard (a homage to Pasolini's *Salò*, 1975). A bowler-hatted businessman wearing callipers wastefully tips grain away, while a tramp is bombarded with credit card advertisements. Refugees wait in silence at a quay but where are they going? A bare-chested and tattooed young man injects himself with drugs in a derelict building. Little English Morris dancers beat Spencer violently with sticks. A fragile naked figure clambers through junk and detritus. Masked and uniformed, SAS-style terrorists (the establishment) round up young civilians (including punks) at gunpoint; Tilda Swinton performs a whirling dervish dance before a glowing bonfire, against a red and yellow sunset. National unity, monarchy and Christianity are attacked, symbolised by the Albert Memorial. Men in white frocks row a boat across the Thames and illuminate the night sky with flares. The soundtrack repeatedly (and ironically) calls for job creation, between ranting Hitler speeches. Most of the exterior location, bombsite and rooftop footage is shot in Deptford and Rotherhythe (south east London). The largely hand-held camerawork is frantic and frenetic.

Made in Thatcher's Britain, *The Last of England* is a violent, scathing and relentless attack on everything the government and class-ridden establishment represents: a portrait of England in decadence and decline (punk/Post Industrial concerns entering content as well as form). The past/archival footage is not nostalgic, but traces Britain's recent, largely ignoble history, a dreary history of hypocrisy, greed and repression. Beautifully composed poetic imagery is juxtaposed with shockingly brutal scenes. It's a mesmerising, hypnotic and thought provoking film, sometimes depressing and seething with anger.

Notes

1 Derek Jarman, *Kicking The Pricks* London: Vintage, 1996. p.160–173.

Downtown Upheaval: NYC 1975

An Interview with Amos Poe

Jack Sargeant

"The scene definitely started

snowballing. CBGB's was clearly where things were happening, from the very first time we played there. We were really unique. There was not another rock'n'roll band in the world with short hair. There was not another rock'n'roll band with torn clothes. Everybody was still wearing glitter and women's clothes. We were these notch-thin, homeless hoodlums, playing really powerful, passionate, aggressive music that was also lyrical ***Richard Hell on Television***

I wanted to make something indigenous to New York that anybody could make ***Amos Poe***

Blank Generation opens with Patti Smith; several different performances are cut together, including a poetry reading. The camera does not rest, rather it zooms in and out, cutting between an audience perspective and from behind Patti on stage. A similar hand-held appropriation of direct cinema style continues for the rest of the movie. This serves to create a sense of immediacy as well as a feeling of frenetic urgency, as if by spending too long luxuriating on one shot something transpiring elsewhere — just out of view — may be missed. A man runs through downtown New York holding a portable TV, his T-shirt bears the legend 'Johnny Jewel.' Cut to an elegiacally thin Television, all bone and sinew, their guitars chiming in ravishing, discordant harmony. This is the sound of music being invented. The Ramones opens with a close up of Dee Dee, pulls back across Johnny and finally settles on Joey. There's an emphasis on the blur of hands across the guitar strings shot in tight close up, matched by cinematic blur as the camera races around the stage, trying to find a focus. There's too much action. The speed of the music, the intensity and brevity of the songs coming so abruptly after Television's minimalism, jars the viewer. The cinematography emphasises this as it jumps from musician to musician, until it frames the entire band. It becomes apparent that this isn't a bunch of poets, this is a gang. Johnny rolls back and plays, Dee Dee bounces, and Joey leans forward. Their T-shirts, ripped jeans, and grubby fucked sneakers all become focal points. This is the whole thing. Restless camerawork, driven by the same manic energy of the performance.

Talking Heads' Psycho Killer sees David Byrne's jerky movements, twitches and nervousness as the band emphasise the song. This is the antithesis to The Ramones' cocksure swagger. Tuff Darts sounds like Stones outtakes; Poe starts filming the audience, zooming in on their disinterested faces. The audience are all sitting down at tables. Somehow it doesn't seem as energised. The scene cross fades into Wayne County: different performances (one in blonde wig, one in bigger darker wig), different outfits. Wayne appears confrontational — sneering, thrusting his/her crotch, radiating pure fuck-you attitude. Cuts to older man in flasher mac and no trousers chasing a girl into her apartment, then back to Wayne in a full horror show outfit that seems to be made from trash, waving a toilet plunger; County's glitter theatre/Warhol roots are clear. A door with 'Blondie HQ' spray painted on it opens. Blondie fool around on the fire escape and in the streets. This is cut with footage of them playing live. Even at this early stage there is something too clean, too pop about Blondie. Even in the grotty nightclub darkness Debbie Harry radiates a painful beauty. Harry Toledo and sixties throwbacks, such as the Marbles or Shirts, are caught next, but there is less of a sense of energy — these bands lack the raw power of their contemporaries; they seem flat when compared to the other bands here; in the final eventuality not everybody makes the grade. During the Shirts' set the camera prowls through the crowd, familiar faces — Richard Hell, Debbie Harry — laughing, smoking, drinking; this is the scene. The New York Dolls play but are lost on a gigantic stage. There's no real atmosphere. Finally, The Heartbreakers play Blank Generation and the future becomes clear.

The end credits see the titles spelled out in magnetic-fridge-style plastic letters across a black leather jacket, a low budget reference to the opening credits of Kenneth Anger's *Scorpio Rising* (1963), with its title marked in silver studs on the back of a biker's jacket. If the black biker style leather jacket was already the icon of rebellion and outsider status, other images in the film would soon join this lexicon of individualism. The images in *Blank Generation* — sneakers, skinny arms, spiked hair — are punk iconography in the making, the street on the stage; punk before it had even been shat out screaming into the world.

Jack Sargeant Tell me how you became involved in making *Blank Generation*; it started with meeting Richard Hell...

Amos Poe It was 1973 or 74. I started working at this company, New Line Cinema, which was at the time this small company that had offices on University Place and 13th Street, and there was a store a couple of blocks away called Cinemabelia which had posters and film books — all kinds of stuff like that. It was run by a guy named Terry Ork, and there was this kind of crazy looking guy working there and after he'd seen me in the store for a number of times we'd start talking. If there was a [Robert] Bresson retrospective or a [Jean-Luc] Godard retrospective at Carnegie Hall Cinema I'd see him there, we'd start talking. And he was Richard Hell.

At the same time I hired a guy at New Line to sort of be my assistant there and that was Ivan Kral, who was basically also a musician at the time; he was into glam rock and Iggy, but he was also classically trained and he had emigrated from Czechoslovakia. So I started hanging around more music things with Ivan and I started filming some stuff; I had a 16mm camera at that time.

And, almost simultaneously, Richard told me he was forming a band. I didn't know he was a musician, and I told him; he says, "Well, not yet, but I will be, once I get on stage." And I knew he was writing stuff, short stories and stuff, and I guess he'd written some stuff with Tom Verlaine, and the band was Television, and they were about to play their first gig at CBGB so he told me where that was, and it was like pretty close to my house. It was still basically a Bowery bum bar, but the guy who owned it, Hilly [Krystal], was really into music, country, blue grass, that kind of thing. But it was basically a place where you could get a beer for fifteen cents, a shot for forty-five cents, something like that. And that was the first time I saw Television play and I think it was their first gig.

And that's when you decided it was worth filming all of this stuff?

Well, I was already making films... Super-8... this was just like a continuation. Something interesting to look at through the camera; obviously once you add music to the image then it really pops, you know. So that was kind of the approach from the film side. And Ivan, we went somewhere, I can't remember where it was now, maybe St Marks Church or something — we heard there was this poet called Patti Smith who had a guitar player and piano player and that she was putting her poetry to music. So we went to see Patti and that was also an epiphany. It all kind of accelerated I think from that point on, it was almost like there was an energy nexus or something where different artists and things all seemed to fit, everything seemed to fit right, different film, art, poetry, style, fashion, the whole deal, began to look right, feel right, sound right.

I don't think we had at that moment a conscious decision that we were making a film, we were continually just shooting stuff; I was shooting stuff and Ivan was shooting stuff with silent cameras. And as the scene accelerated, other bands, The Ramones started playing, Talking Heads, Blondie, all that stuff; it just became more and more and more of a scene at Max's, at CBGB, at Mother's and a few other places, and I think what was interesting about it was how that even without cell phones and the internet somehow, you know, jungle drums or something, everybody ended up being at the same club every night. It was kind of a moveable feast. And eventually by, I guess, early spring of 76 we had a whole lot of footage and, for us, also a lot of money invested in this, in labs and stock and that kind of stuff, so we had a closet full of film rolls, and they were all 100 foot rolls, three minutes each, which for The Ramones could be three songs. And the bands, 'cause we knew them from the beginning, most of them were very comfortable with being filmed. Ivan and I had put together the previous year — footage that was the last vestiges of Roxy Music, Bowie — a short hour film called *Night Lunch*. The last images in *Night Lunch* were Patti. And all of the early stuff, Bowie, Roxy Music, all that was colour, and segued into b&w, which is kind of where I was heading to anyway I think.

And that is of course where *Blank Generation* opens.

Right. So we realised this, and *Blank Generation* we wanted to make an hour, as it could sit on one reel that way. [Laughs] But we had the other half-hour of *Night Lunch* so we had a 'feature film,' that would sort of be the segue between one era and the next, and 'course since we had been working in film distribution we knew a lot of theatres around the country and in Canada that had things like the midnight show. Most people wouldn't go to a midnight movie, but people who were out at midnight would go to see whatever it was, *Pink Flamingos* whatever. And, so that was our intention, so we cut the movie in twenty-four hours in the Maysles Brother's studio. Took it to the lab, made a print, and the following week we had our premier at CBGB with Richard's new band The Heartbreakers. So that was a really big night, because obviously everybody who was in the film came to see it and obviously The Heartbreakers, which had Johnny Thunders, Jerry Nolan, Walter Lure, so, in that band there was the segue from the New York Dolls to punk, so it fit the film *Blank Generation* really well. That was a huge night, and we actually opened for them, I think, two or three nights, and basically we almost made our money back in just three nights, which really fuelled our idea that, I don't know, we were professional filmmakers. "Hey we're getting paid for this, who would have thought!"

The sound for the film was dubbed from demo tapes?

Well, yeah, the only record out at the time was the 45" Little Johnny Jewel which was put out on Ork Records, Terry's label, that was the only really recorded thing... and then, Talking Heads' stuff was, I think, a four-track, maybe an eight-track, demo that they did for Psycho Killer, an early version of that song that I actually like the best. And some of the other bands, we had home made demos.[1] The Ramones was recorded on a $20 cassette machine we brought at Woolworths; we thought for The Ramones that may be a good thing. The Ramones didn't have anything recorded at that point. So we used that. Some of the other bands had stuff on reel to reel [tape], but other than Television's Little Johnny Jewel I don't think that there was anything that was 'professionally' recorded. Which, you know, we were just learning ourselves — I am self-taught — transferring it to 16mm magnetic track, cutting it, splicing it. Thinking about it, it seems centuries ago, just the process...

The technology has changed so much; even two years after you made the film you could rent a video camera...

Yes. Well, while I was filming there would be people who would come in and say "Oh, we can get you an Arriflex and sound recordist and da-da-da-da you should be more professional," and you know, the thing was there was no such thing as waiting for tomorrow. It was all about today, it very much about the present. Also I guess I was arrogant enough that when people said, "You can't do it that way," I didn't understand any other way other than the way we were doing it, I didn't quite get it, I wasn't totally involved enough in filmmaking to understand all the things people were telling me that I should be doing, all I understood was what I was doing. But it definitely made me want to do something more.

That was the whole nature of punk: that anybody could get up and do it.

Yeah, well that's why it worked, it was the same idea. The words "it can't be done" or "no" were not viable, they were not part of the lexicon of the time. You could go up, you knew how to play a couple of chords, or you knew how to play bass enough, about what the beat was like... There were some people who were good musicians, but there were a lot of people who developed over time to become decent musicians, but the energy at the time was not about musicianship, in fact I would say it was against that. Which really was what galvanised the whole thing. If people had an idea... I mean The Ramones played what they could play, they would not play extended songs: for one they couldn't, their songs were so minimalist that's what they could do, but what they brought to it was this insane energy, the first few gigs were just like, "Holy shit I never saw anything like that before," which was what it was about.

In 77 when I first started showing *Blank Generation* I was invited by some school in Connecticut to show it, and Pennebaker was going up in his VW van, and I got a ride up there with him; he was showing that Ziggy Stardust film,[2] he hadn't made a print yet, he still had some issues with Bowie about the rights or something, and he showed it on double system, with the film and a full track stereo-mag going in sync, and he brought up his own projector, his own speakers, and I remember how blown away I was by that. Like you were at the concert, it was so good. And next to that *Blank Generation* really kind of sucked. [Laughs]

Once we had made *Blank Generation* we started trying to book it at midnight; because I was working at New Line I knew all the theatres around the country that showed midnight films, that had audiences for it, they would take my word for it, take it for the weekend, and I'd get these calls from theatre owners like "Man, half the people walked out. They wanted their money back. It was out of sync. Oh my God, what a disaster"... There's still people who write in their e-mail when they've seen it "Man, that sucked, it was out of sync, can't you shoot a thing?" They don't get it. They still don't get it. It's an odd thing that that same mindset still exists, less so now but it is definitely there. But we were kind of like, on one hand we'd kind of look at each other, and think "When are we going to make a professional film?" and at the same time we were like "Wow, we really annoyed some people." [Laughs]

What was the bands' response to the film?

The bands were really into it in the beginning, the bands like would see me everyday, and they'd be like, "What are you doing? What are you doing?" "Oh, just shooting stuff" and they'd be like, "cool." Everybody was basically trying to get attention, so if you were pointing a camera at them... I mean different people had a different point of view. I always thought for example that Patti hated me, because every time I pointed a camera at her she just gave me a dirty look. But actually it looked good on film. Years later I asked her: "Patti, did you really hate me?" "No, no, I really liked you, I was just posing for you," I said "Oh okay, you scared me!" Everybody was really into it, the funny thing was most of the conversations I had with most everybody were never about music, it was always about film. With Richard from the beginning we'd talk about French film, the Nouvelle Vague, all that stuff, *Pierrot le Fou* [1965] whatever, Patti was a Godardophile; Hell was really into Bresson. There were people I never even talked to also, I don't think I ever said more than "Hello" to Tom Verlaine, he's very quiet and kind of shy, but, you know, you could talk to Dee Dee [Ramone] a little bit when he wasn't completely wrecked. Johnny wouldn't talk to you. Joey was kind of shy. But Chris [Stein] and Debbie [Harry], they were totally into film.

Obviously Talking Heads and Wayne County, who was an actor, and so on, were into film, so there was a sense that there was something going on that was wider, there was a wider sense of art…

I think a lot of it has to do with the place, whether it was Max's or CBGB, or a couple of other smaller places, but the energy was so intense because everybody was there at everybody's gig, and that was kind of interesting. Even though a lot of bands hated each other I guess, or had attitude about each other, or whatever, they were all there so you'd have double bills with like Talking Heads and Blondie or something there for a while. I think Patti and Debbie never really got on, but other than that almost everybody appeared at everybody's gig.

How come you never shot The Dictators? There seems to be, in histories of the era, bands who get represented in a different way, or as not part of it or whatever… there seems to be a divide…

It ends on New Years Eve 1975, and I think The Dictators didn't play there until 76. And after we finished *Blank Generation* and showed it I kind of used up my thinking about that and started thinking about other stuff.

Otherwise you'd have ended up spending your life filming bands?

Yeah. Which is not a bad thing necessarily, but at the time I was into starting a Nouvelle Vague in New York — where the music was going I was trying to translate that into film, I was trying to go a little into another narrative thing. So yeah, it kind of burned me out on that kind of movie.

You called the film *Blank Generation* after Richard Hell's idea of a blank generation?

Yeah. I think from my point of view it was the song that was to me most anthemic. An anthem of what was going on. It delineated the difference between the previous generation and this and I think the reference to me was The Who, you know, My Generation, and I was between those two, my adolescence was more like The Who, and I got the whole idea of it. And it was also about the whole alienation thing and the poetry of it. For me I think it was the poetry that really turned me on to that, because it was really like, "I belong to the blank generation." it's like how can I belong to anything? I am so alienated, I belong to nothing, which is blank. For me, Richard was always the poet laureate of it; there were a lot of good poets, a lot of good writers, obviously Patti's stuff, everybody wrote really well — "Jesus died for somebody's sins, but not mine" is amazing. But, it just encapsulated the whole thing. Ivan and I really had no ... we edited the whole film in twenty-four hours, think about that, [laughs] we were editing reversal film, this was the original stuff, so what we kept and what we threw out, that was it, there was no going back, and we had this much music that we had transferred, that's what it was going to be. And we edited it to the music the best we could. We knew it was going to be called *Blank Generation* from the moment we stepped into the room, and we never really discussed it any further than that. Ivan didn't necessarily like Richard all that much; we just knew that was going to be the name of it. We never thought of calling it Horses or Psycho Killer, *Blank Generation* that was going to be the name of it. I think I met Richard first, and I could tell what he was going for, the poetry, the music, the performance, the ripped clothes, the whole thing, he just epitomised for me the whole picture. I just got into it through Richard. Before that I was just making films that were like Stan Brakhage or Michael Snow. Classic experimental cinema, although within that world I was alienated, because everybody in that world said my films were trying to be too narrative, and that was a no-no in the experimental world. And I knew I wasn't of that generation, and I knew I wasn't going to fit in with them, because I had a narrative sensitivity.

Were you aware of the west coast — San Francisco — and London scenes?

Not initially, certainly not the west coast until a year or so later, until fanzines, because they were contacting me about showing the film, stuff like that. I definitely thought it was something that could take off. And then of course London hit — London was just like, it blew New York out of the water. London took it to the next level, that was amazing to see. I remember going to London in 1977 — the first film festival I went to was in France, and I couldn't afford to fly to Paris, so I flew to London. I remember the Scala Cinema, and there was a guy there, he contacted me and then he showed *Blank Generation* in London, and I hung out, saw Siouxsie and the Banshees, The Clash, kind of amazing. And there was an office across the hall and the guy there had a band, a trio that was going out on tour, and they needed an opening act but they couldn't afford another band; they were wondering if they could use my film as the opener, and that band was The Police and they used *Blank Generation* as the opener for their tour.

Then I was already on a different part of the trip — from a filmmaker's point of view it wasn't the sort of thing that was turning me on anymore.

Notes

1 Television released Little Johnny Jewel in 1975; Richard Hell and the Voidoids released Blank Generation in 1976, the same year as fellow CBGB regulars The Ramones, Talking Heads, and Blondie released their debuts.

2 *Ziggy Stardust and the Spiders from Mars* (1973).

The Don Has Taste

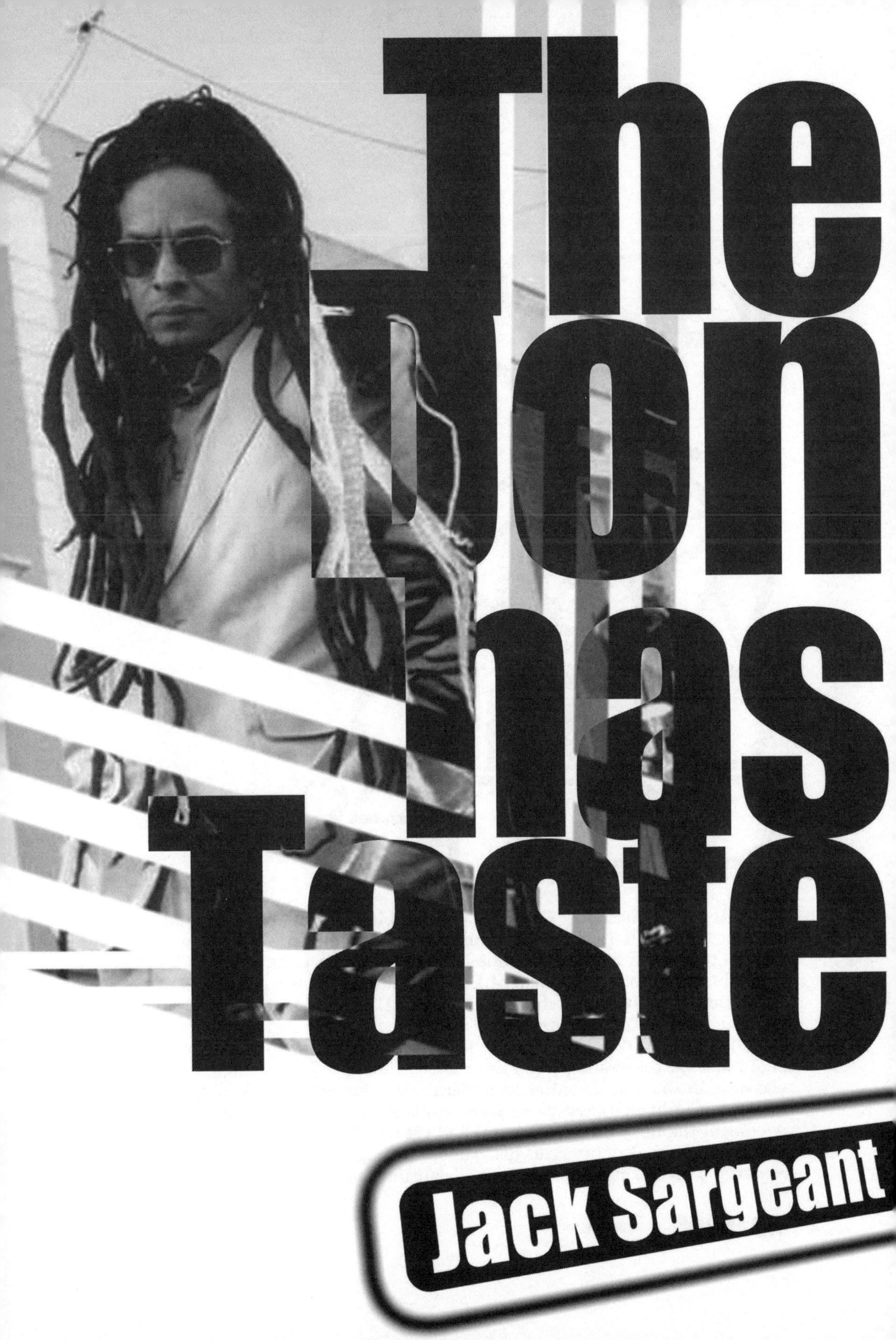

Jack Sargeant

In 1975 Don Letts worked at hip clothes

store Acme Attractions, where he would play reggae records loud, drawing attention to himself, gaining a reputation as a DJ. It was natural that when the Roxy became London's premier punk venue Letts would be asked to be the resident DJ. Here during the early months of 1977, Don Letts introduced the audience to the bass rumble of reggae and dub, undoubtedly having some influence on punk and post-punk's sonic palettes: "I'd get in about 7:30... the club was open until about one: I just sat there and played the records I liked."[1] Like punk, reggae was seen in the mid seventies as underground, outsider music, as rebel music, but unlike punk, records were available; most of the punk bands playing at the Roxy (and elsewhere) had yet to release records.

Don Letts also brought his camera to gigs, shooting bands on Super-8, a format he describes as a "beautiful medium." In 1978 Letts used this footage at a ratio of "nearly 1:1" to produce *The Punk Rock Movie*, a film that illustrated the emergent London punk scene and included The Clash, The Slits, Eater, and numerous others. Following the success of this film he shot music promos for numerous punk and post-punk groups including Public Image Ltd, The Clash, The Slits and The Pogues.

Letts has produced numerous other documentaries, including the film *Punk: Attitude* (2005), which views punk as part of an ongoing gesture of rebellion, empowerment and inspiration. His most recent film — *Sun Ra: The Brother from Another Planet* (2005) — focuses on outsider jazz genius Sun Ra.

Jack Sargeant You came into punk obviously as a DJ, to you, as first generation Black British — obviously you are British but you have this other cultural heritage...

Don Letts Let me tell you, you have to understand, as you said "first generation Black British" or "British Black," which people roll off the tongue now, but back in the mid seventies that was a really confusing concept, because there was no blueprint, it was totally new fucking territory. So we were like what I would describe as a lost tribe, the only real sort of inspiration/information that we got was through records that were coming up from Jamaica, you know. Through that we learned about our culture, also through that we started to wear our rebel hats, if you know what I mean. Our parents had come over on the whole Windrush thing on the promise of the multicultural dream, which obviously wasn't panning out for them; they were basically getting fucking screwed. And you have also got to remember that in America at this time there was all the Black civil rights things going on, and that was filtering over to the UK as well. And we are kind of arming ourselves with all of this information, even though the way we sort of developed in this country was totally different to the whole American thing. I mean the way I describe it is my forefathers were dragged kicking and screaming to America, but my parents bought tickets to the UK.

So, "first generation British Black," got a punky attitude, although we don't realise that is what it is at the time, in the way black music constantly has.

Well, the whole sound system scene in Jamaica, where nobody else is going to do it, you have to do it for yourself....

That's right. I maintain that the development of reggae music itself was punk rock. I mean basically there was a mood out there which wasn't being addressed by the popular music at the time, which was the R'n'B stuff coming in from the US, and the Jamaicans set about creating their own soundtrack, which dealt with themes like how the fuck they were going to live. So that was basically a punk rock thing, as far as I was concerned, in a way. I touch on that in *Punk: Attitude*.

Anyway, here I am, early seventies, black sort of rebel dude, looking for a way to express myself. Mid seventies punk rock happens. And all of a sudden I can sort of see a direction, because of the DIY thing. I mean, the DIY thing has always been integral to the developing world, but DIY in the developing world or third world or whatever the PC term is, is a method of survival, when punk rock exploded on the scene; I can see a way of not only surviving but actually bettering my situation. My white mates, as the story goes, the popular music of the time, the stadium rock, wasn't talking about how people actually felt on the streets, about the social political economic climate of the time, and basically my white mates didn't have a soundtrack that expressed how they felt. I did, I had my reggae music. So, they set about making their own soundtrack: of the people for the people by the people.

And the thing about the punk rock energy, it wasn't just about music, the thing I found interesting was it was all inclusive; punk rock said "If you've got an idea you can be part of this thing too" and that is another reason why I think it has such a lasting legacy, it wasn't just about loud guitars, photographers, filmmakers, fashion designers, graphic designers, poets, journalists — it was a complete subculture. The story goes that people saw The Pistols play or The Clash play and the next day a thousand bands started, which was partially true, but the truth of the matter is that a lot of people walked away from those gigs fired up and inspired and they took that attitude and it informed whatever they did.

So, punk rock is happening in 1975, my mates are picking up guitars, the energy is getting so intense that I want to get involved — it was a thing where you either got involved or you got fucking run over, you know what I mean? So everyone is picking up guitars and pretty soon the stage is full up, and Don Letts wants to pick something up too.

Now, I had been inspired visually, I don't know why, fuck knows how these things happen, by films like *The Harder They Come* [Perry Henzell,1972]; they were obviously very important to me, if for nothing else they gave a visual aspect for my culture, because before we were just getting the music, the 45s from Jamaica, and all of a sudden there is a visual accompaniment. And this is pre-Bob Marley actually. So *The Harder They Come* was really inspirational to a first generation British Black. What I got out of it beyond the obvious cultural information was that you could use media to not only entertain but also convey information, to actually say something, and it was a combination of *The Harder They Come* and actually another film, which was a late night cult film in the mid seventies, *El Topo* [1969] by Alejandro Jodorowsky. I must have gone to see it every month for a year, and to this day I still don't know if I know what the fuck it is about. In fact I just brought a copy of it in Japan. But between these two films, and reggae experience and the whole punk rock explosion, Don Letts reinvents himself as a filmmaker. I pick up a Super-8 camera and decide that's how I am going to express myself. No formal training, making my problems my assets, which is another punk rock thing. I believe that a good idea attempted is better than a bad idea perfected. This is all stuff I learned through punk rock.

So I start filming the bands that I kind of liked. It's pretty ropey, I don't know what the fuck I am doing, all I can do is focus and point the camera in the right direction. But I think my closeness to the scene got me to places that other people can't get, and I had taste — I know who to point the camera at.

That's one of the things I notice with *Blank Generation*: there's some great bands like Television or The Ramones, but there's also some bad bands.

I was filming things that turned me on, for whatever reason. In that remit though, there were things that I thought were absurd, crazy or just fucking outright funny — Johnny Moped comes to mind. Who was like he'd escaped from *One Flew Over the Cuckoo's Nest*. I mean it is all part of the story. It's all tarted up with rose tinted spectacles now, but it wasn't all Pistols and Clash; for every one Pistols and one Clash there were fifty really duff bands. You mustn't forget that.

Anyway, I am going around filming the bands I like: I remember filming The Clash at the Roxy — Harlesden, not the Roxy I DJ'd at — the line up was like The Clash, Buzzcocks, Slits and Subway Sect, I mean, what a fucking line up.

But wasn't it four of your mates' bands?

No. They were... it's hard to explain it. They were mates, I did know them as friends, but they were particularly cool mates. It was that London thing, where I was working at the Kings Road, Chelsea, and formed an alliance with like-minded people. And like I said "Don Letts has taste," so that worked out okay. But I remember filming that gig, Roxy Harlesden, The Pistols at Screen on the Green.

That was Sid's first gig right?

No. Oh Yes! That's right. It was, fucking hell, I forgot, it was so long ago. The Clash at the Rainbow... Obviously I filmed a lot of stuff down at the Roxy, I went out on tour with The Clash. I went out on tour with The Banshees, Heartbreakers... Anyway, I am filming all of these bands, and I read in the *NME* "Don Letts is making a movie." And I am like... "Oh, that's not a bad idea, I'll call it a movie." And being particularly punk rock I called it just *The Punk Rock Movie*.. Next thing I know I get a write up, in fact the cover story of *Time Out*, and then it ends up running for six weeks at the ICA. Broke all the box office records and all that shit. It was quite funny because I was showing it on Super-8, my original, because there was no negative, and I am running this thing every night and it's getting trashed and it's breaking down while I am showing it, and I am having to re-splice it together and stuff like that. And that was my foray into film, in a nutshell.

You shot it all on sync sound Super-8?

Yeah, yeah.

So you weren't able to remix it or anything like that?

No, it's exactly what it was. And the funny thing was that when you shot at 24fps the Super-8 cartridges lasted about three minutes, and it was really fortunate that all the punk groups, everything they had to say, fitted into that time. You know what I mean, the perfect format for punk rock. It was bloody expensive back in the day, I can't remember what the total cost was, but by the time I processed the whole shit, it probably cost about £15 for three minutes.

How did you finance it?

Used the money from Acme Attractions, because I was managing Acme Attractions with Jeanette Lee, and we just used the money from the till. It wasn't like financing the film, it was like something I wanted to do, so I blagged the money somehow and filmed the bands; there wasn't a master plan. I was riding the wave of energy that was punk rock, and the alliance of energy of my reggae groove and the whole punk rock thing.

The next thing that happens from that is that I am obviously getting friendly with these bands — The Clash, John [Lydon], The Slits, whoever — and when these bands did get signed up, or started getting signed up, some of these bands would turn around and say "Alright Don, have a go at making our videos."

Right, because that's when you made The Slits film.

The first one I made, I think, was Public Image's debut, which was called Public Image, then I did The Clash's London Calling. And actually went on to do all The Clash music videos.

You went on to make the film about them, *Westway to the World*.

Yeah. Then I remember going to Island [Records] when The Slits were signed up and saying, "Look, give me a couple of grand or something," and I'll make what was going to be a long form music video, and the thing hasn't been invented then, and I did this thing called *Slits Pictures*. Which took five grand, maybe even less, man, and did sort of video type things for each song; we didn't do every song on the album because the record company wimped out. Now of course that is standard shit. But this is way back; I can't remember when the album *Cut* came out, but this is way back. And I think I did video type things for six songs. It was about the ideas. And again if I hadn't have done that there'd be no visual record of The Slits.[2]

I remember doing a Linton Kwesi Johnson video, *The Great Insurrection*, for a grand just because I wanted to do it because he was such an inspiration to me, and again I don't think he made another video in his life.

It was always like that DIY thing, making your problems your assets, using the medium to communicate ideas. That's what I got from punk, individuality and empowerment.

That's something that in a way I think had an even bigger impact in America with the whole hardcore scene, where you get all of these record labels: Minor Threat having Discord, Black Flag and SST…

But that independent record label thing really started over here.

Maybe, but the Americans really ran with it.

The Americans sort of maximised it just by nature of them having a sort of underground network. The hardcore thing in the early eighties kind of went underground; it was ignored by the music business, but through the groundwork that was established by people like Black Flag, and especially Minor Threat and bands like that, the whole thing ended up emerging as Nirvana nearly ten years later. You can't take that away from them, and that was all part of the whole punk DIY ethic.

And in America, rather than reggae there was a link to hip hop and rap.

In *Punk: Attitude* I maintain that hip hop was nothing but black punk rock. It was. And, as with all of these things it's become part of popular culture, and now hip hop has become hip pop, you know with fucking Snoop Dogg and Puff Daddy instead of Chuck D and KRS-ONE…

More depoliticised…

It happens to everything. People forget punk rock became nonsense in, I reckon, about eighteen months — the minute that Bill Grundy thing happened it was all over. All the smart people moved on. I maintain that music and ideas got a lot more interesting in the post-punk scene…

That's when you get Public Image Ltd and This Heat and…

The Pop Group. But we needed the punk rock thing to wipe the slate clean. You can't take away from that. But some people kind of got trapped by what they saw as a punk definition: mohawks and safety pins and nihilism and that's not what it was about. It was about, like I say, freedom and empowerment.

Does it ever worry you that when you are asked to do something like *Punk: Attitude* you are getting roped into nostalgia?

Well, I don't see that as a nostalgic film. When they asked me to do that my initial thing was, "Oh fuck, not that again," and then I went away and wondered what the constant fascination was, and it occurred to me that really what we were talking about was counterculture. The counterculture is an ongoing dynamic. And the trouble with all this over-analysis of the seventies punk movement is that it trivialises a bigger idea. The bigger idea is that it has continuity; in my film I include the fucking hippies as punk rock, or the birth of the hippie movement anyway. Once people understand that it doesn't become this weird thing that began and ended in the late seventies, it has continuity, and if it happened before it can happen again and, like I say, when you look around it sure fucking needs to. So the punk rock I am talking about is a living thing, a little lost at the moment if you look at popular culture — especially that's coming out of the west — it's kind of a little redundant, it's kind of regurgitating the same old shit, the same thing, but the world's a big place. I keep telling people that punk attitude is like the Force in *Star Wars* [laughs] — you can't stop it, you've just got to look in different places. Anywhere that hasn't had MTV rammed down their throat for twenty-five years, that's a start; I believe that the creative, interesting ideas of the future will come from two sources: the amateur and the naïve. If you want to be on MTV or in the top forty you've kind of been castrated before you've got off the starting line. Punk rock was about new values, and we need new values now. If you want what the Man is offering, you are kind of fucked.

It goes back to Little Richard or whatever… everyone focuses on the seventies, but as you say it's part of a continuum.

The last documentary I did was on a guy called Sun Ra.

I love Sun Ra…

As far as I am concerned: punk rock, totally punk rock. Here is a man coming out of the jazz tradition — all of a sudden he says, "I am going to bring in a moog synthesiser and electronics," and everyone is like "You can't do that"… That is punk rock and that was like in the fifties. He had his own record label in 1956, hand drawing the sleeves and selling them at gigs. That was way before The Buzzcocks, way before

Minor Threat. There you are: continuity. Not just one moment, it can happen again and again.

Like I say, that is really important, because once you get your head around that you can be part of that; it no longer becomes this dead thing conveniently packaged that you look back on, which is very nice for the Man by the way, because he doesn't want anybody to come along and rock the boat, they got rocked once before. Once people understand it's a living, ongoing thing you can be part of, then the playing field gets a little more exciting again. That is what my film *Punk: Attitude* is about — it isn't about something to look back on, it's about something to look forward to if you are brave enough and have a good idea.

Notes

1 Don Letts quoted in Jon Savage, *England's Dreaming: Sex Pistols and Punk Rock*, Faber and Faber: 1991, p.300.

2 The Slits' *Cut* was released in 1979.

Crass: Anarchism in the UK

Alice Banned aka

Gavin Mitchell

"Let me say, at the risk of seeming

ridiculous, that the true revolutionary is guided by great feelings of love **_Che Guevara_**

One band, more than any other, came to dominate the post-punk scene. Through the combined use of music, literature, graphics and film, they relentlessly exposed the dissimulated horror and hypocrisy of 'decent' society. They had phenomenal record sales, yet have all but disappeared from history. During the time in which Thatcher's government busied itself destroying communities, this band was pivotal in trying to build an alternative. You've doubtless guessed the band is Crass.

Named after the Bowie lyric "The kids was just crass," they formed in 1977, inspired (so I'm told) by The Fall, and in opposition to what they perceived as the professionalism of punk by bands like The Clash.

Crass emerged not from the punk/classic wastelands of urban decay, but a well-established hippie commune in rural Essex! Crass consisted of a core of eight to ten people: Penny Rimbaud, drums; Steve Ignorant, vocals; NA Palmer, guitar; Eve Libertine, vocals; Pete Wright, bass; Joy De Vivre, vocals; Phil Free, rhythm guitar; G Sus, graphic design; and Mick Duffield, films. The music was as brutal and uncompromising as the message. The message was avowedly libertarian, anti censorship, pacifist, but above all, anarchist (that's anarchism not anarchy). The targets of their rage were just about every social institution you can think of: family, religion, state, politics, monarchy, law, media, military, music biz, entertainment, school, prison, factory and the office. (As Godard says in *Tout Va Bien*, "Where does the revolution start? Everywhere at once!") In the copious literature that accompanied their records and gigs, they rigorously and persuasively delineated the unpleasant truths that these institutions each seek to conceal. In short, they wanted to rouse us out of the misery and apathy to which we had been condemned, to raise consciousness and expectations, to engender an attitude which questioned authority in the pursuit of responsibility and honesty.

They formed their own record label, Crass Records, despite the risk of becoming capitalist wankers, as it seemed to be the least bad option facing them at the time. Records were always marketed at less than retail price, which incurred financial loss but earned them respect and a sizeable fan base. Crass Records were distinctive, not just by price, but also G Sus' amazing photo-montage record sleeves, which opened out to become provocative posters, creating a corporate image, or as they'd say in these vile times, a recognisable brand. In a spirit of generosity, Crass Records provided a platform for around 100 other bands who without their support would never have been heard. (Agreed, not all of them should have been…) The most famous malcontent from this milieu is Björk, whose Icelandic punk band K.U.K.L. released an album on Crass Records in 1983, long before she hiccupped her way into the charts!

For seven years Crass existed as a beacon for free thinking, radical debate and direct action campaigns: the funding of Rape Crisis centres and Peace News, and amassing a 'bust fund' for any 'friends' who fell foul of Lilly Law in the course of covert operations. All of this in addition to graffiti campaigns and media hoaxes.

As a snotty little fifteen year old, I last saw a version of Mick Duffield's *Choosing Death* at a Crass gig in 1981, mere months before the start of the Falklands war. If I cast my addled brain back, I think entrance was £1.50, which included three bands — Crass, D.I.R.T. and Annie Anxiety, plus Duffield's film. In addition, there were stacks of pamphlets, non-copyright reproductions of obscure anarchist books and a punk disco! This certainly was fun under crisis: we were halfway through Thatcher's vicious first term, and just around the corner from George Orwell's fabled year of totalitarian meltdown. Over the previous two years, sixty per cent of the country's industrial base had been wiped out, causing massive unemployment, and the Cold War, which had just entered its most deadly final phase, provided the perfect backdrop. Comprehension of the information war we found ourselves in never seemed so vital.

Christ the Movie is a compilation of three Duffield films — *Autopsy,*

Choosing Death, and *Yes Sir I Will*. In the course of these dishevelled thoughts, I'm going to attempt to discuss the first two. Not out of laziness, but that I detect a difference between the first two and the latter. *Yes Sir I Will* comes over more like a conventional music video, albeit rather extended. *Autopsy* and *Choosing Death* stand out as films in their own right, worthy of appraisal. The visual style of these films is disjointed and non-narrative — classics of the 'scratch film' genre. By that I mean a type of film making which comprised mainly of visual sampling, collaging disparate odds and ends of existing films and advertising with original footage, thus subverting their meaning, to make something new.

Autopsy — sequence of events

Super 8 footage. Shop windows, mannequins stare pretty vacantly. Road drills. Cut to Crass live. From the soundtrack this is pretty early 77 or 78, possibly the Roxy club. Cut to Steve and Eve discussing the 'suicides' of Enslinn and Baader. Shadowy figures stalk office space. Then explosion/flash, flash again. Faceless crowds in the supermarket. Richard Millhouse Nixon on the soundtrack discussing the merits of nuclear arms proliferation. The frame then erupts into a vortextural effect, blistering before the eyes. Incredibly beautiful, as if the celluloid is a blast victim. Cut to butcher's shop window display/atrocity. Cut to a visit to the Elgin marbles. Soundtrack is Talking Heads' Psycho Killer. A spiky haired oik peruses the line of statues. Pavlovian security guard bristles with empty indignation — a conditioned response. Cut to Crass live again. Severe jump cuts and oblique framing, into long montage sequence of shots including, US military, London stock exchange, cheesy seventies porn, family beach holiday, abattoirs, Group 4 security, a body leaping from skyscraper, the houses of parliament dissolving into the war graves at Flanders. Return to final section of Crass live. Shooting is ultra oblique, with seventy per cent of shots in almost total blackout. The rest appear as if taken in mid pogo! Cut to blackout. Voice-over extols the virtues of "systems, smooth running systems," intercut with an audio loop of Thatcher's voice: "No one wants it more than I do," laid over machine gun sounds and children's screams. The End.

Choosing Death — sequence of events

Title hisses over video feedback backdrop. A hand turns a key in ignition switch, display lights tell us 'system ready.' Cut to extract from sixties shockudrama *The War Game*. Cut to abattoir's vacant production line. Jump cut to seascape footage, all churning waves and seagull sounds. Cut to commercial for Dewhurst's, the family butcher. Return to abattoir production line, this time brimming with unidentifiable body parts. Cut to preposterous promotional film material which I'll call 'keeping up with the Jones'.' This involves two married couples worrying about their mortgages, and simultaneously engaging in a *who has the best kitchen* competition. (Think *Abigail's Party*, sans irony.) Return to seascape, violent waves batter stark, grey cliffs. Cut to hanging animal carcasses, reminiscent of Soutine's paintings. Next, intercutting the Jones' and abattoir footage. This time large circular saws are being applied to dead cows. Dylan Thomas (I think) is the soundtrack. Jump to footage of muddy fields strewn with piles of sandbags, redolent of WWI trenches. Soundtrack has switched to Chamberlain's declaration of war with Germany. Cut to actual WWI footage — explosions, senseless troop manoeuvres. Return to the Jones'. The newly weds bemoan their finances, mortgage etc. Slow motion Dewhurst butcher shoves a plate of chops under female customer's nose. This scene then freezes and is intercut with an image of the human foetus. Still photograph of cosy domesticity; woman sits on the floor at the feet of a man, in front of blazing gas fire. Montage of shots: butcher/abattoir/missile silos, jump to stringing-up of Nazi collaborators, echoing the earlier shots of hanging animal carcasses. Cut again to the Jones', this time discussing DIY/home improvements — "That new kitchen you've always wanted!..." "...You could get yourselves a supplementary mortgage!" Cut to slowly setting sun; a glowing orange disc against a lead grey sky. Hump Back whale-song is the soundtrack. Jump cut to ignition sequence. A housewife peers from an upstairs window/net curtains, as a man below starts up a car. Cut to crash test laboratory. Soundtrack is a loop of American man: "It's just like cranking a car, you turn a key." Presumably he's talking about firing a nuclear weapon, as cold war rhetoric is then espoused — "We're gonna blow them up to stop them blowing us up!" Cut to the Jones'. Older wife brandishes carving knife at hubby and declares, "Think of the value it'll put on the flat!" Next, at the abattoir they're sharpening filleting knives, before setting about another cadaver. Cut to footage of American nuclear weapons installation. Cut to graveyard scene. The camera pans up to reveal tower blocks, as if growing out of the graveyard. Or are the graves detritus fallen from the towers? We see the two together, highrise and six feet under in the same frame. More military and abattoir intercutting. Soundtrack is a neurosurgeon braying on about what a wonderful procedure leucotomy is (that's lobotomy's sister act)! Jump to a clip from HM Government's *what to do in the event of nuclear attack*, film *Protect And Survive*.

Next up the Jones' feeding their children and packing them off to school. Cut to American military installation. Soldiers going through nuclear-strike drill. Soundtrack is talk of collateral damage — that's civilian death to you and me. Stern military types stare intently, intercut with the Jones' and their dream kitchens. Cut to crash test lab antechamber. Here we see boffins in white coats affix limbs and occipital regions to the crash test dummies. (I'm drawn to thoughts of models backstage at fashion shows having finishing touches, accessories and jewellery attached.) Cut to slaughterhouse interior, busy butchers cleave giant, fleshy bodies. Next to car rental office, female client and rep. Jump cut to woman driver harassed by vans and lorries on the motorway. Cut to crash test car smashing, at moderate speed, into a brick wall. Jump to moonrise followed by scene of leafy idyll, all willows and chestnut trees. Cut to trolley of steaming offal in abattoir interior, intercut with slow motion crash test footage. Next, cold war pundits prevaricate about the finer points of mass destruction, intercut with WWII Japanese nuke victims, a foetus, the Enola Gay, fighter planes and pilots. Jump cut to command centre. Cut to the Jones' comparing appliances in kitchen superstore. Then a crash test dummy is strapped into the driver's seat and tested to destruction. Intercutting drivers, vehicles and motorways. Cut to pigs being thrown into incinerators, intercut with shots of Action Man and assorted children's toys. Next, return to the Jones', the kitchen conflict is escalating! Jump to fighter planes, then aerial views of motorway intersections. A Roll's Royce driver crashes dramatically, the shot lingers on the twisted wreckage. Return to nuclear-strike drill. Earnest young men turn switches, ring bells and twist dials in this deadly simulation. Cut to CND rally, then, back again to the earnest young men. Jump cut to TV footage of cruise missiles ranging above an expanse of water. Soundtrack is pigs screaming in an abattoir, then sirens. Back again to the Jones' now in their respective kitchen heavens. Camera pans across still image of Hiroshima — post nuclear blast, intercut with more sound advice from our friends at *Protect And Survive*. Cut to military types and medics discussing radiation sickness, the mounting refugee problem and the difficulties involved in obtaining reliable body-count statistics. Jump cut to photo of Thatcher in flack jacket with army cronies, triumphal visit to the Falkland Islands — after the killing stopped. Moonrise, synth tones on soundtrack. Blackout. The End.

Let's get personal

From Giuseppe Archimboldo's disturbing portraits to William Burroughs' cut-up technique, there has always been something unsettling about the collage/montage form. Its fragmentary nature speaks directly to our sense experience, as, if you think about it, our experience of reality is largely fragmented. The brain could be envisaged as a kind of collage, many disparate elements lying alongside and overlaid on one another. Memory exists like a series of snapshots or short clips. The radical potential of this form is by now a modernist convention. The quasi-mystical revolutionary Walter Benjamin believed that collage/montage, as an art form, had the potential to "...blast open the bourgeois continuum of history." This was said in the context of the 1930s as the Nazis rose to power, and the photomontage posters and book covers of John Heartfield bitterly railed against Europe's descent into fascism. I think it's beyond obvious to mention that Crass' graphic artwork owed much to the influence of Berlin Dadaist Heartfield's work as we descended into Thatcherism... But how could I resist?

Thinking back, this must have been my first exposure to avant-garde film. It's been interesting watching them again. Having seen quite a bit more of this sort of stuff in the intervening twenty-blah years, I was unsure if Mick Duffield's films would stand up to scrutiny. Gladly, they more than withstand it and I'd go so far as to say these two little films are a pair of absolute gems!

My reading of these films owes a huge debt to the cinema of French radical Chris Marker, the scathing political commentary of *Le Fond De L'air Est Rouge* (1977), and his best known film *Sans Soleil* (*Sunless*, 1980). In this radical travelogue he uses the devices of collage, montage, fragmentation and spacio-temporal dislocation. In the course of his travels in Japan, the narrator is drawn, through banalities, to consider the presence of "small fragments of war, enshrined in everyday life." In a similar vein, I believe Mick Duffield is pointing out that small fragments of death and horror are all around us. Through the consumer system, we are all inculcated in the barbaric practices that reinforce it. Just about everything we have comes via the military, and only makes its way to us once all fatal potentialities have been exhausted, and all avenues of cruelty have been fully investigated. Mick Duffield's message, I believe, in these two films (but especially *Choosing Death*) is that the processes and products of dehumanisation are omnipresent. The motives for this are the urge to replace life with money, to substitute experience for empty exchange, to equate the human emotions with the logic of profit and loss. The successful indoctrination of these ideas leads to a subtler cruelty. Once all of life is allotted its rightful economic value, we have, unnecessarily, reduced ourselves to mere terms within a transaction and in the process all human relations become cheapened. So as a counter-strategy Mick Duffield offers different sets of equivalences — competing neighbours/the arms race; the production line/motorway; civil society/crash test dummies; politics/the cemetery; property/children; the atrocities of war/slaughterhouse/death camp. That even the unborn and the dead are circumscribed. Duffield rightly locates Thatcher's doctrines of individual choice and competition, as the divisive agencies par-excellence. The shopkeeper's daughter had accounts on us all.

Watching all the carnage in *Choosing Death* recalls a Francis Bacon interview, where he eloquently sets out his thoughts on the subject:

> I've always been very moved by pictures of slaughterhouses and meat, and to me they belong very much to the whole thing of the crucifixion... Of course, we are meat, we are potential carcasses. If I go to into a butcher shop I always think it surprising that I wasn't there instead of the animal.[2]

Bacon isn't presenting us with a sentimental identification, nor a resemblance, but a profound identity. Through an appreciation of the animal's suffering it becomes human, just as when we suffer we are reduced to the condition of beasts.

The two major spectres that have haunted modern cultural consciousness are the Holocaust and the atomic bomb. How could there be poetry after Auschwitz? How could there be beauty after Nagasaki? As contexts changed and the imminent Cold War danger receded, one could be forgiven for thinking these films a little hysterical. But consider, there were an alarming number of near-miss nuclear missile incidents in the early 1980s; it's well documented that history proceeds not so much by strategy, as fuck up! Cue Chernobyl... The point of all this: "You have to make a friend of horror."

As for the man himself, Penny Rimbaud, in his book *Shibboleth*, writes of Mick Duffield:

> Mick's first visit [to the commune, c.1972] followed a period during which he had experimented with acid... His first works, filmed on b&w stock and painstakingly coloured by hand, were as complex and as fascinating as the young man himself... Without appearing to take his eyes from his editing screen, he could read several books at once and later would be able to discuss the content of them all... Mick went on to create more and more intricate movies, developing a style that was to become seminal to the 'scratch' movement of the early eighties.[3]

His deep sense of enquiry occasionally bordered on obsession. On one occasion he ate a diet of only brown rice, solely to gauge the effects on his metabolism. After fourteen days, he had to abandon it as he very nearly died! For three days he suffered serious fever and ate many, many chocolate bars.

The tide definitively began to turn on Crass around the time of the Falklands war in 1982. Thatcher's eagerness to wage war rather upped the ante. The realisation hit them that the State is all too ready to play much rougher than they ever could, and what they had to offer in comparison seemed rather pale. Prosecutions for blasphemy and obscenity came thick and fast. Added to this was the growing contradiction of their situation. A band with an Agitprop agenda, espousing anarchism, freedom and the ultimate authority of the self, playing to an audience that mostly wanted just to follow. They attacked institutions, yet had become one. This must have been anticipated as the project always had, for obvious literary reasons, a self-destruct date of 1984. For seven years they had done everything in their power to put forward ideas for creating a better world. Trying to reclaim life from the politics of fear and envy, maintaining honesty and integrity throughout. To live outside of the law, you have to be honest.

Mick Duffield's films are a reinforcement of this position and testimony of their time, and indeed our own. As I look around, the culture of conformity and mediocrity has never had it so easy. The alloyed pleasures of the shopping mall — terminal voyeurism, passionless and joyless — reign supreme. The amazing thing is the extremity required to illuminate the banality of horror.

Notes

1 This nuclear war survival guide, in the form of a public information film and accompanying booklet, was in reality, nothing but a bad joke, the like of which only the establishment is capable. It was full of absurd advice. For instance, in the four minutes between warning and enemy strike, the public were advised, amongst other things, to whitewash their windows and make nuclear fallout shelters under kitchen tables! Jolly good luck! This kind of nonsense, of course, came from a bunch of people who, in the event, would be safely holed up in government shelters, having kept the locations of said shelters secret from the civilian population!

2 Source unknown.

3 Penny Rimbaud aka JJ Ratter, *Shibboleth: My Revolting Life*, AK Press: Edinburgh/San Francisco, 1998, p.62–63.

Klub Feet, Kon-certs, Kameras & Quiffs

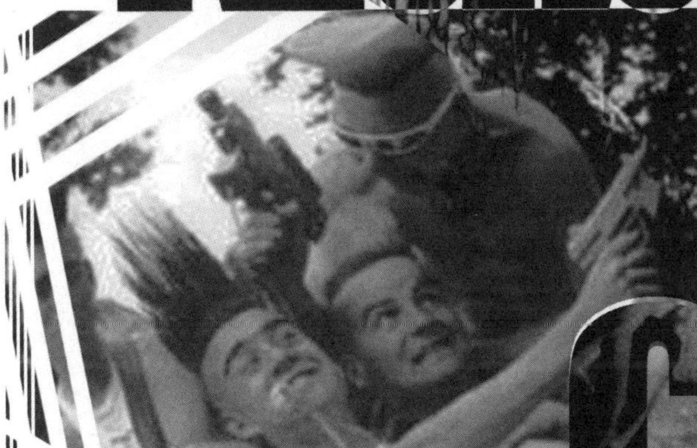

Richard King

I don't remember exactly

when it all started. I just remember being stuck in the middle somewhere: performing with The Turnpike Cruisers one week, filming the next. No one else was really that interested in the scene: it must all have seemed too dodgy and unprofitable. This was good news for us lot — the Jettisoundz video label — as it landed us with some really exclusive footage of the music phenomena commonly referred to as psychobilly, trash or garage punk. It was all a bit of a lark and a bloody good excuse to get completely off your head whilst earning. It's amazing how smoothly the whole thing ran. It's even more amazing how we managed to perform so well and make such bloody good films of the gigs.

The Klub Foot at the Clarendon Hall in Hammersmith was then the premier venue for psychobilly concerts in Europe. It was chocker every Saturday. Tattoos and monster quiffs for boys and girls alike. The ultimate in seedy venues, run by the unhinged for the entertainment of the unhinged. No wonder nobody ever reviewed a gig there.

I remember sitting on the platform in an alcove at the side of the hall that served as a merchandise stand. We had just finished filming The Meteors for the umpteenth time. I was chatting to a spotty faced youth with a foot-long bleached quiff and a black chicken bone hanging from his ear.

It was purist talk: Thunderbird vs 8.5% cider; Skitzo vs Restless; were The Cramps still acceptable role models; pills and brown ale; the Warehouse at Leeds, Hummingbird all-dayers. It was serious competition. A crucial game of 'done it, seen it.' But I was winning. I was it.

A tall, dark and poorly-looking figure staggered through the entrance opposite. It was Jean-Jean, the only black guy in France to successfully join the nationalist party. He was skeletal and fucked. He wasn't welcome at the Klub Foot. Rumour had it that he and a bunch of his Parisian cronies had kicked the drummer of a support band to death during a fight at an early Meteors gig. There were plenty of rumours like that flying about. But having come across the French contingent of the 'Wrecking Crew' on several previous occasions I was tempted to believe much of what was alleged.

He was after a freebie. I did my best to ignore him; I was on a roll with the spotty faced youth and still had a couple of anecdotic aces up my sleeve. There must have been at least eight of them. All in security shirts, all moving towards us quickly in a big bunch, each carrying a bat or lump of wood. They came on fast. We both rolled backwards onto the platform knocking over a merchandise stand. I sprang to my feet and braced myself for a good beating. But they had no interest in us. They just piled on top of Jean-Jean and began pounding him about the head and body as he struggled vainly to escape. Blood squirted. The near empty hall rumbled with sickeningly hollow thuds. It was over in seconds and the black Parisian rag doll was dragged from the hall in cortege silence, leaving behind a scarlet snail trail.

We gathered a few T-shirts up off the floor and handed them to the merchandising guy. Then we calmed ourselves with several large bites from a fresh bottle of red label Thunderbird. "The Long Knives gig at Leeds Phoenix," resumed the youth. "Now that was a dodgy fuckin' gig!" "Yeah!" I replied. "We played it."

To be honest, violence at the Klub Foot is not so much legendary as mythical. Jean-Jean's pummelling was by far the worst incident I ever witnessed there. Besides the odd scuffle — which, let's face it, you get at any gathering — the crowds were generally well behaved. It was a hell of a lot more dangerous playing out of London. There was a lot of respect for the old Clarendon both as a venue for bands and as a centre for the psychobilly movement. The gigs there were second to none that I've witnessed before or since. You just burned up completely. There was a constant stinking drizzle of condensed sweat; the walls were soaking to the touch. No one kept still in the main hall. They were all flinging themselves and their friends around the floor dangerously, or heading back and forth between the bar and hall with plastic beers and bottles of warm brown ale.

A sea of tattooed mutants. The women far more frightening than the men. And up on stage there would be some amphetamine-crazed weirdos screaming rock'n'roll atrocities, machine gunning bastard hillbilly riffs and battering the fuck out of bombed-out double basses. There were some genuinely crazy individuals amongst them. When filming the bands at some sort of ABC Records showcase, it was my job to change tapes at the side of the stage. Early on during the gig Demented Are Go's drummer, Ant, latched onto me, or rather he latched onto my vodka.

"You know why we're the maddest psychobilly band in the fuckin' world?" he slurred, passing the bottle back. I took a healthy draught of the white spirit and did my best to look thoughtful for a few seconds: "Always wondered about that." "'Cos we take more fuckin' acid than anyone else." He patted me on the back like a Druid who's just revealed the meaning of life to his protégé and sloped off in search of drumsticks. He later told me that their lead singer was so out of his brains on stage that he had completely forgotten about the pound of raw pig's liver he had stuffed inside his pants for extraction at a salient point in the performance. I kept hold of my vodka after that.

There was a constant and furious rivalry between all the bands. Everyone claimed to have invented psychobilly. Everyone accused everyone else of ripping them off. They each had their own distinctive image: from the Wham-like presence of Restless to the 'Gothic' hauntings of Coffin Nails. But everyone felt part of something exciting; everyone bought each other's records.

It never ceased to amaze me how such a seedy club could pack 1,400 people into the same building so consistently. Every Saturday night, hordes of the disciples of rabid rockabilly would converge and pay homage to their weekend idols. Young guys told you horrifying stories of P. Paul Fenech wielding a malicious guitar. Girls fantasised about getting inside Pip Guana Bat's surfing shorts. It was as if there was a kind of twisted camaraderie at work. This was the ultimate psychobilly gig. And there we were, right in the thick of it all. Leaping about dangerously on stage, dodging flailing guitar necks or crouched amongst piles of knotted cables in a pool of potentially lethal sweat. Once things were under way you just had to go along with the madness or fry…

John Bentham on autopilot, strutting fearlessly along the edge of the stage, unable to see what he was filming because his glasses had steamed up. He carried on regardless, his eyes stinging with perspiration as hopeful stagedivers heckled him or stabbed him in the ankles with table forks. Now and again John would head towards me screaming, "Hold this, I need a piss." I would be left in charge of the stage camera and shoot a few upside down and vague swirly images that would never be used. When he resumed his position there were always a good few mouthfuls gone from my bottle. Karen Bentham getting far too serious for her own good. Rushing from machine to machine in a futile effort to tell what was going down. Tus Murray trying desperately to get a good sound through headphones that were too feeble to be heard when the bands were playing. Bob Robinson and Mark Chapman at their cameras, completely deaf to any instruction as they teetered precariously on makeshift pedestals that stood in the midst of a writhing mass of steaming bodies. Steve Borsley or Philip Litterick barging their ways back and forth from station to station, in an attempt to relay inaudible messages or scrounge beer and cigarettes. It was all very haphazard. No one really knew what they were doing and no one really cared. We simply knew we had to get the job done.

We were not merely making films of the bands; we were being part of the film. We were making history. And watching those films you can almost see the excitement on screen. You are not just watching a video of a gig; you are at the Klub Foot sweating and being jostled. I'm glad that no one else took any notice of it all, because knowing what I do now about the music business I reckon anyone else would probably have fucked it all up.

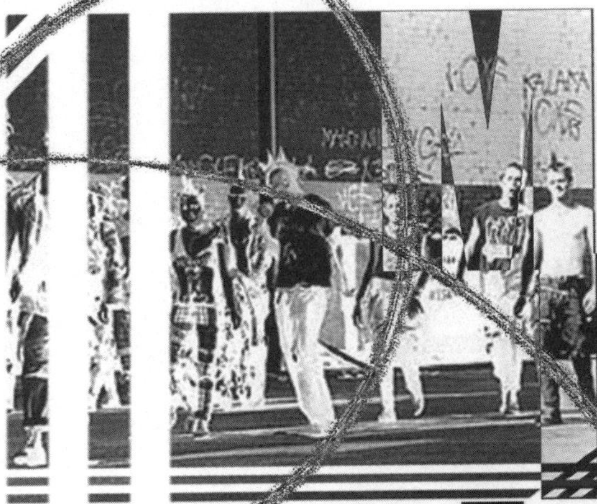

Punk must be humiliated so it may Survive:

Three Movies by Penelope Spheeris

Lance Sinclair

"There's no more brotherhood shit."

It's not like we're all grooving on the same vibes any more. Everybody's grooving on different vibes. Ugly vibes. ***Claude Bessy***

We can watch things without being infected by them. Given the smallest flex of internal discipline, we can process and codify information by pulling it out of its initial context and taking from it what we need. Were we unable to do this, at least comfort can be taken in that we would most likely not be into punk rock. Like any initially maligned culture, punk has, prior to its successful immersion by the corporate entertainment machine into a cutesy option for over-sensitive teens, been the enemy of the media and has primarily been used as a scapegoat for clichéd notions of anti-social terror (the *Class of 1984* [1982] is populated by a particularly malignant and baffling strain of psychopath/dandy punks), and at worst as an ugly-peacock paragon of clownish ignorance (Kelly Enema, anyone?). In the eighties, if you wanted data on punk, turning an eye towards your local video store could yield meagre but valid results.

From this cesspool of misinformation and insults, we can find the truth if we keep our eyes sharp and our bullshit detector tuned.

Penelope Spheeris crammed so much detail and affinity with the LA hardcore squatter community into her film *Suburbia* that the weak, unresolved script, poor acting and overwhelmingly cuddly subtext are dominated and swept aside by the vicious energy and peaking fury of the action playing out for us. For those of us living oceans away from the centre of our cultural world, reading about this in *Maximum Rock'n'Roll* was a long stretch of satisfaction from the fix of seeing how these people spoke, moved and dressed. While punk must always have individuality running through its veins, there is a certain amount of adherence to uniform about it. Without this, it couldn't be defined; and punks do love to have people looking at them, whether they admit it or not. In *Suburbia* we can study the DC-style bald fighting guy; the Rolling Stones/TSOL drug-stupor dealer snake; the cute semi-goth raggedy girls; the proto-crust loner or the sub-Rollins philosopher tough guy. Laid out for the viewer is the rich tapestry of American punk at its pinnacle period of 1982 to 1984. It was a dirty, thrilling and invaluable document for those attempting to walk whilst wearing boot chains.

The essential element of punk haunts the script as well. Cynicism, social decay and the banishment of expecting anything from society are the concrete foundation of these people, however in only a few years time we can see the punks of Spheeris' *Dudes* (1987) run straight to the fuzz at the first hint of violence against their persons. The Dada-esque raids on suburban homes, stores and yard sales are a reminder as well that being punk was once about the kind of anarchic and creative civil disobedience long washed away from the template used now, and recurring only in less satisfactory glimpses in the most abstract *Jackass* sketches, buffeted there by a safety net of prepared and paid legal teams.

Suburbia doesn't pretend that our protagonists are of a heroic or noble quality. They're consistent in that each of them is a monumental fuck-up, hence the uniform T.R. (The Rejected) logo burned into their flesh, or as one redneck would suggest: "What's that T.R. stand for? Totally ridiculous?" Unlike the revised history some would like to embrace, punks of the time were as sexist, racist and homophobic as the next man, if not more so in the extreme hardcore circles. (Race problems had already reared their head in the earlier *Decline of Western Civilization* (1981) documentary, where problems with "black kids" and "niggers" abound.) They destroy their own live scene through thoughtless brutality towards one another, and more savagely still towards outsiders who would dare to breach their sanctum, outlined with perfect unadorned clarity through the unrepentant sexual assault on a pink prom queen who fate cruelly drops into their midst. White boy Jack Diddley, unofficial boss of the crew, hates his stepdad not only for his status as an LAPD pig, but for the fact that he's black. One teen runaway is so horrified at his father's gay leanings that he's driven to the roach-infested hellhole that is T.R. house, rather than tolerate manlove in his otherwise caring, pleasant household. At least the pampered brat is suitably distraught when his new semi-autistic girlfriend overdoses. "Twenty-five black triangles, I had them and now they're gone," mourns the token drug guy.

They were born to lose, and *Suburbia* will not cop out by offering us a brighter future. The truth that these are bad times and this shit is only getting worse, while not a comfort, is the only option when given the alternative of safe entertainment and philosophy, stroking the hair of its listeners while silently easing the pistol to the back of their neck. That the residents of this cursed suburbia have problems and fatal flaws is the major point in the film's favour. There should be no heroes; these characters in bands or on television are not somehow inherently better, more talented or more profound than us. Seeing these people as movie stars or harbouring any faith in them would fly in the face of the kind of bemused nihilism feeding and pouring from the scene of the time, a spirit captured with the keen and unforgiving eye of its precursor *The Decline of Western Civilization*.

> I feel very violent. I feel like I'm doing something I'm good at.
>
> The only performance that makes it and is a success is a performance that causes total madness.
>
> As dumb as you are, even you will remember this.
>
> ***— dialogue from Decline of Western Civilization***

That which Spheeris was so careful to fictionally present to us in *Suburbia* is spread wide and examined for what it really is in *Decline*, a document unrivalled for its vitality and ugly glory. Uncomfortable people in dangerous surroundings, taking bad drugs and doing unpleasant things, is the norm here.

Live performances from Circle Jerks and Black Flag, chaotic and energised, leave the viewer reeling over twenty years later; kids joyfully reminiscing about playing with corpses, big trouble with law enforcement and "throat cancer port" are a taste of the black treats *Decline* has for the world.

Waves of disgust and self-hate recur throughout the film, which is a factual document of events in the Californian hardcore community from December 1979 through to May 1980, told through the voices of a wide spectrum of players, from senselessly hateful street punks to dubious club owners and ranting propagandists. As a companion piece to Leonard Schrader's nightmarish documentary *The Killing of America*

(1981/82), it paints a vision of a country at war with itself, seemingly rushing towards self-obliteration as the only solution to the ennui gripping its populace and slowly suffocating each and every one of them. In this it becomes the most important piece of punk cinema from the eighties, presenting its subject matter in a global, distanced perspective and offering apologies to neither spectator nor participant. Violence, physical and mental, is how ideas are communicated here. Power is taken and all comfort is fleeting. The fascinating, doomed Darby Crash is the saddest little orphan boy ever to carry a razor or blow a stranger for drugs. Darby's self consciousness and self respect appear lost in a maze of debauchery and pain that make his filmed live performance with The Germs sick, compelling viewing. It's all fucked, and it's all of our faults. It's a sentiment the film *Dudes*, still years in the future, would state more explicitly, yet with such a lack of conviction as to be heretical.

Hilarious and scabrous, we meet Frenchman Claude Bessy, who edits the essential *Slash* magazine as well as fronting the art/punk combo Catholic Discipline. His radioactive wit is a joy and his obstinate refusal to cave in to the already encroaching tide of bullshit surrounding his culture laudable: "I have excellent news for the world! There's no such thing as New Wave, it does not exist. It's a figment of lame cunt imagination. It was the polite thing to say when you tried to explain you were not into boring old rock'n'roll, but you didn't dare to say 'punk' because you were afraid to get kicked out of the fucking party and they wouldn't give you coke any more." Bessy truly does not give a fuck for the feelings of those exposed to his art, seeking only to provoke and distress.

Black Flag, who would go on to become the band that would move hardcore into new, unprecedented territory through both their unrelenting work ethic and frightening creative leaps, are even at this early stage obviously on a different level to their peers. Their poet/warrior ethos is made clear in both Chuck Dukowski and Greg Ginn's seemingly light-hearted on-screen interviews. Underneath their easy-going chat is the steel will to power that remained through to their demise some six years later, isolated and light years distanced from their peers.

In a film quivering with highlights and personalities, it's Fear that finish the proceedings with what must be the most representative footage of the era in their shambolic, hell-for-leather glory. Gleefully violent, crass and offensive, Fear tolerate nothing less than submission from the now familiar faces we see in their audience. Their deliberate dismissiveness of the Californian scene and anything except themselves is backed up by the power and ferocity of their music, minds and fists. Witnesses are taunted and then beaten for daring to reply. There's no love or empathy here; these are people in a cage chewing their own hides like zoo animals. This shit is hardcore.

Cue *Suburbia* and things are cool but on a downer. By the time we roll around to 1987 things are not looking so good. Black Flag, Dead Kennedys, Fear and the Misfits are all history. A peak has been reached, and while the spirit of punk is carried into new places by an array of bands as diverse as Butthole Surfers, Poison Idea or the Melvins, there is a feeling that maybe the gold rush is over. Hello *Dudes*.

The primary message of this pedestrian exploitation film is that the punk rock phenomenon is essentially without purpose. Those that follow its codes are merely manifesting their bone-deep cluelessness, apathy and socially pampered alienation to no effect except that of the most minor kind of annoyance to Joe Public. Its protagonists complain almost without pause about the kind of trivial quandaries faced by any mall-dwelling teen. "Music's fucked, girls are fucked," whines our hero Jon Cryer, while drunkenly wallowing in his own peppermint-flavoured misery, all the while remaining oblivious to the fact that punk rock allows us the freedom to create our own music, in place of what we might deem 'fucked,' and that his perception of women is based on rejection and embarrassment at the hands of an overtly slutty, primped Madonna c.1983 clone.

He and his cohorts are consumers, not creators or participants. In this fashion, *Dudes* is a chilling vision of the future of punk, where kids get to play dress up in the most predictable manner until some kind of real purpose makes itself clear to them. The flawed, but iconic, players of *Suburbia* are long gone from this scenario. Forget about starting a collective farm, all ages venue, publication, label, clothing line, or any number of avenues. Like a generation of children whose cultural diet consists of television and annual corporate rock festivals, these worthless posers are unable to look past their own self-inflicted troubles to any larger truth. Complain, use it for all it's worth, and get the fuck out, is the modus operandi of our band of friends, and get the fuck out they do.

Joined by gurning sidekicks Daniel Roebuck and Flea, our man Cryer heads out from New York City to the shores of LA with nothing but a Volkswagen Beetle, a pittance of cash and the type of arrogant, uninformed moxie unique to fake punk rockers and their supposed polar opposite, the jock. The beckoning power of Hollywood is ill defined, but one gets the feeling that it offers more glamorous surroundings to flounce about in, perhaps without the constant threat of running into Agnostic Front or the Cro-Mags, who would doubtless make fine sport of our trio of clowns (Roebuck at one point pines for the opportunity to meet saccharine horrors The Go-Gos). It's here, in the space and limitless, terrible freedom of Middle America that *Dudes* takes on more mythic dimensions and we meet the true star of this miserable show.

Lee Ving, who we've already been introduced to in unforgettable fashion in Spheeris' *Decline* as the sadistically intelligent frontman of Fear, is the only reason copies of this film should remain in circulation. We should look past the banal plotting and dialogue of this movie to what hopefully lies in its guts. Viewed as a portrait of the violence and vitality of punk being chemically castrated, it has much to say.

While our fancy trio camps roughshod in the desert at the halfway mark of their cross-country trek, they fall under midnight attack from Ving (think a more muscular Charles Manson) and his band of psycho cronies. Ving's attitude towards, and treatment of Cryer *et al* is so appropriate and immediate it is truly poetic. Like a flaming shovel of justice, this icon of everything American hardcore was about — originality, fearlessness, viciousness, danger, nonconformity — sweeps down on these faggots and crushes them like the bugs they are. The image of Lee Ving and Flea (who has been scurrying for his life like a fox under the hooves of its pursuers), eye to eye, with full understanding of where this must end, is by far the most satisfying ten seconds of *Dudes*:

> VING [with pistol trained directly between Flea's popping eyeballs]: You sorry sack of shit.
>
> FLEA [knowing, finally, that this is it]: Oh, fuck you!
>
> [Bang]

Here, in perfect simplicity is one of the most important lessons of punk. It has many positive, society-friendly elements to it, but at its core it is nihilist in approach. It should be harsh and unforgiving. It should not be something we can just buy into. Ving here is the teacher and he is, in the harshest way possible, schooling us. Despite having briefly played in Fear and making an appearance in *Suburbia*, Flea was at this time already responsible for the Red Hot Chilli Peppers, one of the most important bands in the cause of assuring dumb shits that punk rock was okay for them to get into. Ving is fighting a losing battle, but every piece of suffering counts, and he is going down swinging. Violence is exclusionary, and this elitism keeps art pure. This unappetising premise is precisely the idea. By weakening, punk killed itself through distillation. Witness the front maintained by skinhead or European black metal culture in the name of preservation. People are less willing to fuck around with a culture that will punish transgressors. Hardcore in general once subscribed to a 'trial by fire' ethos that kept it strong, but by the time *Dudes* crawled out of the focus board meetings in the late eighties, might was no longer right.

It is Ving's attack that finally shows these poor children the light. Flea's "Fuck you!" is a gleam of realisation, although too little and too late, that his softness has been his undoing. The overwhelming apathy that had been the burden of his surviving travelling mates is replaced by the thirst for vengeance against Ving. Through suffering and fear he has taught them. It is this pain, and the desire to share it through his destruction, that has made them whole. They were phonies, and he has given them the gift of brutal truth.

The truth is also more mundane. *Dudes*, in the real world, is a cheaply made quickie aimed squarely at the straight to video/drive-in audience, in which punk rock is merely another ill-researched gimmick along with its supposed paeans to classic western and road movie genres. Watching it unfold from that perspective reveals to us the grotesque homogenisation of punk as poodle-esque haircuts, glam rock accessorising and (barring a truncated pre-credit appearance from The Vandals) the overbearing stench of LA cock rock dominating a scenario that plays on a supposed punk rock premise. The infection of such virulent influences suggests a patient who's given up the ghost at preserving any remaining hope or dignity.

In the interior world of *Dudes* however, Lee Ving is now the last definition of true hardcore and the only way to self realisation, while a recent adjunct to the proceedings in the form of Catherine Mary Stewart as the protecting, providing, downright motherly gas station owner the boys stumble across, provides the dilemma all young punkers must face: do I do this thing for real or do I stay with the comforts and security of my mommy?

As is the case with ninety-five per cent of their wounded antelope peers, they'll choose flirting with the deeper world for a tad before they get their fill and return home to the blanket and the teat. This is what is going on here, and has continued in popular culture since — you can now flirt with this shit. It's for sale. There's no risk or abrasion involved and never has been for Cryer and company. In a world as damaged as this, their all-encompassing dilemma was boredom, and the stultifying lack of interior spark to be able to combat it. Real trouble is rude, messy and unwelcome, and it upsets them to the core of their small-child-with-dropped-ice-cream souls.

So the 'bad guy' is vanquished, and his lessons remain unlearned. After dipping his toe into a world of experience, trauma and limitless possibility, our pansy boy returns to the womb, imagining that he is somehow better for flirting with danger and potential glory. A generation of blood, volume and ideals tied up in a neat package for some bored, fussy gimp to play with and discard, as he will with all things presented to him.

What's to be done? Pretenders spew their evil mimicry from every television, radio and arena stage across the western world for the fleeting enjoyment of tomorrow's corporate machine parts, while the only innovators pushing their art forward languish in obscurity waiting to fade so that these fucks can co-opt their works and sell them as well? There are no new ideas here, there's no threat and there's no humility or recognition of roots as seen in genres as divergent as reggae or metal. Random violent attacks on the part of extremist factions have only resulted in their dissolution and pariah status, so why not call the whole mess done with? That a movement founded on lack of faith, brotherhood, concern or responsibility has become this circus is the coldest pyrrhic victory of all. What sort of serious recognition could have been hoped for, aside from that of children who would be just as easily fulfilled and excited by a stock-car race or a man being fired from a cannon? It was never meant to last, to be lauded, congratulated or admired. A fire may clear a crop or destroy a city: it doesn't have the capacity to care what its effect might be. As for punk, know that it hated you, though only fractionally more than it hated itself.

The Next Decline: A conversation with Penelope Speeris about The Decline of Civilization Part III

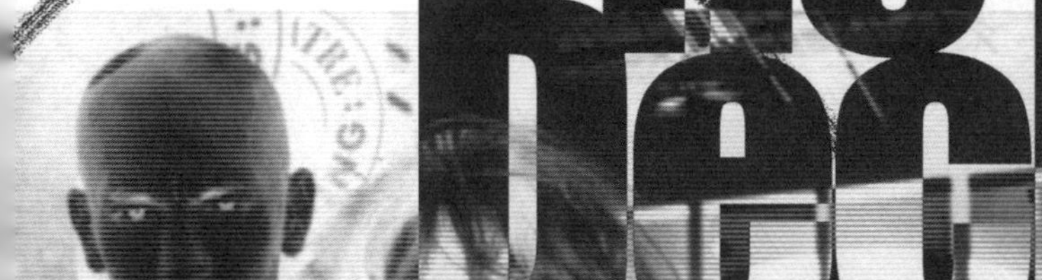

Mark Hejnar

I remember taking a date

to a screening of *The Decline of Western Civilization*. I did a punk rock radio show with two friends called Fast'n'Loud and we were starting a small DIY record label in Chicago at the time. I had already seen the film several times and loved watching The Germs, Black Flag, Fear and X on the big screen. I took this young socialite who wanted to learn about this 'punk' thing, figuring my knowledge of the subculture would ensure a path to her bedroom. The movie scared the shit out of her: "You know these people! You like this music! Why would anyone want to make a movie about such filthy, worthless pigs!" Needless to say I never got any skin but, twenty years later, *The Decline* is still my favourite punk rock documentary. And idiots still raise the same questions about director Penelope Spheeris' latest installment, *The Decline of Western Civilization Part III* (1998). Similar to *Part I*'s completion when Darby Crash dies of an overdose, *Part III* has its share of casualties: one participant is murdered by another and a guitar player dies from an asthma attack.

Spheeris directed underground classics like *Suburbia*, *The Boys Next Door* (1985) and a metal version of *The Decline* (*The Decline of Western Civilization Part II: The Metal Years*, 1988) before going on to Hollywood blockbusters like *Wayne's World* (1992). Spheeris screened *Part III* to sold out houses at the Fifth Annual Chicago Underground Film Festival (CUFF) and received the Best Documentary Award; a testament to the idea that a successful commercial director can retain her integrity. Spheeris made a short presentation before the film:

> I did this film because I took an overdose of some weird drug at the Burning Man Festival. I didn't take it, someone slipped it into my beer and I was so fucked up. I woke in the morning and decided I needed to make *The Decline Part III*. I financed the whole thing myself, that's how screwed up I was. At first I figured everyone knows *The Decline Part I* and *II*, so I'll be able to make a bunch of money on this one. But once I started shooting I realised I couldn't do that because it ended up to be about a bunch of kids on the street that love punk rock music but who are homeless. As a result of the whole experience, I decided whatever money I made I would give to a charity for homeless and abused kids. Anyway, I made a bunch of money making those stupid shit comedies I do, but hopefully we can recycle it into something that really counts.

Half of CUFF's *Part III* proceeds were also donated to a local charity. I enjoyed meeting and talking with Penelope over the course of the festival and this interview was conducted over the phone a few weeks later.

Mark Hejnar In *The Decline of Western Civilization* and *The Decline Part II*, the concentration is on the bands, while in *The Decline Part III*, it's on the fans. Is this how you originally intended the project?

Penelope Spheeris Yes, I saw a second cycle resurgence with punk rock, the type that happens after generally fifteen to twenty years. But I realised the music was exactly the same as it was in 1978, so I couldn't concentrate on that. But in 1977, when we first heard the Sex Pistols, that was a kind of music you had never heard before, and I don't think we have experienced since. Not even with the techno wave or with industrial noise music. It was such a drastic departure from convention. So I wanted to concentrate on these homeless kids that took the look and the political and social philosophy of the original punks and brought it into the gutter. [Laughs]

The *Decline Part I* was very positive — the people are trying to create something active — while in *Part III*, these kids seem so hopeless.

I agree. In *Part I* they were hopeful because they knew they could do something different and put their stamp on the world, which they did. Punk rock did make some changes; unfortunately, the most obvious changes are in fashion and style. But their commitment to anarchy and chaos is most admirable and that leaves some sort of impression.

When we chose the title *The Decline of Western Civilization* twenty years ago it was a joke. I didn't think it would become this profound prophecy.

Even if these kids worked really hard they can't have much of a life. It's unfortunate; they can't go to school, they don't want to work for $5 an hour because they're usually too smart. They just check out, and that's too bad. These are the people my heart goes out to.

From your film, if I was to attribute a reason why these kids react like this, I'd say lack of family structure and a history of physical or sexual abuse.

They're kind of related aren't they? I think you are absolutely right, but I believe we must consider a few other things. I'm not trying to let the parents off the hook because there is no excuse for mistreating your child, for not guiding your child, no excuse. But this generation of parents had to start working so hard to just stay afloat, to survive and maintain, to put food on the table. As a result, they didn't have time for their kids. And the critical thing is they never imagined the fallout, the tragedy that would result from not giving their children love and attention.

If there's any lesson to be learnt from *Part III*, it's that without proper parenting and love and time devoted to your children, it's going to backfire and make your life miserable, if you care at all.

A lot of these kids just take off so it doesn't matter. I always end up feeling so much like a doom-sayer in these interviews...

I look at *The Decline Part III* as a warning. Years ago there was a Brazilian film, *Pixote*, about all these little kids running around on the street, stealing food to survive, running around in packs...

Hanging out with prostitutes and becoming child pimps...

...And what's wrong with that? And then the cops start shooting the kids, and the storeowners beat and chase them, and this film was made about twenty years ago [1981 — MH], and I remember thinking this could never happen here, but it has. Go to any midwestern Middle America town and ask people if this is a possibility and they'll still say no. But I think in the next ten years we'll see the truth and that's the tragedy.

That people refuse to recognise it can happen here in the US?

That there'll be so many kids out there on the street, wandering around with no food or shelter; a pack.

A pack that'll replace itself, since as everyone in the film says, they expect to be dead in five years.

Oh yes, it'll replenish itself easily, there's a major supply, unfortunately.

Do you think Los Angeles is particularly bad?

These gutterpunks are very nomadic, they wander around. It's a natural urge at a certain age to leave the nest and see the world. It's an instinctive drive, but it's magnified and exaggerated in these kids because they don't have any home, and if they do, they just want to leave it. So they all get out there and start to roam and meet up in different cities. So to say it's Los Angeles specifically is incorrect; seventy-five per cent of the gutterpunks I know are from elsewhere. Many parts of the country are conducive to external living.

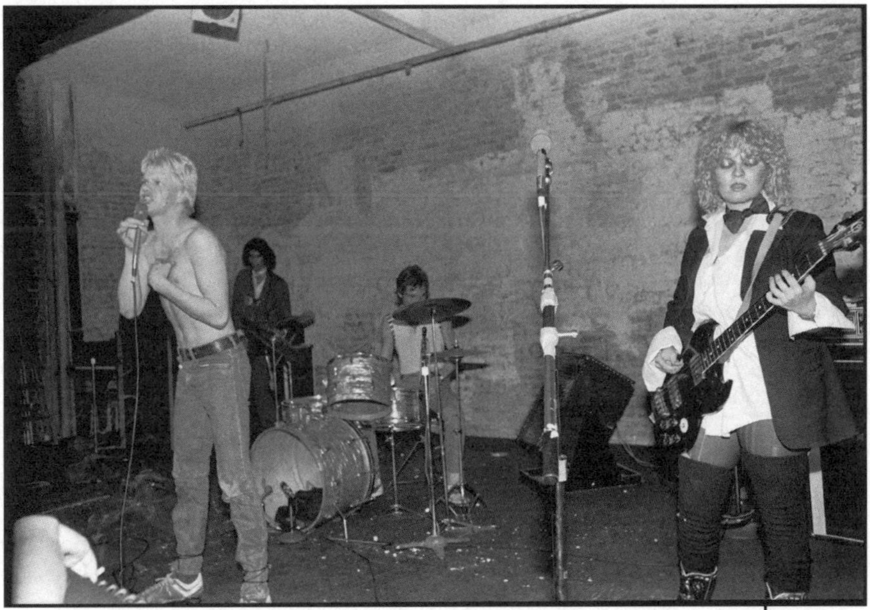

The Germs at The Mabuhay, 1977, one of their first shows in San Francisco (with a different drummer). Photo Ruby Ray

In all three of *The Decline* films everyone hates the police but the second biggest enemy appears to be skinheads.

Cops and skinheads; the far right and the far left, for my money. The cops are their enemy because they like to hassle them. Besides, it makes the kids feel brave and what have they got to lose? Go to jail and get a hot meal and shelter, a night off the street and you can go back to your friends and tell 'em you're a hero. I didn't interview any of the skinheads because I didn't want to take the chance that some vulnerable young mind is going to see the film and imitate them. Just like I don't do violent films when I work in Hollywood, I didn't want to portray skinheads in *The Decline*.

A police officer in the film says the gutterpunks are just demanding attention they never received as kids. Do you agree?

Yes, totally. I can say that without feeling like I'm putting them down because I spent most of my life that way. Trying to look and act different, something that would cause even strangers to give me attention. My mom was a pioneer. She had to take care of four kids without a husband so she had to work too much and totally ignored us, and then there'd be an occasional stepfather that beat the shit out of us. What else could it be? Why else would someone feel that they had to stand out in a crowd if it wasn't from an insecurity about being ignored? As an artistic statement? No. It just furthers my argument, which is: why can't we be responsible parents and take care of our children and choose to break the abuse chain?

Now I get accused, Mark, of taking these kids off the hook and not letting them have any of the responsibility for this, and I don't mean to because I do think young people can choose to make something of their lives. It's difficult to not look at the world in a totally negative way when you've been mistreated. Considering the way I was treated, I should be dead or in jail by now. I've taken a very large lamp and clubbed it over a stepfather's head; he was passed out drunk and I was mad because he beat me up. He could've been killed or I could've been in jail for my whole life. I was fortunate enough to be able to direct my anger in a constructive instead of destructive manner. If I can be any sort of a role model or example for kids, that'd make my life worthwhile — to say, okay, well she had a really bad time but she didn't go down that black path. I gained a lot from having been treated like that. The Chinese have an expression: you can't say if something is good or evil until your time has passed. Things that happened that are very bad have happened for a reason and it is a positive reason; you just have to let some time pass.

People accuse you of glorifying these kids; where do you think this comes from?

Here's what makes me angry: when people who have comfortable lives criticise these people and don't take the time to stop and understand them. It's just too easy and lazy to dismiss another human being because they are in a less fortunate situation. I don't doubt these kids can be aggressive and cause trouble and that some people are targets for these kids, especially if you try to be real hip around them. The question is why did they choose you?

Did anyone accuse you of glamourising the metalheads in *The Decline Part II*?

No, not really, because they sort of hung themselves. I didn't try to put down heavy metal music because I really like it. I was offered the job of directing *Spinal Tap* and I turned it down; I like the music too much to make fun of it. So, no one ever accused me of glamourising metal kids, but they did on *Part I* and they did to a degree on this one, but not so much. I guess with age you acquire credibility.

And you've also noticed if someone tries to fuck with me, I really lay into them. I have a short fuse on that one, so don't start with the "Why do you glorify these animals?" because I'll jump all over you.

Note

Photo on p.117 Penelope Spheeris and Sin from ***The Decline of Western Civilization Part 3*** at the Chicago Underground Film Festival, August 1998. Photo © Mark Hejnar

What do we Love, what do we hate, what do we love to hate and what do we hate to love?

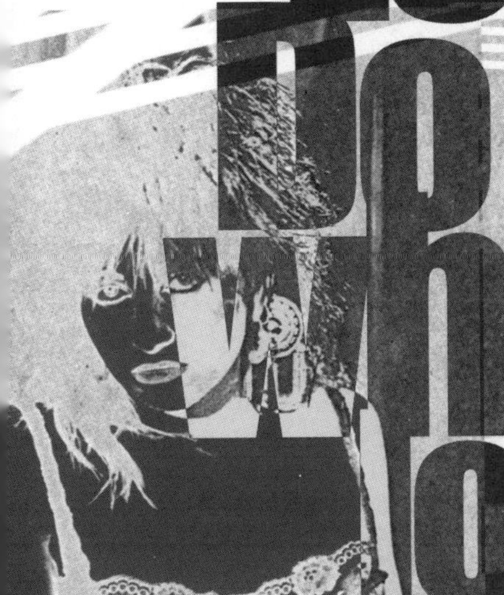

Tessa Hughes-Freeland

[The following chapter, written by Tessa Hughes-Freeland, an active participant in the downtown New York underground/independent film scene, offers a 'snap shot' circa 1979–92. Some of the films described here were never completed and some filmmakers subsequently gave up filmmaking. Readers interested in pursuing this area of research are advised to read Jack Sargeant's book *Deathtripping: the Cinema of Transgression*.]

A certain breed of post-punk

ideology was rife in New York in the eighties. Synthesised with graffiti, rap, vestigial seventies disco and the entrails of sixties psychedelia, it gave way to a curious cultural climate. By the mid eighties an artistic scene was booming downtown and it was being acknowledged by the world. Creative people of all disciplines were coming out of the woodwork to enjoy exposure, recognition, fame and maybe even fortune. The doors were open for everybody and anybody who cared. A burgeoning art scene was being co-opted by the media and, in turn, a self-perpetuating market developed. It became fundamentally commodity based. Artists, dealers, and real estate companies all made money. Such was the superstructure of the 'East Village Scene' to which so many were attracted.

How did filmmakers fit into all this? There was a sense of community and an active subculture that pre-existed the supposed birth of the East Village. Rents were cheap and affordable. New clubs and venues were opening every month. A hybrid culture was becoming official in the radical, multi-ethnic bowels of the metropolis where welfare families, illegal immigrants, pimps, prostitutes, drug dealers, drug addicts, poets, hippies, Satanists, writers, musicians, painters and performers all lived side by side in an area where drugs and violence prevailed.

Films being made in this community were underground; expressive of a state of mind rather than a state of the art. They represented anti-establishment attitudes blended with personal visions. The outrageousness of Andy Warhol's Factory environment and its transformation into punk nihilism paved the way for experimentation of all kinds.

A relationship between filmmakers, musicians and performers developed mainly because they hung out together. The punk scene was totally anti-art and anti-acceptance. The current bands like Suicide, DNA, Teenage Jesus and the Jerks, The Contortions, Richard Hell and the Voidoids, Bush Tetras, and the Heartbreakers rocked the New York clubs. The clubs were a happening scene; Max's Kansas City, CBGB, Danceteria, Club 57 and later the Mudd Club played host to a whole cast of characters. It was in these clubs, rather than in cinemas or alternative spaces, that Eric Mitchell (*Underground U.S.A.*, 1980), Amos Poe (*Unmade Beds* [1976], *Blank Generation* [1976]), James Nares (*Rome '78,* 1978), Charlie Ahearn (*Deadly Art of Survival, Wild Style*), Beth and Scott B (*G-Man* [1978], *Black Box* [1978]), Vivienne Dick (*She Had Her Gun All Ready* [1978], *Beauty Becomes the Beast* [1979]), Manuel De Landa (*Ism Ism* [1979], *Raw Nerves* [1979/80], *Harmful or Fatal if Swallowed* [1982]) and M. Henry Jones (*Go-Go Girl, Soul City*) showed their films.

Super-8 film was cheap and cameras easily available. This opened up the possibility for anybody to make films and conceive of their use in a way that had absolutely nothing to do with Hollywood in production, form, content or ideology save for a type of genre exploitation or image plundering, which, taken out of context, served to make a statement.

There was always something going on in the clubs. In the early eighties at Club 57, Danceteria, Pyramid, No Se No, Mudd Club and Limbo Lounge there was something happening every night: bands, performers, films, art exhibitions. The boundaries between disciplines broke down completely and people worked together. Activities ranged from multi-media extravaganzas to solo acts. For anybody working with film, or anybody who had a camera or just got hold of one, the subject and content of what they did with it became an extension of a lifestyle. As more and more people did things with film a community gelled. The best way to understand how this came about is to look at some of the individuals involved, who together constituted a vibrant film community.

Fuelled by a plentiful supply of low rents, drugs, talent, time and a seemingly inexhaustible array of marginal characters ready and willing to do just about anything in the name of celluloid glamour, Richard Kern's life in the mid eighties was wild. Hunting and hunted, Kern was into something that creatures understood. A bare-faced parody of human extremes was tangible to those possessed of a certain twist of mind or like inclination. He was exploring the raw meat of human nature and made no bones about it. Coming from a background of photography and fanzines with self-effacing names like *Dumbfucker* and *Valium Addict,* Richard's sharp eye, menacing vision and incisive wit produced films that not only let hell run loose, but also kept a finger well on the pulse of a delinquent American teenage psyche. However unsettling, psychotic or distorted the content of Kern's films may be perceived as being, visually nobody ever looks bad. He is technically proficient: inventive camerawork, imaginative lighting and fast paced editing contribute to the dynamic and compelling nature of his films. Working only in Super-8, Kern's narratives and characterisations are direct and concise.

In the early eighties he made *Goodbye 42nd Street* (1983/4) and *Zombie Hunger* (1984), which both suggested an interest in sex, drugs and violence. He also did a number of expanded cinema performances of *Blood Boy*, which varied in content but usually involved Brian Moran naked, pouring blood over himself and included acts of terrorism, interrogation and assassination.

An affiliation with punk music and attitude became an integral part of Kern's films. A story of sexual obsession, *Right Side of My Brain* (1984) was co-written with Lydia Lunch and features Lydia Lunch, Henry Rollins, Foetus, Norman Westburg and others, with music by JG Thirlwell and Dream Syndicate. Dispensing with any irrelevant subject matter, it focused on the pursuit of realising sexual desires.

Specialising in paring down human relationships to their most basic elements, *Manhattan Love Suicides* (1985) is made up of four short stories of seedy lives ending in suicide by different means. Simultaneously horrific and hilarious, these stories have a cartoon-like quality in construction, as in the characters' exaggerated behaviour, appearance and expression. It is a b&w film portraying a b&w world.

The people Kern played and worked with were always close to each other. Kern's collective *Deathtrip* films attracted people like a magnet. They were ready and willing to participate in and perform full scale, large screen acts of erotic indulgence, humiliation, degradation, self-destruction and mutilation. *Submit to Me* (1985) and *Submit to Me Now* (1987) are like visual diaries, documents of those who passed in front of Kern's camera and through his apartment life. In a sequence of tableaus devoid of backgrounds or storylines, the focus is on individual acts. A cinematic emphasis through intrusive and authoritative camerawork, polychromatic lighting and kaleidoscopic editing results in an ocular assault of prurient psychopornadelia. The films are prefaced by an explanation: "The characters portrayed are suggested to R. Kern by the actors illustrating them either literally or subliminally." The words SEX/HATE, SEX/DEATH and DESTROY confirm a punk aesthetic (of sex, hate, death and destruction).

Those who act in Kern's films reappear with some frequency: Lung Leg, Lydia Lunch, Clint Ruin, David Wojnarowicz, Tommy Turner, Cassandra Stark, Audrey Rose and Nick Zedd have all worked with Kern in different mutually creative capacities. Kern worked with Lung Leg on her film *Black Monster* and Tommy Turner on *Simonland* (1984), while *Thrust in Me* (1984), one of the *Manhattan Love Suicides,* was a collaboration with Nick Zedd.

You Killed Me First (1985) was based on mixed autobiographical experiences of a number of Kern's friends. A nightmare of domestic suburbia, it was initially shown as part of a collaborative installation with David Wojnarowicz, who also plays the father in the film. It starts with a leaf-strewn floor interspersed with mangled metal parts, shifting to a scene of a murdered family viewed through a breezeblock wall. Examining these physical remains and the story leading up to it, *You Killed Me First* explores the alienation of a teen spirit.

Lydia Lunch and Richard Kern joined forces again in 1986 to make *Fingered*. Also featuring Emilio Cubeiro, a local performer who wrote his own dialogue, *Fingered* dives in at the deep end, hard and fast, and never comes up for air. Like most of Kern's narratives in naturalistic settings, *Fingered* is b&w. *You Killed Me First* stands out as the only colour narrative in a naturalistic setting with dialogue so far. Kern tends to favour colour for his tableaux, creating moods and lighting figures in a disconcerting spatial void.

Richard Kern is an incredibly prolific filmmaker. He has made sixteen films to date and is working on a seventeenth as I write. *The Evil Cameraman* (1986–90) picks up where *Submit to Me Now* left off. The film involves a transformation: a few years in absentia, there is a marked contrast between two phases. His encounters with girls in the later part of the film become acts of persuasion rather than brutal and forcible. Many have focused on the blood and guts violence in Kern's films rather than on the humour. In *The Evil Cameraman* humour comes to the fore. It is packaged and distributed — under the name of *Sex vs. Guns* — on one video tape alongside *King of Sex* (1987), *Pierce* (1986) and *X=Y* (1990): a crucial and effective way of getting films 'out there.' In *X=Y,* Kern addresses the question of violence on a societal level rather than in terms of personal obsessive self-destruction. At the end of *X=Y* Tomoya, a Japanese girl, offers a gun on a folded American flag up to the viewer.

Sex and fetishism prevail as Kern continues to explore taboo subjects. Kern chose *Scooter and Jinx* from Sonic Youth's album *Goo* to turn into the film *Money Love* (1991). It portrays a lesbian encounter which requires money. Money also appears in a transaction in *The Evil Cameraman*; possibly a reflection of Kern's concern for the source of money for his films, now mostly from Europe and not the American grant system — trying to untwist their dainty white knickers — or from any other source. Nudity is pretty taboo in the nine-to-five world but Kern celebrates the beauty of the human body and its sexuality in action. In *Tumble* (1991) the athletic eroticism of Linda Serbu's movement is doubled by his classic disorientating camerawork. He uses his camera like a subversive weapon, penetrating exterior appearances and opening our eyes to the world of a fantastical reality.

In *Catholic* (1991) and *Nazi* (1991) Kern cracks through exterior preconceptions and makes lighthearted fun of stereotypical labels. One label wrongly attributed to Kern by some is that of misogynist: a seemingly groundless accusation because men and women are treated alike in his films. *Horroscope* (1991) is a short humorous narrative that incorporates female fantasy and male stereotypes. In his 1992 film *The Bitches,* a kind of pornographic parody, the girls are on top and in control, echoing and reversing the sexual dynamic of *The King of Sex*. So, does this make men victims?

Kern is an intense and prolific filmmaker: putting his work on videotape and DVD makes it available to millions and expresses a commitment to a brand of filmmaking that can only be encouraging and inspiring to others.

Cassandra Stark is a filmmaker whose psychological inquiry is fraught with religious and ritualistic overtones. Her films are poetic and disturbing in their expression of human responses and behaviour. Her first short Super-8 film, *Dead on My Arm* (1985), was quickly followed by *Go To Hell* (1986) made with Nick Zedd. *Wrecked on Cannibal Island* (1986) is more sophisticated and uses sound portraying the obsession, loneliness, fear and fascination inherent in many relationships. Stark investigates abnormal behaviour; conditioned responses become more personal and questions of what is actually normal disappear.

In *We Are Not To Blame* (1989) the unconventional relationship between two sisters is made more understandable as we learn about the characters' alienation, isolation and their common basic human need for familiarity. The two sisters wreak appropriate revenge on one of their abusive husbands, played by Richard Kern, by tying him up on the roof for a long time. Stark's films contain an intense personal vision also present in her paintings, writing and music. When Menace Dement, Stark's band, plays there are projected visuals by David Schmidlapp. In front of these contrasting urban and primal images, Stark rocks and sways with guarded gestures. Her performances are another expression and extension of an aesthetic that is both gentle, vulnerable and somewhat deranged.

Breaking down the barriers between film, performance and music, Kembra Pfahler has found a new name for her work: Availabism, basically meaning working with anything available. Surfboard baby Pfahler was performing at all the small downtown clubs in the early eighties. 'From the manual of action' came performances with names like *Reification Playground at Armageddon* (1980), *Murder Mysteries at Limbo Lounge* (1984) and *Tribute to Rudolph Schwarzkogler* at No Se No.

Working with her longtime partner, Samoa, their performances involved mysterious rituals and psychosexual symbols all dazzling with glamour and glitter; a Las Vegas showgirl run wild and rampant. Kembra and Samoa made performances with tools that were available to them, so when a camera became available film became another medium to explore. This enabled her to have more control and freed her from the annoyance at others trying to sell recordings of her performances back to her. Kembra Pfahler's Super-8 films are colourful, elegant, hallucinatory, melancholy and fun. *Cornella, Story of a Burning Bush* (1985) is the most simple: a depiction of a flower growing out from between a pair of upstanding thighs, it appeals to a primeval state.

Bodily adornments and bizarre physical feats are used as means to explore themes of duress and disorder in *Mild Seven, The Cowboy Stories* (1986): with her feet attached to bowling balls, Kembra raises herself up off the ground using two long poles as her only means of support. This act later became part of a self-styled Diet Pepsi commercial. In a 1987 performance entitled *Pussycat Bladder Waste*, she performed a bloodletting ceremony, only recently replacing blood bags for the real thing. The film *Historical Beauty Treatments* (1986) depicts the natural sources and visceral procedures involved in beautification throughout the ages. As an expanded cinema performance, *Craftmatic Dreaming* (1987) was never executed twice in the same way.

Kembra Pfahler's idiosyncratic alter ego Abra Kedavour, inspired by the Ed Wood Jr penned movie, *Orgy of the Dead* (1965), is just one example of her versatile persona as a minor cultural icon. She appears as different personalities in a variety of films: *The Splatter Movie* and *Purgatory Junction* by Mike Kuchar, Jerri Rossi's *Anima Sola*, Ari Roussimoff's *Shadows In The City* (1990) and Nick Zedd's *War Is Menstrual Envy*, to name but a few. Now she is working with a band The Voluptuous Horror of Karen Black. Body paint, fright-wigs, crazy imaginative props, headdresses, and lurid, sexy costumes are characteristic of this band which has Abra Kedavour, Samoa, Annabelle La Fleur, Squeaky, Matt Black and others as members. One of their songs, Going To Alaska, is constructed totally out of Karen Black's dialogue in *Five Easy Pieces*. Pfahler conceives of the songs she writes as little movies: visual and narrative. *Neiborachie* was originally to be a film about a shy living room entertainer, suffering from stage fright so severe he murders his one on one audience members. The name of the band was chosen by Mike Kuchar, and the song Diane is an ode to him. It is during this finale song that Kembra 'does the eggs': she performs a headstand and Annabelle La Fleur Rabbit, or another assistant, smashes paint-filled eggs in her crotch. The one time I saw a man assistant, it was Joe Coleman fearsomely going for it with an eggbeater. This, and other onstage antics of the glamorous nine-member theatrical rock band, has been released as a film, *The Fear of a Karen Black Planet* (1992), under the aegis of Pfahler and with the aid of Steve Doughton.

Steve Doughton comes from a painting background and in the early eighties he was making fetish dolls. He made a number of short films early in his life, which directed his interest towards sci-fi, or as he prefers to call it now, Psi-fi-chedelic. His attraction to Hollywood films stems from them being a fertile, plunderable or exploitable resource, sexist imagery *et al*. Shooting from the TV, he samples images and works with opticals and matts in un-split Regular-8, worked with yet further to create a fly eye effect. His imagery is very psychedelic and perfect material for ambient expanded projections.

Being of a cosmic tendency, he fuses science fiction, fantasy, alchemy and nature. *Forming* (1987) is a science fiction study of entropy and *Pixilation* (1989) is a sci-fi fantasy with an entropic theme: a space alien and an elf adventure through Bedrock City and the Enchanted Forest, Oregon. *Hand of Doom* (1976), one of his earlier efforts, has a slightly more tangible premise: a teenage junkie scores a bag of dope, shoots up, overdoses and dies. *Meug* (1990) depicts the experience of a guy who sits in front of the TV smoking pot, eating and dreaming: the limits and expanses of a couch potato lifestyle. As well as working on *The Fear of a Karen Black Planet* — which for his part, he more specifically describes as two music videos (*Mr Twighlight* and *King of the Sea)* shot in Super-8 — Doughton has been working on *FEo2*, starring Kembra Pfahler. This nature film in Yellowstone Park contains four commercials about the

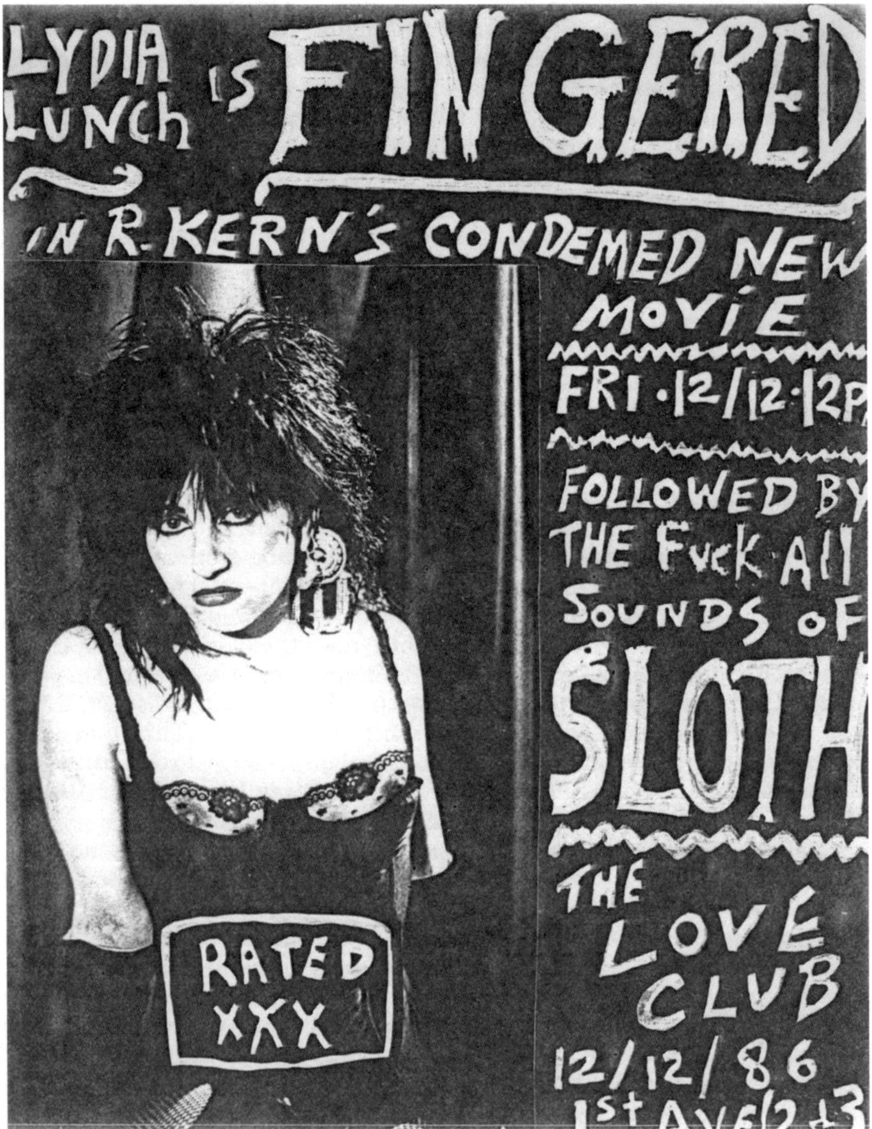

Flyer for Richard Kern's *Fingered*

smithing of iron and ends with a Busby Berkeley-esque dance number with kaleidoscopic choreographed space aliens.

Bradley Eros' films and expanded cinema performances experiment with the visceral and technical elements of film. Using still images, found footage, redefined effected video and self-shot film, the poetic nature of his work is substantiated by equally haunting soundtracks. A previous collaborative relationship, Erotic Psyche, consisted of Bradley Eros and Aline Mare. Mare now lives in San Francisco and her most recent piece is a video *S'Aline's Solution*. Now, Eros collaborates with Jeanne Liotta. Their films and performances are dark, mysterious, biomorphic, psychedelic and subterranean. Utilising optical printing and re-photography, most of the films are Super-8, though *Fungus Eroticus* (1990) was printed onto 16mm. Eros and Liotta describe themselves as "media mystics investigating cycles of decay and regeneration in the body and the world." The freedom of working with various elements means that every performance is different in some way. They incorporate their films into their performances, which are named in the same spirit: *Liquid Hardcore Mystics, Wandscape, Techno Spiritus* and *Turning the Dragon Inside Out*, to name but a few.

Essentially experimental, environmental and ephemeral, their work is different on every occasion, yet a sensory essence is always present. Their conception that images are infinitely versatile and mutable, challenges the notion of film as an object that is transportable and finite. The arena in which Eros and Liotta work is one of breadth, dealing with correspondences and associations that are mystical and sensual.

Ela Troyano puts a truly flexible approach toward moving pictures into practice: a campy, glitzy, celebratory outrageousness characterises the aesthetic of her expanded cinema performances. Showing at downtown clubs such as Studio Henri, Pyramid, Limbo Lounge, 8B.C., Darinka and Chandelier, as well as alternative art spaces throughout the eighties and in large dance clubs like Limelight and the Building, now as then, she incorporates film, slides, video and live action into these performances. During these performances the projectors are used like instruments and the resulting visual jam is analogous to a piece of music. In the early eighties Troyano worked repeatedly with John Zorn, whose broken compositions and accumulated sounds were reflected through corresponding images and rhythms.

These performances or multiple projections were contextually varied depending on whatever technical resources were available, and were mostly collaborative. Troyano did a whole series of nights at Pyramid in 1982 with David Schmidlapp. One of the larger of these performances was a four night multiple projection covering three twenty-foot walls. These ambient visuals were in constant motion for six to eight hours each night. It was a collaboration between Troyano, Tessa Hughes-Freeland, Andy Soma and Stephen Hoiman at the Kitchen for 8 B.C. Nights in 1986. Implementing a barrage of up to sixteen projectors, the visuals were spontaneous and aleatory. They were often long, varied in degrees of intense lyrical grooviness and were interspersed with flashes, vibrating rhythms, cuts and bursts, refractions and fusions. They involved just about anything that was projectible: feathers, creepy plastic insects, gels, mirrors and broken glass. One epic psychedelic multiple projection at Chandelier in 1986 ended when the dancing girls abruptly stopped, resulting in the image of their voluminous red ball gowns melting.

Blonde Voodoo (1987–89) and *Playboy Voodoo* (1991) are extensions or self-perpetuating encapsulations of multiple projections. They serve dual functions: not only can they be shown as individual films but also they can provide yet more density during multiple projections, thereby facilitating less equipment. *Blonde Voodoo* is figurative and abstract, and displays Troyano's personal iconography and techniques. Almost all the objects to which she finds herself attracted relate to her native Cuba. One glass object is a perfume bottle dispenser, which belonged to her mother, being one of about ten items the family could bring from Cuba.

Playboy Voodoo is a collaboration with Tessa Hughes-Freeland. It combines two films (one of which is already superimposed), slides, gels and other techniques and methods resulting from the multiple projection experiences. The imagery in this film is sexual, fantastical and oneiric.

Working in 16mm, a fascination with looseness, experimentation and a spontaneous method of working is fundamental to Troyano's approach. In 1983 she made *The Bubble People*, a double projection of two unedited reels with two soundtracks. A variety of sets were put in a room, actors and crew came together and just shot. The camera was centrally positioned to allow maximum range of activity between the continuous sets and the actors chosen and informed of an idea. Phoebe Legere plays the Bubble Goddess, a teacher/Marilyn Monroe character, who comes to earth and teaches everybody to be like her. Jack Smith also played the same role on a different day and Phoebe stepped in again. In fact, anybody who came to the set could potentially appear.

For *Totem of the Depraved* (1984) — a film in four sections, featuring Nick Zedd, Phoebe Legere, Gia Gamba and James Richardson — Ela had a definite idea of different cinematic approaches for each section. Parodying Andy Warhol's *My Hustler* (1965), Nick Zedd has sexual encounters with all the characters. Gia was found on the day of the shoot, and James Richardson was just asked to show up. This spontaneity was intentional and a small scripted segment was an idea Nick wanted to try. A related section, *David Does Venus*, is an encounter between Carmelita Tropicana and David Crocker, a guy who wants to be a successful performer.

Carmelita Tropicana, "a sort of low rent Carmen Miranda (no fruit)," stars again in *Loisaida Lusts* (1985). This film has more of a conventional format and was written and directed by Ela Troyano and Uzi Parnes. Although fictitious, *Loisaida Lusts* behaves like a commentary on a specific time.

Troyano's collaborations with Carmelita and Uzi extend into performance and theatre. *All New Red Hot* (198?), performed at Uzi's club Chandelier, maintained a consciousness of Ela, Camelita and Uzi's cross culturalism. Similarly, the plays at P.S.122, *Candela* (1988), and *Candela y Azucar* (1989), have a high camp style that pokes fun at aspects of both Cuban and American socio-political issues. Once having been described as Cuban-American, Troyano is not alone working in this realm of fiction and social satire; being bi-lingual, sharing two cultures and a like sense of not belonging, she says she is Cuban and was raised in the USA, but choses to call herself Latino as a political statement.

Troyano's *Once Upon a Time in the Bronx* (1992) was inspired by a visit to a gallery that featured dolls dressed as rappers and homeboys, made by Ricky Rodriguez. What started out as an idea for High-8 video generated interest and developed into a larger 16mm project. It is an upbeat story of two young Puerto Ricans dealing with problems common to Latino kids growing up in the US — a lack of opportunities, teenage pregnancy, few role models. It is the story of Rafael, a homeboy immersed in the hip hop culture of the Bronx, and his cousin Edward. The film features rap songs by Latin Empire, who also play the two main characters. Presently, Troyano is working on a film about the life of Camelita Tropicana.

Cross-dressing, role reversal and questions of sexuality appear continuously in Troyano's films and collaborations with Uzi Parnes. Parnes' Super-8 pornographic parodies, *Girls Can't Help It* (1986), *World Peace* (1987) and *Squalid Salad* (1988), go to make up the trilogy entitled *Maneaters*. The scenes of male rape and dominant women castrating various men are very funny: special effects and a happy soundtrack lighten a hard message.

A Queer Love Poem (1991) intersperses homoerotic imagery with words from a poem. Gentle, wistful and more lyrical than the *Maneaters* trilogy, the arid Hollywood musical disco soundtrack is complementary rather than ironic. Parnes also continues to work in expanded cinema performances and theatre with Carmelita Tropicana. His most recent production, *Carnival*, mixes humour and historical fact.

As early as 1968, James Harding was making sci-fi monster movies with GI Joe dolls. A giant fly threatens earthlings with doom in *The Attack of the Giant Fly* and *Return of the Giant Fly*. In 1979, Nick Zodiak was showing his Super-8 punk feature *They Eat Scum* in the clubs downtown. By 1983, he had completed a vehemently probing pseudo-propaganda 16mm short called *The Bogus Man* (1980), an ambitious camp horror feature, *Geek Maggot Bingo* (1983), and transformed his personality into Nick Zedd. Politically concerned from the start, an anarchic, inquiring character was at work. Acutely aware of the fragile nature of parody, *The Bogus Man* and *Geek Maggot Bingo*, although quite different in content, both contain a pervading element of absurdity that subverts the genre they allude to, whilst simultaneously exploiting it. Well versed in shock, horror, B-movie comic book culture and camp, the initial popiness of Zedd's imagery gives way to awkward decadence.

A shift occurred when Zedd made *The Wild Wild World of Lydia Lunch* in 1983. This Super-8 portrait is very personal and emotionally expressive rather than blatantly entertaining; it is more experimental in form, provocative and humane, and features narration by Lunch reading from her diaries.

In 1984 Zedd put out the first issue of *The Underground Film Bulletin*. Frustrated by the local press and the closed-mindedness of the alternative film spaces in the area, he, like others, went into action, realising that to make a point, or to attract attention to himself and other filmmakers, the energy had to come from within the community. Using the alter egos Orion Jericho, Rufus Jacoby, Ernie Birk and sometimes Nicola Zedd, he substantiated and perpetuated his concept of a cinema of transgression. This was an artful means of packaging a movement, of which — in writing about it — he became self-appointed spokesman. In *The Cinema of Transgression Manifesto*, Zedd declared: "There will be blood, shame, pain, and ecstasy, the likes of which no one has yet imagined. None shall emerge unscathed."

The Underground Film Bulletin was eventually a massive

exercise in self-promotion. Following the example of his Dada and Surrealist forebears, Zedd created a vehicle, which, for want of a better description became considered a movement. The self-consciousness of this movement eluded many who were embraced by Zedd; many were so deeply entrenched in transgressive lifestyles that, like madness, it wasn't really possible to recognise it as such.

Connecting with other filmmakers, Zedd pursued sexual experimentation as Nicola Zedd in *Me Minus You* and a variety of other expanded cinema performances. As Nicola Zedd, he collaborated with Richard Kern for *Thrust In Me*, a film in which Nicola kills herself, followed by Nick getting a blow job from her and jerking off over her corpse. Nick and Nicola also appear together in Kern's *King of Sex*, courtesy more movie trickery.

Seeing Kern's *You Killed Me First* reminded Zedd that narrative film need not be commercial length and, returning to a 16mm scripted narrative, subsequently made *Police State* (1987), which was based on personal experience.

More recently, *Whoregasm* (1988) and *War Is Menstrual Envy Part 1* and *Part 2* (1989 and 1990), are non-narrative and unscripted. According to Zedd, his choice of subject matter is no longer dictated by reason but by some unseen force. He claims that *War is Menstrual Envy* is a product of anticipating war and a wish to remind the public that war is about bloodshed and is not glamorous, artificial or symbolic.

Prior to 1984, the film shows and expanded cinema performances that were happening in the clubs and other available spaces downtown were arranged and organised by the filmmakers themselves. At the Reel Club, which was at Danceteria and then at Club 57 until it was closed, anybody who showed up with a film could be included in the programme. The Reel Club also had cameras, which could be borrowed to make films. Screenings at Rafik's OP screening room were regular events, and Nancy Coleman's *Late Show* series featured B-movies, obscure documentaries, archival pornography and animation. As people hooked up with one another more and more happened.

During 1982–83, Tessa Hughes-Freeland organised a series of weekly shows at Limbo Lounge called Films in Limbo, and also a weekend marathon, Celluloid Cantina. Ileana Montalvo, Ela Troyano and Hughes-Freeland, in conjunction with the 309 East 4th St. Housing Fund Corporation, organised Street Movies, a night of short films in Spanish and English along with children's films, which took place in a lot between C and D. All of these events were community-oriented and included films made by people in the neighbourhood. In 1984 Michael Limbo was moving Limbo Lounge into a large old garbage truck garage on 9th St., when Troyano came up with the idea of a three night extravaganza that became the First Annual New York Film Festival Downtown, taking place at Limbo Lounge that October. It included thirty-six filmmakers and showcased the different ways in which they were working in the medium: not solely traditional films, but slide shows, expanded cinema performances, unfinished works or works in progress, 3D slides, home movies, dance with film — basically any kind of moving image that used projected light.

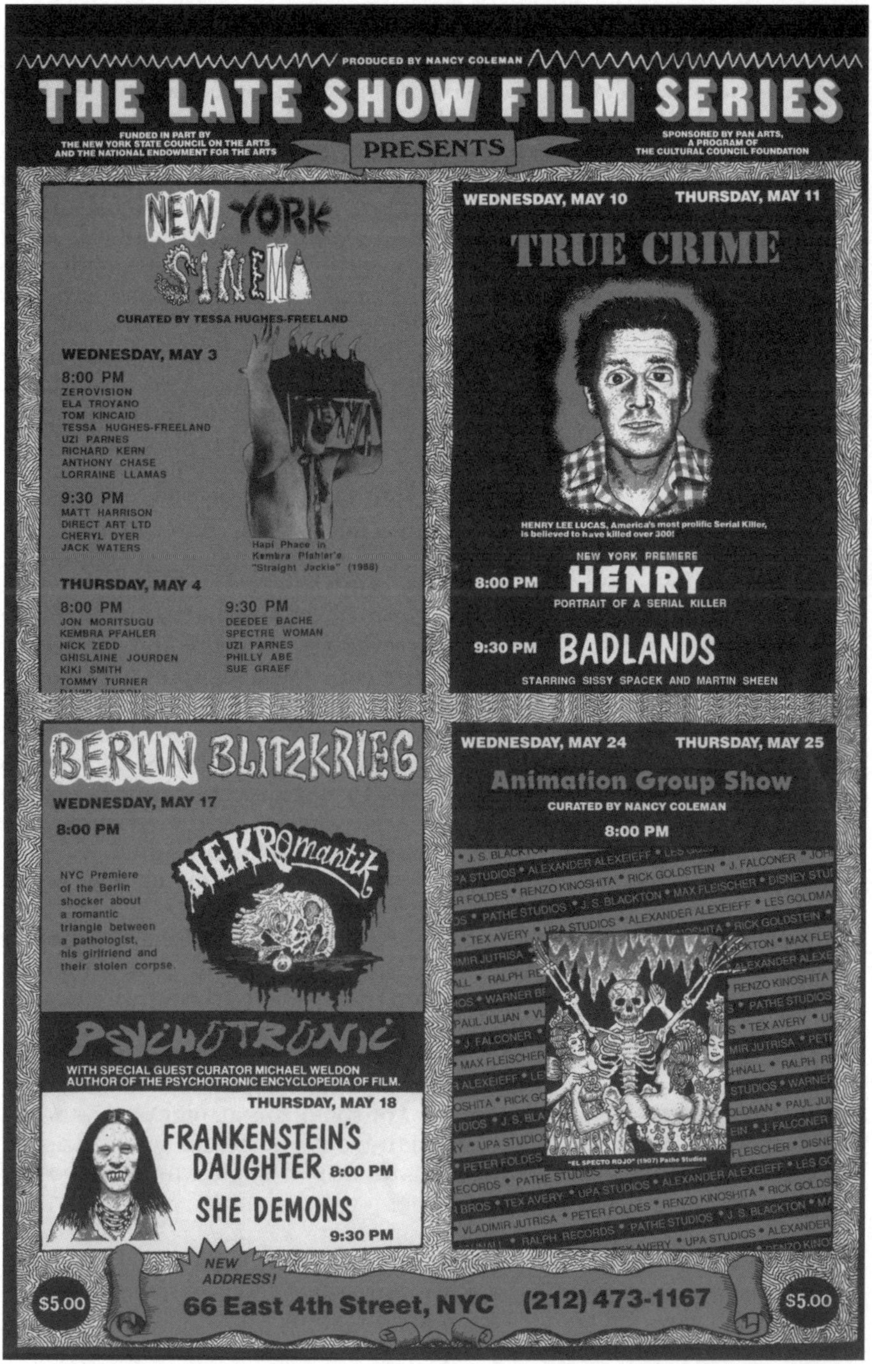

Late Show Poster © Joe Coleman

The New York Film Festival Downtown took its name from the established festival uptown, providing an alternative that immediately followed the official event, complete with champagne opening, awards ceremony and later the addition of a Master of Ceremonies. The New York Film Festival Downtown took place in clubs since clubs were loose and informal and could deal with the complicated technical set-ups required, as well as being the environment in which most of the filmmakers had previously showed their work. Alternative spaces were not only ill equipped but were generally unwelcome to certain brands of filmmaking. Some years, the New York Film Festival Downtown brought its own PA and equipment into otherwise raw spaces like Charas in 1986 and, before it opened in 1988, Harbar Hall.

As the popularity of the New York Film Festival Downtown grew, between 1984 and 1988, so did the exposure of many of the filmmakers involved. Patronage included curious European film programmers and a few like minds from across the Union, which in turn lead to programmers organising tours in Europe and, alongside sparodic screenings across the US, the world of New York underground film began to spread.

In a film community that was part of a larger creative community, there were many interchangeable or multidisciplinary roles: people acted in one another's films, exchanged ideas and helped each other with technical aspects. Those who cared helped by providing showcases for film and also writing about it. The steady gentrification of the area, which changed Loisaida or the Lower East Side into the East village, put economic pressure on the whole community. Stricter law, licence and code enforcement resulted in many of the small clubs having to close down. Rising rents made it imperative to have some form of reliable income (film wasn't it), and AIDS awareness grew as the virus became more manifest and more and more artists and performers died.

With the pressures of environmental and economic change, some active members of the film community left town, while others changed their working methods. Lung Leg, maker of weird and wonderful movies like *The Worm Movie* (1985), *Sun Puppet* (198?) and *Black Monster* (198?), as well as being a poetess and actress in Richard Kern films, went travelling and ended up in San Francisco.

Where Evil Dwells (1985), co-written and co-directed by Tommy Turner and David Wojnarowicz, is a metal drama capturing the suburban Satanic teen spirit. Based on the story of Ricki Kasso, eighteen year old murderer and spiritual leader of many Satanic teens in Northport, Long Island, the proposed feature length, Super-8 epic was described by Tommy Turner in 1986 as coming from

> ...actual events leading to the murder of Gary Lawers and Kasso's suicide and experiences David and Tommy went through as teens, some they wish they had gone through: Black Sabbath, AC/DC, Angel Dust, vandalism, the occult, animal torture and human torture. The suburban teens are trapped. They fill their dull lives with action and fantasy. Ricki's father beats him and he substitutes the Devil as a role model. Ricki only craves for all the power in the world.

Many were involved in the making of *Where Evil Dwells*; one scene offering a portrayal of Hell became a community event with the distribution of flyers requesting 150 extras for the shoot in an abandoned warehouse in Williamsburg. There were pyrotechnics and extreme physical atrocities, courtesy Survival Research Laboratories, who made the explosions, and Mark Gabarino, who did the special effects. Scott Werner starred as Ricki, Baby Gregor as Gary Lawers, Joe Coleman as the Devil, and Rockets Redglare as — of course — Jesus.

According to Turner, he and Wojnarowicz made the film because "most of the kids involved in this lifestyle are too out of their minds to get a camera and shoot it themselves."

Where Evil Dwells is a logical successor to Turner's own *Simonland* (1984), a film based on cults and mass suicide, such as Jim Jones' Jonestown, Guyana. Never completed as a feature, *Where Evil Dwells* does exist as a half-hour trailer (the rest of the material reached an ill-fated destiny in an inferno on 13th Street). As with any major project, shooting was a long process, during which Tommy Turner and Tessa Hughes-Freeland made *Rat Trap* (1986), a twisted drug movie containing images of animal torture and human self-destruction.

David Wojnarowicz's Super-8 *Fire in My Belly* (1987), combines footage shot in Mexico with images from his own personal iconographic vocabulary. An artist in all disciplines — painting, writing, photography and film — Wojnarowicz's work is highly individual, accessible, angry, compassionate and beautiful. Parts of *Fire in My Belly* have been reused in multi-media installations by the artist. Wojnarowicz has also made films with Phil Zwickler amongst others.

Similar to Super-8 in the late seventies, the upsurge of video during the eighties opened up new possibilities for filmmakers, not only in the utilisation of video and TV imagery in films — pretty much taken for granted nowadays — but also in terms of distribution and reaching a wider audience. The boundaries between film and video may have broken down somewhat in many areas, but technically there remains a major difference between the mechanical aspects of each medium.

M. Henry Jones is an animator. His experiments have been so extensive and thorough that he practically earns the title of inventor. In the late seventies and early eighties, he made the pop and optically beautiful *Go Go Girl* (1978) and the stunning, colourful stroboscopic *Soul City* (1977–79), featuring The Fleshtones, amongst other films. Over the last few years, one of his many personal projects has been *The Well* (1992), for which all the preliminary elements were produced in film. Despite having intended to make *The Well* in video, Jones soon realised that forcing a film rhetoric onto video was counter-productive and not viable; he claims that the elements could never have been done in video, and consequently *The Well* has actually metamorphosised from a film into a video.

The difference between an electronic video pulse and an animation field would have little consequence to those working in video, but Henry is essentially interested in optics, colour, synesthesia and their psychological affect. In film, the effect of overlaps of color on the retina is essentially stroboscopic, but in video it is a smooth continuous stream. In *The Well*, the dissolves have a morphing effect, a continuous link between things that are similar. The colour effects are blended as opposed to stroboscopic. *The Well* is not only about psychological nuances through colour effects, but also iconography. *The Well* was animated by Susan Tremblay and was created for the absorption of the masses. Henry wanted the imagery to be simplistic so that the dynamic colour effects could manifest themselves in a pure fashion. Henry Jones decribes his intent in filmmaking by quoting the late Harry Smith: "The purpose of film is to put you to sleep, thereby creating a false dream state." Henry strives to create an oneiric affect in the viewer.

Henry Jones' films are not rock videos. He considers psychedelia in the sixties as purist; as technology developed and progressed, a barrage of images ensued, blended together using Freudian psychology in an insulting way. Henry claims his films are "based on mood, not on someone's underpants." *The Well* will be a visual song, with colour equalling melody and iconography, words matching with dissonance and harmony, never in two identical combinations. The song is by Amy MacMahon and is sung by Angel Dean.

Jones' interest in 3D has not only been the focus of a number of expanded Go Go performances, combining dancers and 3D slides, but has also led to his experiments with P. Anthony Munn, Gary Darrow and Arby Schumann in Depthography. Depthography applies a lenticular process to a way of making 3D pictures viewable without special glasses. When one walks by, they are progressively flat, then 3D, then animated, then animated in 3D. Depthography enables the creation of an animated image, that is not projected, to become animated paintings or film paintings.

Video has a life of its own that does not really become obvious until one actually works with it, as evidenced by filmmakers who have worked in both film and video mediums, such as Charlie Ahearn and Beth B. The cultural terrorism to which Super-8 lends itself so well, exists multifold in video. Ahearn's two recent videos, *Doing Time in Times Square* and *Jane in Peepland*, may seem like a far cry from *The Deadly Art of Survival* (1978) but behind the camera the same mind is at work. Beth B.'s videos *Belladonnna* (1989), *Thanatopsis* (1989) and *Stigmata* (1991) have socio-political affinities and some structural similarities with her previous Super-8 films, but now more developed and complex. Both Beth B. and Charlie Ahearn have directed 35mm features, and may again, but continue to work on a personal uncommercial level.

It is commonplace for filmmakers to use video to edit and distribute films and some have chosen to work completely in this medium, considering High-8 video as more versatile and affordable than film. Many film festivals are still leery of, and do not accept, Super-8. Short of blowing Super-8 up to 16mm, video may provide an alternative means of presentation. Charles Pinion — whose script *Killbillies* was intended for Super-8 and at one time looked like it may be a 35mm feature, but as of writing still only exists on paper — made a Video-8 film, *Twisted Issues*. For immediacy's sake he shot another High-8 horror video entitled *Red Spirit Lake* (1993). Annabel Davies, co writer on *Red Spirit Lake*, is currently in post-production of *Dirty* (1992), a collaboration with Tessa

Hughes-Freeland. Loosely based on a Georges Bataille story, it deals with aspects of obsession and degradation. Joe Christ, who broke onto the film scene with the self-mutilation short *Communion in Room 410* (1988), made *Speed Freaks With Guns* (1991) as a combination video, including re-shot film.

In his other films such as *La Belle Fleur* (1986), *Whipoorwill* (1987) and *Star Spangled Bush* (1991), Carl George has mixed the fanciful with the political to point the finger at racist, fascist, and minority categorisations. The intimate and matter of fact manner of Carl Michael George's *DHPG Mon Amour* (1989) locates the extraordinary conditions of living with AIDS in the late eighties. It is a short Super-8 documentary home movie that follows domestic preparations for a barbecue and the elaborate drug ritual necessary for the self-administration of DHPG, a treatment for CMV Retinitis. The film's emotional power stems from a high degree of intimacy that is both moving and disturbing, and couldn't have worked in 16mm. However, for screening at the New Director's series in 1990, it had to be blown up to 16mm. Similarly, Richard Kern's *Fingered* had to he enlarged for inclusion in the Berlin Film Festival in 1987.

Despite external changes, filmmakers in New York continue to make films. Although some left town, others still appear, and films are still shown in the small clubs and bars downtown. The New York Film Festival Downtown 1990–91 took the form of a series at Webo, a now extinct performance space. Ela Troyano produces La Misma Onda, a showcase for Latino film and performance at P.S.122. There was a two night film series at CBGB's gallery presented by Natural Process; Matthew Harrison's Film Crash circulates shows of primarily 16mm film in various venues, and the Anthology Film Archives reopened in 1989, after being closed for seven years. Run by Jonas Mekas, a very open-minded person and filmmaker himself, Anthology Film Archives provides a place for many filmmakers to show.

Objectively and subjectively the people and places that made up a film community during the eighties have changed. If the places have gone the people remain. A generation of filmmakers, who in the early eighties were in their twenties, are now older. It's the beginning of a new decade and what have we got? Not money, that's for sure. The government grant cutbacks and restrictions are not new to anyone, yet an interest from Europe and Japan provides hope. Alyce Wittenstein — maker of the stylish and accomplished 16mm science fiction films *Betaville* (1987) and *No Such Thing as Gravity* (1989) — is at present making *The Deflowering*, the third part of her trilogy *The Propaganda of Progress*, which will be released as a feature. Wittenstein recently returned from a tour of Japan, as did Cassandra Stark from Italy, Richard Kern from Denmark and Germany, and Ela Troyano from Spain.

Nothing can replace the experience these filmmakers written about here have gone through, nor the omnifariousness of their film work. They, as well as others like Michael Wolfe and Jon Moritsugu, are dedicated; motivated by a need and desire to express themselves, they continue to make films and show them just about any way they can.

Postscript
Ela Troyano

> I come from a nuclear family. I was the substitute for the son
> **Tessa Hughes-Freeland**

Dirty, Tessa Hughes-Freeland's most recent work in collaboration with Annabel Davies, is also one of her most narrative films to date. She claims, though, that "it doesn't succeed as such... it is much more a depiction of some kind of degradation of another human being." Obsession is depicted literally through shifting points of view. The lovely, vulnerable, blonde heroine (Marti Blue) staggers through lush surroundings intercut with her own distorted perceptions under some kind of substance abuse. *Dirty* (1982) is subtle, visceral and unique in eschewing either a moralising or glorifying tone. Like *Rat Trap*, a collaboration with Tommy Turner that bombards the viewer over and over with drug related images, *Dirty* is provocative in its treatment of subjective emotional reality. When asked why she is attracted to obsessive themes often considered negative, she pauses to think, explaining that she doesn't find these areas negative per se, adding that "the sex, drugs, and rock and roll stigma fascinates everyone because it corresponds to a primal instinct that society tries to repress."

Baby Doll (1982), *Play Boy, Playboy Voodoo* and her expanded cinema performances all comment on the sex industry. At first she used the porn imagery as an element of surprise, but soon realised it was all too common even on TV. What interested her was the "ridiculousness" or "corniness" of porn scenarios: "The totally stereotypical fantasy roles in the media, either macho roles or totally feminine females." As she explained: "...the simplicity of it is ridiculous. Human beings are not so simple". Though Hughes-Freeland's work defies simple categorisation, as does much contemporary cinema, it could be loosely defined as falling within three styles or work processes; documentation of gallery installations sometimes with added fictionalisation; live multiple projection shows or expanded cinema performances; and completed films or videos which use multiple image processing, that are formally structural or more narrative in content. Though Hughes-Freeland claims that she sees herself as someone who "constructs" out of images she is attracted to, she concedes she has become more interested in her own images: "It's subtler: choosing to shoot one's own stuff is more specific and more personal."

Levity and Mystery: an introduction to the films of Billy Childish

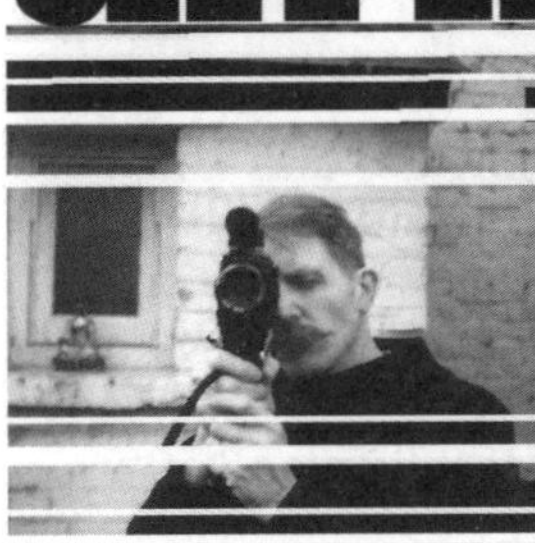

Neil Palmer

Punk rock has long since

become an umbrella term for outsider creativity worldwide, and Billy Childish's creative-individualist stance has been and continues to be a factor in defining what punk rock means. Childish's music, painting and writing have long been subject to investigation in various magazine articles and documentaries, but the films he's made and in which he has participated, from 1979 to the present, remain virtually unknown and he has not discussed them at length before now.

Billy Childish is known primarily for the music he's made with various groups over the years including, among many others, The Milkshakes, The Mighty Caesars, The Headcoats and, until very recently, The Friends of the Buff Medway Fanciers Association (The Buff Medways for short). He's respected on his own terms by those who buy his records and go to see him play live, and also holds a place in the wider public gaze through the periodic citation of his music by more popular artists like Nirvana, Beck and the White Stripes. He is also known as a poet, novelist, painter and print-maker in his own right, again through his own efforts in organising exhibitions and shows in Europe and America, and through the work of others, including Kylie Minogue, who was inspired by *Poems to Break the Hearts of Impossible Princesses* (Hangman Books, 1998), but most notably through the work of Tracey Emin, his ex-girlfriend, with whom he has had an ongoing public battle over the provenance of her confessional art.

Childish's confessional style tends to affirm by default a sense that creative acts can be considered as truly expressive only if they come from a near-separatist individuality. However, his work is rife with contradictions that are introduced as purposefully as the didactic, scything couplets of his song lyrics, and force the listener, reader or viewer to regard his as a purposefully reflexive individualism. While Childish's songs are often didactic, a swift re-reading of his novels reveals juxtaposed sentences that mimic the jarring of contradictory thoughts and his poems often end with a coda, or punchline, that negates the preceding text and at times undermines his individualist voice with reflexive comment. However, given Childish's striving to establish the separateness of his individualism, the greatest contradiction in his work is surely the least commented upon: that is, his continual affirmation of the group ethic of cultural production, whether in creating a record label, publishing books, or playing beat music or punk rock.

Childish has said that he has enjoyed creating clubs and societies since he was a child, and whenever he is putting himself to the fore in songs, poems or novels, he always does so in the knowledge that without others — even if they are his subjects — he would be standing silent. For example, he has always worked within an established circle of friends and acquaintances, centring on a hard, provincial town with its own distinct identity, which is reflected and discussed in all his work. The strong, often local, 'supporting cast' is a vital element in much of his work. Nowhere is the collective nature of Childish's work more apparent than on film, whether as an actor in short films made by Eugen Doyen, a long-time collaborator who has also produced many photographs of Childish's various groups and projects for record covers and publicity purposes, or as a director, camera operator or participant in the 8mm shorts of the Chatham Super-8 Cinema, which has been operating in the Medway area since 2003.

I interviewed Billy Childish in May 2005 at his house in Chatham, a very short taxi ride from the rail station.

Neil Palmer Tell me about punk rock movie making...

Billy Childish Punk rock movie making is getting an old Super-8 camera from the flea market — or in our case get your mate to get one who hasn't got any money at all, get him to get all the gear together and then make films on it, because he's already started doing it. It's the same as recording. The reason we use film is because it looks better. There's more awareness, in a way. It's chuck-away, but it's not. The amount we spend on stock, we could buy a pretty good quality video, but video doesn't look any good. I believe in the limitation of something being the thing that makes its importance. We have to choose our shots, we don't cover ourselves very much. If the film in a cartridge doesn't come out, we've lost all the close-ups, for instance. And one camera only. Simon [Williams, along with Wolf Howard, the third participant in the Chatham Super-8 Cinema] has since got a Super-8 and Wolf's got a spare, but that hasn't got such a good depth of field, so we only ever use one when we're shooting.

How are the Chatham Super-8 Cinema films put out?

They're not. They're shown occasionally if we're doing a Chatham Super-8 Cinema night — we show them with our rickety old projector — or up at my friend's house and invite a few people. Lately, we've been showing a few if we do a reading. We've done that for a few years.

Wolf, Simon and me are the Chatham Super-8 Cinema, which still seems to be Hangman Films, for some reason. Simon's got a projecting DVD, so if we edit things on DVD we can show them as film through the projector and do more sophisticated edits. Don't forget that the reason that we do the transfer straight from the film straightaway [the original projection is filmed with a DVD camera] is that it costs nothing. We can't have anything that costs money, apart from film stock, which is

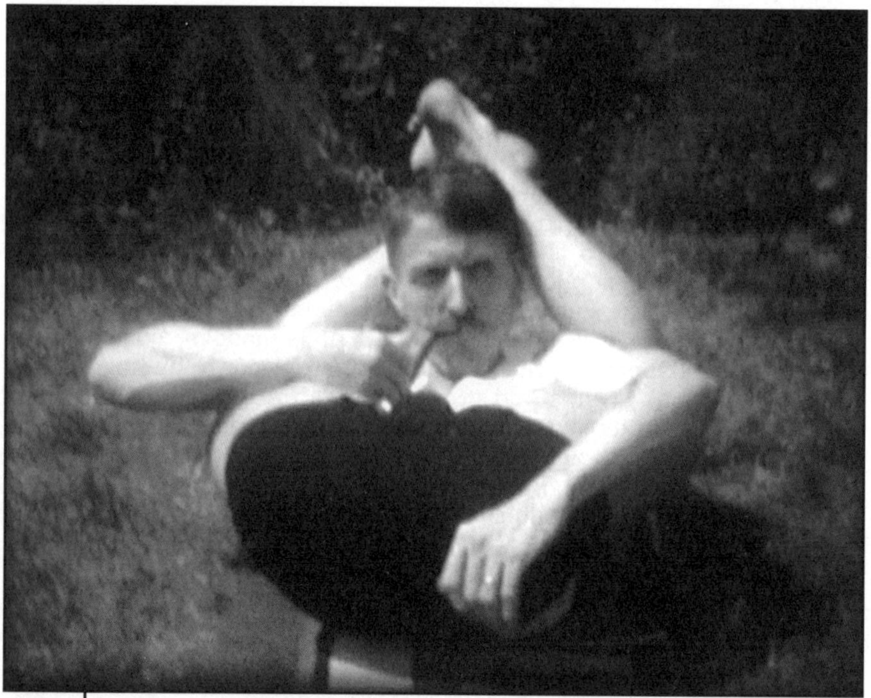

Childish with pipe in Smoking Yoga

expensive enough.

These Chatham Super-8 Cinema films will come out at some point, but we're holding them back because Simon's doing a documentary about me — it's been an on-goer for a bit — and wants to utilise elements of all those things.

[The Chatham Super-8 Cinema (CSC) has been going since 2003. Its main participants are Billy, Wolf Howard, drummer for The Buff Medways and former drummer for 1980s and nineties groovers, The James Taylor Quartet, and Simon Williams who works for BBC Collective. Their films have not been distributed widely and continue to be shown at dedicated CSC film nights, performances by The Buff Medways and at Billy's poetry readings. The CSC makes films that, like Childish's short poems and punk rock tunes, do not outstay their welcome; it's all about getting on with it. The group has produced eight films since 2003, including three promotional films for The Buff Medways: *Troubled Times* (2003), *Punk Rock ist nicht Tot* (2004), *Medway Wheelers* (2005), *Brass Monkey* (2005), and a poetic documentary of a large scale re-enactment of the Mons retreat in August 2004, filmed by Billy, who participated in the event. Its other films are conceived more spontaneously, with Billy contacting Wolf or Simon and suggesting a filming session.]

I'll ring Simon up. I said to him a few months ago, "Let's go and make a film, it's nice weather." He said "What shall we make it on?" I said "I don't know, we'll find out. There'll be a bike ride involved and I'll go and do something." So me and him go out and just make a film in an hour or so. He filmed me on my bike. I said "I'll go to the war memorial and get on the bike." The war memorial's in a few of the films. He films me parking the bike and getting off. I said, "Now I'll get out my notebook and write something." So I did that and then drew a picture. Then we did a macro shot, because Wolf's old camera's got a macro thing. Then I wrote down 'The Man with the Gallows Eyes' and said "There's the title of the film." I draw a picture, then do a poem or a song and we'll fit it to the film. I've since written a poem and a song called The Man with the Gallows Eyes and the new selected poetry is going to be called that. So now all we'll do is cut that film together and see if it's a poem or a film by cutting it together. I've got to record the song in a week or two — a blues song — and see what fits.

Our stuff is very unaware of itself and very un-self-congratulatory. I don't even consider myself a musician, so I'd never consider myself a filmmaker. All the Chatham Super-8 Cinema is, is that we've got a broken Super-8 camera, a broken tripod and a bad projector.

The only bit of kit that's any good is some stuff that Simon's got. It just happens that he's moved in up the road and he's got this gear and he wanted to make a documentary about me. Me and Wolf are making these funny little films and he said "I'll transfer them." We said "Okay! Great!" Wolf edits our Super-8 stuff together with cellotape. We don't have leader tape, we have cellotape to do the editing. Wolf's the most ham-fisted person I know, and he strings these films together. Me and Simon do the editing up the road, but Wolf does the editing on the real Super-8 stuff. We don't even get a look-in; we don't know what we're going to get, and Wolf's not sure whether the cellotape's going to come off during the showing.

People say I like shit painting and I don't like taking any care over anything, whereas actually we [the Chatham Super-8 Cinema] take a great deal of care over all of it, because we know what we want the thing to look like. We've just got the sense to use materials that enhance what we're looking at, rather than degrading it. Video is like plastic carrier bags. There's millions of them and they're blowing all over the countryside and ruining it, whereas ours is an old, good standard canvas bag we bought from an ex-army shop in 1962 and it's still going. It's not disposable.

[Reflecting the process and reality of film is a primary concern for the CSC. Its movies are made entirely within the limits of the technology at hand, and that precludes the use of additional lighting. In *The Artist Goes to Work* (2003), filmed in late wintertime, the presence of winter daylight affords just sufficient brightness indoors to light Childish as he gathers his things, walks to Victoria Gardens over the road from his house, stands in the newly fallen snow breathing fog and paints a picture in oils of the bandstand against this white background.

Similarly, *The Shave: The Excelsior, or Signalling and Shaving Mirror* (2003) features Childish in his back garden in daylight, demonstrating the proper use of a shaving kit. This part of the male grooming process, as realised by Childish, is about the shaving mirror reflecting a job well done by a practised hand and is altogether a more expert operation than the shoddy job in Scorsese's student film of a similar name and subject (*The Big Shave*, 1967).

Since being forced to leave St Martin's school of art, Childish has spent his time veering away from theory, towards the reality of process. He provides ammunition with which others may attempt to shoot down the totality of Pierre Macherey's assertion that the text says what it does not say, and offers sometimes unreasonable, though not irrational, experience-based counter-assertions that enable others to bear down on Derrida's or Foucault's premature pronouncements on cultural production as a supplementary social-cultural activity, rather than one that is expressive, immediate and affective. However, the truth of Childish's films, as with his other work, is that the activity itself should be considered as much as the artefact produced. In Childish's method of operations, the intent and material are essential component parts of the context of production.

Since Childish doesn't talk readily about theoretical context, it is difficult to do more than offer his words and modus operandi as a series of counter-positional statements against theory. It would be wrong to do that without a caveat, however, because he speaks for himself and requires no one else to do so for him. In fact, his need to explain the practicalities of producing his work — the reality or truth as he sees it — so that people may understand more clearly the intent behind his work, surely makes it plain that his anti-theoretical position should not be mistaken for philistinism, as art careerism and marketing, in the vein of Damien Hirst or Tracey Emin.]

You don't just chuck this stuff together by accident. I remember seeing an interview where you talk about Thee Milkshakes making a £2,000 bit of equipment sound like five bob. But you know the sound you're trying to get.

With sound you want excitement, with film you want mystery. With sound you want excitement and you then have to work out what does that and helps that, as well as the performance and the gear you use. We don't use valves because they're old fashioned, we use them because they sound better. We don't use analogue because it looks better, or we think it's fancy; it's because it sounds better. We wanted to know why old recordings sounded better. You want to know why things look better on film? It's because they're on film. The thing helps it, it brings out the depth. Film helps bring mystery; video makes it look plastic and glued to your eye.

When I record an album I've got two mics and I've got to get the guitar on one and a balance between the bass and drums on the other, and it's got to be right. When we recorded The Buffets album [Julie, Debbie and Delia from the A-Lines doing Buff Medways numbers], since we had two days and they had one afternoon to rehearse, I recorded it on a sixteen track, down the studio, which I usually dub on afterwards. But I know the engineer, how to use that equipment and how to make the thing sound okay through their gear and it'll be good. But the real point is that it's much easier and quicker to use his gear. We didn't have time to do it properly. If you're going to do it on half-track, you've got to do it right. I didn't have time to do it right.

We don't try and make gear sound crap, we try and make it sound good. Sometimes limiting the thing and taking it down means a lot more hard work, because then I've got to dub the stuff over, fill in any gaps that I want filling and then we've got to physically record it and physically re-record it. This is the same as the Chatham Super-8 Cinema stuff. It's got to be redone. It takes so much longer. But we're using this really basic equipment, because that stuff has got the look, and the whole point of film is another world. The whole point of sound is it's another world. If you make it sound 'this world,' then it's very fucking mundane.

We only used one cartridge on *The Impossible Shoulder Leap of Death* (CSC, 2003), because that's all it needed. When me and Wolf make a film, they're much more slung together. When I want Simon involved, he'll usually say to us "How about shooting this, or that?" If I'm doing a film on my own, I'll shoot what I think is necessary. The stuff me and Wolf do has much more levity to it.

How do you feel about putting stuff on DVD?

I don't have any problem with technologies that are used. I don't like technologies that dictate. CD is okay, but it's a crap technology. It's okay as a storage medium, although I've suggested that it's probably not even that good for that. I reckon most of this stuff will be degraded and lost in the future. Luckily, we've got our stuff on real film and real analogue. Analogue is the only way to really store it. But so that people can get access to these things, we're forced to use this stuff and we're not fussy about it. I could, if necessary, use a video recorder. I've never used one, but I could probably make a film on a video recorder that's okay because I've got the discipline to make it okay, and I could record digitally okay, because I've got the discipline to do it. I could go in and use all this fancy gear because I know when to say no and when to limit the use of that stuff and how to put some sort of interface into it to not make it sound so bland and boring. But it would be a fucking sight more work to do, to then step it into that, because digital recording will always remain cold.

[The other-worldliness and levity of the Chatham Super-8 Cinema is most apparent in its more spontaneous short movies, *The Impossible Shoulder Leap of Death* (2003) and *Smoking Yoga* (2005), in which Childish appears as a type of latter-day Victorian film pioneer. In the brief *Shoulder Leap*, only a minute long, he squares up to the camera in a vest and army surplus tropical fatigue shorts, preparing himself for some immense task and commences a run-up, which ends with him leaping on

Wolf's very broad shoulders and both of them turning to face the camera triumphant, the impossible feat accomplished. *Smoking Yoga* is a more exotic piece that features Billy as a late nineteenth century muscle man in a smoking cap, mugging to camera and performing some of the more difficult yoga positions while smoking decorously. Each position is announced in chalk on a blackboard.

The CSC is an ongoing project that enables Childish to exercise his visual imagination as he sees fit.]

This new film I want to do will be called *I Love That Girl Ammonia*. It's about a girl who goes and washes her sheets in the River Medway — we'll film it backwards, so they come out spotlessly clean. There's this song that goes with it. We'll have Nelson in there as well. Perhaps I should keep it quiet. It's a little turn around from normal... Okay, I'll tell you. Really, the idea's Tracey's [Tracey Emin]. I wrote I Love That Girl Ammonia [featured on Billy's 1989 Hangman album, *I've Got Everything Indeed*] and she suggested doing this film. So it's a nice twist on events that this is the first time I've ripped her off.

What happened was that there was this song and I was thinking about making this film. Then my mate was round and he was trying to apply for a grant, so we thought we'd try and get a grant — put in a bit about the regeneration of Medway and tie it into Medway's naval past. The film starts out with a black screen and writing saying "HMS Trafalgar was laid down in Chatham in 1759," or whatever, "This ship went on to become Nelson's flagship at the battle of Trafalgar." Then we have a man in Nelson's uniform with a telescope, looking. Then there's a view through the telescope of my wife, Julie, doing this little Polish dance she does along the top of a hillside. Then below that there's me singing "She eats Ajax..." Then we have a film of her doing her nice dance and me singing the song. Then she goes down, washes the sheets in the river and brings them back. Then the song ends and you're back to Nelson folding his telescope away.

We put on the form that we wanted to make this film. I don't know if you've ever seen grant applications and the sort of gibberish people write. We've written all this stuff down: like it's about regeneration, about the EEC, about the war and healing and cleansing.

Memory, narrative, regional politics...

Yeah, but this is the film they're gonna get — sort of Benny Hill. I'm keen on Laurel and Hardy and Benny Hill, really.

What about other filmmakers?

I used to be on friendly terms with Mike Leigh, who'd read my poetry. I said I'd send him the films, so I sent him *Cheated* and he sent me a postcard, which said: "Better than most things you see on television. Ciao baby." [Leigh signs off with Billy's character's catchphrase in *Cheated*.]

I hate him.

I can understand that. There's something really sick about it.

I think Mike Leigh's saying "Look at all these stupid people."

I don't know if he does that. I think it's just that it's mannered and overworked. I think there's some really great bits in some Mike Leigh films and I don't think he has that much disregard for people. I've heard that argument. I just think it's laboured, incredibly laboured and you don't notice. Some of the early films have a lightness and more spontaneity. *Nuts in May* (1976) is a good laugh. You've got those great scenes, like the one where — in the one on the estate — where the family are all signing on and the bloke goes in and says he's got a job spying on people who work there.

Meantime, with Phil Daniels.

Yeah, it's got bits that are genuinely funny. But the problem is... I saw the new one [*Vera Drake*, 2004]. It was really interesting. It had a bit about them making it at the end — talking about it and how he builds the thing up and rehearses and rehearses and rehearses, and they learn it all and they do this and discover that. I thought, my God! You can imagine my reaction to that, because that is the absolute antithesis

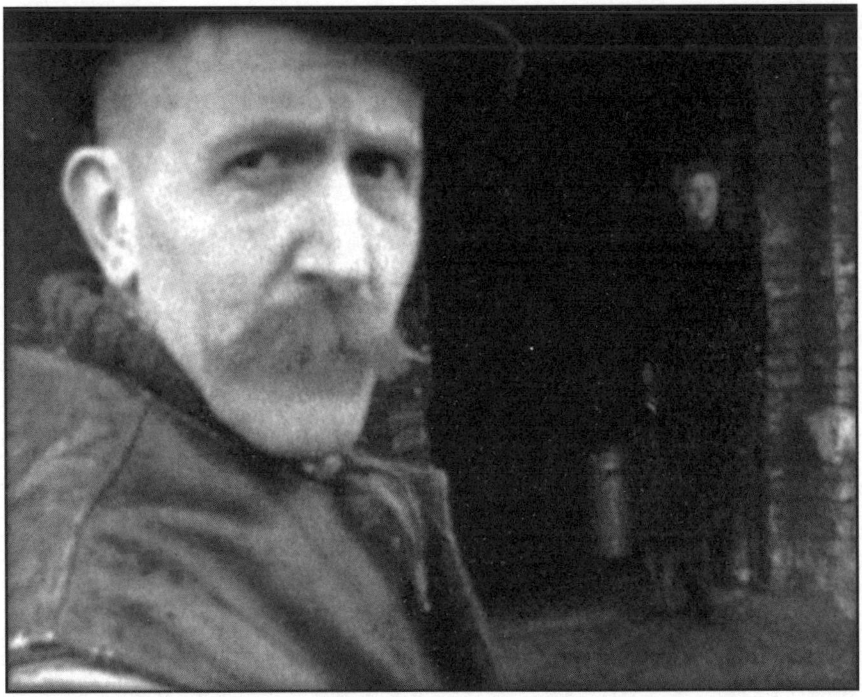

of everything I do, which could attract me to it, but actually makes me think that life wouldn't be worth living. And then you realise why the films have got this strange, turgid, depressed atmosphere. It's not because he's laughing at the people, it's because the thing's been fucking nailed to the ground. And it's meant to be spontaneous.

It's a perversion of improvisation.

Yeah. When I realised that, I suddenly thought that's why they've got this hideous atmosphere — that weird, depressive atmosphere — it's because he's nailed them to the cross. It is sadistic in a way. It's got no light or life. It's the absolute opposite of how we [the Chatham Super-8 Cinema] make a film. The idea is that the film will make itself if you let it. A painting will make itself if you let it. Mike Leigh's films are under ten tons of varnish.

I think his films have a strong humanitarian feel to them and are actually quite upbeat. It's probably the way he makes them that ruins them, which is a strange thing to say, because the way he makes them is probably the whole essence of it. What he should do is make the film with a set of actors, rehearse them up, get the film finished, show it to a bunch of actors and then film it again with people who've only done it once. Then it might be bearable.

My favourite would be Laurel and Hardy: Stan Laurel. I like some Hitchcock, but I have to leave the room because I don't like suspense. It actually drives me crazy — absolutely, I cannot stand it. Laurel and Hardy do it a bit, because it's like, "Oh, don't do that." But their suspense is more bearable. I find suspense tough. *Taxi Driver* is a good film, I like that. My favourite film is *The Life and Death of Colonel Blimp* (1943). I like *A Matter of Life and Death* (1946).

A Canterbury Tale (1944)?

I didn't like that much; I didn't like the lack of acting and story, and that American in it got on my nerves. There's a couple of others that I like. *Black Narcissus* is great and there's another earlier one that I've seen — I'm not very good with names — that's filmed out on an island in the German Sea — the North Sea — and it's about these people who just... it's one of the first things he did.

One of my favourite films is that good and evil fighting with Mitchum, *Night of the Hunter*, by that English bloke they never let make another film, that poof who played the hunchback [Charles Laughton]. That's a good film. I like the story in films. The only thing that makes a film any good is if you care about what happens to the person, and if you don't, it doesn't bother me; I can't be arsed.

And Larry Clark?

I'd never heard of him, but he asked if he could make a film of *My Fault* with me [Childish's first novel, published in 1996].

Have you written the screenplay?

I wrote a thing that he said would do as a screenplay. He liked it, but I don't think other people accepted it. I didn't know what a screenplay looked like. He rang me up and invited me to see a film of his [*Bully*, 2001] and that he wanted to make a film of my book. I thought *Bully* was a good film — quite disturbed.

So he's not dragged you into that world.

I don't think he can drag himself into that world, from what he tells me. He came over and I was meant to have dinner with him again and he punched out the distributor, Hamish MacAlpine; he broke his nose and threatened to kill him. He ended up in Tottenham Court Road police station and his film was withdrawn from the festival by this bloke, who was the person who bankrolled Tracey's endeavour on the silver screen [*Top Spot*, 2004], which was apparently a pile of shit.

So we're not going to see a film of *My Fault* any time soon?

I wouldn't have thought so. He maintains that he's going to do these things, but when anyone says they're making a film I just smile smugly and walk away. Films are the least likely things to happen out of everything.

Any others?

Someone wanted to make *Notebooks of a Naked Youth* and they've got the rights to that, but they couldn't find anyone to write the screenplay and they wouldn't allow me to write it, because they think I'm not up to it. That's all very well, but they can't get anyone who will do it. I'm really easy going. If I wrote a screenplay, it would be no problem whatsoever to change anything, but those people don't have a certain *je ne sais quoi.*

So are films of *A Hangman Triple Bill* Eugene Doyen's?

Yeah, they're totally his. *The Man with Wheels* [an as-yet unfinished poetical-biographical film about Kurt Schwitters, filmed in 1979] is a bit of a collaboration. The other things are very much Eugene deciding that he can make films using me because I'll put up with it. Eugene was doing photos and he was interested in making films. I think he did little bits of film — you'd have to ask him about what films he did before — but I had an idea about doing a thing about Kurt Schwitters and I'd written these poems. Eugene probably suggested "Why don't we make a little film of it?", so we made this film called *The Man with Wheels*, which is a little bio about Kurt Schwitters. We did the film, but we never got it edited or got it sorted out. I think a version of it exists, but it was never shown. I published this little book of poetry. I was away in Germany, but my girlfriend at the time gave it to Ernst Schwitters, who was over in London and said to send his best regards to Mr Childish, which I was very proud of, because I was a big fan of Kurt Schwitters.

[*The Man with Wheels* is filmed in a white box Merz made, by Eugene Doyen; a rented house in Rochester; and outdoors in around Rochester and Chatham. Against the constant ticking of a clock, Childish reads his poem about Schwitters, sometimes to camera, but mainly as a voiceover with backwards images of Childish climbing stairs and riding bicycles in the streets of the area and around The Lines, in the hills above Chatham, to the accompaniment of WWII air raid sirens. In another version of this film, Doyen reads the poem. Neither version has been completed and it remains a rare, largely unseen item of Childish-abilia.]

That was that really, then Eugene came up with the idea to do this film based on me and Tracey, who was my girlfriend a bit later on, after I got chucked out of college. Tracey was studying fashion at Medway — must have been there at the same time as Eugene was. I sort of hooked up with her after I got chucked out of St Martin's. I think she subsequently left the fashion department because she wanted to be a painter or something.

How did you get to know Eugene?

I used to do my fanzines up at Medway College at the time. I'd already left about two or three years before. I used to go in and use their Xerox facilities in the library — it was cheapest. I used to have problems getting my poetry magazines done. Eugene was the social secretary. He went up and did photography about 1979 to 1980. I think I was at St Martin's. I used to get the fanzines done up there, but then there was a problem with getting the Xeroxes done. Someone introduced me to Eugene and I met him and he said he'd do them for nothing. He said he'd speak to the Student Union and they said, "We've got to vet this poetry and see if it's publishable." He said "Well, are you poets?" They said "No," so he said, "Well, how do you know whether it's publishable or not? It's nothing

Childish and Wolf Howard perform *The Impossible Shoulder Leap of Death*

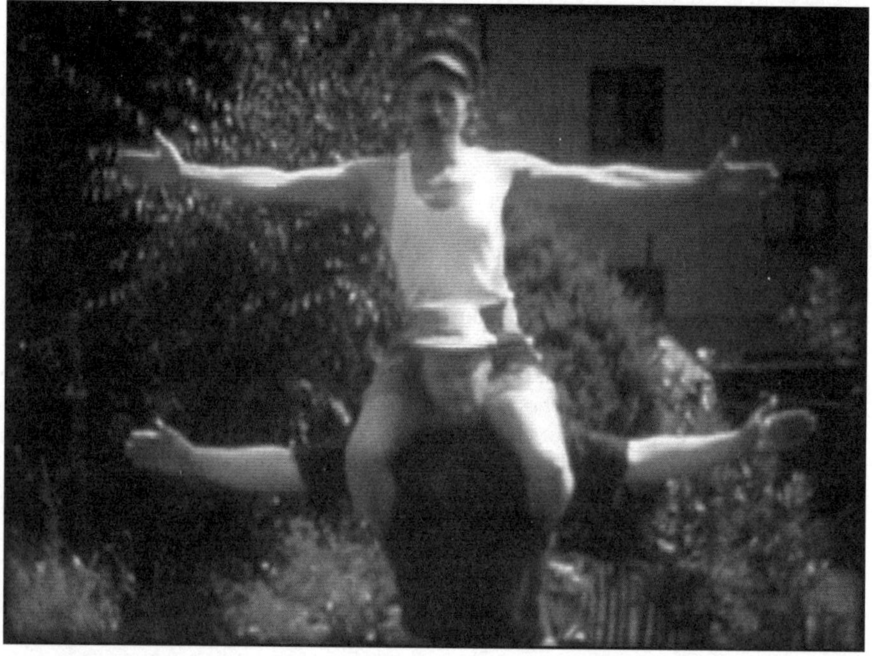

to do with you. You either do it or you don't." I remember a little cassette player he used to have and he'd secretly record people while they were talking, which people used to get really angry about.

Including you?

I think he was recording stuff. I'm not sure if he wanted to write things down later, or what. Then he was involved in photography. He wanted to take some photos and I got him to take photographs for my little books and what have you.

I've seen some photographs on the covers of Milkshakes albums.

Yeah, he was keen on photography. Actually, he was one of the reasons I got chucked out of St Martin's, because the Union were allowing my poetry books to be printed there and that's why they were confiscated. The librarian said they were obscene and they gave them to the head of the college, who refused to let me have them back and then I didn't have my work for St Martin's. I was told I could submit my poetry fanzines, or magazines, as work. That led to me getting chucked out, because my tutor called the [Medway] college and their Head called the Head of St Martin's and wanted to know why I was doing this obscene poetry.

I don't want to put words into his mouth or anything, but the problem is in art schools, you don't meet many creative people, or people with ideas, there's nothing there. At our college they didn't do painting or art, it was much more mechanical and also nobody's actually doing anything, so they're not even pretentious art school people, they just don't do anything and don't have any creative interest at all — don't even pretend to, like they do at St Martin's.

So you're saying that he [Eugene] had to do something because he was at art college?

No, he wanted to do something. He was like me: he went to art college to meet creative people and do creative things, which is very naïve, because that doesn't happen. But I did things and was interested in things, so Eugene wanted to make these fanzines and was like, "We'll do it. I'll give you the money from the Union." He wanted to make a film and he's got to get someone to be in them, so he may as well have someone who likes things. I like Kurt Schwitters, so alright, we'll make a film about Kurt Schwitters. I was interested in this other stuff. I think he needed people who'd put up with the hours.

I noticed that in *Quiet Lives* Tracey's got a stylish early sixties look.

That was probably directed more. She used to make these pencil skirts. Eugene would have asked her to dress a bit like that probably, because what happened was, it turned out not to be such a film about me and Trace. Eugene wanted to do this film about... Because another one of my interests was the Moors murderers, and Eugene decided that he wanted to make a film and rather than make a film directly about something, which is always fraught with problems anyway, let alone if you're doing the Moors murderers, to do a film based on those incidents. So really, it was meant to be based on that. He had different bits of script worked out: there was the grandmother who lived upstairs which was similar — they were meant to be living in the grandmother's house — and all sorts of gruesome stuff.

I thought it was kind of a perverted kitchen-sink drama.

Well, I think that's the same idea!

[*Quiet Lives* (1982, collected with *Cheated* and *Room for Rent* in *A Hangman Triple Bill*) is a tightly drawn, even more claustrophobic, version of early 1960s kitchen sink dramas, such as *Up the Junction* or *A Kind of Loving*, where two people's dysfunctional personal and social lives draw in around them. As with its cinematic prototypes, the quietness of domestic life equates not so much with peace and contentment, as with a total failure to communicate anything other than self-destructive loneliness and obsessional physical desire and emotional need.

At one point, as Lauren, Emin's character, is on her hands and knees cleaning up the mess Ian has made, he mounts her back, grabs her neck and whips her behind with a chair leg, shouting, "Whoa, horsey! Whoa, whore." She complains at his language and he replies, "Don't tell me what to say," and chokes her with chair leg, then shouts, "Are you dead? I'll give you a poke with me stick later, if you're good." Later, in bed, Ian asks for sex, saying "Don't you want to be broken in?" Lauren rolls over, then wrinkles her face, saying, "Ian, that's not right."

The implicit subtext of the insane love of Ian Brady and Myra Hindley, the Moors murderers, and the public nature of the difficult relationship shared by Childish and Tracey Emin, makes *Quiet Lives* a unique, parallel-text document. Childish does not acknowledge that he is actually acting in any of the films comprising *A Hangman Triple Bill* and offers a reason for the shortcomings of these films.]

I can't act, but Eugene found out that I didn't ask stupid questions. When we were doing *Quiet Lives*, Tracey would be asking lots of questions, like "Why is that there? That wasn't in the last shot." He said "We can't see it in the camera." "Can't we move this there?" "But that wasn't there last time." I don't do that, because I understand that the camera saw something different. That was my only plus point, because I can't act at all but I am willing to do what he wants and to not ask questions. So then we were working out who's going to give their time and do it.

The reason they've really got big problems, those films, is that I'm not, Tracey's not, Kyra's not, directed at all, because Eugene spent no time directing; he was trying to make the camera work. Actually, by the time we did *Room for Rent* he helped a little bit and he'd do a little bit of directing. But you had to go cold into this stuff. I had no acting experience at all and you've got to remember the next scene and try and learn stuff — and you weren't being helped by the director at all, because he was trying to make the camera work and dealing with all of this stuff. There was no delegation. It used to be horrendous.

I was wondering about this, because the personas and characters — because you're acting — are so different in the [*Hangman*] films. It's not just you saying your lines to camera. I thought that you were taking direction.

There was some direction, but not much. Eugene would try and get us to do something, but then you're left to it.

Ian, the male character, is self-taught; he's always got his head in a paperback and walking ten steps ahead, crane-like, marching, almost goose-stepping.

I wasn't trying to really get hold of Brady. I know that one of Brady's favourite films was the one in Vienna, with the big wheel and Orson Welles in it — *The Third Man* — and he really liked that speech that Orson does, but he didn't realise that it was a bit silly. He thought it was reasonable. He was really into the Third Reich, Ian Brady. He's got the same name as the character [in *Quiet Lives*].

Eugene wrote various versions of this script, but I never saw a completed one.

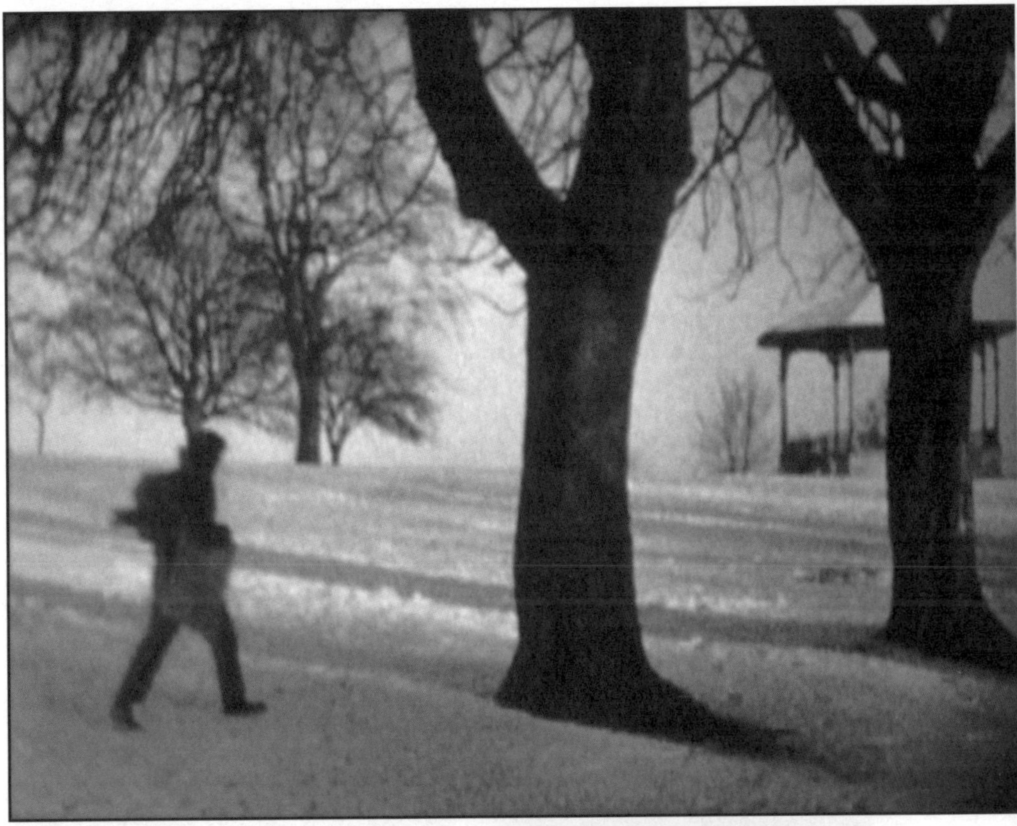

In a way, I think Eugene was looking for some work to do. Whatever thing I happened to be vaguely interested in, I thought that I'd do that, because I'll get him to do it. He wanted to make a film.

I think when we did *Quiet Lives* we were doing eighteen or twenty hour shoots. The camera was making a huge amount of noise and had to be wrapped up in huge amounts of clothing to keep the noise down, because we were doing lip sync. We had problems with light. We borrowed someone's front room — I think Eugene's downstairs front room — but he had other people living in there (it was rented accommodation up May Road) and we had to buy all this junk that we had to smash up.

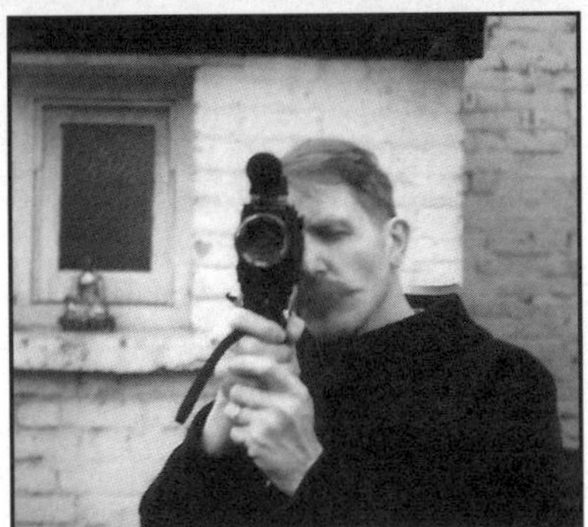

Childish in *The Artist goes to Work*, and (inset) with Super-8 camera

Tracey Emin is best known as an artist with an internationally acclaimed reputation and she has made at least one film that has been widely distributed (*Top Spot*, 2004), but *Quiet Lives* was her first film and stands as the only visible marker of the beginning of her career as an artist.

Tracey is very, very intolerant of working and doing anything. I remember one time I came back from a break [during the filming of *Quiet Lives*] to get a cup of tea, because I lived down the road in May Road as well. I had a rented house. It was the cheapest place to live in Medway at the time. I came down the road and next thing, Tracey was at the door crying her eyes out because she'd been whingeing — she whinges all the time — and Eugene had picked up a tripod and thrown it at her. I had to spend an hour or so getting her to go back.

Has Tracey ever shown *Quiet Lives* as part of her work?

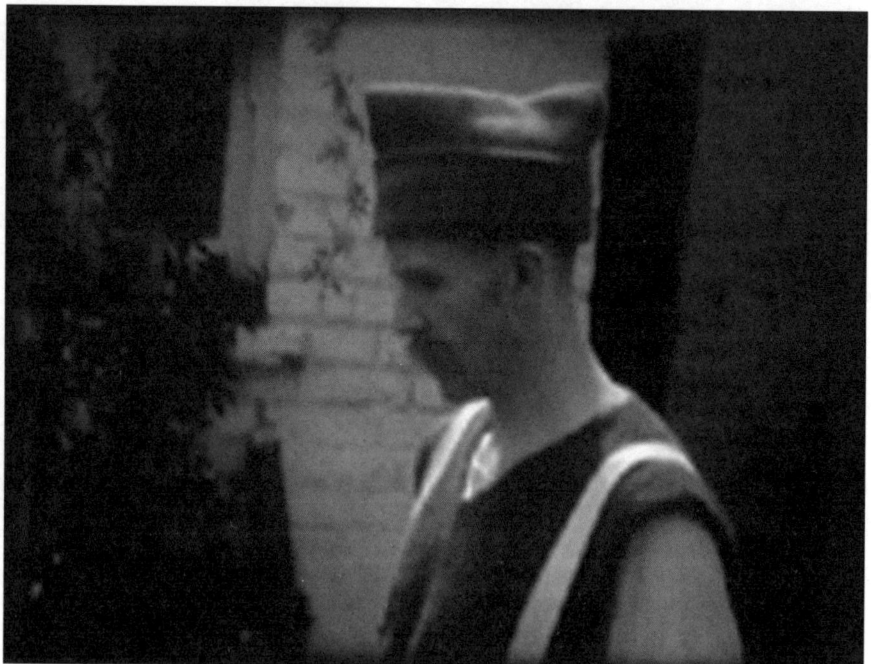

The Shave: The Excelsior, or Signalling and Shaving Mirror

Tracey's very keen to edit out any of that period. She doesn't even mention that she worked for Hangman Books as the administrator for four years, and seeing that she says that her work is confessional and based on the written word, that's quite an omission.

Eugene's got an incredible temper. When we did *The Man with Wheels*, I wasn't behaving properly and hadn't been there and he stopped talking to me for three months. I had to make him talk to me. He'd already been talking about buying this axe to kill me with and he wanted to get one with a rubber handle, 'cos you don't lose your grip if the blood gets on it. This is why Eugene stopped making films, because it's too stressful.

[In addition to *A Hangman Triple Bill* and the Chatham Super-8 Cinema productions, Billy has been involved in the making of a couple of documentaries: *Billy Childish vs Dr X*, and several short Super-8 movies with Sexton Ming.

Billy Childish vs Dr X was made in 1989 by film students who asked Childish to participate in a documentary film about his work. Characteristically, Childish dominated the project and even ended up interrogating himself in the voice of Dr X, sneeringly asking questions, such as "You publish your own work. Now, between you and me, this is because no-one's fucking interested, right?" Childish's answer to the question, "Tell us about punk rock," shows the consistency of his approach: "Punk rock was about the only decent thing that happened culturally in England for a long while… it only lasted for a little while — and then it was a lie. It's self-made, home-made stuff. People doing what they wanna do, rather than what everyone else wants them to do, without need of subsidies. Well, apart from the dole, of course, and they ain't letting us have that no more."

Among the poetry reading and walking around post-industrial Chatham to the sound of his own music, there are two short films attached to *Dr X*, *Muscle Horse* and *The Slap of Wild Bellies*, both featuring Childish and Sexton Ming. *The Slap* commences with Billy in a fez, smoking a pipe, with "KILL" written on his forehead and a painted-on moustache, watching enviously as his then-girlfriend Kyra de Coninck [formerly in charge of Hangman administration] dances lasciviously in a gold belly-dancing costume with Sexton Ming, who is also gyrating his belly wildly to the sound of a Turkish tune that Childish had been introduced to by Tracey Emin. Kyra eventually kneels and licks Ming's hairy belly button, whereupon Billy becomes agitated and, crouching, begins to move in an approximation of dance.

Muscle Horse is a grainy, b&w static-camera movie set on the mist-covered hills above Chatham, with a heavy horse grazing in the background and Sexton singing in an impassioned voice to a pump organ accompaniment. Sexton wears a papier-mâché horse mask and Billy has on a crow's head and an overcoat split down the back, for ease of flapping. The washed-out, faded dark of *Muscle Horse* plays on the grotesque, folkloric use of animal masks, but supplements those evocative symbols with funny sexual gestures to produce a canny mix of humour and wonderment.

Childish's band, Thee Headcoats, was also asked to appear in a movie by Alex Chandon and Josh Collins, who worked in a space in the same Victorian factory building once occupied by the now famous Toe-Rag recording studio in the early 1990s.]

We appear as a group playing in that awful *Perv Parlour* (1995). But I don't think people would ask me [to appear in their movies] because I'm not easy-going enough. If we get asked to do gigs and festivals, I don't like doing things with other people and where there's no careful control. I don't go to parties, so films that are done like parties I wouldn't do.

Not part of a gang.

No, I'm not very good at that. I would consider doing stuff, but one thing I really have a problem with is David Bowie. I don't like these people who think that because they're half-baked popstars they're even going to make it as half-baked actors. I think you have to put a lot of work into acting and that's probably one of the reasons I'm not interested in it.

Bruce [Brand, long time Childish collaborator] did a bit in *Perv Parlour* and *Pervirella*.

They asked someone like Bruce because he's more of a party animal. They wouldn't ask someone like me, because I've got opinions. I won't go along with the flow. Graham Bendal did a documentary on a home camcorder type of thing and it's coming out on Cherry Red [*Billy Childish is Dead*, 2005]. He did interviews with various people [including Shane MacGowan, Larry Clark and TV art historian, Matthew Collings]. That was a very, very strange experience. I've probably got a copy of it, but he's mad and tells me I'm not allowed to show it to anybody. There's all sorts of madness involved in that. You wouldn't believe it.

Filmography

The Man with Wheels 1979, 16mm, written by Billy Childish, directed by Eugene Doyen

Quiet Lives 11 mins, 1982, 16mm, written & directed by Eugene Doyen (collected in *A Hangman Triple Bill*)

Cheated 16 mins, 1986, 16mm, written & directed by Eugene Doyen (collected in *A Hangman Triple Bill*, or *The Hangman Trilogy*)

Billy Childish vs Dr X 1989, VHS, edited by Billy Childish, Andy Crabb & Sheena Daly (Super-8/B&W); also edited by Andy Crabb, Sandra Jean Cossou; produced by Sandra Jean Cossou & Sheena Day. Directed by Andy Crabb

Muscle Horse 1989, Super-8, (included in *Billy Childish vs Dr X*)

The Slap of Wild Bellies Super-8, VHS, (included in *Billy Childish vs Dr X*)

Room for Rent 26 mins, 1991, 16mm, written & directed by Eugene Doyen (collected in *A Hangman Triple Bill*, or *The Hangman Trilogy*)

Crying Blud 1992, Super-8 (promotional film for Billy Childish & the Blackhands)

Perv Parlour 1995, 16mm (featuring Thee Headcoats)

The Artist Goes to Work 2003, Super-8/DVD, Chatham Super-8 Cinema

The Flying Mustach 2003, Super-8/DVD, Chatham Super-8 Cinema

The Impossible Shoulder Leap of Death 2003, Super-8/DVD, Chatham Super-8 Cinema

The Shave 2003, Super-8/DVD, Chatham Super-8 Cinema

Machonochie's Stew 2003, Super-8/DVD, Chatham Super-8 Cinema

Smoking Yoga 2003, Super-8/DVD, Chatham Super-8 Cinema

Troubled Times 2003, Super-8/DVD, promotional film, Chatham Super-8 Cinema

The Genius of Billy Childish 200?, Super-8/DVD, Cherry Red, CDMRED262 (live film of Thee Milkshakes & Thee Headcoats)

Punk Rock ist nicht Tot 2004, Super-8/DVD, promotional film, Chatham Super-8 Cinema

Brass Monkey 2005, Super-8/DVD, Chatham Super-8 Cinema

Medway Wheelers 2005, Super-8/DVD, promotional film, Chatham Super-8 Cinema

Billy Childish is Dead 2005, directed by Graham Bendal, Cherry Red, CRDVD86

Ornithology Or The Birdman 2005 (1989/90), directed by Eugene Doyen, Hangman

Brass Monkey: A Documentary 2005, directed by William Hamper , Hangman

Talking Heads: Stop Making Sense

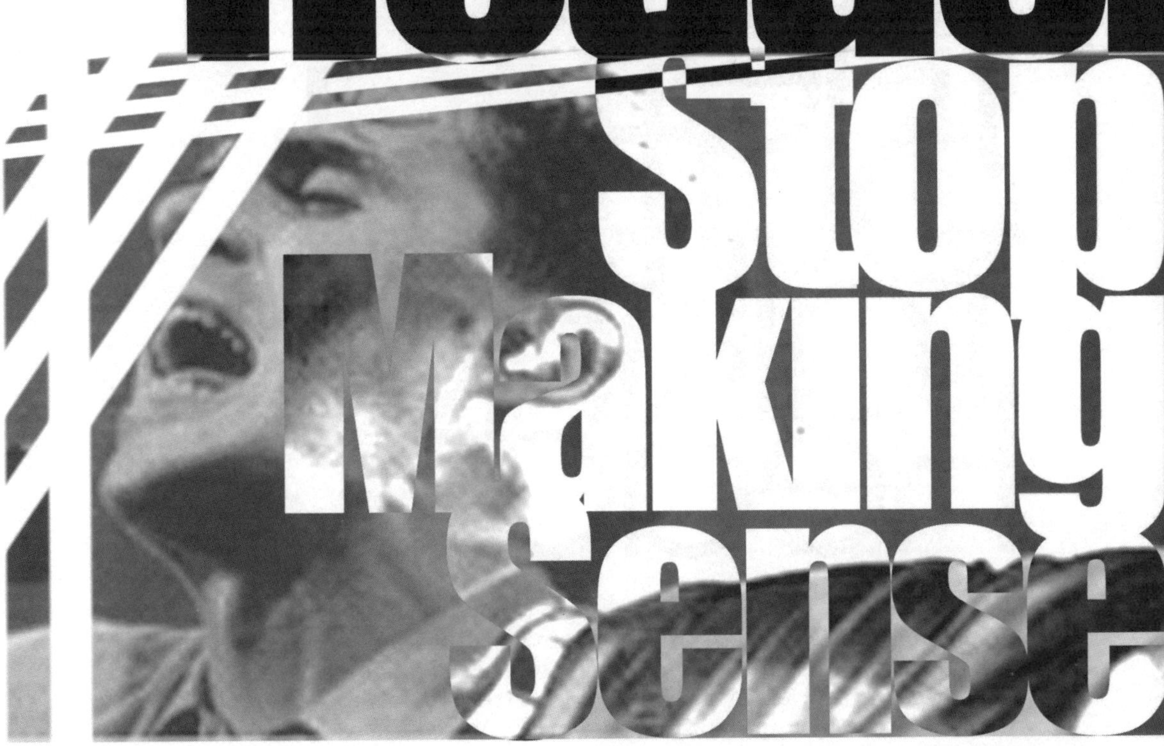

Chris Barber

From the outset, Talking Heads

championed the DIY aesthetic, in common with other new wave and punk bands. All four musicians in the band shared an obsessive interest in avant-garde and experimental art, theatre and music — especially with contemporary minimalist or post modernist concerns. While David Byrne wrote most of the band's lyrics, they experimented with alternative techniques of musical composition. During their most innovative period, each musician would take the lyrics or song theme and produce their own musical accompaniment, isolated from the others. They would then meet and force the four sections together through rehearsals, until they obtained a composition that satisfied all.

Director Jonathan Demme began by making slick, low-budget exploitation films, like *Caged Heat* (1974), a violent women in prison flick, and *Crazy Mama* for Roger Corman in 1975, a Ma Baker gangster romp. His contribution to *Stop Making Sense* (1984) should not be over-esteemed or underestimated. The band themselves, Byrne in particular, were well informed and experienced in modern art and experimental theatre, as well as musical performance. Byrne already had a fairly detailed idea of how the film should look and sound, even down to completed storyboards. But Demme efficiently picked up on the effects Byrne wanted and achieved these with slick mastery. Further, Demme developed a smooth and productive working relationship with Byrne, who took Demme's own suggestions seriously and happily incorporated many of them.

Title credits flash across a darkened stage as the live roar of the audience grows in anticipation. David Byrne's feet (wearing white trainers) stroll across the empty box stage, wearing a light cotton two-piece suit. He carries a ghetto-blaster in one hand and has a guitar strapped over his shoulder. Byrne approaches the solitary microphone centre-stage, "Hi, I've got a tape I want to play," he says, quoting a line from David Cronenberg's *Videodrome* (1982), stands the ghetto-blaster on the stage and switches it on...

The stage area is deliberately bare and derelict, free of sets and props at the gig's outset. This is an efficacious concept, similar to avant-garde theatre techniques developed by Bertolt Brecht. As other performers, props and instruments are gradually added to the *mis en scene*, as they are required for the show, the spectator's attention is concentrated on the process of making music and performing. You get to see precisely what, and who, does what and how, unburdened by showy distractions — a demystification of the production process.

> Can't seem to face up to the facts,
> I'm tense and nervous, can't relax,
> Can't sleep, head's on fire,
> Don't touch me, I'm a real live wire ***Psycho Killer***

An electro-rap rhythmic beat wafts through the arena (actually the beat is being played backstage, not on the ghetto-blaster) and Byrne grips his TR808 acoustic guitar, revivifying the first song David Byrne ever wrote for the band, Psycho Killer. *Qu'est que ce?* Byrne claims he wrote parts of the song in French and English, to suggest the "internal head state of a demented person"; he envisaged it should sound like an "Alice Cooper song," but "more introspective" and "sophisticated." At the end, Byrne performs his 'spastic dance' — based loosely on dance steps from a Fred Astaire movie — deliberately traversing a wide semi-circle, covering the full area of stage space.

Tina Weymouth's bass riser is efficiently wheeled on stage, and the ghetto-blaster removed by a roadie in black overalls. All the stage crew wear similar black overalls throughout, an idea borrowed from traditional Japanese theatre, to enable the spectator to identify and so choose to see through them, as if they're not there. Weymouth enters stage right in a blimp suit and joins Byrne front-centre, collecting her bass. They sing Heaven, their existential angst song from the *Fear of*

Music LP, which was partially inspired by the gay London nightclub.

During the last verse, the drums riser is wheeled on behind the duo (a conceit is used solely on Heaven; Weymouth mimes while an anonymous vocalist sings behind the scenes). Chris Frantz enters between songs, taking position with a brief drum roll. The three players are spotlighted, poised on stage... and they're off. Thank You For Sending Me An Angel kicks in with its up-tempo punkish galloping rhythm; a hand-held medium camera shot pans a circle around the drummer at work. Frantz says this part of the movie best evokes the spirit of their 1977 performances at New York's CBGB club.

Jerry Harrison joins the original Talking Heads line up and the workman-like performance continues into Found A Job. Risers are wheeled into position alongside the drums, adding synthesisers and bongos. Close-up and medium shots of the performers are cut to static long-shot of the show from the rear of the auditorium. Byrne claims the repetitive, trance-like extended instrumental section at the end is a homage to the composer, Steve Reich.

Percussionist Steve Scales sits on a stool at bongos. Two fabulous, grinning soul vocalists (Lynne Mayberry and Edna Holt) assume positions at Byrne's right hand. Straight into Slippery People, with its funky dance rhythm and shrill backing vocals; medium shots from the wings capture interaction, intercut with hand-held/trolley facial close-ups, emphasising the performers' changing expressions. Despite the absence of narrative, the spectator becomes involved, acquainted with each 'character' as they interact and party together. In the instrumental interlude, Byrne faces Mayberry and Holt (with their swinging, long and bouncy hair styles) mimicking each other's exaggerated dance gyrations. Byrne refers to his 'Duck' dance.

> Put away that gun,
> This part is simple
> Try to recognise
> What is in your mind **_Slippery People_**

Burning Down The House follows; Byrne says the song's nucleus is based on a chant at a Funkadelic gig, but "most of the song does not make logical sense, just a series of statements... surprised it worked." Bernie Worrel joins the line up on his synthesiser riser; Harrison moves to downstage guitar and Weymouth swaps to mini keyboard. Byrne does his 'knock-knee' dance to instrumental close. Reflecting their recordings — the *Speaking In Tongues* album — the band's original four-piece line up grows to eight musicians.

For Cities, Alex Wier joins with guitar, completing the nine-piece onstage ensemble. On this lively number, Byrne, between singing, provides a variety of tightly rehearsed body-action routines (these began as improvisations but were formalised for performance). Incredibly this Cities slot was cut from the original US theatrical release; thankfully most available versions now include it, although not necessarily here, in its intended slot. Despite the lack of real narrative, the juxtaposition of facial expressions and group interaction shots unfolds a cast of characters for the film audience.

Life During Wartime is next. Revivifying the track from the *Fear of Music* LP, Byrne claims it's a New Orleans song written in New York; the scenario describes ongoing urban warfare campaigns by the Baader-Meinhof group, Patty Hearst, and Weathermen. Byrne has already ditched his jacket and is still pouring sweat from earlier onstage gymnastics. For this final instrumental crescendo, he hands his guitar to a roadie and joins musicians jogging on the spot, and then, incredibly, he runs two circuits around the whole stage.

> Heard of a van that is loaded with weapons,
> Packed up and ready to go
> Heard of some gravesites, out by the highway,
> A place where nobody knows
> The sound of gunfire, off in the distance ***Life During Wartime***

"Does anybody have any questions?" Byrne asks the applauding audience. Blackout [although the film is edited together like one lengthy concert, it actually comprises of sequences from three live gigs, performed in Los Angeles], and the seven-piece band rejoin onstage. Drum intro rolls as three towering projection screens, each displaying various words on a red backdrop (like ONIONS, PIG etc.), illuminate for Making Flippy Floppy. Weird keyboard solo as spotlight follows Byrne (now with swept-back, greased hair) who sits up suddenly out of the darkness, to begin singing.

After another blackout, rear stage mole-lights fade in slowly, accompanying a minimal and suspenseful instrumental intro, as Byrne enters the stage brightly illuminated by a hand-held spotlight. The spot projects his towering shadow onto a back screen (expressionist style). Byrne's voice acquires the timbre of a sleazy, quivering, southern US drawl, as he renders Swamp. His enacted physical awkwardness (like dragging a dead leg) and exaggerated gesticulations bring menace to this theatrical persona. White stage lights flood all the musicians for the final chorus, ending in total stage blackout.

What A Day That Was starts suddenly out of the blackness, with its fast, up-tempo guitar riffs. All the performers' faces are illuminated individually from below by cold, bright Tunksten film lights, out of the darkness. Individual face-on close-ups — especially Byrne's wide eyes and manic mouth movements — create mask-like silhouettes, resembling a cross between Bela Lugosi pics, Munch's *Scream* and a Beckett performance. The song's urgent intensity completes the nightmarish imminence of the spectacle. Only white stage lighting is used throughout the film, but the cornucopia of different light effects is astonishing and induces strong emotional responses in the spectator.

> There are fifty thousand beggars, roaming in the streets,
> They have lost all their possessions; they have nothing left to eat,
> Down comes a bolt of lightening, starts an electrical storm
> Causes a chain-reaction… a time for big decisions ***What a Day That Was***

A lounge table lamp with tacky lampshade, placed centre-stage, glows out of the darkness; cosily positioned and softly lit around it is a lounge sofa, rug, and dining room table and chairs. In the background, giant projector screens alternate slides of apartment blocks and body parts. Contrasting with the previous song, the instrumental intro is warm, serene and laid back. For This Must Be the Place (Naïve Melody), the band assembles in a cosy semi-circle around the lamp prop, Byrne in a casual, buttoned blazer. The figures appear almost motionless, casually nodding heads and using minimal gestures in their playing. Static long-shot from the rear of the auditorium cuts back to medium shots from the stage. Throughout the film, there are almost no audience shots until the final number, giving you (the film audience) the feeling of being there. Apparently, during the film's first theatrical release, cinemagoers not only clapped and cheered between songs, but also sometimes left their seats to stand and dance in front of the screen. For the second instrumental section, Byrne casually plays with the table light (re-fitted with brighter flashlight bulbs, all other lights are dimmed) gently tilting it back and forth.

> Home is where I want to be
> But I guess I'm already there ***This Must Be the Place (Naïve Melody)***

Blackout, set props cleared (all the blackouts between songs are tightly edited in the movie, so the performance appears virtually continuous, effortless and seamless). Once In A Lifetime follows; calibrated spotlights again highlight the musicians individually, against darkness. Byrne appears in a straight suit and pressed shirt, wearing thick framed *Joe 90* style spectacles. Resembling a Pentecostal church preacher (whose performances inspired the song's delivery), Byrne, twitching and vibrating, looms gaunt and tall from the blackness, adopting a monotone voice to deliver a fiery sermon (song). The gospel-rock melody picks up and shuttles along with its gospel backing vocals on the chorus. Byrne remains convincing, raising his right hand in divine gesture. Musicians appear spotlit in rising rows (mounted on hidden tiered platforms), while backing vocalists lie backwards to rise stiffly upwards, as if entranced or possessed. The trolley or hand-held, onstage camerawork was well rehearsed, requiring few cuts to other cameras during this number.

> And you may find yourself behind the wheel of a large automobile
> And you may find yourself in a beautiful house, with a beautiful wife
> And you may ask yourself — Well... how did I get here? ***Once In A Lifetime***

Only now does the film's intoxicating spell begin to loose its grip on the spectator, becoming just another concert movie. The band breaks down, as an understandably frazzled and shabby looking Byrne wafts through a solo guitar-wank. Blah blah, he clears off stage, making way for Weymouth, Frantz and The Tom Tom Club; rear stage projectors screen cut-up and blown-up bits of their album cover, flashing strobe and disco lights litter the stage, seemingly positioned with careless abandon. Genius Of Love is whimsically played (loosing the taut, funky depth of the album version). Weymouth bounces around with guitar in some sort of frenzy, and "Check it out" chants fail to sound remotely like James Brown; but at least the performers seem to be having "Fun, nasty fun…"

Things improve substantially when the familiar Talking Heads line up returns to the stage. Girlfriend Is Better, reminds us these whities really do do disco: "We're being taken for a ride again." Byrne wears a gigantic two-piece suit (made for the film to look several sizes too big). This simple theatrical-prop trick, the suit that allows the wearer's tiny head and hands to poke out, adds a patently absurd and wonderfully surrealist touch. A stagehand crouches before him pointing a sun gun light upwards at him, projecting his gigantic shadow onto the backdrop.

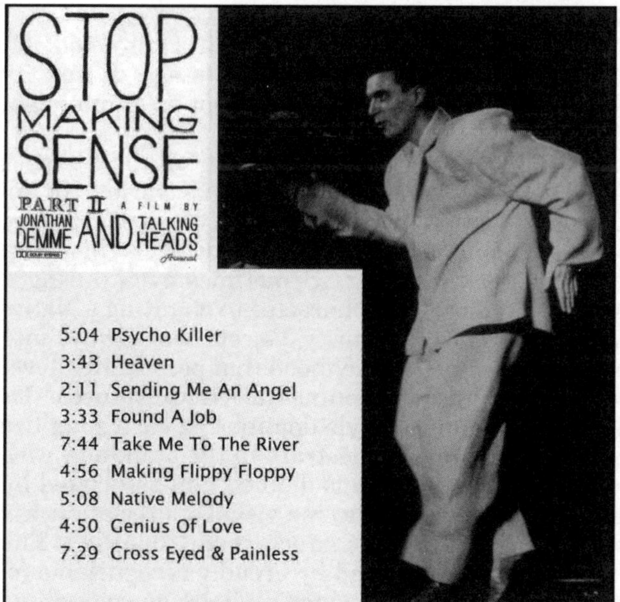

German bootleg album sleeve of the *Stop Making Sense* film soundtrack.

Byrne deliberately moves slowly, making exaggerated 'wiggle' dance gestures.

Back in New York's late 1970s new wave/punk explosion, several new wave bands jointly augmented a campaign, promoting rock music to a scene dominated by disco. Talking Heads discovered they were associated with vociferous bitching against soul/disco music. The band repeatedly expressed their fondness for disco, increasingly absorbing its influence into their punk legacy.

Finally, a seemingly endless presentation of Take Me To The River wails pleasantly on… and on. Eventually Byrne introduces the full stage line up, individually by name, as each plays a clipped roll call (jazz style) or pulls a goofy face for the camera. The whole stage set is bathed in light, backed up by full on house lights, as a long-shot from the rear of the auditorium captures the whole scene, complete with party ambience, before cutting to a mixed montage of live audience shots, technicians and even a couple of fag cameramen. Cross Eyed And Painless plays out to closing credits.

As mentioned, Cities was cut from some versions of the movie, as was a medley of Big Business and I Zimbra. These have been restored to most currently available versions, although — as with Cities — not necessarily to their intended slots. For each of the three filmed gigs of which the final movie comprises, seven cameras were used in different positions. At least one is hand-held, another possibly mounted on a moveable platform (for use onstage). The most productive fixed positions are either in the wings or machine-mounted front-of-house cameras. Dramatic shot contrasts are achieved by seamlessly inter-cutting between these cameras.

The location is LA's Pentages Theatre in Hollywood. All the risers, equipment, instrument logos etc used on stage during filming were painted black beforehand, and stage sets kept as minimal and simple as possible.

Beyond the music performance, most of the stage spectacle is dominated by Byrne's ingenious antics; his variety of minimal but effective costumes, props, hairstyles, wacky voices, facial expressions and dance movements. He radically transforms his stage persona, changing identity for each song. (Sometimes even during a song, like Swamp, from creepy sleazeball character to chanting a Native American tribal dance.) This multiple identity concept was always integral to the band's music, inspired by the likelihood that personality develops largely via relative cultural and environmental circumstances. They express this through a specific music style dominating each song (from country & western to contemporary orchestral). In the punk/new wave tradition, the Talking Heads music canon is defined and associated by difference — not similarity. Byrne renders a cine-visual appreciation, assuming and acting out a variety of different characters and identities. Further, these performances tend to be inspired by broadly recognisable (or ordinary) social stereotypes, a familiarity which invites some empathy.

You Got Bad Taste

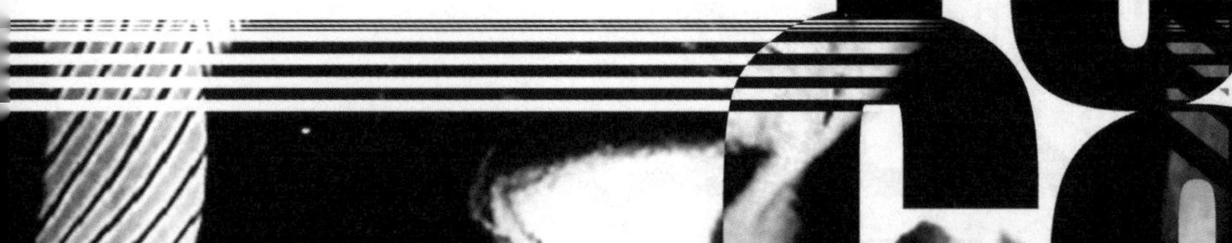

Chris Barber

Punk cinema is not a new genre,

nor an original approach to filmmaking. It doesn't represent a significant break with pre-punk cinema and wasn't inspired or augmented by punk rock alone. There's no manifesto or agenda to establish, delineate or lay claim to the punk film heritage. Punk cinema pre-dates punk rock, with examples dating back to silent movies... That is, films exemplifying the formal concerns of punk.

Punk subculture as an eclectic, late twentieth century phenomenon, was partially inspired by cinema. Some controversial or cult films were icons for adolescent punks. You would be hard pushed to find an ex-punk rocker who didn't rave about *A Clockwork Orange* and *Taxi Driver*. Or ask any punk cine-auteur to name the filmmakers that most inspire them and a handful of directors are repeatedly named (Buñuel, Vertov, Godard, Waters, Warhol…). This chapter forms a brief introduction to the roots of punk cinema; the directors, movements and films that most inspired or influenced punk filmmaking, or achieved iconic or cult status among the punk movement.

Shock tactics; all-out assault on the spectator's gaze; the unfamiliar and unexpected; absurdity; the senseless; chaos and confusion; laughter; destruction; revolution; Freudian dream analysis; challenging censorship; *l'amour fou*; convulsive beauty... Luis Buñuel was a surrealist and filmmaker from Andalusia, Spain. While living in Paris with the other surrealists, he enlisted the assistance of Dalí (as co-director), Max Ernst and other artists, to make the first surrealist short film. In b&w and silent, Buñuel presents montages: edited sequences using different formal patterns; abstract, associative and narrative. When first screened (in Paris) the film caused a riot.

Sex and violence are the central recurring themes of *Un chien anadalou* (1928): a young woman and a man (played by Ernst) keep trying to have passionate sex but their efforts are constantly interrupted; a woman's eye is shockingly sliced apart (in close-up) with a hand-held razorblade; diegetic time-span is lost; there are ants all over the place and a cow on the bed; two priests tied to grand pianos with rotting horse corpses on top are dragged across the floor by a determined young man...

Now it's widely recognised as one of the great cinematic masterpieces, still wonderfully weird and a little shocking. Buñuel and Dalí followed up with *L' Âge d'or* (1930) — again, it's weird, elliptical and dream-like, but more polemical. Buñuel went on to direct a plethora of surrealist and avant-garde feature films in Mexico and France

In his autobiography, *My Last Breath*, Buñuel says:

> I love my dreams, even when they're nightmares, which is usually the case... *Un chien anadalou* was born of the encounter between my dreams and Dalí's. Later I brought dreams directly into my films, trying as hard as I could to avoid any analysis. "Don't worry if the movie is too short," I once told a Mexican producer. "I'll just put in a dream."[1]

The Surrealist and Dadaist art movements are largely taken for granted as having a significant impact on punk subculture. It is a challenge to find any director who doesn't mention Buñuel in general, and *Un chien anadalou* in particular, as formative influences.

German born Hans Richter is another surrealist film director, who engaged other Dadaist and surrealist artists in his productions. He sometimes allows for more non-figurative abstract imagery than Buñuel, but tends to undercut the playful shock potential of this by over sign posting these sequences with conventional cine narrative devices. His most renowned eighty minute feature, *Dreams That Money Can Buy* (1946), is a prime example. The bulk of the film consists of five unrelated sequences, each devised and directed by a different artist: Max Ernst, Fernand Léger, Man Ray, Marcel Duchamp and Alexander Calder. Duchamp's sequence is a hypnotic dance of spinning discs; Ray's section turns the audience on the audience, depicting a cinema audience actively following their film's instructions, and so on. But Richter links each episode with a wacky story about salesmen starting a business to capture and sell other people's dreams. The film remains conceptually innovative and influential, particularly among punk directors.

In his book *The Struggle for the Film*, Richter states:

> To varnish our lives with entertaining stories is too petty a task for this mighty technology... if it is to grow to artistic maturity. Let it... be allowed to participate in the intellectual conflicts of the age, let us dare apply this technology to shape genuine emotions, thoughts and ideas: to shape social life; it will be stimulated... and manage to change... to an instrument of genuine imagination.[2]

Jean Vigo is a French anarchist and surrealist director. He led a fairly dismal life and died young, making just a few films. His short film *Zéro De Conduite* (1933) is set in a boy's boarding school, where the masters are predominantly sadistic fascists, hypocrites and bullies. The pupils (from whose viewpoint the audience watches) creatively plot to terminate their suffering and revolt against the system. In the film's climactic scene, the boys play-fight in the dormitory, bursting pillows, filling the screen with feathers like a magical snowstorm. Vigo also scripted the film, which was considered too subversive and banned until 1945. Editing is rough'n'ready and its message iconoclastic, but it is hugely influential, most obviously on Lindsay Anderson's *If...* Punk director Julien Temple even made a film about his hero, *Vigo: Passion for Life* (1999).

For a decade or so after the 1917 Bolshevik Revolution, the Soviet Union hosted a remarkable period for what Lenin called "the most important art... film," not only via its plethora of maverick film directors (like Eisenstein and Pudovkin), but also through the cultural debates it inspired about the meaning and purpose of film: the LEF forums. No filmmaker or intellectual made a more significant contribution to both film theory and practice than Siga Vertov.

Vertov was already established as a popular documentary filmmaker and Futurist polemicist when he directed his silent, feature-length documentary film *Man with a Movie Camera* (1929). Basically, the film is a day in the life of a Russian city, but it moves at a frenzied pace of perpetual motion. There are no actors or individual heroes, but crowds of people going about their business. All the footage is shot on location in working towns and the contribution of Vertov's assistant cameraman, Mikhail Kaufman, is essential. Careful selection of shots, fast editing, slow motion, freeze-frame, associative and elliptical editing, flashbacks, fast-forwards and montage are just some of the cinematic devices Vertov utilises.

Eisenstein famously criticised Vertov's films as "formalist jack-straws," implying they comprise pointless technical experimentation and trickery and are devoid of content. But Vertov recognised you can't have form without content, and vice versa. Time, space and motion are central concerns of the film, which suggests their collapse into a relativist world of flux. What's more, despite the bitchy criticisms aimed at the film by rival filmmakers, who predicted the Soviet people would not watch this sort of film, *Man with a Movie Camera* attracted massive audiences, becoming one of the most popular Soviet films ever made.

I am cinem-eye. I am a mechanical eye. I am a machine, show you a world such as only I can see **Vertov**

Italian Neo-Realism

When Italian film director Luchino Visconti made *Ossessione* (1942) in Mussolini's Italy, its gritty realism and sordid plot distracted censors from its allegorical attack on fascism. Following Italy's liberation from both homegrown and German fascism, Visconti's film inspired a new generation of intelligent, angry, and socially committed filmmakers. Rosselini's last days of war sagas and Vittorio De Sica's *Ladri Di Biciclette* (Bicycle Thieves, 1948) were filmed in b&w, used deep focus photography throughout, made extensive use of long-shots and long-takes, with minimal camera movement, cast ordinary people rather than actors, and concentrated on simple stories based on the real lives and hardships of the urban poor. The result was a documentary-style realism, which continued to be developed through to the early 1960s, by movie maestros such as directors Pier Paolo Pasolini (*Accatone*, 1961; *Mamma Roma*, 1962), and Federico Fellini (*La Strada*, 1954; *Nights Of Cabiria*, 1956).

In France, Andre Bazin's circle of intellectual film critics championed the technical innovations of Neo-Realist cinema, claiming it introduced 'democracy of the gaze' to the spectator (based on dubious phenomenological presumption). Radical filmmakers in Britain and France were quick to recognise the potential of gritty social realism, sexual tension and brutal violence to transform their respective film industries, but first they had to get past the censors. Gradually, kitchen-sink realism became an integral part of serious British filmmaking, a tradition compatible with many punk filmmakers.

Meanwhile, Pasolini and Fellini in particular had widened their social conscience lenses to explore the street life of prostitutes and vagrant youths. Recognising the broader poetic licence their perfected techniques offered, when infused with psychoanalysis, Fellini turned his camera on the filmmaking process (*Eight And A Half*, 1963), and Pasolini on mythology (*Oedipus Rex*, 1967).

The French Nouvelle Vague

Whatever the strengths and weaknesses of critical film theory, as advocated by Bazin and co., it unquestionably made a monumental contribution to cinema by inspiring several young critics to become radical film directors: the French new wave. Jean Luc Godard transformed filmmaking forever with *À bout de souffle* (Breathless, 1960), bringing location shoots, hand-held camera, jump-cuts and pop art to the screen, portraying the reckless crimes and love life of a young gangster (Jean-Paul Belmondo). Further, Godard's amiably anarchic cop-killer anti-hero challenged the censors with (then) cutting-edge depictions of sex and violence.

Godard and his contemporaries also made an asset out of low budgets, resorting to endless cheap innovations, while intellectual concepts from modern art and radical politics are unashamedly utilised in film form and content. *Alphaville* (1965) turns existing Parisian locations into futuristic science fiction landscapes, with a noir existentialist detective. *Le Mépris* (Contempt, 1963) explores the exploitation, production and marital problems that beset a film director. *Pierrot Le Fou* (1965) has an obstreperous young couple, suddenly leaving conventional jobs, home and marriage and taking to the open road on a crime spree. Their blood-drenched victims provoked the censors, to which Godard shrewdly responded, "It's not blood, it's red." *Weekend* (1967) deconstructs civilisation, film form, language, revolution, and just about everything else… Famously, Godard said: "A film should have a beginning, a middle and an end, but not necessarily in that order."

Saturday Night and Sunday Morning (1960)

Czech born director Karel Reisz established his filmmaker credentials in Britain, as a leading member of the Free Film movement in the 1950s. This group of directors was committed to transforming British cinema, to portray social realism and everyday life. *Saturday Night and Sunday Morning* is based on Alan Sillitoe's novel and stars Albert Finney as a Nottingham factory worker. Probably the most enduring of Britain's first generation of kitchen-sink dramas, the film champions its working class hero, his contempt for bosses and authority, and his sexual immorality. It also challenged censorship of its time.

The Battle of Algiers (1965)

A b&w Italian production, lasting 135 minutes, this remains a benchmark of documentary-drama/political filmmaking. Set in Algeria in the late 1950s, director Gillo Pontecorvo utilises documentary and news archive footage, intercut with interviews, dramatic re-enactments and location footage. It's the immaculate editing of different material into a seamless complete feature that makes the whole film convincingly resemble a documentary. The events leading to Algerian independence from France are shown, including interviews with leading figures on both sides, creating the appearance of balanced and unbiased reporting. The film was banned in France for several years.

If.... (1968)

Lyndsay Anderson is surely one of the most talented, exciting and innovative British film directors ever, but his preoccupations with film theory, theatre and television direction sadly limited his output of feature films. The son of a serving British army officer in India, Lindsay came to Britain to enrol at Cheltenham and later Oxford (experiences which inform *If....* He was a leading proponent of the documentary realist-inspired Free Cinema, directing *This Sporting Life* in 1962. *If....* is probably his masterpiece and the first in an angrily polemical, allegorical and poetically biographical trilogy, starring Malcolm McDowell (followed by *O Lucky Man!* in 1972, and the much maligned, punk masterpiece *Britannia Hospital* in 1982).

Partly inspired by Vigo's *Zero De Conduit* and Godard's cinema, *If....* is an anarchic film, which pits lads in a traditional British public boarding school against their iron-rod authoritarian and hypocritical

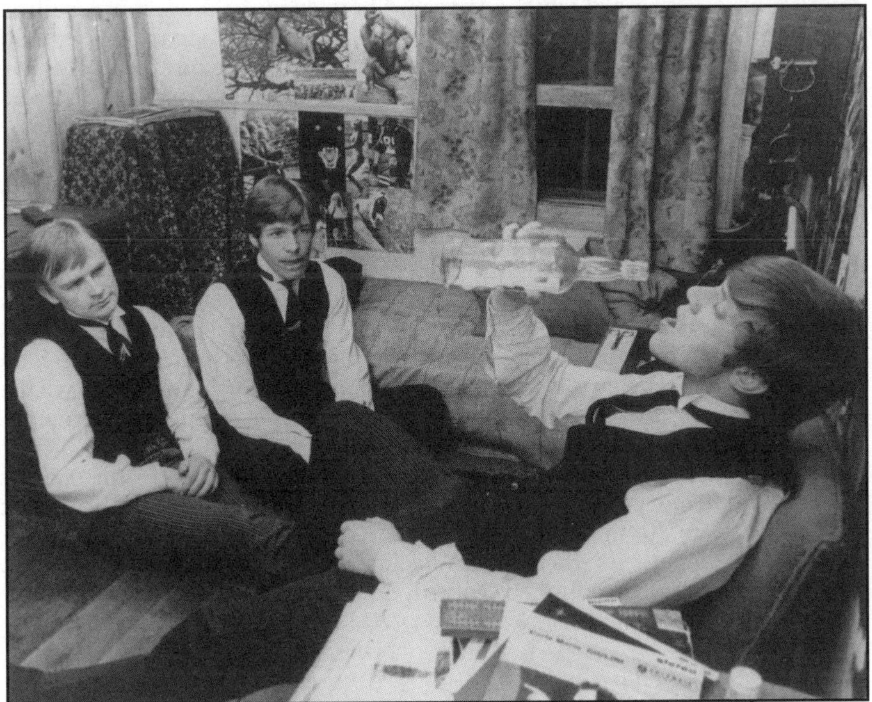

British public schooling; Malcolm McDowell swigs from the bottle. *If....*

masters. The class system, British nationalism, and the fascistic underpinnings of imperial authority are exposed and intelligently attacked; so is the hypocrisy of sexual morality, through sympathetic depictions of gay relationships. Chapter divisions are used throughout, along with other playful theatrical distancing devices, and sequences oscillate between colour and monochrome. The film's celebratory climax shows a group of youths forming an armed, anarchic, urban guerrilla squad, instigating a revolution by embittered pupils against their parents and school authorities. An extraordinary and prophetic (undoubtedly inspiring many pre-punk kids) British film, Anderson proclaimed "It's something like *The Writing on the Wall.*"

A Clockwork Orange (1971)

Director Stanley Kubrick was a renowned cine perfectionist, who loved to challenge social taboos with intellectual and aesthetic mastery. His adaptation of the Anthony Burgess sci-fi novel, about violent youth, creativity and the human condition, is perhaps the ultimate cult movie. Set in a supposed not too distant future, Thamesmead in London, a then modern council estate, provided the ideal location to shoot much of the film. Young Malcolm McDowell (the young rebel star of *If....*) was well cast as Alex, a violent delinquent and gang leader of the droogs. In their boots'n'braces, pressed white shirts and bowler hats (the latter recalling those wretched yobs who used to hang about the city!), gang-slang, and Alex with his thick black eyeliner, they set a fine example to twelve year old future punk rockers. Never has any movie better aestheticised brute violence, or so thoroughly mastered the audience's point of view and empathies, to deconstruct conventional prejudices (persuading the spectator to adopt Alex's warped and sadistic, but also creative, perspective).

The caricatures representing various facets of British authority/ establishment are immaculately conceived. Cynical abuse of power is exposed to ultimately equate the brutality of both criminal outsiders and legal guardians: its expression shown to be easier and carry less responsibility, by operating within the 'system' than outside. The substantial hypothesis is a warning: tinkering with human nature with a view to social improvement can have far more catastrophic consequences than accepting negative creative expression.

The controversy surrounding the film's release and subsequent withdrawal from public screening in the UK all added to the film's mythical status. Actually, Kubrick himself ordered the film to be banned, shifting the debate to whether his decision was provoked by the media reaction, personal threats he received, or wilful capriciousness.

Cabaret (1972)

Bob Fosse directed this sensational and unique musical adaptation, based on Christopher Isherwood's volumes of short stories set in 1930s Berlin, about the period's short-lived, pre-Nazi, innovative and satirical live stage culture. Musical and performance routines (inspired by the likes of Wiell and Brecht) are built into the film's diegetic plot (contrasting with Hollywood's conventional musical genre). Liza Minnelli bristles with talent and exudes sensuality as a cabaret performer; Joel Grey presents a masterly head of (stage) ceremonies; and Michael York is a typically English and easily shocked young visitor, quickly corrupted by divine decadence. The impending spectre of Nazism and its socio-political dynamic is intelligently examined and contrasted against the sexual permissiveness of the bohemian subculture. Dramatically filmed and choreographed stage routines dominate the film's highlights, whose visual impact, lighting and make-up left a lasting impression on future punk rockers (like Siouxsie and the Banshees).

Eraserhead (1976)

While all the movies, film movements and directors listed in this section can be shown to have directly impacted on punk cinema, the release of two new films in 1976, coinciding with the advent of punk/new wave subculture, perfectly captured and spoke to the mood of the time. Both *Eraserhead* and *Taxi Driver* achieved cult status with young punk and new wave audiences; aspects of each were adopted by, and influenced, the nascent subcultures. Controversy surrounded both films, dividing film critics and audiences alike; each was widely considered to be shocking and to have broken new ground in filmmaking. Although both films are American, neither production was made in Hollywood. Both are now widely regarded as classic films, but neither was acknowledged as such until much later, when the film establishment was replaced by a new generation.

Eraserhead, David Lynch's cult black and white, surrealist horror film took some five years to make and was all shot at night.

The soundtrack is almost as stunning as its visual impact: a collage of sounds sampled from various unusual sources and often pitched at unusually high or low frequencies. Industrial or factory sounds are, claims Lynch, his favourites (suggesting a mutual affinity with the new wave). Independently produced on a low budget, nightmarish and elliptical, the basic plot tackles the fears of a young man who has got a girl pregnant and must suddenly transform his life to become a husband and father.

When the baby is born a monstrous, foetus-like freak, sick and continuously whining for attention, it is the stuff of nightmares: fear of sex, flesh, women, adulthood, responsibility, life, death… just about everything. Visually the film comprises stark post-industrial landscapes, claustrophobic minimal living spaces and infinite nothingness; people co-existing through mutual alienation and misunderstanding. And the horror — a bizarrely disfigured baby, decapitation, sickness, oblivion… all to make pencil erasers! Among the movie's many new wave fans, David Thomas, the front man in Cleveland's band Pere Ubu (about as hardcore avant-garde new wave as you get) based his towering high-quiff hairstyle on *Eraserhead*'s Henry (Jack Nance), which became an icon of their stage performances.[3]

Taxi Driver (1976)

Quite simply, *Taxi Driver* is one of the handful of movies by which cinema should be defined. Italian American, New York born and bred, film director Martin Scorsese was a student of the New York actor and independent filmmaker, John Cassavetes. Both are especially concerned with portraying urban streetwise realism, and the lives of people in their inner city neighbourhoods, mythologising their lives by highlighting the frequently overlooked surreal and absurd moments.

Young Robert DeNiro gives one of the finest method acting performances ever, as Travis Bickle, starting a new job as a New York

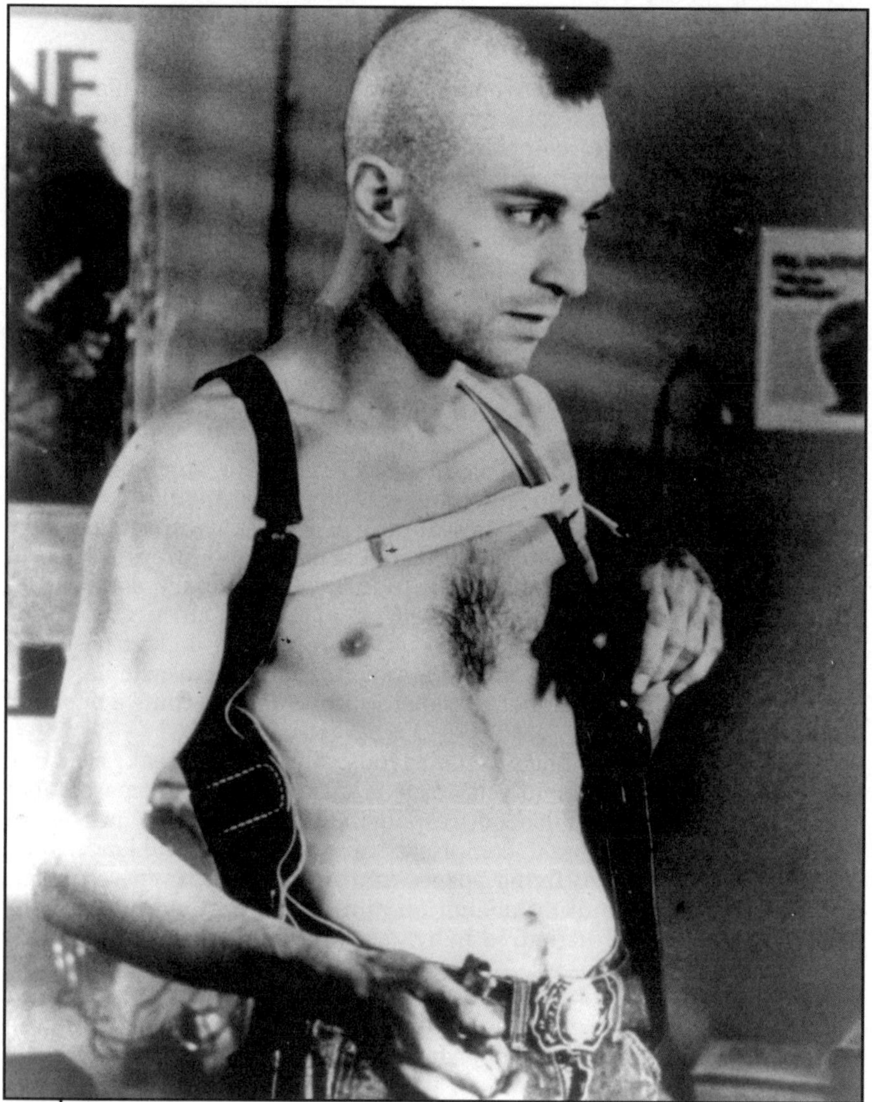

Robert De Niro in *Taxi Driver*

yellow cab driver. Bickle to many is a psychotic loner, introvert and misogynist, with sociopath tendencies. Some could argue he is a cool existentialist rebel, in search of a cause? Perhaps he's just the guy next door: self-loathing, lacking in confidence, full of contradictions, just trying to do the right thing in a contradictory world.

Travis is not good with words, he has trouble communicating. He is also evasive and cagey What has he got to hide? He's not unlikeable, he is sometimes amusing, but at whose expense? Is he grinning with you or at you? These are the questions he evokes. His facial expressions are equally confusing: one moment his eyes meet yours, the next, it's as if he can't see you. For an instant, he smiles with radiant alacrity and then his lips almost quiver uncontrollably. Even his body language is contradictory, slumping like a rag doll, and then robustly standing to attention:

"Education?" asks the cab controller, completing Bickle's application form for him.

"Uh… some," he replies.

His inquisitor glances up. "Are you moonlighting?"

"Um… I just want to work long hours… What's moonlighting?"

"Religious holidays, festivals — when can't you work?"

"I'll work any time, makes no difference to me."

"Any districts, neighbourhoods, you're not prepared to go?"

"I'll work any time, any where."

"Okay, you get the night shift."

In the first few minutes, the simple and minimal establishing sequence in a working cab office, photography, script, acting and direction combine to conjure an atmosphere of menace, intensity and imminence that grows and intensifies as the plot develops. You're kept in nail-biting suspense and the more you learn, the more unpredictable events become.

When initially released, the film was a hit with reactionary audiences, whooping and clapping the vigilante style bloodbath. After attending public screenings, Scorsese expressed his indignation over this response.

Throughout the film, the stark deep focus and crisp naturalistic photography repeatedly blends into sequential moments of total abstraction: a melange of coloured streetlights, reflections, rain and water patterns, shadow, extreme close-ups, obtuse camera angles and movement. With his last soundtrack before his death, composer Bernard Herrmann (famous for his Hitchcock soundtracks) provides perhaps his best work, unusually minimal and haunting. Paul Schrader's superbly existential script became a joint effort on set, with input from Scorsese and De Niro's improvisations. In keeping with their characters, De Niro and Keitel antagonised each other on set, developing a genuine mutual dislike, which reverberates in their performances.

The most obvious iconic punk images in *Taxi Driver* occur towards the end during the bloodbath, when Travis appears on screen sporting his slick Mohawk. The mohawk has associations dating back to Native America's Mohichans. The few who survived the colonial wars between the French and British were wiped out by the US government's clandestine genocide policy. This is 1976 and in Britain, punk rock is just making the news and nobody has mohawks yet; but clean-shaven, with his shabby, ill-fitting combat jacket and shades, Travis Bickle is setting DIY punk style, perhaps the first onscreen punk icon.[45]

"You sure don't look hip…" Another proto-punk concern in *Taxi Driver* is the negative portrayal of hippies. Personified by Harvey Keitel as a pimp, he is clearly a ruthless exploiter at the very least, employing sexual liberation rhetoric and emotional conceit to manipulate the girl. Punk-style political cynicism is also expressed in the Palentine character: a sleazy master of rhetoric, hell-bent on personal power, whose policies are nothing but hollow spin. Further, political cynicism is given a social

dimension by attacking both liberal and reactionary sentiments. Urban street cred is another punk expression central to the film. Travis exudes punk attitude, contradictions and all, through his social alienation, nihilism and contempt towards authority. Finally, in its representation of both sexual decadence (particularly the young hooker) and hardcore violence, *Taxi Driver* goes out of its way to provoke censorial reaction and expose social hypocrisy.

No Laughing Matter: Proto-Punk Comedy Shockers

John Waters cult underground movies, *Pink Flamingos* (1972) and *Female Trouble* (1975), are independent, low budget productions — shocking, controversial, transgressive, anarchic, sick, violent, surrealist, camp, challenging censorship, exuding street cred and redefining bad taste. By the time punk arrived, Waters was ready to move on, but in a gesture of solidarity, he cast a punk rocker in his final punk movie, *Polyester* (1981).

Born in 1946, from childhood Waters felt alienated from his straight-laced, middle class parents. He boasts that, from 1964, he indulged in heavy drug taking which impacted significantly on his early films. A year later, he was expelled from college in New York for narcotic consumption. Typically, he called in the local press and embellished his activity into a hysterical drug scandal. However, he and his streetwise friends were not comfortable with the 1960s hippie counterculture. His formative cinematic influences include Andy Warhol, Jean Luc Godard and Herschell Gordon Lewis.

John Waters began making Super-8 shorts in his youth; his earliest film (he claims) is *Hag in a Black Leather Jacket*, shot in 1964. *Roman Candles* followed in 1966. Living in Baltimore, Maryland he soon acquired a 16mm camera and befriended an entourage of weird and fantastic friends — sort of proto-punks — who appeared in most of his early films, most famously Divine, as well as Mink Stole, David Lochary and Cookie Muller. His first 16mm film was *Eat Your Makeup* in 1968, followed by *Mondo Trasho* (1969) and *Multiple Maniacs* (1970). In 1972 he completed his shocking cult feature *Pink Flamingos*, climaxing with Divine eating dog's excrement. The film attracted a cult following on the late night/underground circuit; *Female Trouble* followed in 1974, and *Desperate Living* in 1977.

In 1981 (the year *Polyester* was released), Waters published his first book, *Shock Value*, in which he writes:

> I've spent the last three years putting together my new film, *Polyester*... It's scheduled in production in October 1980, stars Divine and Tab Hunter, is budgeted at $300,000, will be shot in 35mm, has Michael White (*The Rocky Horror Picture Show*) and New Line Cinema as executive producers, and utilizes one of the most ludicrous promotional gimmicks of all time. The plot dealing with alcoholism and divorce in a comic vein, can best be described as *Father Knows Best* gone berserk.[6]

Polyester (1981)

IT'S A REAL STINKER! Director John Waters — the living maestro of shock cinema and transgressive trash — presents a punk 'comi-trag' satire and camp melodrama, the only movie made in Odorama (replete with scratch'n'sniff smell cards). Starring Divine (the world's favourite transvestite) as Francine Fishpaw, Tab Hunter (as you've never seen him before), Edith Massey, Mink Stole (two veteran Waters movie beauties) and punk rocker Stiv Bators (of The Dead Boys and later The Lords of the New Church), *Polyester* features music by Chris Stein and Michael Kamen, with a song by Debbie Harry of Blondie.

Underlying all the 'shocking, controversial, transgressive, anarchic, sick, violent, surrealist and camp' strategies employed by Waters in his movies up to *Polyester*, ironically Waters has a highly responsible socio-political agenda. He literally shocks us into challenging and questioning our own prejudices, while cautiously neglecting to provide alternative, and equally invalid, dogmatic resolutions. He frequently uses characters within the script as vehicles to express radical polemics. In *Polyester* for instance, Francine's teenage daughter Lulu (Mary Garlington) speaks out against the anti-abortion lobby, a crucial issue in the US. In his earlier movies, Waters has used similarly bombastic shock tactics to challenge 'conventional wisdom' concerning other issues, like recreational drug use and Christianity. In *Polyester* these issues remain committed social concerns for Waters, but Waters opts for more subtle counter strategies.

Odorama was dreamt up by Waters, his first idea on the movie. Its inspiration came from 3D cinema, with its red and green spectacles, and William Castle's movie gimmicks, like the tiny electric shocks felt by the audience via wired-up cinema seats while watching *The Tingler* (1959, also the widening screen effect). Waters saw Odorama's subversive potential as a direct assault on the audience; a sort of Brechtian/surrealist inspired, Situationist, agit-prop theatre device. Significantly, from this perspective, Odorama stinks of punk shock tactics.

Polyester, like the preceding Waters movies, shares punk's absolute contempt for hypocrisy. Punk and Waters also share their commitment to shock tactics — a strategy that instead of seeking compromise to avoid conflict, exaggerates or sensationalises a potential threat (as perceived by others), forcing each counter position to its own provocative apotheosis. 'Provocative' here refers to the point where any belief, turned in on itself, cracks under the weight of its own contradictions and tautologies, provoking the believer to question her/his own prejudices and reasons.

Much of *Polyester*'s inspiration is homage to Douglas Sirk, the master of melodrama, and director of classics *Written on the Wind* (1957) and *Imitation of Life* (1959). *Polyester* continues to exude the punk attitude of his previous movies and brazenly employs shock tactics, but it marks a significant shift in direction. Next, Waters made his last movie with Divine, *Hairspray* (1988). After that, there was only one direction to go — towards convention. *Cry-Baby* (1990) satirises teen exploitation/delinquent movies, with Johnny Depp at his youthful best. *Serial Mom* (1994) features former SLA (Symbionese Liberation Army)

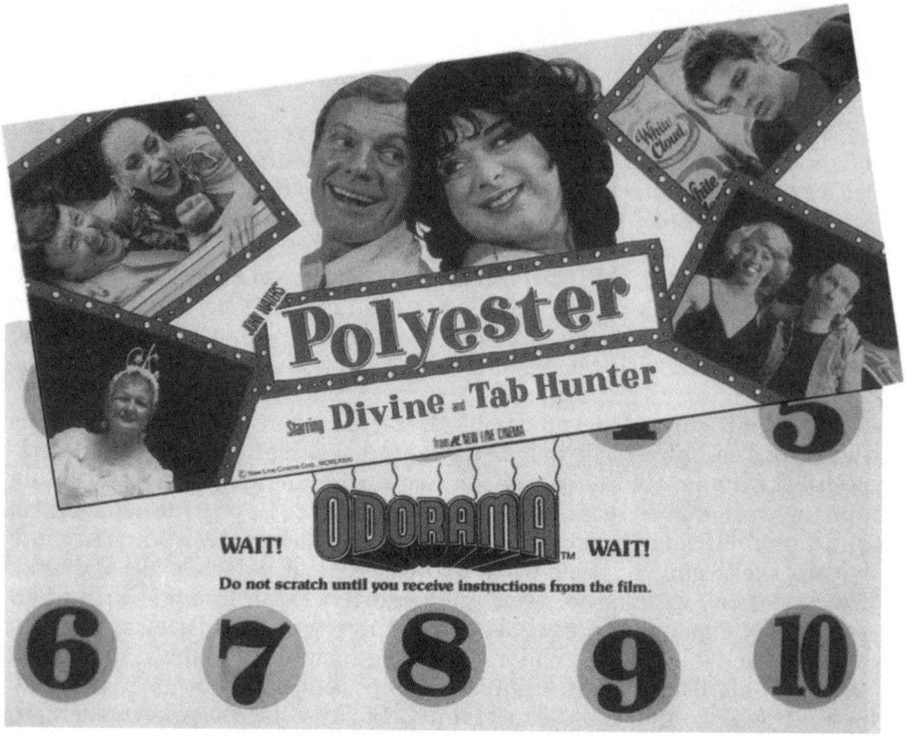

urban guerrilla and fugitive, Patty Hearst, in a hilarious female serial killer romp. *Pecker* and *Cecil B. Demented* are his recent movies — toned down maybe, but still innovative and mischievous. Waters also followed up his book, *Shock Value*, with another — *Crackpot* — and even guest-starred in one of the finest episodes of *The Simpsons*.

RIP Divine... one of the great stars

> My *Gone with the Wind* would be *Polyester* I guess, wouldn't it? **Divine**[8]

Glenn Milstead was an effeminate schoolboy from Baltimore, frequently bullied by other kids. But when their mutual friend, Carol, introduced him to another schoolboy, John Waters, the pair instantly hit it off. Glenn's best friend was a lad named David Lochary, but the group bonded, a repertory group adopting the name, Dreamland. After seeing Glenn in drag, Waters named him/her Divine — after the tranny thief and shit-kicker in Jean Genet's novel *Our Lady of the Flowers*. Divine was eager to pose for John's camera and proved to be quite some discovery, growing into 300 pounds in weight of pure excessive transvestite. From *Roman Candles*, Divine appeared in eight Waters movies. But until *Polyester*, he claims he just played himself in eccentric performance pieces; playing Francine in *Polyester* engaged him in developing his acting skills. (Divine was a big admirer of Elizabeth Taylor.) From there, Divine later won character parts in features by other directors, including *Lust in the Dust* (1985) and Alan Rudolph's *Trouble In Mind* (1986). Further, Divine developed a modestly successful career as an electro disco singer and live performer, including a live tour of Europe's clubs.

In *Multiple Maniacs,* Divine assembles a gang of queers, junkies, fetishists and perverts into a sleazy carnival freak show, "The Cavalcade of Perversions." They embark on a proto-punk mission to shock and outrage decent people. Pre-punk sensibility is also at the forefront of *Pink Flamingos,* when Divine and her trailer-park family of reprobates compete to become the filthiest people alive (culminating in Divine's notorious, real dog shit eating display, as requested by Waters and shot in a single take, from arse to mouth, so to speak). While *Pink Flamingos* is undoubtedly the most renowned Waters/Divine movie, real aficionados maintain the proto-punk *Female Trouble* is the real masterpiece.

Indeed, it is cogently argued that *Female Trouble* should be recognised as among one of the finest films ever made. Apparently, after the film was screened in Cannes, Jean-Luc Godard claimed he had spent his whole life trying to make a film like it. The story follows Dawn Davenport, played by Divine, charting her path from her days in high school as a disruptive pupil, to her tragic execution in the electric chair. Dawn runs away from her strict parents who refuse to understand her and negate her individualism. The final straw is when they neglect to give her the fashionable cha-cha heels she had long coveted, telling her, "Nice girls don't wear cha-cha heels!"

Before playing Cuddles, Francine's only loyal friend and ally in *Polyester*, Edith Massey was (briefly) the singer for Jan and the Rockajets, a butch female band. John Waters says:

> When punk first came out, I suggested to Edith she adopt this look for novelty reasons. Edith is about as far from punk as you can get, but she realised it was a good gimmick and would make good copy for journalists who were always searching for a new angle to write about her. She retrieved her old leather S&M outfit that she wore in Female Trouble from mothballs, glued a spider on her face, collected some original music material, and began to tour the country as the Queen of Punk... Since Edith is the first to admit she can't sing a note, her show had the appeal of a Mrs Miller-Florence Foster Jenkins goes punk.[9]

A real woman, lesbian and star — one of the biggest! — she's the Egg-lady, Divine's mother, kept in a playpen, in *Pink Flamingos*. She's Aunt Ida, Divine's mother-in-law, chucking acid and losing an arm in *Female Trouble.* In *Desperate Living* she's Carlotta, the evil Queen of Mortville.

Desperate Living is an allegorical lesbian punk fairy-tale. Peggy Gravel, the crazy, neurotic wife of a wealthy senator, accidentally kills her husband, so is forced to go on the run with her fabulous fat black lesbian maid. After escaping the clutches of a lingerie-wearing motorcycle cop, they cross the border into Mortville, a lawless anarchic state. There's a lot of wild, pussy-bumping lesbo action and a great ramshackle town. But the town is ruled by a thoroughly nasty and bad natured Queen, who lives in a fairy-tale castle on high and constantly terrorises her subjects, making them conform to stupid ordinances (like

Backwards Day) at her whim. But the revolution is coming... Look out for the sensational wrestling contest, with its eye gouging and eyeball stomping sequence.

Pepi, Luci, Bom Y Otras Chicas Del Montón (1978)

Although made before *Polyester*, it was several years before this Spanish punk comedy was widely shown, but when it was, *Pepi, Luci, Bom y otras chicas del montón* was pushed as a John Waters style cult movie. So, placing it after John Waters in this list seems an appropriate position.

This is the debut film by Spain's best-known living director, Pedro Almodóvar. From the late 1980s to 1990s, Almodóvar gained international recognition as one of the world's finest moviemakers. This acclaim is well deserved for some of his later films. But despite being a damned good directorial debut, *Pepi, Luci, Bom...* is a flawed film. Had it not been for Almodóvar's later renown, it's unlikely it would have been seen outside Spain.

However *Pepi, Luci, Bom...* is inescapably a punk comedy and Almodóvar claims that when he first conceived it, he was entirely driven by his obsession with punk culture. It had minimal to no budget, looks extremely rough, is replete with DIY innovations, and contains punk rockers, punk rock and art design. Further, it plays heavily on cheap shock tactics. The John Waters association is pertinent. It's interesting to see many ideas that Almodóvar would develop in later films. He has said about his debut:

> *Pepi, Luci, Bom y otras chicas del montón* belongs to the punk years. When I started writing the script I used a lot of punk ideology; the aggressiveness, the social corruption that punk stood for... [The film] was written in 1978, influenced by the punk movement, but the punk aspects were transformed by the story. It was a way of looking at punk in the way it was lived here, a more positive way, more like pop.[10]

The time and place in which the film was made is crucial in this instance. Spain's notorious and murderous dictator, President Franco, died in 1975; he had single-handedly ruled the country with an iron rod of right-wing Catholicism since the 1930s. Shortly after his death, Franco's supporters attempted a military coup, which thankfully failed. From 1978 to 1980, when *Pepi, Luci, Bom...* was made, the Spanish people were still undergoing the aftershock, enjoying previously unknown freedom and transforming their country. Even before the Spanish Civil War, the country never built a significant film industry. The most famous Spanish director, Luis Buñuel, made most of his films in Mexico or France. Homegrown film production during the Franco years was confined to reams of ridiculous nationalist propaganda movies. Post-Franco, Spain had far more important things to deal with than building a film industry. Besides which, there had been the death or imprisonment of generations of artists and intellectuals capable of creating truly international cinema. Decades of strict censorship had deprived the people of access to the best of world cinema, so there was a lot of catching up to do. In this context, the real extent of Almodóvar's achievement in breaching the cutting-edge of international filmmaking is remarkable.

Despite the problems confronting Spanish filmmakers, for anyone who had experienced life under Franco, change really could only be for the better — and so it's hardly surprising that, in spite Almodóvar's commitment to punk, the anger and attitude are reduced to affectation in a joyful, frothy and playful expression.

As a female 'buddies' movie, *Pepi, Luci, Bom...* recalls Jacques Rivette's *Céline et Julie vont en bateau* (Celine and Julie Go Boating, 1974). The form of *Pepi, Luci, Bom...* is more like a series of sketches related by the same cast, than a developing narrative. DIY improvisation within mise en scene is phenomenal; much of it looks like it was filmed in various mothers' lounges, which after a while adds an almost surrealist incongruity to the proceedings.

The episodic sketch structure is also notable for the film's one omnipresent theme — sex. In juxtaposition with the alternating roles of each character, from sketch to sketch, the whole movie can be seen as a series of constructed erotic role plays: hetero/homosexual, couples/groups/individual (masturbatory), exhibitionism/voyeurism (directly engaging the film spectator), active/passive, sadistic/masochistic, etc.

Deployment of camp performance and kitsch set design recall Waters, but the rendering of shocking moments, whether performed for real or constructed, highlight the core affinity with Waters. In *Pepi, Luci, Bom...* the woman on woman pissing/water sports scene (a double whammy, for the real action and the female protagonists); the vomit or Roman shower exhibition in the theatre aisles; giving a blow job live on stage before a large audience; the excessive violence by a brute against a woman in the prolonged rape sequence... All of these displays are simultaneously exciting and repugnant to the spectator.

Pepi, Luci, Bom y otras chicas del montón was shot entirely in Madrid, still amidst the celebratory radicalism of the Franco aftermath. It's a comic look at how different personas (alternating strengths and weaknesses) cope when they commit themselves to chance, suspending reason and restraint to follow instincts and passions. (Herein lays a comic conceit, because it neglects to deal seriously with consequences and responsibility.)

Almodóvar has always maintained that without the help and commitment of Carmen Maura and Felix Rotaeta, who appear in the film, the film could not have been made. Initially the project had no financial backers at all. But Maura and Rotaeta provided Almodóvar with contacts, eventually involving over 100 people in the production. Nobody profited financially from the film.

The resources were simply never available on the production to shoot anything as depicted in Almodóvar's original script. Throughout shooting, Almodóvar had a day job to maintain, working for the National Telephone Company. Every morning he would re-write the script, while at work, to suit the available resources. Shooting took place in the afternoons and at weekends. The first complete version lasted forty minutes, but was too short, leaving too much open. Almodóvar soon sketched a longer, more complete story, but having filmed everything thus far according to budget limitations, there was no cash for more filming. It took another year before Almodóvar found a young Catalan producer, Pepe Corominas, willing to team up and complete the film.

The final version lasts eighty minutes and involves many of the youthful, new generation of creative talents emerging in post-Franco Madrid; many of whom subsequently achieved national or international notoriety, and several talents who formed the corps of Almodóvar's later entourage.

Essentially optimistic, the film presents Spanish culture at a crossroads and the spectrum of possibilities reaching out before it. As Almodóvar says, it "is funny, clever, out of place, modern, uneven, subversive and immoral." Indeed, its willingness to leave its jagged edges and faults exposed and open to criticism, highlights the production process over end product becoming, for punk sensibility, its strongest asset!

One of the film's most radical, subversive and punk-oriented achievements (especially significant in Spain) is in the centrality and options afforded to women. This is achieved without recourse to dogmatic political correctness but instead with punk matter of fact depictions. This reflects punk's egalitarian attitude regarding sex and sexuality, which is more relevant to today's post-feminist social sensibility than the proscriptive PC feminism, which dominated socio-political discourse in the early 1980s. Further, this punk attitude towards sex and sexuality has remained a defining motif in Almodóvar's later films.

Notes

1 Luis Buñuel, *My Last Breath*, London: Fontana Paperbacks, 1985, p.92.

2 Hans Richter, *The Struggle for the Film,* Aldershot: Gower Publishing, 1986, p.164.

3 In the UK, this writer cannot recall any screenings of *Eraserhead* prior to catching it at the 1978 London Film Festival.

4 Less known and tragically beset by distribution problems since its making in 1971, so virtually unknown to nascent punks, is Jodorowsky's *The Holy Mountain*; a should-have-been proto-punk masterpiece, featuring a stunningly punk character sporting a mohawk.

5 If you really want to get hairdo-anorak, there's a distinction between mohawk and mohichan cuts defined by whether the tail extends down the back of scalp.

6 John Waters, *Shock Value*, New York: Dell Publishing, 1981, p.226.

7 Ibid, p.128.

8 Jack Stevenson, *Desperate Visions 1: Camp America,* London: Creation Books, 1996, p.98.

9 Waters, *Shock Value*, p.184.

10 Nuria Vidal, *The Films of Pedro Almodóvar*, Instituto de la Cinematografía y las Artes Audiovisuales, Ministerio de Cultura, 1988.

Pissing in the Kitchen Sink

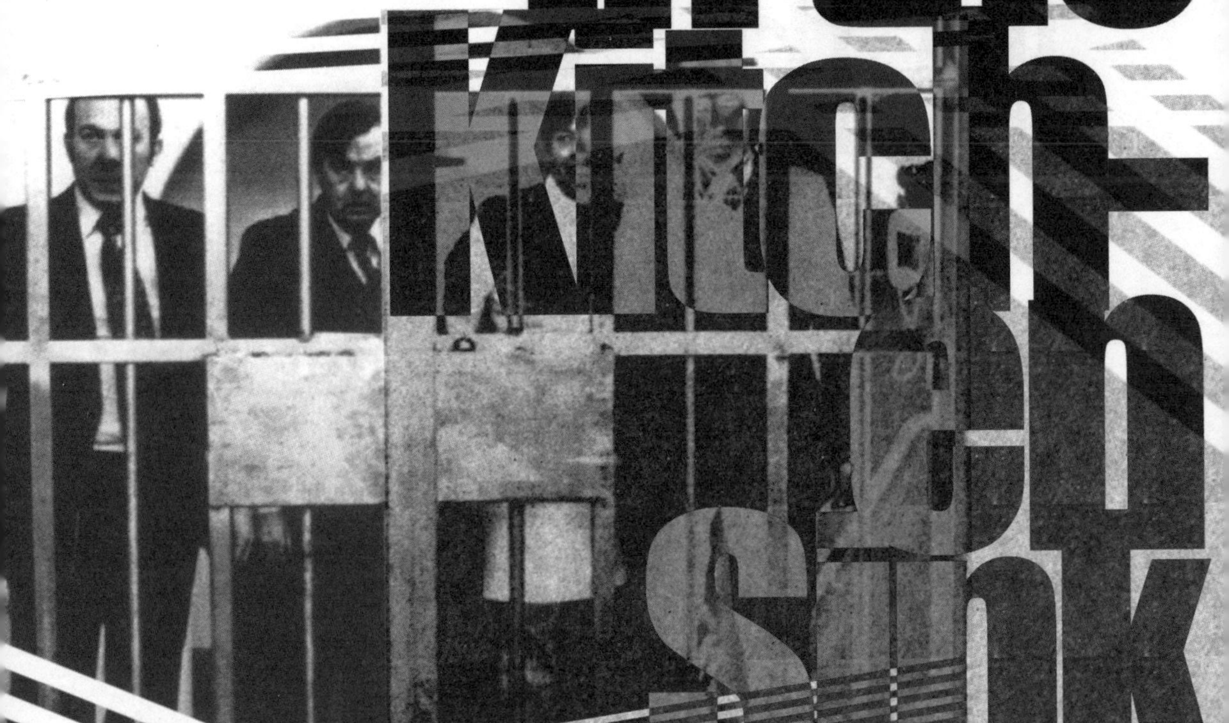

Chris Barber

In the post-war years, radical

Italian filmmakers used techniques associated with documentary to initiate a new expression of socially aware, realist cinema. Known as the Neo-Realists, they utilised aesthetic criteria, analogous with the Marxist critic George Lukacs, to create the quintessential European art movie. Britain had established a strong tradition of socially aware, documentary filmmaking since the founding of the BBC, with noted producer/directors like John Grierson. From the 1950s, largely thanks to the influence of John Osborne's play *Look Back in Anger* (1956), British fringe theatre was transformed into an arena for experimental socio-political agit-prop. By the early 1960s, angry, shit-kicking playwrights like Joe Orton and

Harold Pinter were incorporating elements of Beckett-style absurdity into their working class, kitchen-sink drama. The Free Film movement drew on all these influences to produce a new and angry style of British cinema. Realist, kitchen-sink drama became the dominant, avant-garde alternative to the popular mainstream, in British theatre, television and cinema (typified by Ken Loach from the late 1960s).

Early kitchen-sink realism is gritty, low budget, innovative and experimental in form. It shamelessly promotes working class culture, challenges censorship of sex and violence, promotes didacticism, unsettles the spectator, and exposes the contradictions and hypocrisy of unjust society — all proto-punk objectives. But despite occasional proto-punk breakaways like Lindsay Anderson's *If....*, strict, dogmatic adherence to outmoded 'realist' constructs eventuated in reams of repetitive films that were little better than soap operas, floating like decaying food scraps in a bowl of cold and festering washing-up water.

Tainted by punk attitude and sensibility, angry and innovative British filmmakers like Alan Clarke, Mike Leigh and Stephen Frears decided it was time to pull the plug and piss in the kitchen sink. By the time *Twenty Four Hour Party People* hit the screen in 2002, depictions of social realism were turned upside down. This chapter looks at the way punk attitude transformed, revivified and put the avant-garde back into British social realism.

Borstal Breakout

Advocating a tough, streetwise and anarchic attitude, British punk rockers had a natural — if slightly romanticised — affinity with young offenders. Vocalist Jimmy Pursey and Sham 69 bombastically express this in their punk anthems Borstal Breakout and Hersham Boys. Sham 69 gigs soon became rallying points for alienated and criminalised youth, particularly skinheads. But the band's initial excitement turned sour with the growth of racist and fascist politics amongst their fan base.

There were few precedents in cinema that explored the experiences of juvenile offenders in the penal system, with a couple of notable exceptions. Luis Buñuel, in Mexico, made a remarkable contribution. *Los Olvidasdos* (The Young and the Innocent, 1950) utilises stark social realism, with occasional surrealist moments, in a brutal Cain and Abel type story (with unexpected twists) about two struggling street urchins. Motivated by poverty and deprivation, they turn to crime. The younger is apprehended by the law and sentenced to a young offenders institution. But when he is trusted to venture outside with his guardian's money, he is himself mugged by his former pal. This is soon the least of his problems in a world where any hope of redemption is pure fantasy.

Francis Truffaut's *Les Quatre Cents Coups* (The Four-Hundred Blows, 1959) is an outstanding depiction of a twelve year old boy's delinquency in Paris. Scripted by Truffaut, based on his own upbringing, it stars a young Jean-Pierre Leaud as the wayward schoolboy. The title derives from the French expression for the period of adolescence when lads are expected to be problematic and rebellious. But as the film shows, expected does not mean accepted, and after his petulant parents tire of his confused state and lawbreaking, they escort him to the local police precinct to be placed in a reform school.

But it was in Britain, during the punk era, that television director Alan Clarke made the issue centre-stage. When Clarke made *Scum* for the BBC in 1977, his employers were shocked by its gritty documentary style realism and uncompromising violence. They banned it and forced Clarke to make substantial cuts. *Scum* later got theatrical distribution. In 1981, Clarke returned to the violent borstal world of young offenders in *Made in Britain* (1982), with a tough skinhead anti-hero.

Clarke was born in Seacombe, near Liverpool. A bricklayer's son, he worked as a labourer and insurance salesman before serving two years national service in Hong Kong. He emigrated to Canada to study acting and directing, returning to Britain in 1961. Clarke chose to pursue his directorial career in television, believing that it offered unique opportunities to expose and explore social exclusion. From 1969, he worked for the BBC, directing numerous TV plays and programmes.

He wanted to offer a voice to poor and wretched social outcasts, developing a stark, gritty, hardcore realist, documentary style. Clarke's concerns coincided with punk subculture in the late 1970s, culminating in one of the most controversial British films ever — *Scum*. Appalled by the production, the BBC banned it and Clarke had to re-make a tamer version, screened in 1980.

Made in Britain was also produced for television and, together with *Scum*, Clarke directed two of the finest, most realistic and controversial youth films to come out of punk Britain. Both films expose the nihilistic hopelessness of dispossessed youth, each depicting a microcosmic metaphor encapsulating society as a whole.

Clarke directed two other features, the all but forgotten *Billy the Kid and the Green Baize Vampire* (1985), and the delightfully sordid sex-comedy, *Rita, Sue and Bob Too* (1986). His many television productions pertained to a diverse array of sources, from Solzhenitsyn stories to Arthurian myths; he even directed a production of Bertolt Brecht's play, *Baal*. In 1989 he directed *Elephant*, an allegorical TV film about violence in Northern Ireland, which later inspired Gus Van Sant's award-winning movie about the Columbine High School massacre.

Scum (1977)

Alan Clarke and writer Roy Minton interviewed former borstal inmates exhaustively, before and while making *Scum*, to recreate situations as accurately as possible. Clarke also formed close working relationships with several of the actors, many of whom were not professional actors, but had relevant life experiences pertaining to events in the film.

Minton based his script almost wholly on factual incidents. In his original script, the character Carling (Ray Winstone) has a homosexual relationship with another inmate, but despite this reflecting real experience, it was considered too controversial at the time and written out. The writer stresses that his basic plot is atavistic, an individual man entering a 'bad' institution. Eventually Carling decides to take control and uses a sock loaded with billiard balls to attack his opponent. Apart from the opening shots in the van, the whole story/film is deliberately confined within the grounds of the institution.

Producer Clive Parsons stated that the BBC decision to ban *Scum* was taken by Billy Cotton; the Board of Governors initially had no objections to screening. Major objections concerned the wrist-cutting sequence; this is where trimming was demanded before its 1979 release. Mary Whitehouse also campaigned to ban the film. Several MPs joined the debate and, while some supported the ban, one argued it should be required viewing for every MP. Further support came from Channel 4, who offered to screen the original production. Because of the duration of the BBC ban, the film rights reverted to Minton and the producers, ensuring its eventual release.

Teen star Ray Winstone, who was formerly a young boxer, won immediate notoriety for his remarkable performance as Carling, the inmates' 'daddy.' In a minor role, Phil Daniels attracted due critical praise as an almost likeably inept bully, leading to more demanding roles in *Meantime* (1983) and *Quadrophenia* (1979). These streetwise youth performances by Winstone and Daniels signalled the potential of a genuinely new generation of British actors that could at last blow away the pompous 'stagecraft' traditions that long dominated the profession. (Clarke again exhibited his young talent-spotting foresight, casting Tim Roth in *Made in Britain*.)

Mick Ford's performance, as Archer, is also notable, but his character is more problematic. From one perspective, his detached individual persona, intelligently determined to antagonise the system, is both worthy of empathy and definitively punk in attitude. He also gets some of the best lines in the film. But this character is also the film's didactic vehicle, the mouthpiece for broader social and political commentary. Further, the drawing of this character, with his slightly hippie-ish/Leo Sayer haircut and polite middle-class affectations, seems less credible in context (it's difficult to believe he could escape being picked on by other inmates). Quite simply, a more streetwise punk-looking character might have better carried the part.

How does *Scum* look now? When *Scum* was made, a heated, national debate was occurring, within politics and the media, about the treatment of young offenders. Law courts had the option of sentencing juveniles to borstals or detention centres (the latter reputedly being the tougher option, based on military training camps). The high rate of inmate suicide in detention centres eventually led to their disbandment. Gradual reform has been implemented throughout the borstals, particularly with regard to bullying. There is now tighter control on the tactics used by wardens, and the presence of anti-bullying officers, to whom victims are encouraged to report incidents, whether instigated by inmates or wardens. This aside, suicide amongst inmates is again rising and current legal trends favour tough punishment regimes, reflecting public opinion; aggressive inter-racial divisions among inmates are still a major problem. Overall, the stark realism, deep focus and brutal violence of the film, as well as its broader social critique, mean *Scum* has dated surprisingly little, remaining shocking and disturbing.

Scum writer, Roy Minton, tried his hand at a girls borstal script with *Scrubbers*. Directed by Don Boyd, this curious film was released in 1982, starring Amanda York.

Made in Britain (1982)

Tim Roth makes his superb screen debut as Trevor, an obstreperous, aggressive and racist skinhead, who is also stubbornly intelligent. Throughout the (made for television) film, cinematographer Chris Menges concentrates on close-ups of Roth's snarling face, complete with swastika tattoo on forehead, making the most of small-screen limitations. Appropriate stomp-y Oi-skin/punk theme music is provided by the Exploited. The brute ambiance of documentary realism and Roth's 'feral' performance makes for uncomfortable viewing, particularly from a finger-pointing liberal or Politically Correct perspective; infusing the film with hardcore street-cred and punk attitude.

1981 seems to have been a vintage year for borstal movies. *Pixote: A Lei do Mais Fraco* is a Brazilian feature, directed and written by Hector Babenco. It's a kiddiesploitation film, which sometimes seems to try a little too hard to shock. Filmed to look brutally real, it's about a pre-adolescent boy, living for drugs and violent crime, on the streets of Sao Paulo. Predictably, he's eventually apprehended by the law and sent to a juvenile penal institution that makes *Scum*'s borstal resemble Disneyworld.

Who Killed Pixote? Fernando Ramos Da Silva, the very young and naughty kid plucked from the streets to play Pixote, won unexpected and ultimately tragic post-movie notoriety. His real life decline into misery and death at the hands of the police itself provoked a Brazilian feature length documentary over a decade later.

Bad Boys (1983)

Not to be confused with the film of the same name from 1995, this *Bad Boys* (1983) was directed by Rick Rosenthal. A brutal urban street gang war rages between two rival teenage gangs. After gang leader (Sean Penn) gains the upper hand during a scuffle, his rival gang leader takes it personally, ruthlessly pursuing a vendetta. Violence escalates causing the death of Penn's girlfriend. Penn is distraught, but his killer rival is arrested and sentenced to a juvenile correction centre for another crime. Penn gets himself caught so he can be sentenced to the same institution to avenge his lover's murder. Life inside is rougher and tougher than either lad had bargained for. All the lads must be constantly on their guard and no one can trust anyone. Vicious attacks and murders by fellow inmates are virtually a daily occurrence and the wardens don't want to know. After enduring some mean borstal situations, Penn and his rival get to fight it out, with only one walking away.

This is about as close to an American attempt at *Scum* as you'll find — if you can find it! It's a pretty obscure youthsploitation movie. American editing gives this a racy pace, sometimes bordering on comic strip machismo. However, it's a genuinely gritty and seriously violent movie, with real street cred.

The Firm (1989)

Alan Clarke's penultimate film is an excursion into the enigmatic world of soccer hooligans. These sad and confused — but extremely dangerous — lads may be too old for borstal, but you wouldn't think so from their behaviour. There's no hint of Clarke's uncomfortable empathy here; instead it provokes viewer discomfort via a total absence of empathy. Gary Oldman's character is a yuppie estate agent by day, soccer-lout Napoleon down his local pub at night; his turf is under siege by rival team psychos. Delusions of grandeur restrain Oldman's counter attack until his enemies are walking all over him. After the Stanley knives come out to perform instant facial surgery on both sides, Oldman realises only the most extreme counter attack on his enemies will rescue his collapsing reputation. Luckily, under his bed at his parent's home, in his Union Jack flag drenched childhood bedroom, he has a case bulging with nasty weapons. After a bit of bloodletting and totem initiation nonsense to enrol a new recruit, he gets his troops psyched up, armed to the teeth to wreak violent mayhem on his enemies. More violent and obscure than his previous films, Clarke encapsulates the viewer in this detached world: a silent voyeur, both close to and distanced from the action.

Don't worry about the government

Mike Leigh's *Meantime* and Stephen Frears' *My Beautiful Laundrette* (1985) share many concerns. Both are early 1980s low budget British features — London based kitchen-sink dramas that owe more to developments in British fringe theatre during the 1950s and sixties, than they do to cinema. Each film was produced by the newly augmented Channel 4 television station, which was targeting alternative and youth audiences.

Both *Meantime* and *My Beautiful Laundrette* reflect streetwise punk attitude in the decline, and aftermath, of punk. Punk as a movement always identified with working class culture and by 1978, punk's front line had aligned itself with left-wing political causes in one guise or another (like Rock Against Racism and the Anti-Nazi League). So a significant blow was taken when Thatcher's Conservatives won the 1979 general election; whatever solidarity existed among punks was smashed by the reactionary social policies of a far right-wing government. While *Rude Boy* had remained safe and boring in its adherence to kitchen-sink dogma — failing to keep up with changing socio-political dynamics — these two films each observe Britain's rapidly changing climate, and offer voices of resistance. Both suggest that (following the decline of class solidarity and the extended family) camaraderie and intense friendship might offer the last stand against exploitation. Each also considers the changing face of employment, urban life, class, race, and the family.

The son of a doctor, Leigh spent most of his childhood in Manchester's working-class neighbourhoods. Later he enrolled in the Royal Academy of Dramatic Arts, but his fascination with actors and acting was tempered by his wish to develop technical skills, and he ultimately transferred to the London Film School.

These childhood and educational experiences form the basis of Leigh's later preoccupations in his films. Like Ken Loach, Leigh was greatly influenced by *cinéma vérité* and fly-on-the-wall television documentaries, as well as French Nouveau Vague films (particularly Francois Truffaut in Leigh's case). Both directors want to engage the spectator in the real, grassroots day-to-day lives of the contemporary working class and socially deprived. But Leigh excludes Loach's well-defined political agenda, favouring detached ambiguity, making it more difficult for the spectator to draw clear-cut conclusions.

Leigh is also deeply concerned with the process of acting and the way roles are constructed. He developed a method of working closely with actors and actresses in theatre workshops, experimenting with improvisation techniques. Skeleton plot scenarios were selected from newspaper stories and developed spontaneously with improvised role-playing games. There are similarities with playwright Edward Albee's approach (like *Who's Afraid of Virginia Woolf?*, 1966). Further, Leigh works individually with each cast member alone, asking them to make lists of relatives, friends and acquaintances, listing notable characteristics for each of them. The list is then discussed in detail with Leigh, gradually excluding inappropriate names, until only the character best suited to the skeleton scenario remains. The actor/actress then assumes this role, attempting to think and act as their character would in real life; then the whole cast is brought together to act out events.

The first play Leigh filmed was *Bleak Moments* in 1971. Leigh married actress Alison Steadman, who stars in the BBC television production of Leigh's most famous play, *Abigail's Party* (1977). But it is in his 1983 television film, *Meantime,* that Leigh captures the anger and nihilism of social exclusion in punk Britain. Leigh continued to work in theatre between making TV films (including *Nuts in May* [1976] and *High Hopes* [1988]). His productions won much critical acclaim and, in 1993, his feature film *Naked* got a theatrical release. *Naked* is his most punk and nihilistic film, alongside *Meantime*. In 1996, his *Secrets and Lies* won massive critical acclaim and box-office success; unexpectedly, the film was a big hit in the United States, winning an Oscar. Leigh staunchly refused lucrative film offers from Hollywood, insisting he had no interest in directing major films; he continues to make innovative 'small' intimate films.

Meantime (1983)

Meantime was filmed on 16mm, produced by Graham Benson as a Film on Four (Channel 4) for Central Television. It involved new producers;

BBCTV produced Leigh's previous films. Channel 4 was a new entity, establishing itself when *Meantime* was made. The timing was unfortunate for Leigh because, several months after filming, Channel 4 announced its intention to distribute feature films and began shooting movies on 35mm.

Photographed with precisely observed naturalism by Roger Pratt, using real locations, *Meantime* captures perfectly the bleak desolation, boredom and hopelessness of life on Britain's kitchen-sink estates in the early Thatcher years. Detritus litters the paving, graffiti conceals walls and the lifts are too dark to see much, but at least you can smell the piss. This is real life for many in the urban wastelands, as punk sounds fade into the distance.

Meantime was Leigh's thirty-sixth production scripted via his improvisational acting method (and his thirteenth film to date). On December 1, 1983, it was first broadcast on Channel 4, having been premiered at the 1983 London Film Festival. As well as attracting substantial critical appraisal from movie reviewers, it provoked in-depth features in the *New Musical Express* and *The Face*.

In the book *The World According to Mike Leigh*, biographer Michael Coveney quotes Leigh as saying about *Meantime*:

> That is how life is for many, many people... I had this terrible flat, with a bath, no shower, over a shop... I was in the bath, listening to the radio very early in the morning, and this story came on about two unemployed kids in Warrington or St Helens or somewhere who had committed suicide. And I thought — I always go through something like this — what we're doing is irrelevant. That's what we should be doing. Something about unemployment. We were two or three years into Thatcher, it was already an issue, and it lingered in the back of my mind.[1]

Gary Oldman reveals his diverse acting skills as Coxy, the skinhead, switching comfortably between being a psychotic menace and just downright wacky. He went on to play Sid Vicious in *Sid and Nancy* (1986). In 1987, he told *Blitz* magazine that Sid and Coxy shared many characteristics with which he could identify from his own youth. During rehearsals for *Meantime*, in a Hackney factory, Oldman was nearly blinded in an accident. Tim Roth threw a bottle, which hit a fluorescent lighting strip and shattered glass onto Oldman's head. He was rushed to hospital and Roth claims stitch marks are visible in some scenes in the film.

Presumably excited by Leigh's demands on actors, all the performances in *Meantime* are simply immaculate. But shining brightest is Phil Daniels as Mark, the unemployed, streetwise youth, who exudes punk attitude and stands up for his principles. Daniels is from King's Cross, London, trained at the Anna Scher School, and based his character on an acquaintance living in the flats where he grew up. He has suggested Mark was a difficult part "because Mark would always say something to top someone else."

In 1986, *Meantime* was enthusiastically received at the San Francisco Film Festival, with commentators suggesting its suburban world presented a visual parallel to lyrics by the Sex Pistols and The Clash.

My Beautiful Laundrette (1985)

Stephen Frears was a Cambridge law student. He trained as a director in theatre at London's Royal Court, serving as assistant director to Lindsay Anderson and actor Albert Finney. In 1966, he began working in the film industry as Karel Reisz's assistant director; their working relationship continued until 1972.

Frears directed his first feature, *Gumshoe*, in 1971, starring Albert Finney; it's a hardboiled detective drama. For the next thirteen years he prolifically directed plays and films for television, working on about thirty productions. A few of these attracted outstanding critical acclaim, including his 1979 television movie, *Bloody Kids*, a doom-laden story about urban adolescents on the rampage. It was justifiably considered worthy of a limited theatrical release and became a minor cult film.

In 1984 he directed *The Hit*, a likeable little movie about a British gangster (played by Terrance Stamp) on the run in Spain from a hit man. But it was *My Beautiful Laundrette* (1985) that established his reputation as a world-class director. Over the next six years he directed four highly regarded movies, *Prick Up Your Ears* (a biopic about controversial playwright Joe Orton), *Sammy and Rosie get Laid* (both 1988), *Dangerous Liaisons* (1988) and *The Grifters* (1992).

Frears has stated he's interested in making films about different cultures and from different perspectives, often by positioning himself in the audience. He is renowned for surprising the spectator with unexpected and unconventional plot twists, which still retain their verisimilitude, despite frequently manifesting absurdist or surreal elements. He also has a knack for finding extremely talented and innovative scriptwriters, with whom he works closely.

He is most comfortable making 'small' films in Britain, with modest aims and budgets, but surpasses these limitations with innovation. His best movies also confront pertinent and contemporary socio-cultural issues. These credentials fall within the orbit of punk cinema, as realised by Frears in his minor masterpiece, *My Beautiful Laundrette* (1985). Beyond the political dialectics of class, race, gender and sexuality, and despite the importance given to these issues in the film, the essential message in *My Beautiful Laundrette* is about personal loyalty — more particularly the strength and power of loyalty to confront and resist exploitation. This message is imbued with a sense of desperate urgency appropriate to the time, because when all other strategies have failed, loyalty may offer the last chance to withstand the struggle. Further, it recognises loyalty is not an easy option and cannot be taken for granted. It necessitates deep personal commitment and, after the collapse of less personal expressions of resistance (like solidarity), loyalty (camaraderie) may offer the last chance in the struggle for integrity.

My Beautiful Laundrette sets itself crucially in the time and place where it was made. But, importantly, it suggests that the broader implications of the struggles and strategies involved are timeless, eternally part of the human condition. In one form or another, there has always been (and probably always will be) exploitation and resistance: a profoundly Nietzschean observation. The specifics of politics and morality are transient and mutable, but their expression in some form is deeply rooted in human nature, perhaps even defining humanity itself.

Such pedagogical interpretation is hardly needed or relevant to enjoy the movie, which is replete with more immediate concerns — a generosity of spirit offering almost everyone something to latch onto or empathise with. But its underlying nihilistic cynicism regarding hope, change and 'progress,' while advocating "optimism of the intellect" (as Antonio Gramsci referred to it) is a profoundly punk sentiment; likewise its manifestations in the quotidian streetwise world of ordinary lived experience. It's as basic as washing your dirty laundry!

Hanif Kureishi's screenplay is outstanding. Essentially it's a farce, but drenched in the sort of anarchic irreverence found in Joe Orton's plays. In 1986, the screenplay won Kureishi an Academy Award (Best Original Screenplay) and the New York Critics Circle Award (Best Screenplay).

My Beautiful Laundrette opened just after the peak of AIDS hysteria, in a social climate of hostility towards homosexuality and gay liberation. Frears is not gay, but his concerned, enlightened, queer-punk perspective, proved unexpectedly popular with audiences, not only in Britain, but also in Europe and the US.

Where will it end?

Early in 1976, punk rock was essentially a London thing. But in February, Howard Devoto and Pete Shelley travelled down from Manchester to London to see a Sex Pistols gig. Devoto and Shelley had formed a band called the Buzzcocks the previous year. Within weeks of returning to Manchester, they organised two Sex Pistols gigs at the Lesser Free Trade Hall. Among those who attended were a local television presenter, Tony Wilson, Morrissey (later of The Smiths), and two geezers who would be galvanised to form Joy Division (after Warsaw and before New Order). Manchester's homegrown punk scene was about to explode into action. *Twenty Four Hour Party People* (2002) is their story…

Director Michael Winterbottom was born'n'bred in Blackburn, Lancashire, in 1961; once Britain's industrial heartland and what would become the stomping ground for the real twenty-four hour party people, mythologised by the film. He began directing — on *directing*, with a couple of films on the renowned Swedish director, Ingmar Bergman. Other early television credits include episodes for popular serials, such as *Cracker* for ITV in 1993, and the BBC drama *Family* in 1994. The following year, Winterbottom directed a feature, *Butterfly Kiss*, a controversial British road movie about a couple of lesbian spree killers. Also in 1995 was *Go Now*, a romantic drama with multiple sclerosis and Robert Carlyle. His other titles include *Welcome to Sarajevo* and *I Want You*.

It is in *Wonderland* (1999), a story of life on a kitchen-sink council estate, that his ability to present realist drama with a fresh, contemporary eye is fully realised. He followed this with *The Claim* (2000), *In This World* and *Heartlands* (2002) and *Bright Young Things* (2003). 2002 was a busy year for Winterbottom, who returned to his Manchurian youth to direct (and edit) *Twenty Four Hour Party People*. Further to the movie's meticulous appreciation of punk aesthetics (exhibited both in form and content), Winterbottom's direction suggests awareness of an extraordinary diversity of cinematic techniques and traditions.

The director expresses an appreciation of European art cinema of the 1960s and 1970s, in particular the films of German director, Rainer Werner Fassbinder. Winterbottom credits Fassbinder with an ability to portray "real life" in the "recognisable world," capturing "elements of normality". Fassbinder was a prolific director throughout the 1970s, making innovative, low budget features, which range from prosaic product to movie masterpieces. He was a bohemian outsider, queer and alcoholic, with a pessimistic, radical intellectual sensibility which found expression in his films; he was also a talented actor and accomplished playwright. Jean-Luc Godard greatly influenced Fassbinder, who developed his own independent film factory (similar to Warhol's set-up). It relied on the collective efforts of his friends, many of whom were actresses, actors and cine technicians. Many of his films exhibit his remarkable ability to sensitively capture the gritty, obsessive and often sordid, quotidian lives of ordinary or socially excluded people. Fassbinder also had a knack for capturing the surreal and frequently cruel fringes of harsh reality. His films include *Fear Eats the Soul* (1974), *Satan's Brew* (1976) and *Querelle* (1982).

Winterbottom surely realises "Fassbinder's simple directness" for observed reality in *Twenty Four Hour Party People*, with the additional achievement of making this appear effortless. It's notable in the cock-crowing children's television jingle when Curtis tops himself (the broadcast of which, apparently, coincided with Curtis' actual death); in Joy Division's dressing room after the club riot, and in the absurdly mundane encounters that frequent Wilson's television job.

The director helped to provide a substantial amount of informative material about making this movie. It's duly noted this is his most personal film to date, and that he, like many others in the north west, used to watch Wilson's local reports on TV. Winterbottom also shares with Fassbinder an "obsession with truth and detail, cinema that's felt and thought about." But Winterbottom also recognises the insidious limitations and traps which impede this objective, necessitating that to best achieve this, you cannot take it too literally; perspective is relative. He claims most of his inspiration comes while working on-set: ideas and parameters considered *a priori* are often seen from a different perspective in the working environment.

Winterbottom determines to ask the spectator difficult questions and provoke serious thought throughout. Unlike many of his predecessors in this tradition, and in tune with the time, Winterbottom understands that he can fail by overusing audience distancing devices, alienating the spectator instead of inspiring recondite consideration. To this end, he uses his eclectic awareness of avant-garde techniques with cautious abundance, realising that pleasure can be the most provocative tool.

Alan Partridge... Steve Coogan... Could the real Tony Wilson please show himself...?

Steve Coogan is renowned for his many comic personas on television, in particular regular slots alongside Chris Morris, and his own BBC series, playing bungling radio DJ, Alan Partridge. Coogan personifies dry, sardonic wit, with deadpan delivery and post-modernist ambiguity for the post-ironic age. His star casting as Tony Wilson in *Twenty Four Hour Party People* received wide critical acclaim. Many of Wilson's closest associates stated Coogan's portrayal perfectly captured the real Tony Wilson.

The real Tony Wilson was born in Manchester. In the early 1970s he got a job as a journalist for Granada Television, who shifted him around over the years as a presenter on various programmes, including the station's weekly rock music slot, *So It Goes,* which in 1976 happened to coincide with the emergence of punk rock in London. Wilson was one of the many in Britain at that time who was bored and dissatisfied with what was going down and was waiting for punk, or something like it, to happen. And when it did, he seized the opportunity to expose a bigger audience to what was happening on music's cutting edge. He was also helping the bands get wider exposure, when most of the media was closing ranks and denying airtime.

With Wilson, it was also personal. He was well informed and kept up to date with what was going on in politics, the arts and music. He had a good education and was aware of obscure, alternative and underground subcultures (like Situationism, comprising an exclusive group of revolutionary artists and intellectuals, whose complex philosophy had a significant impact on the Paris student riots in 1968).

He went to the first Sex Pistols gig in Manchester, claiming what he saw was "nothing short of an epiphany," and realised he was in a position to promote this exciting phenomenon. Over the next few months, *So It Goes* televised live performances by the Sex Pistols, Siouxsie and the Banshees, The Stranglers, The Clash, The Jam and more. This wasn't enough for Wilson; he wanted to be more involved and set out to open a punk venue. At Manchester's Paradise Lounge, the landlord was prepared to hire out the venue one night per week, on Fridays; Wilson called it Factory Club Night. New punk bands were forming all over Manchester, and this was the venue they needed to perform.

From that first wave of new punk bands, Wilson recognised the potential of Joy Division (who actually hassled him for gigs). He wanted to do all he could to help them develop and became a sort of surrogate manager, a role he would undertake for varying periods with many bands over the next fifteen years, in particular New Order and the Happy Mondays. But he also wanted a band he could mould from scratch and take on a fully committed management role; A Certain Ratio fulfilled this function.

The Factory name and idea would endure and expand, becoming an umbrella organisation that would facilitate a variety of associated functions. It appealed to Wilson because of its denotations with Andy Warhol's Factory in New York, a source of inspiration for him.

It was the Buzzcocks who really set the agenda for Manchester's first wave of punk bands. Howard Devoto recalls the release of their *Spiral Scratch* EP (early 1977):

> There were no record labels up in Manchester then... A lot of people in our situation would have realised... But we had some other sort of wherewithal, which made us borrow money from Pete's dad, book a recording studio and have records made.[2]

The Buzzcocks did it themselves, inventing their own record label, New Hormones. Boon recollects "There was a feeling... that the record could illustrate part of the 'do it yourself' Xerox/cultural polemic that had been generated." Even the picture sleeve, of the band mounting some statue, was snapped on a Polaroid camera. Musically, "it took about three hours, with another two for mixing"; sleeve notes give it to you straight, how it was done, literally listing the production process.

Now we can cut back to Tony Wilson, the importance of Manchester's early punk scene, and Winterbottom's sensitive direction (pertaining to both form and content) of *Twenty Four Hour Party People*; there was nothing new about independent record labels (Virgin, for example) when Factory suddenly gained status as the radical chic vanguard of punk rock production. To believe that is just crude snobbery. But the Buzzcocks had achieved something far more radical and useful; Wilson and some of his contemporaries like Joy Division were among the first people to fully understand this and recognise its further potential. This was the truly innovative dynamic that Wilson was looking for and would enable him to play a significant part in Manchester's punk and post-industrial renaissance.

Thankfully, the history and significance of punk rock, in all its diverse expressions, has found its perfect commentator and spokesperson in author Jon Savage. Savage summarises the full importance of the Buzzcocks' DIY record production and distribution process in ten words:

> Its aesthetics were perfectly combined with the means of production.[3]

Thus Tony Wilson (and Alan Erasmus) embarked on creating Factory Records: a new and independent record label, recording studio (selecting the finest music/sound producer, Martin Hannett), in-house niche marketing, design and packaging facilities, and a uniquely alternative internal working/management structure (whose faults could sometimes be as disastrous as its achievements could be inspirational). The Factory process would also lead to The Hacienda venue.

Don't give up the day job! Whatever parallels can, but probably shouldn't, be drawn between Wilson's and Warhol's Factorys, at least Wilson, unlike Warhol, didn't end up on the Factory floor with his body bleeding and torn by seven bullets (although he sometimes came close!). Now Wilson's back, working at Granada TV, which is cool because whatever mistakes were made handling other people's cash, he didn't siphon off a private stash for his personal comfort. What worth the cultural legacy — *Twenty Four Hour Party People* says it all — and a fuckin' good time was had by all!

Twenty Four Hour Party People was a brash and audacious project from its inception, especially in British cinema. The task of realising relatively recent historical events, in a feature length movie, is usually only attempted to exploit the immediate aftermath of a media deluge still fresh in the minds of the mainstream British public — like Sheila Payne's prostitution scandal in *Personal Services* (1987) or

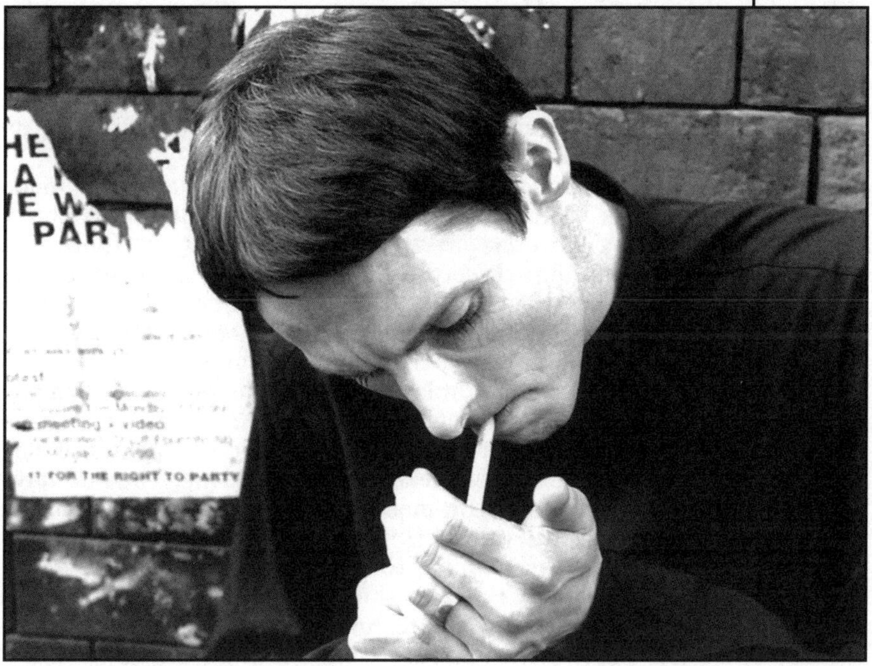

Sean Harris as Ian Curtis; *Twenty Four Hour Party People*

the Nick Leeson merchant banking fiasco in *Rogue Trader* (1999). Or where public interest in recent history has been sustained or revived by later events (*The Battle Of Britain* [1969] covering events continuously revived in memorials etc, or *The Krays* [1990], gangsters whose prison sentences were effectively served, entitling them to seek release). One major hurdle is that many of the people/characters involved are still alive. No movie will please everyone concerned and some related persons might be upset by depictions, publicly contradicting and protesting against the screening of such a film, or even seeking legal injunctions or financial compensation. So when dealing with living histories likely to attract only minority or specialised interest, the risk is just too great. The best you can expect is a rigorous documentary, relying on original archive material and corroborated testimonials, to override objections and provide cost-effective material resources.

Twenty Four Hour Party People managed to involve all the real, living characters portrayed and, unusually, win universal favour for the end product, attracting only minor, well-meaning criticisms. For example, Peter Hook (the real one) of Joy Division/New Order, commented on the film's humour, saying the musicians took themselves more seriously at the time than depicted.

Any attempt to recreate living history in a feature film is bound to require creative compromise and innovation — mythologising — that presents the spectator with a cut-down, elliptical and enjoyable representation of actual events, ideally conveying the authentic intensity and spirit of their actuality, and exciting broader or renewed interest by creating mythology. In other words, transforming social history into cultural mythology. Even Hollywood movie corporations are reluctant to produce living mythologies. Oliver Stone's *The Doors* (1991) is an excellent and pertinent example of mythologising living history with only obscure cult appeal and turning it into a successful blockbuster; however, this was only possible thanks to the determined efforts of its already commercially successful director.

So it's remarkable that *Twenty Four Hour Party People* was made at all, being reliant on Winterbottom's determination and the economic advantages of filming with the latest digital technology — there is a tradition among great film directors of mastering cutting edge cine technology to realise new visual potential, like John Ford's use of deep focus. Technology aside, another notable achievement of *Twenty Four Hour Party People* is the innovative diversity of techniques employed to embellish its mythology. One notable example is the inclusion of cameo appearances by real people historically associated with the story. These appearances include Mark E. Smith, the vocalist and songwriter of The Fall (originally associated with Manchester's punk scene, The Fall have subsequently remained one of the most obscure and innovative music acts for over a quarter-century), and Howard Devoto (original singer and songwriter in the Buzzcocks, who left to form Magazine).

Twenty Four Hour Party People is shot on digital video and remains a cutting edge example of how this technology can be used in cinema — only one other digital video feature comes to mind as its technical equal: Jean-Luc Godard's *Eloge De L'amour* (2001). Everything about it is slick: contrast of colour, fast editing and montage, smooth, often hand-held, camerawork, depth of field, seamless special effects, shot variety, audio quality, occasional use of split screen and monochrome photography, title sequence, use of overlays, transfer of material filmed on other mediums, and so on... Technically it's a *tour de force* — the shape of things to come? The cutting edge of British cinematic social realism has ditched the old sink and refurbished the whole fuckin' kitchen!

Notes

1 Michael Coveney, *The World According to Mike Leigh*, London: Harper Collins, 1997, p. 171–2.

2 Jon Savage, *England's Dreaming*, London: Faber & Faber, 1991, p. 296.

3 Ibid, p. 297.

Punk-sploitation

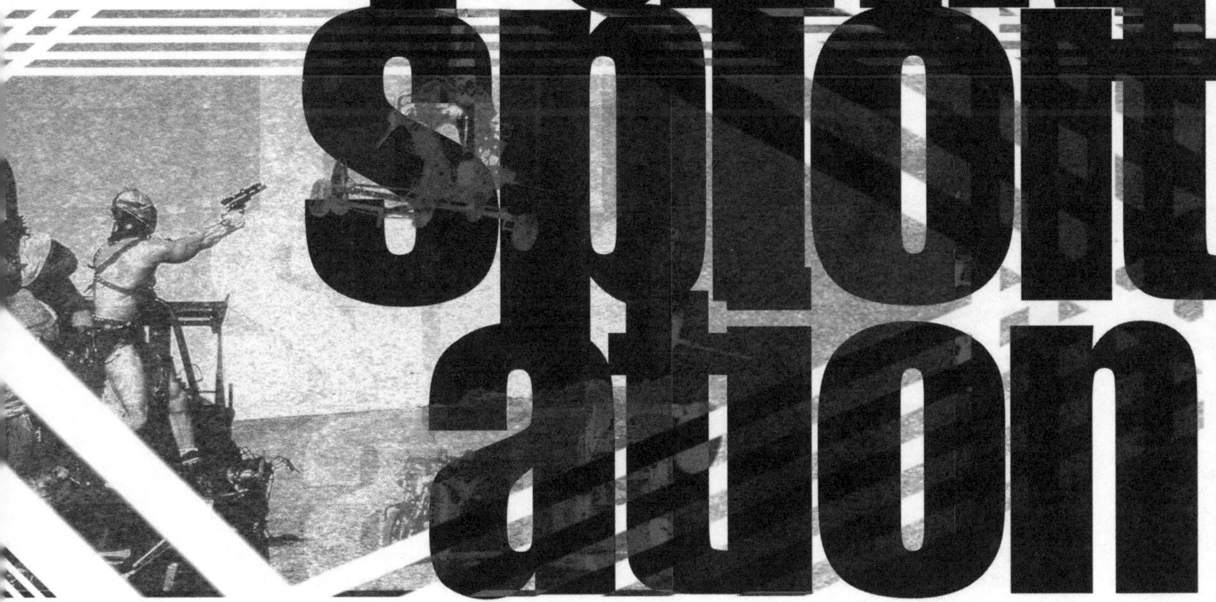

Chris Barber

Since *The Wild One*, youth trends

have provided a lucrative market and inspiration for low budget filmmakers. Punk is no exception, finding expression in the horror and science fiction genres as well as youthsploitation.

The Driller Killer (1979) is an outstanding example. Abel Ferrara, the director (under the alias Jimmy Laine) stars as Reno, the Driller Killer. This low budget punk splatter movie is one of the most notorious and controversial psycho films ever made — thanks to the British media's 'video nasties' campaign and the British Board of Film Censors (BBFC) video ban. Actually, the film depicts a serious and realistic account of an ordinary guy's breakdown into madness. None of his victims are women, breaking dramatically with genre conventions in a film that suggests the influence of Polanski, Godard and Warhol, as much as Scorsese's *Taxi Driver* and Tobe Hooper's *The Texas Chainsaw Massacre*.

Ferrara also wrote songs performed by the film's punk rock band, who are central and noisy protagonists in the plot. Gritty urban street-cred captures New York's real seedy underbelly, where the poor, wretched and homeless are left to rot. There's social commentary with attitude amidst the misery of a daily struggle for survival in a sink or swim society. The film shocks not only through its visceral violence, but also via hallucination montages. Some details pertaining to Reno's life and relationships are blurred, adding to his intrigue and displacement and echoing Reno's state of mind; his own sense of confusion and turmoil over his identity. His uncertainty and feelings of ineffectiveness are a source of anxiety, contributing to his mental breakdown. Ferrara's unique vision expresses the anger and indignation of the punk generation with singular intensity.

Death Warmed Up (1984) is a New Zealand production and a punk psycho-zombie flick: an innovative, low budget, exploitation genre-buster, with a healthy balance of shock tactics, splatter, sadism, nudity, profanity, body counts, psychedelic effects, nihilism and misanthropy. It's directed and co-scripted by David Blyth, maintaining tension and pace throughtout its eighty-five minutes. Michael Hurst stars as Michael Tucker, a petulant, belligerent, antipodean cross between blond-haired/ blue-eyed Aryan beast and shit-kicking punk with attitude! He begins by blowing away his parents with a double-barrelled shotgun, after he has been molested and brainwashed by a mad scientist intent on turning mental patients into rampaging zombies. Michael Heath co-wrote the screenplay with Blyth, and David Huggett's slick'n'quick editing sustains the zippy pace. This is cheap, rip-roaring, nasty, punk fun from start to finish. It rips off just about every cult, American sci-fi and horror movie of the previous decade, jumbles them all up and re-presents them with shameless, low budget, innovative panache.

Mad Max (1979)
Mad Max 2: The Road Warrior (1981)

Skin-tight black leathers and glistening chrome zips, trooper boots and spiky haircut, surviving alone in the post-apocalyptic wastelands — the ultimate action punk *ubermensch*. In the not too distant future, civilisation has been destroyed by total world war and oil is worth more than human life. Some dream of a new start beyond the struggle for survival, while marauding tribes of nomadic punks have alternative plans…

Essentially a genre-busting cliff-hanger/action movie (and they don't come more action-packed) set in a post-industrial dystopia, *Mad Max 2: The Road Warrior* (1981) is a contender for best Australian film and contains some of the finest movie stunts seen on the screen. It is also one of only a few movie sequels to improve on its original, *Mad Max* (1979). Starring the young, ruggedly sexy and little known Mel Gibson as Max, George Miller directs both films, mythologising the future as hyper-real medieval sci-fi, on a Nietzschean existentialist highway to nowhere — an ultra-violent brave new world where survival of the fittest is the order of the day.

Max hits the road (in *Mad Max*) as a happily married small town Australian cop and father, suddenly forced to deal with big crime

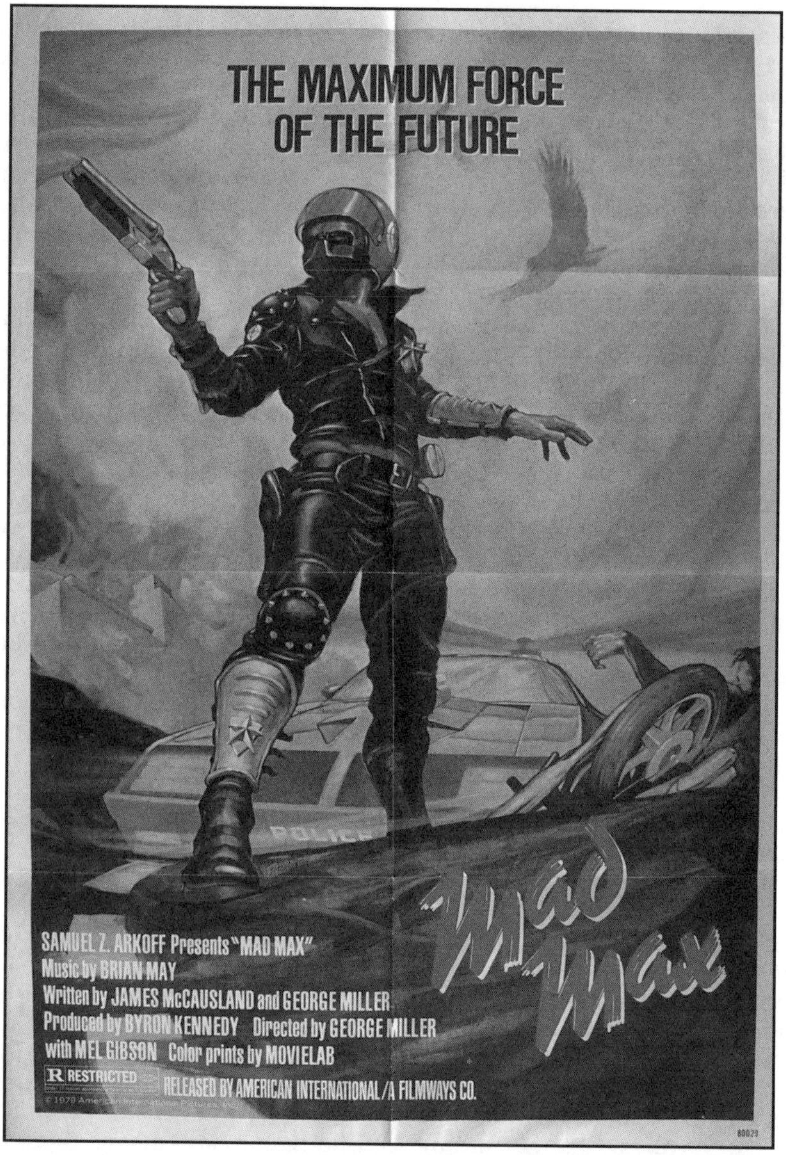

problems (with barely a hint of his later punk attitude and street cred). With the world's oil supply almost depleted, international superpowers struggle for control of the diminishing resources, culminating in a super-war of mass annihilation. No one escapes the fallout of anarchy and violence, even in the remote outer-regions of the outback, where patrolman Max and his old guard colleagues naïvely believe they can still uphold peace and order. But the Glory Riders motorcycle gang hits town, a ragamuffin alliance of criminals that regards the highway as *their* territory (a power metaphor) and ultimately massacre Max's wife and child. His life, love and future decimated, the angry Max ruthlessly avenges the murder of his family, signalling his own irredeemable arrival as Mad Max (in every sense).

Max (in *Mad Max 2: The Road Warrior*) is the ultimate comic strip punk caricature. It's not just his DIY punk-style clothes and haircut, it's also his attitude. Max resists identifying with structured, organised and hierarchical groups, and the ethical codes that define them, whether survival of the strongest, a nostalgic drive to rebuild the past civilised order, or a quasi-mystical/religious search for higher values. However, he has a conscience and makes sacrifices for others when he considers it fair or practical: an outsider and lone, existentialist warrior.

The hyper-real is a modern representation: more real and more explicit than we are capable of perceiving while engaged in the action. This is how *Mad Max 2* captures and depicts a punk, post-industrial and post-apocalyptic dystopia. For all the comic strip clichés, choreographed action sequences and fast editing, it seems all too real (allegorical). It ambushes the spectator's consciousness via the visceral nastiness of the violence, through the simple and eternal Darwinian survivalist options, the *being-in-itself-for-others* functionality of objects (recycling etc); it's apparent in the combination of dark and deep-rooted paganism, medieval functionalism, referential contemporariness, and future practicality, which pervades this film (post-history as pre-history as mythology).

Max is beyond good and evil; he is amoral. Notably this amoral, non-judgmental perspective is what encapsulates the spectator in the whole film:

> Mel Gibson called his character "a closet human being" who doesn't want to be involved with other human beings because he believes an emotional investment will be too painful and also compromise his chances of survival... He is destined to roam the wilderness alone because he is still tortured by demons of the past... If Max is grand enough to be designated a hero, he would of course deny it... One of their common traits is that they are often reluctant to assume the status of hero.[1]

Liquid Sky (1982)

When New York's chic new wave becomes old news, the decadent narcissism of blank generation doom and gloom turns in on itself... there's nowhere left to go except sex, death and outer space. *Liquid Sky* is a truly unique and extraordinary little film, a real oddity abundant with punk/new wave sensibility. It encapsulates the viewer in its own world, on its own terms. A low budget independent production, it's experimental and cunningly innovative. Made in New York, *Liquid Sky* is directed by Slava Tsukerman, a Russian émigré — an alien — who had lived among New York's bohemian subculture for five years, simultaneously thriving on its creative energy while critical of its perverse nihilism.

In addition to co-writing the script with Tsukerman and Nina V. Kerova, actress Anna Carlisle plays the two central characters, punk girl Margaret and new wave lad, Jimmy. Both characters are top New York new wave glamour/fashion models that are promiscuous and bisexual; each is self-obsessed and feels threatened by the other. Marge is also a junkie and in a long-term lesbian relationship.

Liquid Sky was made on a meagre budget and acting, or lack of, is where the film's limited resources are most obvious. Carlisle's spellbinding screen presence — in both roles — is a real treat. Originally from Connecticut, Carlisle moved to New York to enrol in the School of Visual Arts, intent on becoming a painter. But alternative visual media excited her more, learning holography and making videos for exhibition galleries. Her tutor, Bob Brady, encouraged her to develop her acting ability, and she landed a modelling job with New York's new wave agency, La Rocka, who integrated performance art and fashion modelling for designers like Zoran and Julia Morton. Carlisle's acting skills in the self-directed Super-8 film, *Fish*, were enough for Tsukerman to offer her the leading role in *Liquid Sky*.

The photography and camerawork throughout the film are mesmerising and superior to many movies boasting twenty times its budget, due to the efforts of another Russian, Neyman, who had directed photography and handled the special effects on movies prior to *Liquid Sky,* including *Soul* (1975) and *Mayakovsky Laughs* (which garnered international acclaim for its technical dexterity and experimental formalism). In *Liquid Sky,* Neyman employs panning camerawork, close-ups, unexpected angles and cheap technical tricks creating a unique saturated sci-fi look.

Set in New York City's fashionable, decadent and bohemian punk club scene, the young inhabitants are all too narcissistic and self-absorbed to notice the alien invasion in their midst. Aliens possess special powers, and have flown their saucer from the furthest reaches of the universe. They consume and thrive on the energy exuded by drugged-up youths when they're fucking. Energy peaks at the point of orgasm. Of course, the punks' sexual proclivities are as polymorphously varied as their spiky haircuts and chic make-up. There are allusions to Andy Warhol's Factory circuit: the continuously drugged-up punks can't resist posing for flashing cameras and swooning admirers. Since every night is party night, the aliens can gorge themselves with alacrity. At the moment of orgasm, the victims suddenly vanish in a psychedelic pyrotechnic flash.

There are several superbly choreographed futuristic nightclub scenes, and a bizarre original electro soundtrack. A variety of innovative, low budget special effects are used to disrupt events with colourfully abstract psychedelic storms. Designer make-up, customised punk costumes and chic interior set-designs combine throughout to make a hypnotically watchable whole.

The three-way joint script/screenplay is laden with much crass dialogue, perhaps due to the director's limited English at the time. Tsukerman also worked on the joint music score, with Brenda Hutchinson and Clive Smith; the plodding, dated, droning synthesiser racket — minimal with occasional Baroque flourishes — is frequently annoying. Acting (except Carlisle) is ridiculously camp and calls for improvement.

Looking at the film now, over twenty years after its very limited

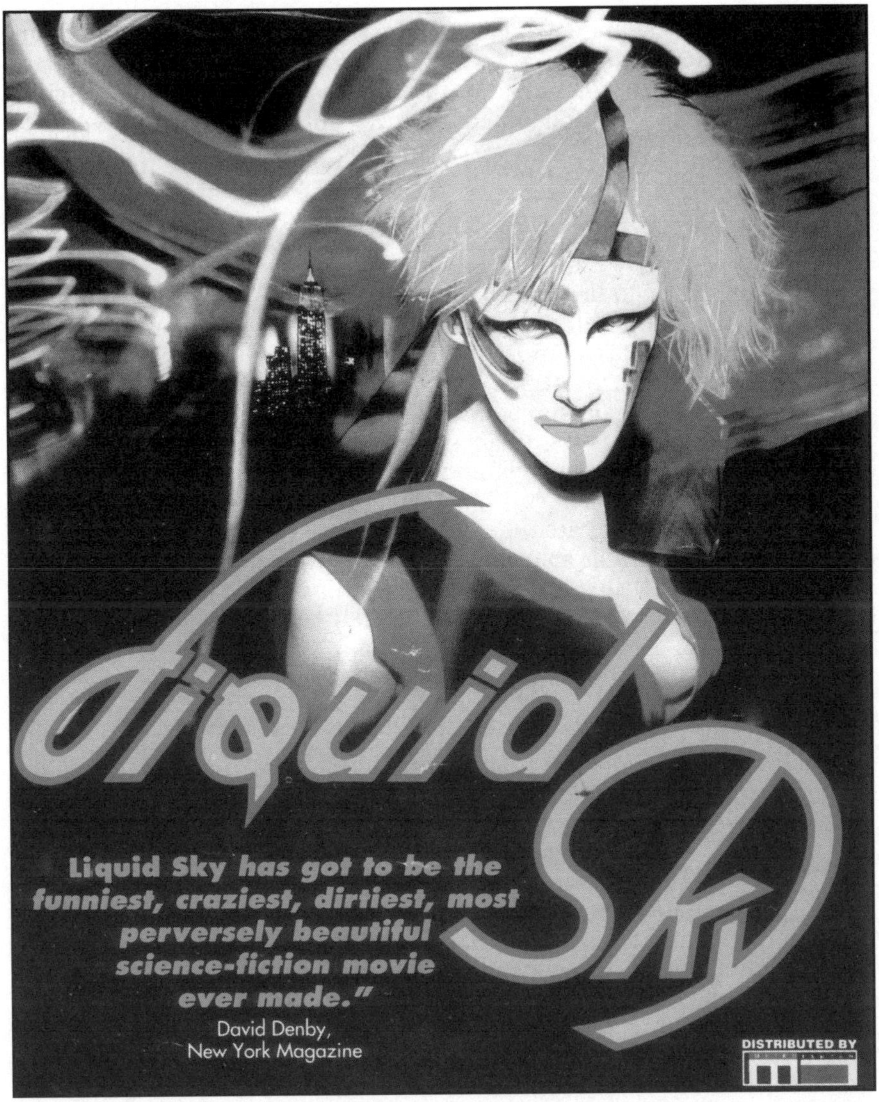

alternative cinema circuit release, *Liquid Sky* remains a visual feast. This is particularly impressive for a science fiction flick, largely inspired by its contemporary, new wave chic aesthetic sensibility, with a production budget that was more virtual than reality. Its flaws can be overlooked as adding to the overall cult eccentricity, and its criticisms transmute into creative credits — apart from the minimalist and repetitive synthesiser soundtrack, which remains obtrusive, despite its (presumed) futuristic intent. This is not just a consequence of the availability of vastly superior electro music/sound production technology, but also a reflection of artistic music trends peculiar to its time and place.

The creative renaissance inspired by New York's new wave/punk rock subculture of the late 1970s maintained an avant-garde edge with a more purist industrial/post-industrial aesthetic into the 1980s, recognising the potential of electro/synthesiser music. This facilitated a conjunction with the dogmatic minimalism fashionable among the city's high art and critical establishment. Hence contemporary composers like Steve Reich and Philip Glass, and high-concept performance artists like Laurie Anderson, were getting pissed in the same bars as David Byrne and Patti Smith.

This had positive and negative side effects. It continued to be artistically productive and its audience proliferated into the popular mainstream. The quality varied considerably, but regardless increased in value, now able to fetch top dollar. Alternatively — or rather at the expense of its alternative/underground status — the new wave lost most of its street cred, DIY aesthetic, creative anger, suicidal tendencies and relentless existential pessimism. The new wave's new attitude became chic indifference. Thus its alliance with crude camp expression, effete narcissism, and the obscene glamour and fashion industries.

Liquid Sky remains a cult masterpiece because it retains a back to basics new wave formal attitude, while anticipating later developments, and finds no comfortable solutions. What was once a shit-kicking creative subculture with attitude is decadent and selling out. This is New York's new wave becoming everything it started out rebelling against.

Repo Man (1984)

How a sensitive LA punk gets to be a hard-boiled car repossession merchant, hounded by UFO fanatics and Christians, kidnapped by government agents, rescued by gun-toting urban guerrillas, zapped by atomic radiation, and wafted off into alien hyperspace in a 1964 Chevy Malibu...

If you find film auteurism fun or useful, Alex Cox is a punk auteur. Punk rock and attitude are essential to three of his movies (*Repo Man, Sid and Nancy* and *Straight to Hell*) and could be claimed as a leitmotif in all his productions. Cox claims punk inspired him to make films *a priori* and its attitude informs his working approach. That he makes this claim could be problematic, and advocating qualitative improvement from film to film would be a perverse attribute to apply. But such formalities aside, Cox's punk auteurism needn't be controversial.

Cox won a Fulbright Fellowship to study film criticism and production at the University of California, Los Angeles (UCLA), for three years. Cox claims he soon hated LA, but realised it was the place to be to work in film. At UCLA, he was assistant director to Rose-Marie Turko on *Scarred*; Cox also played a porn star character role in this film about street prostitution from a feminist perspective. His own final student film immediately challenges convention by having two titles, *Edge City* (at the beginning) and *Sleep is for Sissies* (at the end). Cox spent two years making it, at a cost of $8,000, largely from his own pocket, which he earned part time doing jobs such as lecturing film students. It's set in LA and stars Cox as an artist living in a near police state (an apt description of LAPD's corrupt politicised policing methods throughout the 1970s and 1980s). The confusing plot is packed with eccentric characters, including an assassin and a bank robber, and ends with Sid Vicious singing My Way.

Between studying, filmmaking and part time work, Cox frequented punk gigs, catching touring British bands and becoming a feature of LA's punk scene. After graduating, he stayed in LA seeking breaks in the film industry, but it proved to be a fairly tough few years for him. He held his resolve by writing film scripts and eventually found an agent, Stephanie Mann, who organised his portfolio and had the connections to circulate his scripts among movie executives. This got Cox some interviews and almost secured deals on a couple of occasions. But as the early 1980s trundled on, nothing quite materialised. Cox was on the verge of giving up when he fortuitously bumped into a couple of former UCLA pals, Peter McCarthy and Jonathon Wacks. They had established a company making commercials, Wacks-McCarthy. They hired Cox as a director and scriptwriter, with a view to expanding the company into producing movies.

Cox enthusiastically began writing a script called *The Hot Club*, based on the short story *Exterminator!* by William Burroughs. The final script was much liked but considered too expensive to make. Cox was asked to write a new, low budget version, recycling sections of his previous script where possible. One of his part time jobs had been as a car repossession merchant; the result was *Repo Man*.

Even then things didn't go as expected. The script floated around for nine months without a deal, before finally it fell into the hands of businessman Michael Nesmith (ex-The Monkees). He was most impressed and had executive contacts at Universal Pictures, who offered $1.5 million on a negative pick up deal. This necessitated that a good approximation of the script had to be completed by a pre-set date, in order to pick up the cash. The deal was agreed and *Repo Man* went into production, but Cox was by now pretty cynical about Hollywood's movie business.

Repo Man's soundtrack includes the pick of West Coast punk bands: The Plugz, Fear, The Circle Jerks (who briefly appear as the lounge band), Black Flag, Juicy Bananas and Suicidal Tendencies, as well as proto-punk trailblazer, Iggy Pop. (Tito Larriva and Steven Hufsteter of The Plugs also provide the incidental Ennio Morricone/spaghetti western style non diegetic music.)

Harry Dean Stanton is superbly cast as Bud: on the surface a cool, cynical, hack repo man, but underneath a paranoid misanthrope who takes affronts to his professional status too personally — Stanton was an ideal star selection, his acting career long associated with beatniks and alternative, offbeat films. Emilio Estevez manages a fine and convincing performance as Otto, the sensitive punk rebel, who is forced to compromise his principles, but in contrast to Bud maintains a professional sense of proportion and dignity. Sy Richardson renders a suitable caricature as Lite, the psychotic repo loner.

Dutch cameraman Robby Muller was chosen because of his previous cinematography on films directed by Wim Wenders and Jim Jarmusch, as well as *To Live and Die in LA*. The production took six weeks to shoot in 1983, and the final cut lasts ninety-four minutes. Initially, Universal

Pictures mis-marketed *Repo Man* as an action movie for drive-ins, and it bombed. Repackaged as an art-house cult movie, it was a huge success.

> I found the idea of *Repo Man* gaining this cult audience quite odd... It's a compendium of weird ephemera... Pop culture aspects of punk rock.
> ***Alex Cox***

Repo Man is replete with pop-cult references. Otto's cynical and detached, but caring and truth-seeking, repo man, is a contemporary variation on the hard-boiled detective of noir novels and movies. Mass paranoia in the US was a common undercurrent in 1950s sci-fi B-movies. But the most explicit reference in *Repo Man* is to the 1955

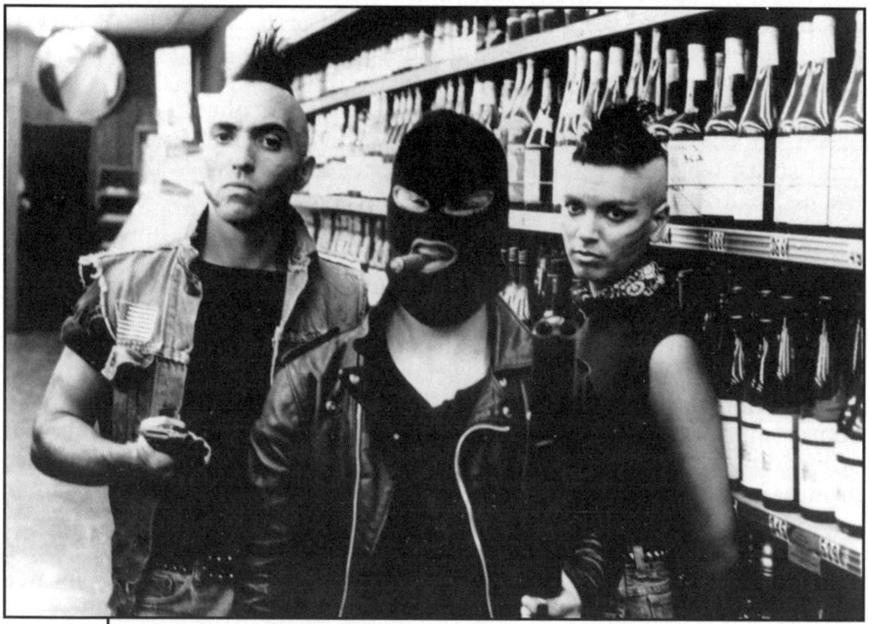

Tough guys and gal (above), and Emilio Estevez and Harry Dean Stanton (next page), *Repo Man*

noir, *Kiss Me Deadly*, by cult director Robert Aldrich; both films concern a powerful, glowing and inexplicable force concealed in a car boot; like Pandora's Box, with apocalyptic potential, it may hold the power to alter the whole course of humanity. Godard's *Alphaville* and *Weekend* also suggest themselves, for their dislocation of time and space by using real contemporary locations, depictions of the hypocritical and fascist undercurrents pervading capitalist democracies, and the omnipotent potential of social fragmentation and chaos. Mass paranoia and government/state secret service surveillance tactics refer to *The Manchurian Candidate* (1962) and *The Conversation* (1974). It's probable *Repo Man* impacted on numerous cult movie directors of the late 1980s and 1990s; Quentin Tarantino, in particular, springs to mind.

One time me and the smooth brother went out on a special fumigation job... This man is a sort of crank... been out here a number of times... claims he has rats under the house... We'll have to put on a show for him. Well, he hauls out one of those tin pump guns loaded with cyanide dust and I am subject to crawl under the house through spider webs and broken glass to find the rat holes and squirt the cyanide into them.

"Watch yourself under there" said the cool brother. "If you don't come out in ten minutes I'm coming in after you"[2]

What remains of *Exterminator!* in *Repo Man*? The Burroughs story (less than half a dozen pages) and Cox's *Repo Man* script are both based on part time jobs undertaken by their writers; both exterminators and repossession merchants are widely regarded as outsider, twilight jobs, evoking two social taboos: dirt and debt. *Exterminator!* is also a volume of stories by Burroughs, and the general wise-assed, street cred tone (see extract above) is reflected in *Repo Man*.

More significantly, William Burroughs is the supreme counterculture guru. The godfather of the beatniks remains a dogmatic non-conformist and social outsider, and anyone with the remotest interest in counterculture is sure to have stumbled upon his legacy. Nowhere has this legacy had more impact than on the punk, new wave and post-industrial movements.

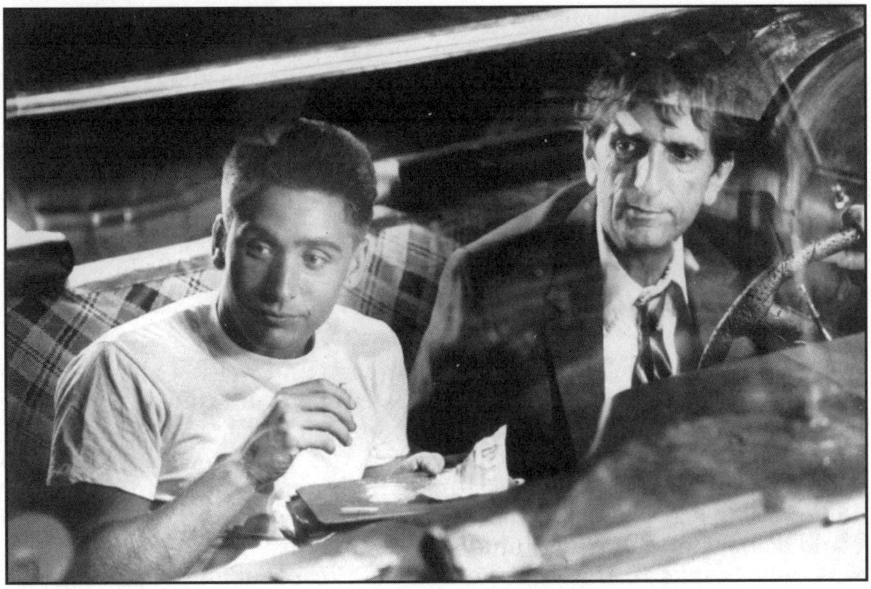

The sinister and corrupt abuse of power by governments as a means of social control and the deployment of science — particularly through surveillance technology — towards this end, as well as clandestine conspiracies between powerful corporate and government concerns, are approached similarly both by Burroughs and Cox. Chaos and lawlessness as antidotes to social order, absurd and surreal aspects of day-to-day life, the constant threat of the bomb (nuclear war), the nightmarish potential of runaway science and self-awareness through vigilant de-programming are all shared concerns. *Repo Man*'s chaotic hospital sequence could be matched by episodes in several Burroughs novels. The film's narrative structure is also episodic and sometimes elliptical, another feature of Burroughs' novels.

Look at the watches... They've got no hands. And there are other subtle prop placements, like a generic newspaper box and air freshener. Bud and Otto taking speed in the car is pertinent in that not only does it keep repo men awake long hours, but amphetamine sulphate is also the illegal narcotic most associated with punks.

More specific to Los Angeles, since 1978 and throughout the years of Ronald Reagan's presidency, the head of the LAPD was Chief Gates, a renowned reactionary Republican and shameless self-publicist. He instituted an exceptionally tough policing regime, defending LAPD's notorious record of racist policing and overseeing a sharp rise in the number of innocent bystanders shot by officers in the line of duty. Black ghettos were repeatedly targeted for SWAT police sweep operations, allowing cops to resort to SS stormtrooper-style mass arbitrary searches of citizens and homes, unrelated to crimes committed. In general during this period, LA was a show town for Reaganomics, instituting massive cuts to public services and transport, forcing the city's whole infrastructure towards the brink of collapse. Demand for cheap labour to do rotten manual jobs attracted an influx of immigrants, which in turn played upon citizens' fear of foreign culture/aliens threatening familiar lifestyles. *Repo Man*'s depiction of LA streets and civil attitudes captures and satirises the city's prevailing mood at this time. Further, the emphasis on automobiles carries broad symbolic significance in terms of corporate America and the twentieth century transformation of the US economy — analogous to the car metaphor in John Steinbeck's *The Grapes of Wrath*.

Blade Runner (1982)

Blade Runner is one of the most widely seen and written about science fiction movies, and whilst a case can be made for its reflecting broader concerns of punk sci-fi (urban dystopian future vision, alienated sub-human outsiders...), its punk characteristics are largely restricted to *mise en scene* (set design, costumes, hairstyles, make-up). Director Ridley Scott had demonstrated that nasty and pessimistic sci-fi movies could achieve blockbuster status at the box office, with *Alien* (1979). It was only thanks to this that he was able to command the budget he required to realise *Blade Runner*. But even then, Scott was forced to release a final cut that significantly altered his intended version, in order to conform to the demands of Warner Brothers. The film initially bombed at the box office, and a campaign against it by feminists for its depiction of violence against women. However, it quickly became a cult movie and attracted highbrow critical acclaim, capturing the trend towards post-modernism. Eventually, its status persuaded the studio to re-release the director's cut.

The screenplay was based on the novel *Do Androids Dream of Electric Sheep?* by Philip K. Dick, a cult sci-fi writer renowned for his excessive use of LSD and speed, and set a trend for later Dick adaptations, like *Total Recall* (1990) and *Minority Report* (2002). *Blade Runner* utilises various formal devices more conventionally associated with film noir thrillers (particularly Godard's *Alphaville*), such as the cynical, hard-boiled detective/cop hero. Harrison Ford offers one of his best performances, breaking his usual tight casting as a conventional good guy action/adventure hero. But the real star of the movie is undoubtedly its (then) cutting-edge, futuristic urban landscape set design and special effects, which transformed the sci-fi genre.

Blade Runner is surely one of the best sci-fi movies ever made. It offers a fascinating discourse on the human condition — existential, psychological and metaphysical. There is nail biting tension, a good body count, beautiful chic violence, a seriously prophetic, considered and largely believable future dystopia, and the chicest punk costumes, make-up and hairstyles on celluloid. It even slots in some outtakes from Stanley Kubrick's *The Shining,* and makes for a cool trip if watched on LSD. But in the final analysis, the punk aesthetic is just a skirt and sweater, an extra morsel of exotic, chic weirdness adding to this eclectic visual extravaganza.

Tetsuo (1989)

Photographed by Shinya Tsukamoto, this incredible Japanese low budget, 16mm, b&w, innovative post-industrial nightmare merges sci-fi and horror. If *Eraserhead* is the industrial avant-garde movie for the 1980s, *Tetsuo* is the post-industrial avant-garde movie for the 1990s. Revivifying themes tackled by director David Cronenberg and in films such as Paul Verhoeven's *RoboCop* (1987), *Tetsuo* is the ultimate cyberpunk movie, with a stomping post-industrial soundtrack. Social alienation and individual identity crisis in urban, technocratic, capitalist dystopia, is the order of the day. The spectator is privy only to the central character's frantic, hallucinogenic, masochistic and sadistic point of view, as he slides in and out of madness and loses control, trapped in a vortex of kinetic, hand-held camerawork. First, his body is torn open from inside by metallic shards, with the mirror reflecting his painful transformation; his fragile delusion of self-control is shattered. Language and the ability to communicate are lost, paranoia intensifies, and his body sprouts cybernetic limbs. His sensuous girlfriend becomes the castrating monster threatening his masculinity and he collapses in fear. Blood turns to oil, his phallus becomes a mighty rotating steel drill, which empowers him to attack and destroy the Other… But as his new cyber strength envelops him, he's forced to recognise he's no longer in control of his own body and bodily functions. Like Nietzsche's *Will to Power*:

> …a monster of energy, without beginning, without end; a firm iron

magnitude of force that does not grow bigger or smaller, that does not expand itself but only transforms itself; as a whole, of unalterable size... enclosed by nothingness as by a boundary... but set in a definite space as a definite force... as force throughout, as a play of forces and waves of forces...[3]

Return of the Living Dead (1985)

Cannibalistic zombies in a gore-drenched, comic strip, rollercoaster splatter movie, hunting punk rockers, with their own punk rock soundtrack! There are shocks galore, razor-sharp black comedy, a matrix of references to zombies long gone and a plethora of zombies with new tricks'n'thrills!

Director Dan O'Bannon's slick horror homage — and 'sequel' to George A. Romero's *Night of the Living Dead* (1968), the cult, independently produced, low budget, monochrome zombie movie that augmented the modern zombie/splatter genre — uses crisp, glossy photography, combined with sharp editing and neat moving point of view shots, to make this one of the finest hyper-real comic strip movies. It looks as effortless as an animated, photographic cartoon strip, with socio-political satire that hits the viewer like a sledgehammer.

The soundtrack comprises American garage-band punk, including The Cramps and some heavy metal. Throughout the first half, there is much playfulness between diegetic and non-diegetic music, facilitated by one character's Walkman and the ghetto-blaster that accompanies the punk rockers wherever they go.

O'Bannon is renowned for writing some of the finest action sci-fi screenplays, including *Alien*. He co-wrote the *Return of the Living Dead* screenplay with John Russo, who had worked on Romero's original *Night of the Living Dead*. A business arrangement had meant that Russo and Romero could work independently to one another on further zombie productions, while protecting their own copyrights. It was decided Russo would retain control of 'Living Dead' while Romero was just 'Dead.' Hence, Romero's own follow-up excursion into zombie land, *Dawn of the Dead,* in 1979. Produced by Italian horror maestro Dario Argento, it was a massive international box-office success. The 'split claim' deal between Russo and Romero saw Romero returning to zombie land once again in 1985 (the same year as *Return*), when he directed *Day of the Dead*, and again in 2005 with *Land of the Dead*.

In the interim, the Italian film industry cashed in on zombie mania with low budget, cash-in zombie features of varying quality, but consistently upping the shock and visceral gore stakes. Among the most worthy efforts are Jorge Grau's *The Living Dead at Manchester Morgue* (1974, Spanish co-production); a spate of films by Lucio Fulci: *Zombie Flesh Eaters* (1979), *City of the Living Dead* (1980), *The Beyond* (1981) and *The House by the Cemetery*; Umberto Lenzi's *Nightmare City* (1980), and Andrea Bianchi's *The Nights Of Terror* (aka *Zombie 3*, 1981). Some of these features attempted to create new variations on old zombie themes. But it was a low budget, American, comic strip, shock and gore galore movie that cleared the way for a new generation of zombie variations: Sam Raimi's *The Evil Dead* (1982). Films that followed and further diverged from zombie convention, include Lamberto Bava's *Demons* and Stuart Gordon's *Re-Animator* (both 1985). While *Return of the Living Dead* offers lots of fabulous little variations on zombie tradition, its distinction is found in the opposite direction, notably in that it is the ultimate self-aware, self-referential zombie lexicon. Russo certainly had the necessary credentials to achieve this in the screenplay. All the deeper meanings, socio-politics and subtexts are on the surface. Political messages and philosophical diatribes — integral to the zombie genre since *Night of the Living Dead* but hidden in the subtext and concealed by metaphor — are utilised in *Return of the Living Dead* as political satire to assault the spectator.

At the beginning of the film, a notice flashes up on screen, informing the spectator that the following story is real, factual. A similar opening message appears in the original *The Texas Chainsaw Massacre* (1974), directed by Tobe Hooper, who was initially slated to direct *Return of the Living Dead*. The film's first meaningful conversation sets out the plot by direct reference to events portrayed in *Night of the Living Dead*. A few names and references were altered to avoid litigation, but essentially that movie depicted factual events. In *Night of the Living Dead*, the zombies are a metaphor for the 'old', 'parental', reactionary conservative citizens — the establishment of the Nixon era coming back from the grave to kill the young. The central, most positive, character in *Night of the Living Dead* is a young Afro-American, a significant gesture at the time (*Dawn of the Dead* also casts a positive, young, Afro-American). *Return of the Living Dead* again features prominently an Afro-American youth as the member of the punk gang who survives the longest. *Night* offers no conclusive explanation for the zombies sudden being there: they just are (it's suggested that a rocket crashed, leaking chemicals). *Return of the Living Dead* makes explicit the US military connection: dangerous chemicals developed by the army to "spray on marijuana or something" (referring to Reagan's War on Drugs policy). There is military insignia on the barrels, and the presence of the General, whose main mission is to locate the chemical shipment and terminate its effect with the military's final solution.

There's also some emphasis on what the living dead feed on when they return; in this movie it's live human brains (as opposed to human flesh in earlier zombie movies), also suggesting that the zombies want to consume and destroy the Other's thought/intelligence.

(The Italians coupled zombies with another sub-genre, the cannibal movie, to maximise exploitation potential, and in so doing help further the traditional horror function of breaking social taboos. Death and cannibalism are age-old social taboos in most cultures; transgression or taboo-breaking is another function shared by some horror sub-genres and punk, and is linked to the human capacity for shock. Anyhow, back to brain-eating zombies...)

Apotheosis seems to be another referential device used in *Return of the Living Dead*, by taking features and concepts touched upon in earlier zombie movies to their ultimate, extreme conclusions, hence segmented body parts that keep moving, zombies that function on basic animal instincts (ability to run, hunt and entrap pray), and, if zombies could talk a little (why not?) they would order food — in this case, cops and paramedics — with free delivery service! There's also resort to question sources again: *why doesn't destroying zombie brains kill them off?* It worked in that damn movie — but not in this one!

The zombie genre has been linked with popular American comic books (such as EC) since Romero's genre definer. When *Dawn of the Dead* was first released, it seemed like the full potential of comic art had been realised on the screen. But improvements in cine technology, and audiences becoming more attuned to genre conventions, allows for faster editing and more ellipsis. In *Return of the Living Dead*, every frame is constructed to look like a comic illustration.

Despite being produced in association with Fox Films, and given its glossy veneer, there's an angry, bad-tempered punk attitude running through this film, which runs deeper than the DIY fashion accessories on the body count fodder punk rockers. It's notable in the arch black humour that has you chuckling at its relentless pessimism; this isn't a cop-out movie, there's visceral gore galore, keenly observed nuances of human fallibility and the appalling potential consequences, Homeric laughter at the realisation that we're all doomed, and complete mistrust and cynicism towards state power structures that supposedly protect us.

Notes

1 Danny Peary, ed., *Omni's Screen Flights, Screen Fantasies*; *Directing Mad Max and the Road Warrior*, New York: Doubleday and Company, 1984, p. 280–286.

2 William Burroughs, *Exterminator!*, London: Corgi Books, 1976, p.12.

3 Friedrich Nietzsche, *The Will to Power*, New York: Vintage Books, 1967, p. 550.

The disappearance and re-emergence of Ladies and Gentle-men: The Fabulous Stains

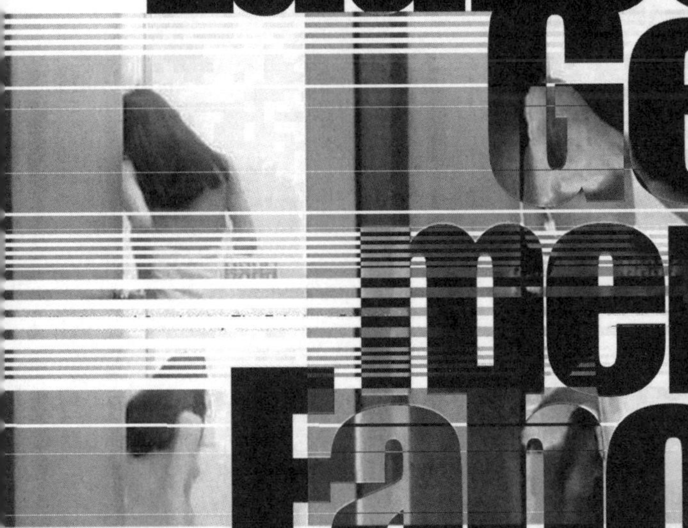

Neil Palmer

Narrative:

After her mother's death, Corinne 'Third Degree' Burns (Diane Lane) is determined to bust out of a run-down Midwestern steel town. Tired of selling hamburgers and further inspired by seeing English punk band, The Looters (with Ray Winstone as Billy, and featuring ex-Pistols Steve Jones and Paul Cook, and Paul Simenon of The Clash), she takes the initiative and gets her band, The Stains, with her sister, Tracy, aka 'Dee Pleated' (Marin Kanter) and cousin Jessica 'Dizzy Heights' McNeil (Laura Dern) in as second support act on a tour with has-been rockers, Metal Corpses (featuring Fee Waybill of The Tubes in his first acting role, as the Metal Corpses singer).

With the Corpses bounced off the tour after the fatal overdose of their bass player (Vince Welnick), The Looters grab the headline slot and Corinne and The Stains get on the tour bus owned and driven by Lawnboy (reggae singer Barry Ford) and start their rise to fame, eventually topping the bill with The Looters as their support band after Corinne successfully hijacks Billy's lyrics and stage act.

Corinne's strikingly individualist gut-instinct feminism is first glimpsed after a brief club performance that highlights the fragility of

The Stains' combined musical talents and reveals the strength of her genius. Her angry response to the dumbstruck, lukewarm audience — "I'm perfect, but nobody in this shit hole gets me because I don't put out!" — sums up her position as a confident, inexperienced and aspiring young woman in a macho music industry. That key phrase also sets the tone for the rest of Nancy Dowd's inspirational screenplay.

With the backing of a local TV news anchorwoman, Alicia Meeker (Cynthia Sikes), and massive support from Stains-uniformed girl fans, the Skunks, The Stains progress from a position of alienation to one of influence. Although the band splits ignominiously after the fans reject the aggressive marketing of their product, the closing credits show The Stains re-formed and acting in a glossy, MTV style promo film, having rejected the gauche, self-created punk dynamic and replaced it with a smooth, professional sound and video-friendly stance.

In one sense, *Ladies and Gentlemen: The Fabulous Stains* is your classic wide-eyed fans-turned-musicians vs cynical music biz characters movie; it is as much about the nuts and bolts of the rock industry — gigging and inter and intra-band politics — as it is about ultra-feminist polemics and the transformative, inspirational quality of bands as perceived by music fans. In that regard, it is a traditional rock'n'roll movie like, for example, *The Golden Disc* (1958), which depicts the struggle for independent production values and marketshare in the early, cut-throat days of the rock'n'roll business in Britain; *Stardust* (1973), with its fly-on-the-wall interiority, or *The Great Rock'n'Roll Swindle* (1980). However, the radical difference is that The Stains sidestep the cynicism of a male-dominated industry and become popular, initially, because of the direct appeal of their feminist sloganeering to girl fans. Even though their final appearance in the film shows that they have become a polished pop act, nothing can alter the fact that, although they have become a part of the industry, they have also successfully decentred it. In the words of the movie poster, "These Girls Created Themselves."

Production

All Washed Up, later re-titled *Ladies and Gentlemen: The Fabulous Stains* (1982), was the first in a two-picture deal offered to Nancy Dowd by Paramount on the back of her success with *Slapshot* (1977) and *Coming Home* (1978). By the time her punk rock movie was in production, she had won an Oscar for *Coming Home*.

Adler had already been the executive producer of *The Rocky Horror Picture Show* (1975) and produced the Cheech and Chong movie, *Up in Smoke* (1978). He was well known as a music entrepreneur, having had chart success with Carole King and the Mamas and the Papas, owned prominent Los Angeles music clubs, the Roxy and the Whisky-a-Go-Go, and was involved with the 1967 Monterey Pop Festival, as well as the 1968 film that documented the event. However, *All Washed Up* was his directorial debut.

Dowd became interested in punk rock in her thirties. Interviewed in Sarah Jacobson's twelve minute TV documentary, *Ladies and*

Gentlemen: The Fabulous Stains: Behind the Movie (1999), she says: "You have to remember that during the seventies, everything in terms of music was junk." She was very aware of the place of women in punk: "There were girl bands right from the get go… and not in the sappy way they had been in rock'n'roll at the end of the seventies."

Dowd expresses her radical feminism through a narrative exploring the creative genius of a group of girls led by a powerful, fast-learning street-smart young woman. However, in relocating the transformative narrative of punk rock from cosmopolitan urban centres to the mid-west (filmed, in fact, around Vancouver), Dowd was reacting to the massive spreading out of punk from New York and Los Angeles throughout the US. *The Fabulous Stains* narrates the clash of different cultures — local, provincial, national, as well as those borne of class and gender — and contextualises the subsequent alienation within punk rock.

Through a mutual friend, Dowd made contact with Caroline Coon, a designer, artist, writer, liberated feminist, co-founder of drugs charity Release, and one of the original chroniclers of London punk rock, visiting her in England as part of the pre-production process.

Coon first introduced Dowd to the major figures in the UK punk scene and took her on a British tour with Sham 69. She became the movie's creative consultant and designed the distinctive make-up, logos and looks of the three bands featured in *The Fabulous Stains*. Keen-eyed punk rock sleuths will have noticed that the briefs-on-the-outside stage wear sported by Corinne Burns was pioneered by Ari Up of The Slits, who subversively sported visible Silver Jubilee underwear in one of Coon's best-known photographs. Coon also assembled Cook, Jones and Simenon — three of the best-known faces of the London punk scene — as The Looters, to back Ray Winstone, the band's singer, who was already known from *Scum* and *Quadrophenia*, both released in 1979.

Coon and Dowd shared a common view of the aims of the movie: "We were all for gender-blur. Male and female don't exist, we want to be equals." Mediating the feminist message through an attractive, recognisable band look was important, Coon recalls, citing The Slits' look:

> I liked the male-female thing, bovver boots and tutus, that lovely thing of young girls wanting to be tough and pretty… It was very difficult for young women, because feminists were hated and feminism was so threatening and the tabloids were setting feminists up as the enemy. [1]

Both Dowd and producer, Joe Roth (currently head of Revolution Studios and former chairman at Disney and Twentieth Century Fox), wanted Jonathan Kaplan to direct, but Lou Adler was appointed instead.[2] Given Dowd's feminist take on punk rock, and with her very recent experience of successful Hollywood screenwriting, it was perhaps inevitable that she and Adler, a face from rock's hippie past, would approach the business of movie-making and the realisation of *The Fabulous Stains* from very different positions. Commenting on Adler's first directorial position, Dowd has mentioned "a lack of professionalism" in the production, saying, "You can't sit there and… expect that it's going to happen. Directing is a skill".[3]

Dowd left the movie before its completion. She told Sarah Jacobson, in *Grand Royal Magazine*, that a camera operator "went to turn the knob on the camera and instead he grabbed my breast… Finally, toward the end, I just left. I think it was the day [Adler] gave Corinne a tambourine and I thought 'Get me out of here.' So I went home." After Dowd quit, Adler renamed the movie by directly referencing the documentary, *Ladies and Gentlemen: The Rolling Stones*, a model of a rock'n'roll film that he and Paramount may have felt more comfortable with.

Despite her absence from much of the filming and from the credits — she used the pseudonym Rob Morton, rather than be directly associated with Adler's version — Dowd's presence is palpable. However, although the alternate title misses the mark by several miles, the powerful didactic message of Dowd's screenplay subverts Adler's attempt to turn the movie a sub-canonical rock artefact.

Caroline Coon agrees with Dowd's opinion of the production. She told me, "I'd never worked in a situation that I so wanted to leave" and confirmed that there was little professionalism on the set, despite an "incredible team." She alleges that "Adler was on the set and didn't know what to do."

She observes that the movie's $5 million budget should have gone further, but claims there was a lot of drug-taking going on, alleging that there was a point three weeks before the end of filming, when the bond was nearly up, and Adler started "tearing pages out of the script" to finish shooting, leading to a movie that was "incoherent on presentation." David Brown, co-founder of legendary LA punk label Dangerhouse, and member of Black Randy and the Metro Squad, featured in the movie, says:

> Every day they would rip a couple of pages off the script, throw those away, do a bunch of coke and try and come up with what that day's script was going to be. [4]

Coon recalls with distaste some aspects of Adler's directing technique, especially regarding the improvised scene in which the Metal Corpses' singer (Fee Waybill) is punched by Billy (Ray Winstone) in an ad-libbed scene. "The director is sniggering and he has to go along with it, because if you complain, you're called a poof… But by that time it wasn't surprising, because we'd seen the way the youth had been treated. I thought you could get better work trusting in the art." Coon claims that the boys in the band were plied with drugs. However, Paul Cook says: "The film people… were thinking we were doing tons of drugs and all sorts of illicit things, when I think it was the other way round… We were quite well behaved compared to them sometimes."

Ex-Pistol Paul Cook and Fee Waybill both say, in interview snippets in *Grand Royal Magazine*, that Adler was a cool character who let them get on with the business at hand. Caroline Coon, however, has no doubt that she and Dowd were "up against that billion dollar sleaze, where powerful men can do what they like."

There was a massive amount of partying during filming. Dowd and Coon recall inviting members of Vancouver's transsexual population to their hotel for after hours entertainment, much to the annoyance of the hotel staff. Diane Lane sums up her experience in an interview in *Behind the Movie*: "I saw the dawn a lot. It's stuff you can only do when you're that age." In the same TV programme, Steve Jones recalls: "There was more sex and drugs going on when the camera wasn't rolling than was in the movie."[5]

Caroline Coon makes no bones about her attitude towards the opportunities afforded by movie-making — "I'm a feminist and I'm going to enjoy myself up to the hilt" — but she hints at an abusive side to the on-set partying, saying pointedly, "We're feminists... adults playing hard with other adults."

If ever there were a fond perception that *Ladies and Gentlemen: The Fabulous Stains* was a naïve product, a lost artefact from the prehistory of present-day feminism and punk rock — two treasured concepts that have long since become accepted by niche media as easy, radical signifiers of past ideological and cultural struggles — that was dispelled by Sarah Jacobson's incisive research. Wider knowledge of the gendered power plays occurring during the movie's production have brought the original point of the writer's feminist screenplay into sharper focus, rather than overshadow it.

Disappearance

Paramount dropped the movie swiftly after its completion and if it had a release it was a very short-run thing. Adler cites poor previews and the difficulties of matching the film to the 'right' audience. Steve Jones, interviewed for *Behind the Movie*, says that it "might have been a bit corny... after the Pistols and the punk thing was kind of dying out." Adler's excuse is, by his own admission, the sort of thing a director would say. Similarly, Steve Jones's opinion may have been coloured by his gradual decentring from the music industry, but he may have a point. The novelty of punk as a pop phenomenon had all but worn out by the time the film had its limited release in 1982–83.

No details of the US preview experience have made it into the public domain and no theatre print of *The Fabulous Stains* has ever made it to the UK, so we can only wonder what the impact of the film on UK audiences might have been. It is anyone's guess how movie audiences recently hit with The Ramones camping it up in *Rock'n'Roll High School* (1979), The Clash living the life in *Rude Boy* (1980), and the rather lame likes of *Urgh! A Music War* (1980), would have viewed another movie dealing with the dirty politics of the music industry from a grassroots perspective.

In retrospect, the sharp writing and didactic political message of *The Fabulous Stains* distinguishes it from the other rock'n'roll movies of the early 1980s, such as *Breaking Glass* (1980), which traded on *Metropolis* style machine-age angst, the imminent totalitarian shadow of 1984, and new wave sounds, to evoke a comfortably recognisable dystopian environment.

The market for punk movies was still strong in the early 1980s, but consumers of punk product had developed a strong sense of authenticity that militated against populist representations and for punk 'originals.' There was continuing interest in the recent history and cultural context of punk rock, inspired by the buoyant live music scene in the early 1980s and the reappearance of images from the dawn of British punk. For example, *The Great Rock'n'Roll Swindle* (1980) was still packing late-night shows around the UK some two or three years after its first release, and Caroline Coon's photobook, *1988: The New Wave Punk Rock Explosion*, was reprinted in 1982.

Perhaps if Adler had stuck to the original script, which, as Caroline Coon confirms, had The Stains arriving "in Britain, with thousands of English skunks" to greet them, the film may have received earlier, wider interest from across the Atlantic. There is an attractive case to be made for an alternate feminist history of the film, for as Coon says, "The girls wanted to be equal. The glamour is in the struggle… In the original, the girls were more aspirational, successful, and go to England to demonstrate their success to The Looters. The competition between bands is what drives it." Coon suggests further that the movie "could have been so much bigger… it could have been fantastic, triumphal, pre-Spice Girls, pre-Madonna."

Re-emergence

Cult movies don't just happen overnight. Beyond their life as independent or studio productions, they are, in effect, made again by fans who invest a lot of time, effort and cultural capital in recreating the film in their own image. *The Fabulous Stains* has become one of the most mythical, inspirational, underground artefacts of the rock'n'roll era due almost entirely to a network of enthused fans, who, over time, have successfully sold the idea of the film to other like-minded individuals and created a market for a product that has never existed except for a few prints available to movie theatres, late-night cable TV stations in the US and bootlegged n^{th} generation VHS or DVD copies.

The re-emergence of *Ladies and Gentlemen: The Fabulous Stains* as a fan phenomenon happened despite, or, perhaps, partly because of, Paramount Studios' decision not to give it a proper theatre life after its perfunctory release in October 1982, and its failure to make an impact during a brief outing on the art house circuit in 1984. Although it bombed in previews and has attracted little more than aloof disdain by mainstream movie critics, its fans have tended to adopt it on its own didactic terms, rather than as a canonical part of the *so bad it's good* trash pantheon.

One reason why this film has gained such publicity recently is the work of the late Sarah Jacobson, an influential figure in independent movie-making in the United States and fan of *The Fabulous Stains*, who undertook extensive research on the movie, leading to an authoritative article in *Grand Royal Magazine* and the documentary, *Ladies and Gentlemen: The Fabulous Stains*: *Behind the Movie* (1999), made with Sam Green.[6]

The Fabulous Stains, written by a feminist, is about young women's success as creative individuals in an industry dominated by men and protected by a male power base, so it is not difficult to understand why some proponents of Riot Grrl mindset in the early 1990s hailed the movie as the prototype for their take on punk rock, feminism and the ethics of independent music production. Tobi Vail of Bikini Kill has said: "It is the most realistic and profound film I have ever seen." In an interview in issue five of *Jigsaw* fanzine (1992), Justin, from the band Unwound, thanks interviewers Vail and Kathi Wilcox for turning him on to the movie: "You said it would change my life and it pretty much did."

A surprising number of commentators insist on perpetuating the historical contention that *The Fabulous Stains* was a Riot Grrl movie made before its time. Although it's true that this movie was a great influence on the style and didactic force of what became known as Riot Grrl, it is truer to say that it served as a contextual reference point for the Pacific North-West independent music scene and for radical feminist and punk rock cultures. On considering the appropriation of this brilliantly written, if inexpertly realised, piece of fiction, it is clear that it has become a beacon of alternate pop cultural history and a plausible cultural narrative for many independent music makers and producers.

Future

The final theatre print of *The Fabulous Stains* is on its last legs and there are currently no plans for another one to be made, or for a DVD release. Despite Sarah Jacobson's best efforts, it is possible that the most unlikely scenario in this age of digitisation and cult fandom — the loss of an acknowledged movie classic — may come to pass.[7]

Notes

1 All quotes from Caroline Coon come from a telephone conversation with the writer on October 26, 2005.

2 *Ladies and Gentlemen: The Fabulous Stains* may be the lowest-grossing movie of Roth's entire career.

3 Sarah Jacobson, 'The Expose of a Cult Phenomenon' in *Grand Royal Magazine*, No. 6, 1997, p.34.

4 Ibid.

5 *Ladies and Gentlemen, The Fabulous Stains: Behind the Movie*, Sarah Jacobson and Sam Green, USA, Documentary, Video, 12 min., 1999. (Produced for Jon Pierson's IFC program *Split Screen.*)

6 While the issue of *Grand Royal* is hard to locate, the documentary *Ladies and Gentlemen: The Fabulous Stains: Behind the Movie* (1999) has been released on DVD as a bonus feature to Sam Green's *Rainbow Man/John 3:16* by Other Cinema DVD.

7 See: **[w]** fabulousstains.com for a Quicktime version of *Ladies and Gentlemen: The Fabulous Stains: Behind the Movie*.

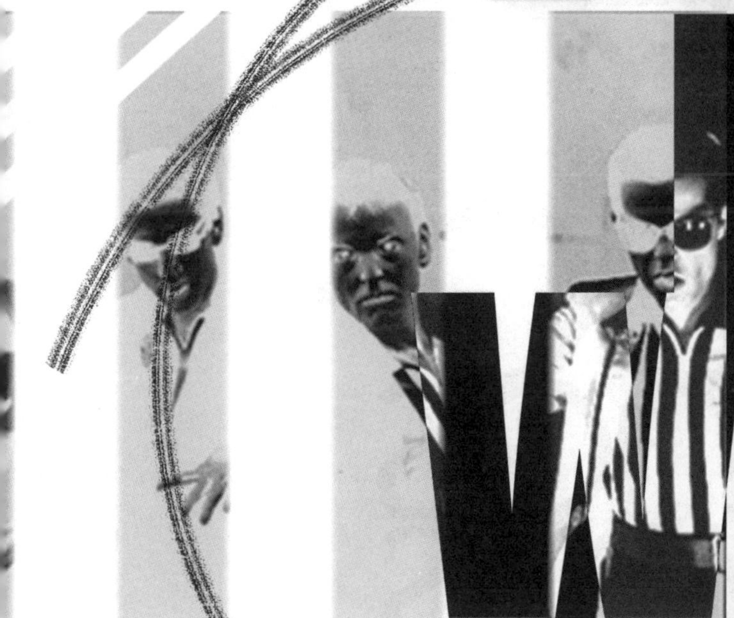

Paying Witness

Jack Sargeant

'The true theatre has always

appeared to me as the exercise of a dangerous, terrible action, where the idea of theatre and of spectacle are eliminated together with those of all science, all religion, and all art ***Antonin Artaud***

Before 1976 the idea of filming a band was too difficult for most people; the industry around the rock giants wanted narrative movies like *Help!* (Richard Lester, 1965) or 'epic,' 'generation defining' documentaries of supposed rock giants like *Woodstock* (Michael Wadleigh, 1970), films that celebrated the obese spectacle of rock'n'roll. Even worse, they made films that embraced a high concept, for example the bloated rock opera *Tommy* (Ken Russell, 1975), or the animated excesses of *Yellow Submarine* (George Dunning, 1968). The majority of music documentaries followed jet-fuelled, high-end tours, for example *The Song Remains the Same*

(Peter Clifton & Joe Massot, 1976), but these movies were rigorous in presenting carefully mediated images. Films showing a less than managed and contrived image of rock bands, such as Robert Frank's *Cocksucker Blues* (1972), which remains effectively unreleased, despite the availability of bootleg copies, or the Maysles' Altamont documentary *Gimme Shelter* (1970), were rare. Invariably, the filmmaker had to work as part of the showbusiness machine rather than as an aesthetic collaborator with the musicians. While a handful of underground or experimental filmmakers made films, often of less known bands, these were rare exceptions to the highly contrived images dictated by the music industry. These notable exceptions include Warhol's footage of The Velvet Underground rehearsing at the Factory, *The Velvet Underground and Nico* (1966); a handful of home movies of the Stooges performing live; Peter Whitehead's Rolling Stones tour movie *Charlie Is My Darling* (1963, although like Frank's Rolling Stones movie this too remains officially unavailable), and Conrad Rook's cult midnight movie *Chappaqua* (1968), which features proto-punk band The Fugs.

Here was a genre of music that advocated a radical independence allied with the creed of self-production. Combined with the ready availability of sync-sound Super-8 film (introduced in 1974), the increasing availability of video cameras, and by the end of the decade the mass distribution promised by home video, it was inevitable that some punks or punk audiences would turn to film. There are numerous documentaries that explore punk, offering it up to the audience as both spectacle and cultural event, such as Wolfgang Büld's *Punk in London* (1978), a documentary that features contributions from the Adverts, The Lurkers, Chelsea, Wayne County and the Electric Chairs, Subway Sect and The Jam, amongst others. Two years later, Lech Kowalski's *DOA* (1980) was released, notable for its depictions of a blasted barely coherent Sid being interviewed while slumped next to Nancy. This ultimately tragic sequence is cut with street punk Terry as he attempts to create his own mark with his band, the comically absurd Terry and the Idiots, who singularly fail to impress at their debut gig at the local pub. Former punks continue to produce retrospective examinations of the period, ranging from Paul Tickell's *Punk and the Pistols* (1995) produced for BBC's Arena strand, which offers a history of British punk, and Don Letts' *Punk: Attitude* (2005), which follows punk to the present day, and includes footage of Bad Brains and The Contortions, alongside interviews with Thurston Moore and Henry Rollins, as well as the more familiar faces.

But these films all offer a context, an explanation, and an interpretation of punk; the music becomes contextualised as part of a wider social phenomenon. In contrast films such as *Louder, Faster, Shorter* (Mindaugis Bagdon, 1978), which offer the performance of the band or bands as their central pleasure, the discourses of punk are articulated not by commentators but by the music and performance itself. *Louder, Faster, Shorter* documents the emergent San Francisco punk scene. This twenty-three minute 16mm blast featured performances by The Avengers, Mutants, UXA, Sleepers, and Dils, all shot during a benefit for striking Kentucky miners that took place in March 1978 at the Mabuhay Gardens, in an event that was organised by Howie Klein, who was rumoured to have been inspired by a visit to England where he saw The Clash. Framed via an industrial sonic soundscape and footage shot from a car as it drives into the city, the live footage is notable for being filmed from multiple perspectives and seamlessly edited together.

The Avengers live at the Mabuhay, 1977 Photo: Ruby Ray

At the end, not of a set but a set-to, the singer jumps off stage

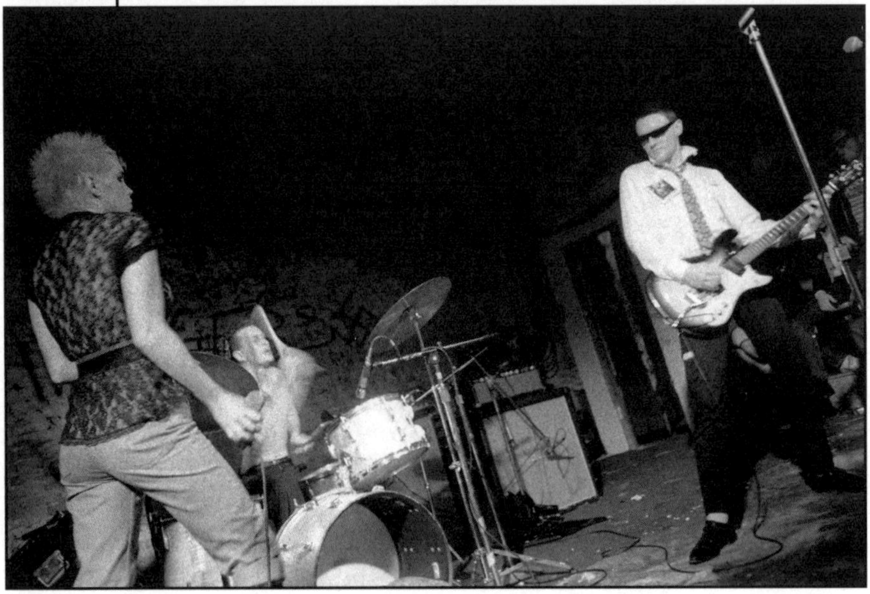

with a helper... and runs through the dispersing crowd to hurl himself at two long hairs responsible for the heckling and the flying glasses. ***Jon Savage*** [1]

We don't want to get like other bands who tend to withdraw rather dramatically from their crowds. ***Jello Biafra*** [2]

Bands like the Stooges, Suicide, Beasts of Bourbon, and yes, The Birthday Party, are the real deal. They are as close as you can get, the fragile line between performance and possession. But the line fragments and shatters, and that is when it happens: that is when art becomes dangerous... rock'n'roll is a music born of inarticulate rage, a primal scream of consciousness and the pain that accompanies such a state. And this state of grace was occupied by both performer and audience. Gut reaction. Animal instinct. ***Rowland S. Howard*** [3]

If punk advocated a new attitude to music production and artistic practice, bands 'affiliated' to punk, or the radical and subversive creative renaissance it inspired, also engaged in a radical new exploration of the nature of performance in a way few previously had.[4] While the rock giants and singer songwriters who dominated the music scene prior to punk maintained their distance from the audience, performing as a spectacle, punk broke down the traditional nature of performance. In part, this breakdown of audience/band divide owed something to the fact that early audiences were made up of other musicians, artists and bands.

However, while the bands were versed in the mythology of rock'n'roll, many were also driven by other notions of performance that sought the limits and embraced madness, from the bloodied rituals of the Vienna Aktionists, to the confrontations of outsider art, to the radicalised high camp of queer theatre. These influences beyond music created new kinds of performances that embraced self-expression, reaching into the abyss, and an exploration of new relationships between the audience and performer.

The Germs threw food around the stage and audience at their earliest shows (later, GG Allin threw his shit into the crowd); conversely, Non performed from the dressing room, not even appearing physically on the stage, and numerous bands and audiences ended up in fights with each other or — as audiences increased — with the police. But some bands took this even further, taking the performance itself out of the club/bar scenario and into a new uncharted territory, taking the performance to an unsuspecting audience.

On June 13, 1978, The Cramps played on a bill with The Mutants at the Napa State Mental Institute in what was described by one witness as "the fuckin' greatest new wave show I've ever seen."[5] The resulting video release, produced by San Francisco based Target Video, *The Cramps Live at Napa State Mental Hospital* (1978), sees a solitary camera shooting The Cramps as they play on a tiny stage before a room full of mentally ill patients. Despite the audio-visual quality being marred with occasional dropouts, the subsequent video — shot in b&w, with one microphone — has become legendary. The one camera perspective acts to punctuate the transgressive, clandestine nature of the event, and neither the video nor the performance can be judged by 'conventional' standards of live rock documentaries.

The video captures The Cramps in finely chaotic form: Lux Interior rolls and jumps around the audience and stage, Poison Ivy is almost unmoving, stoically playing her savage guitar riffs, and Nick Knox holds down the pounding beat; finally there is Bryan Gregory, all hair, cheek bones and cigarette, dancing a sleazy little twist with his spot-painted guitar. But it is the response of the audience that makes this video so exciting and entertaining. At the beginning of the performance the audience engage with the music as entertainment; during Mystery Plane they watch, soon two members of the audience start to dance on the lip of the makeshift stage — one complete with suit and tie appears to be mimicking Lux, pretending to sing the song.

"We're The Cramps, and we're from New York City... Somebody told me you people were crazy, but I'm not sure about that, you seem alright to me..." Lux tells the audience before launching into Way I Walk. More people from the audience start to climb onto the stage: some are dancing around the band, others less certain, stumbling around like heavily medicated zombies. By the third song — What's Behind The Mask? — a woman in the audience has decided to use the vocalist's microphone whenever possible, shouting periodically into it. The camera periodically loses sight of Interior, as the audience scramble over him and he vanishes into the crowd.

By Human Fly, the woman is screaming an improvised howling intro, accompanying the familiar buzzing-fly guitar twang; Interior takes the microphone for the verses, but the woman keeps taking it to scream, shout, grunt and holler whenever Lux isn't using it. Nobody seems too concerned.

The Cramps at The Mabuhay, 1979. Photo: Ruby Ray

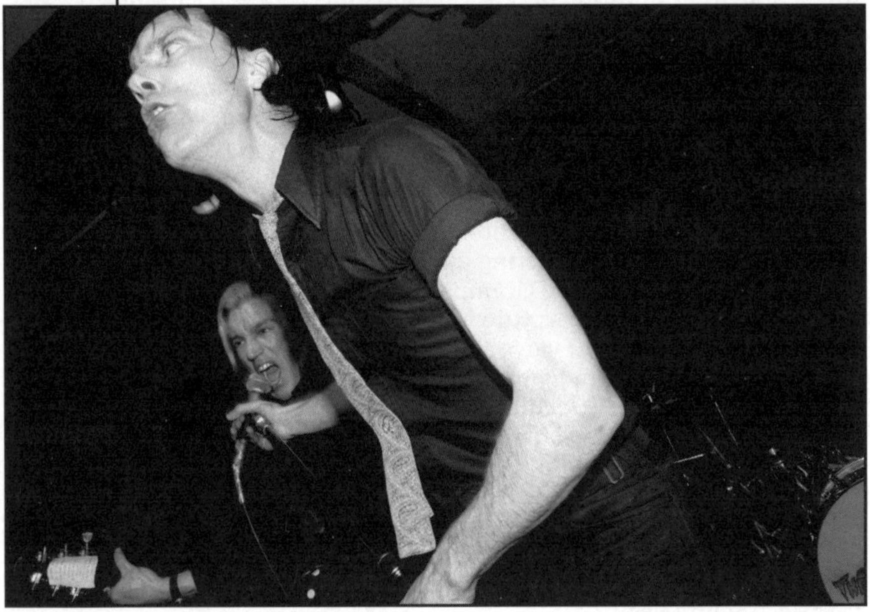

During Domino, Lux takes her in his arms and they dance a frenetic waltz, arm in arm. Lux enters the audience, the woman takes singing duties, a smile flickers across Bryan Gregory's lips. At one point between songs Interior asks the woman: "How do you like The Cramps so far?", to which she replies, after a space of a couple of seconds, "Blaaahhhhhh! I've got cramps!"

As the video progresses it becomes apparent that the band no longer simply control the event or even want to, rather it is dictated by all present in the room — any pretence at a division between performer and audience vanishes. As one audience member subsequently stated: "These guys look like they came out of the T Unit,"[6] the section of the hospital for those deemed to be so 'mentally ill' they would never be discharged. Indeed, at least one audience member wondered if they would ever be allowed to leave.

The madness of the moment, of a garage punk band playing in a mental hospital, of patients and residents enjoying the band alongside a handful of fans who had travelled to the show, has fed into The Cramps' mythology. If ever there were a band who truly revelled in the spectacle of rock'n'roll as madness it was The Cramps, and this event serves as a celebration of their outsider status. The video documentation inspired a re-

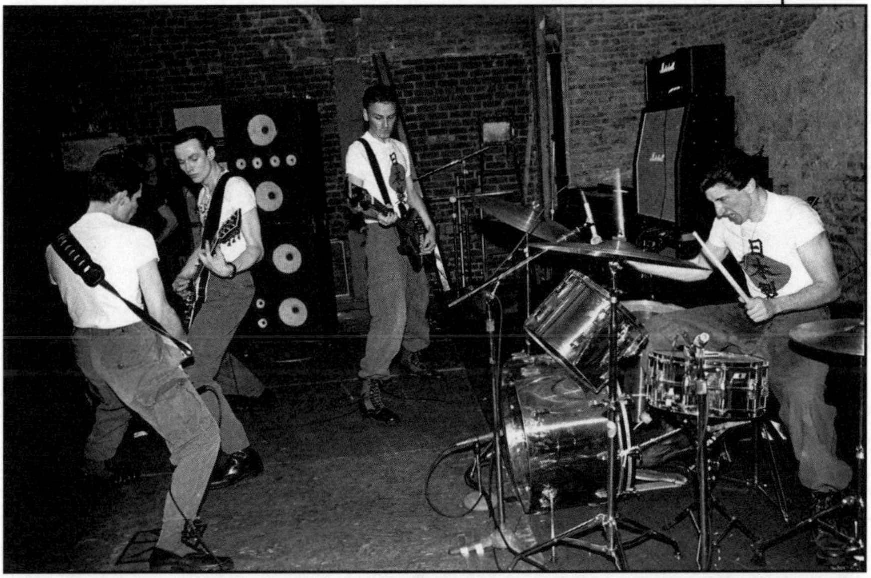

Crime.
Photo: Ruby Ray

enactment in 2004 at London's Institute of Contemporary Art (ICA) by artists Iain Forsyth and Jane Pollard, who re-created the original event, documenting it on film under the title *File Under Sacred Music*.

Equally noteworthy is the footage of San Francisco punk band Crime playing in San Quentin, on September 4, 1978: both the event and subsequent film echo Johnny Cash's performance at the same venue.[7] As Crime's Hank Rank remembers:

> There was a group of subversive artists at the time who founded Museums Without Walls, an organisation dedicated to putting art in unusual places. We were the most notorious band in the city, so we were contacted to play in the Q. Needless to say, we jumped at the chance. Some ideas are too perfect to believe, and this was one. If the authorities at the prison had any inkling of what they were really getting we would have been yanked quicker than Al Capone. [8]

Standing on a makeshift stage in the middle of the concrete prison yard, playing in bright sunshine for the assembled inmates, Crime are resplendent, dressed in matching black police uniforms, black shades, black slicked back hair; with sneers on their faces, they look like a squad of vice cops gone rogue, radiating contempt and bad attitude. Johnny Strike:

Thhrobbing Gristle in Victoria Park, London

> We were very into our look and, early on, in one photo session I wore a police uniform and Frankie a nurse's uniform. Our basic look was all black, leather jackets etc., so it wasn't a big jump for us all to start wearing them. We wore them anytime we went out as a band, causing some problems with the local law, and befuddling a lot of the punks. It caused confusion, which we

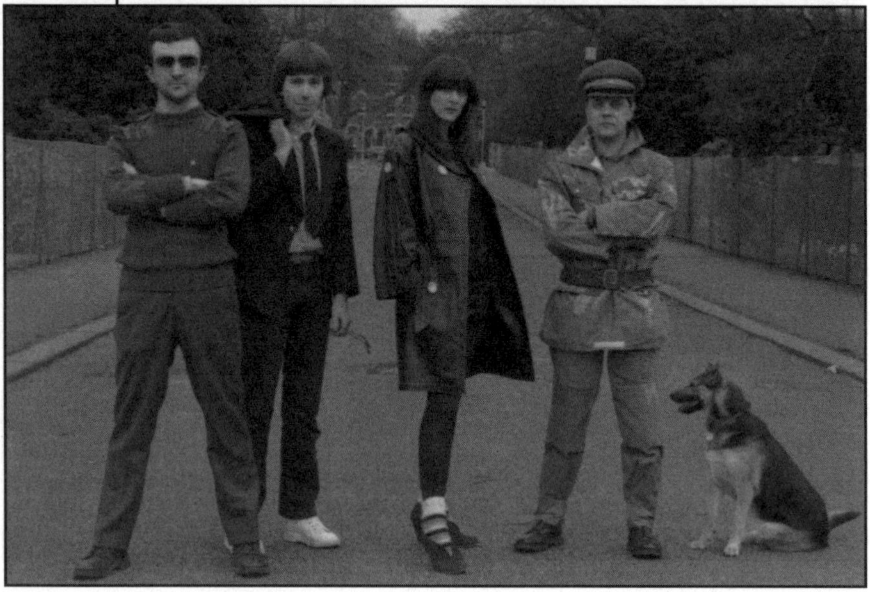

> thought was great. Some people were intimidated, others got angry, others loved it fetishistically.

Having just watched a country & western band, the assembled convicts responded to the quartet of punk upstarts with a combination that was part stunned, part pissed, and part lecherous, "especially watching a couple of our girlfriends," remembers Strike, "who had gotten in [and were] shakin' their butts." The audience reaction was also dictated by the situation: "It's a maximum security prison. Prisoners do what they're told or risk the consequences. There were freakin' guards with riot guns." On the video, prison wardens can be seen watching from the wall, guns in hand. As the camera tracks from band to audience, several inmates rise, all ripped muscles and tattoos; some of those gathered to watch are holding up flyers for the camera. The camera zooms in and it becomes clear that these depict a cartoon of a semi-naked woman behind bars and read "Crime," creating an element of gleefully nihilistic abjection. Here, amongst those deemed as the worst of the worst, holding this poster becomes an affirmation.

Like The Cramps at Napa State, Crime's performance is often mentioned but barely seen, known via reputation rather than viewings. Johnny Strike remembers it "as a fairly shitty show, but quite an experience. It was in the daytime. We were used to sleeping all day. Frankie Fix was so smashed on a pill I'm surprised we made it through the set." While Hank states that the film "stands as document of a defining moment in rock history. It is the most perfect blurring of art and reality ever captured by a moving image. It is our gift to the ages." Thus far available only in various teaser trailers on Target Video products, the entire concert has yet to be released,[9] although it is believed it will finally see the light of day in the near future.

Finally, Throbbing Gristle documented their March 16, 1980, performance at Oundle Public School. If The Cramps found a willing and enthusiastic audience for their B-movie styled garage rockabilly at Napa, and Crime were able to present their sneering attitude punk to a bewildered but wryly amused prison population, then Throbbing Gristle went one stage further, playing to a room of unsuspecting teenage school boys. Invited by Nigel Jacklin, a fan and school pupil, who somehow convinced the school authorities to allow the industrial group to play, the video shows exactly what happens when boys are faced with a combination of gut churning white noise, electronic rhythms, sound loops, and quasi pop-songs such as the hymn to ejaculation, Something Came Over Me. The mere presence of the group's guitarist/cornet player, Cosey Fanni Tutti, serves to create a mix of pubescent sub-sexual yelps and cries of "Show us your legs!" — an almost Pavlovian response to the presence of a female in such an environment, made more strange because her legs are clearly visible as she is wearing a leather miniskirt — later, bolder members of the assembly shout "Strip!"

Although (barely) stopping short of a total riot, the assembled teenage boys ultimately respond to the sound of the group with hoots, jeers, cheers and shrieks. More strange and exciting was the assembled youths' response following nearly an hour of performance. As Throbbing Gristle drive through their set, another noise can be heard on the video, increasing in volume. As the band finally stop playing, it becomes apparent that this is not part of any intended subliminal noise, found tape, or sonic art, rather it is the amassed rich boys responding in ultimately the only way they can understand by singing Jerusalem as a mass hymn/chant.

Monte Cazazza, who also opened for Throbbing Gristle at the school, causing outrage by sitting on stage in a leather chair reserved for senior college staff, filmed the event. The video documents both the performance and, as the set continues, the boys' response. Between songs the teenagers are loud, shouting, chanting and boisterous; however, it becomes apparent that during the songs the boys respond in a combination of pop mimesis, all skinny arms outstretched towards the stars on stage, and bewildered shock, with their upturned young faces blank and uncomprehending.

Unlike the more clearly punk performers whose documentations attempt an unmediated presentation of the performance, Throbbing Gristle understood the power of propaganda and the manipulation of the image, and the video was released having been edited and with images such as syringes, a young woman's bottom in panties, and skulls, superimposed across occasionally colorised footage of the performance.

In addition the video is contextual via the use of footage shot within the school grounds, the corridors, and the dormitories, illustrating the constricted and carefully ritualised daily existence of the pupils. Like Lindsey Anderson's *If....*, the documentary captures the seditionary nature of youth left to its own devices, but the swirling mob chaos of the children reacting to Throbbing Gristle also recalls the feral boys of William Golding's novel, *Lord of the Flies*.

There are other live videos, other performances, but what makes this trio of films so essential is the way in which they document not just a live performance but the confrontational, radical nature of punk and post-punk subcultures. These films act as an affirmation of performance and of aesthetic radicalism, acting as a signature, and allowing viewers to pay witness to unique events.

Notes

1 Jon Savage, *England's Dreaming: Sex Pistols and Punk Rock*, Faber and Faber: London, 1991, p. 240.

2 Marian Kester and F-Stop Fitzgerald, *Dead Kennedys: The Unauthorized Version*, Last Gasp: San Francisco, 1983, p. 53.

3 Rowland S. Howard, 'Gimme Danger!' *World Art*, No. 19, 1998, p. 24.

4 Punk precursors such as the Stooges radically challenged the nature of band/audience relationships, as did The Doors, but the majority of rock bands in the sixties and early seventies still created a recognisable division between performer and viewer.

5 Howie Klein, in Lindsay Hutton, *The Cramps*, undated booklet.

6 Anonymous audience member cited in Howie Klein.

7 Johnny Cash's 1969 performance at San Quentin was filmed for Granada Television. *Johnny Cash in San Quentin* (Michael Darlow, 1969).

8 All quotes from Johnny and Hank come from personal communication with the author.

9 Target Video originally recorded music from 1978 onwards to broadcast on cable TV as well as to release on video.

WILD YOUTH:

Streetwise Punks and Street Gangs, Wasted Youth and Teenage Delinquents, Kids with Attitude... Thrill Crazy and Living for Kicks... Street Cred in Suburbia... Hanging out in your local cinema!

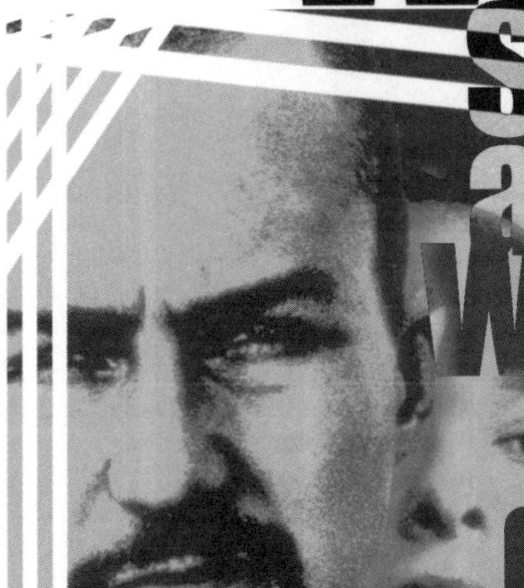

Chris Barber

punk: noun 1. *informal* a worthless person

(often used as a general term of abuse). A criminal or hoodlum. US (in prison slang) a passive male homosexual. An inexperienced young person; a novice. 2. (also punk rock) [*mass noun*] a loud, fast-moving, and aggressive form of rock music, popular in the late 1970s. (*also* punk rocker) [*count noun*] an admirer or player of such music, typically characterised by coloured spiky hair and clothing decorated with safety pins or zips. Derivatives: punkish *adjective*, punky *adjective*. Origin late 17th cent...perhaps, in some senses, related to archaic punk 'prostitute,' also to spunk. ***New Oxford Dictionary of English (Oxford University Press, 1999)***

In the US, the term 'punk' was in general use long before it was adopted by punk rock, most commonly to describe the members of youth street gangs and petty criminals who became part of the urban landscape from the 1950s. This connection in the amelioration of 'punk' was one reason the term appealed to punk rockers. Dick Hebdidge observes:

> This unlikely alliance of diverse and superficially incompatible music traditions, mysteriously accomplished under punk, found ratification in an equally eclectic clothing style which reproduced the same kind

> of cacophony on the visual level. The whole ensemble, literally safety-pinned together... Punk reproduced the entire sartorial history of post war working class youth cultures in "cut-up" form, combining elements which had originally belonged to completely different epochs.[1]

The generation of British youth who reached adolescence in the early 1960s were the first to grow up in a multi-racial Britain. Mods were working class lads who had lived with and embraced the cultural diversity offered by Afro-Caribbean communities, especially the music — modern jazz, soul, ska, and rhythm and blues. Initially inspired to emulate the elegant dress sense of jazz musicians, they wore slick two-piece suits with sartorial narrow trousers, pointed shoes, pressed shirts, thin-cut ties and Parka hooded jackets. Girls dressed boyish with darkened eyes. Both favoured short haircuts for a unisex look.

Most mods lived in London or southern England. They often had a Lambretta GT200 or Vespa GS160 scooter. They lived for weekends, when they popped purple hearts (amphetamine pills) for non-stop partying. Mods provoked public hysteria when their antics made tabloid headlines, following a series of massive gang fights against rockers in popular seaside resorts, including Brighton and Southend.

Quadrophenia (1979)

Franc Roddam directs the ultimate mod mode movie. It's set in 1963, the peak year for mods versus rockers warfare throughout many of England's finest and sunniest seaside resorts. Phil Daniels is perfectly cast as a cocky Cockney mod, becoming increasingly strung out on 'blues' (speed/amphetamine pills, legally prescribed for dieting at the time) and determined to be one of the gang. So it's off to Brighton for the weekend, with a bucket and spade... and a hand grenade! He thrusts himself into the action, determined to bloody his immaculate suit and confused manhood. He succeeds in proving his mod-ness against rocker-ness and is arrested for his efforts. Released in the aftermath, his sense of achievement turns hollow and identity crisis looms. His super-mod idol (played by Sting) is revealed to be a sham and the whole mod fashion fetish turns into fad fetish. There are some cool mod club sequences, and Toyah Wilcox renders a fine supporting performance. The film is loosely inspired by The Who's album, *Quadrophenia*. Aside from this, it's actually a damn fine youth gang flick.

Skinheads are one of the most controversial and enduring youth subcultures, their hardcore image spreading across Europe and the USA. It, too, was an image firmly rooted in 1960s British working class youth, and grew partly as a reaction against hippies. Initially, skinheads were inspired by black Jamaican music (reggae, soul and ska) and proudly defended their growing multi-racial, working class communities. But from the early 1970s, an economic slump resulting in high job losses and unemployment among the working class coincided with rising immigration. Rarely renowned for their deep political insights, skinheads began to blame the growing numbers of Asians and West Indians for the job shortage. This naïve presumption was quickly seized upon by re-emerging far right wing, nationalist and fascist political groups, who further propagated the message, recognising a fertile recruiting ground among disaffected youth. Hence began the long and insidious association between skinheads, dogmatic racist/fascist/nationalist fringe politics, and street violence (an association that took a generation to break in the UK). From the late 1970s, punk rock broadly appealed to skinheads. Many punk bands attracted skinhead contingents to their gigs, including Sham 69, Siouxsie and the Banshees, and Joy Division. At first these bands unwittingly encouraged their new fan base, but when skins were seen to be spreading racism and provoking violence at gigs, punk bands were quick to distance themselves from this following.

Classic skin attire comprises DMs (Doc Martens) or bovver boots (black or ox-blood, with twelve, sixteen, or more, eyelets), skin-tight bleached blue jeans, Fred Perry tennis shirts or Ben Sherman button-down collars, braces (red or white with matching bootlaces, once connoting allegiance to the National Front or British National Party), and green or black zipper bomber jackets; tattoos are very popular. Like later punk rockers, skinhead subculture proved to be exportable, appealing to disgruntled youths in many countries, as did the association between skins and nationalistic/racist politics. Skinhead gangs appeared in the US, Australia, Germany, the Czech Republic and France. Back in Britain, skinhead appeal outlasted its narrow political associations, finding renewed popular appeal on the gay scene. Actually, its growing association with gay fashion dates back to the mid 1980s, and increasing awareness of this probably contributed to the breaking of skin/racist association. Amusingly and less well known, homosexual tendencies among skinheads (in Britain) go back to the late 1970s, but were kept in the closet. As word leaked out, the National Front, a fascist party with a large skinhead membership, became known in some circles as the National Fairies for its clandestine homosexual activity!

It is interesting to compare issues raised by *Made in Britain* (UK), *Romper Stomper* (Australia) and *American History X* (US) — concerns of far-reaching social importance beyond their skinhead orientated plots, and emphatic degrees of social realism. All three films incite controversy and refuse to advocate simplistic solutions to the social problems they expose, utilising formal and stylistic aesthetic devices to this end. The film attracted some very dumb criticism, suggesting they might incite racial violence. Such criticism represents precisely what each film is vigilantly deriding: shortstop thinking. Each tackles head on the thorny and ugly spectre of racial violence, but recognise the insidious limitations of preaching to or patronising its audience. Racially motivated violence is not just the prerogative of naughty boys, whose lackadaisical parents neglected to tell them off. Organised racism has an agenda and attracts supporters because it offers easy solutions to deeply divisive, often complex and far-reaching, social issues. Those solutions are wrong, based on an ill-informed or perverted understanding of real causes. By dictating simple messages to people, fascists and their opponents do the same thing, but use different rhetoric. Each of these films goes further, exposing and exploring underlying social contradictions: there is no instant, quick fix remedy that will terminate the anger and resentment some people feel. They attempt to provoke spectators on all sides of the debate to think about and try to understand the real complexity underlying their existing social aggregate.

The critical theorist Walter Benjamin argued the difference between reactionary/negative (fascist) and progressive/positive (socialist) approaches to art, is that negative art is founded upon the aesthetisisation of politics and positive art is based on the politicisation of aesthetics. Aestheticisation of politics ultimately fails to change life for the better; it merely serves to embellish, elevate and glamorise the prevailing order, and create an illusion to make the spectator believe they can improve their quality of life. The politicisation of aesthetics aims for real, practical change and improvement in the spectator's circumstances; this can only be achieved by provoking the spectator to think hard for her or himself, to work out how to genuinely affect social improvement. *Made in Britain, Romper Stomper* and *American History X* are each productions that attempt to politicise aesthetics. So far as any of them fail by compromising this objective, it is *American History X*. This may be because its star, Edward Norton, persuaded the production company to sack the director, Tony Kaye, while the movie was in production. Kaye had secured a contract guaranteeing him sanction on the final cut. Norton wasn't happy with Kaye's direction and showed the rushes to studio executives, telling them he (Norton) could direct a more commercial final cut. The executives agreed, releasing Norton's final cut, which Kaye subsequently disowned.

Romper Stomper (1993)

A slick and brutal low budget Australian youth-sploitation movie, directed by Geoffrey Wright (who also made *Metal Skin* with Chris Odgers in 1994) and independently produced by the Australian Film Commission/Film Victoria/Seon Films. Russell Crowe plays Hando, a psychotic Nazi skinhead, in the film that made him a star. Beyond being a skinhead youth-sploitation movie, *Romper Stomper* attempts to tackle Australia's social and political problems in a period of economic depression creating high unemployment, while immigration into Australia from surrounding Pacific countries was soaring. Young working class Australians unable to find jobs blame the influx of cheap foreign labour (a disastrously simplistic misunderstanding of international economic circumstances in a nation established by immigrants who substantially wiped out the native population). As previously happened in the UK and USA, skinhead subculture became a breeding ground for reactionary, nationalist and fascist tendencies. In this sense, Australia's *Romper Stomper* is analogous to *Made in Britain* and *American History X*; when first released in Australia, *Romper Stomper* defied expectations. Its appeal was not limited to the youth/cult market — it was a phenomenal commercial success attracting mainstream audiences. Despite *Romper Stomper*'s cinematic embellishments and shocking violence, it depicts events and feelings commonly expressed in Australia at the time.

Romper Stomper wastes no time in getting down to disturbing violence, even before its opening title sequence. Three ethnic youths (a girl and two lads) skateboard along a railway platform and into the subway. Switch to slow motion sound and vision (not as an aesthetic device but to connote the victims point of view — pure fear) as a gang of skin bullies, drenched in skinhead gear and Nazi paraphernalia, lean over them, clearly intent on violence. "This is not your country," whispers Hando calmly to the girl. And thus it erupts, with sustained shocking, brutal and ruthless intensity; a hail of powerful punches, booted kicks and savage abuse. Just to slam home their attitude after the massacre, a close-up shot of a skinhead presents a fuck off hand signal to the spectator.

With a Vietnamese family taking over the local bar, the skinheads find a target on which to vent their frustration, and they plan their attack. The proprietors, however, have prepared for such an eventuality and for once the skins are caught unawares and outnumbered, surprised that anyone has had the audacity to fight back. The story then follows events in the aftermath, with some action 'on the beaches.'

Romper Stomper doesn't patronise the spectator with crass rhetoric or simplistic solutions, but requires the audience to think. Surprising then, that the BBFC thought the film could inspire racist violence. Less surprising that a lawyer defending a racist murderer in a British court case in 2004 claimed his skinhead client was corrupted after watching *Romper Stomper*! One is tempted to conjecture that anyone stupid or sick enough to perceive this film as incitement to violence should be securely locked away for his or her own safety.

American History X (2002)

American History X is a thought provoking and controversial American skinhead film, which contains savage urban violence and is remarkably well shot, directed (at least in part) by Tony Kaye. However, it's also over-long, employs conventional Hollywood audience emotional manipulation techniques, and the arty composition (flashbacks, b&w sequences, and slow motion) seems a little pretentious. The story is set in LA's Venice Beach suburban community, where an economic depression and soaring street crime is dividing neighbourhoods along racial lines. Edward Norton stars as Derek, a convincing angry and psychotic Nazi skinhead, who is left to look after his mother and teenage brother and sister, after his fireman father is killed in an accident. He falls under the influence of a local, middle-aged white supremacist, intent on stirring up racial hatred. Despite the protestations of his liberally minded mother and sister, Derek is idolised by his younger brother, Danny (Edward Furlong). Pumped up for violence and sporting a massive swastika tattoo on his chest, Derek rouses local youths to ruthlessly attack blacks and immigrants. He's incarcerated for three years for murdering a black thief and quickly adapts to the racially divided social microcosm inside the penitentiary. A bright lad, Derek begins to notice social contradictions and hypocrisy among his fellow white inmates, eventually provoking the white group to rape him. Befriended by a black prisoner,

Derek gradually undergoes a conversion of his attitudes, and when released, rejoins his family, committed to extricating himself from the Nazi skinhead group and saving his young brother — also now a racist skinhead — from emulating his mistakes. There's a well re-created Nazi skinhead party scene, with live bands and Hitler posters, from which Norton fights his way out at gunpoint. But it's bound to end tragically, with the sacrifice of his brother to atone his past.

Skinhead Attitude (2003)

This ninety-three minute documentary is a Swiss/German/French co-production. It's directed by Daniel Schweizer and was shot on mini Digital Video. It explores the origins and history of the skinhead movement in the UK and US from the 1960s, and includes interviews with Jimmy Pursey (of Sham 69), and musicians Laurel Aitken and Ian Stuart. The diverse range of skinhead attitudes is investigated, from neo-Nazis to skin fashion victims.

No Skin Off My Ass (1992)
Skin Flick (1999)

Canadian director Bruce LaBruce makes low budget, art/experimental, independently produced films, and is gay, sexuality being a pivotal issue in his work. His seminal influences include Derek Jarman, John Waters and Andy Warhol, and LaBruce identifies himself as a punk filmmaker, starring in some of his own movies. He shoots on Super-8, 16mm or Digital Video, incorporating playful homoerotic sequences that border on pornography.

Two of his films centre on queer depictions of skinheads. *No Skin Off My Ass* is the first film LaBruce directed, in which he also stars as a punk hairdresser. It's shot in b&w, lasting about seventy minutes. This is a fine, subversive and audacious debut film, which cost virtually nothing to make, except for film stock. Essentially it falls somewhere between a rip-off and homage to Paul Morrissey's Factory film, *Andy Warhol's Flesh*, in which the camera sexually fetishises a New York rent boy/hustler, played by Joe Dallesandro. LaBruce substitutes a sexy, baby-faced skinhead (Klaus von Brücker) as the object of his predatory camera. Hairdresser LaBruce picks him up from a park bench, takes him home, bathes and seduces him, then locks him in a bedroom. The guy escapes and visits his lesbian sister, concerned that he found the encounter exciting. "Queers are smart, skinheads are stupid," she tells him, and sends him back. In the skinhead's absence, the hairdresser has been fantasising about humiliating him, but is distracted by the moral implications of his desire. Remembering he is effete and the skinhead is butch further confuses the hairdresser. But they're soon reunited for more games…

No Skin Off My Ass also recalls Robert Altman's *That Cold Day in the Park* (1969). Bruce LaBruce claims "I wanted to make a film that would make a skinhead really mad." After this auspicious debut, LaBruce continued to employ punk aesthetics for his superb *Super Eight and a Half* (1993), an experimental, tongue-in-cheek parody based on the life of Andy Warhol. After directing *Hustler White*, his first colour feature, with a modest budget, LaBruce returned to filming queer skinheads in *Skin Flick*. Sadly, this messy picture isn't worth the DV tape it is shot on. Made in Britain, there are two versions of *Skin Flick*: a substantially censored cut, which got a short release in Britain, and a hardcore pornographic version, which failed to get certificated by the BBFC. Never mind, it's really not worth the effort!

Punk Rockers

Punk was never just a youth fashion trend; it was anti-fashion! Although several internationally renowned fashion designers established their careers on designing punk clothing (most importantly, Vivienne Westwood), punk fashion trends were eclectic, inspired by various unrelated sources and DIY aesthetic sensibilities. Punk rockers utilised and recycled what was cheap, functional and ready-to-hand. In *The Filth and the Fury*, Johnny Rotten explains how the proliferation of plastic black refuge sacks strewn around urban streets during the national dustmen strike inspired him to wear a bin-liner, as a punk statement. The punk singer Ian Drury first wore safety pins, simultaneously as a cheap and practical means to repair old/damaged clothes, and a statement of punk's anti-fashion credentials (zips got similar treatment). Punk's controversial fashion sense also involved shock tactics, to challenge people's fears and thoughtless conformity to socially dictated dress codes. Siouxsie (of the Banshees) highlighted this by wearing a Nazi SS armband during her early live performances, for which she attracted a barrage of criticism. The Banshees were also probably the first punk band to incorporate tartan patterns, especially in punky trousers. Malcolm McLaren and Vivienne Westwood's fashion entourage incorporated bits of leather fetish and bondage gear from Soho sex shops. Many of Westwood's fabulous punk designs collaged bits'n'pieces from a wide range of utilitarian sources. Her 1977 Parachute shirt straps a jump harness to a military shirt; the Two Cowboys 1977 T-shirt was inspired by ripping off fetish wear designs (in this instance the pornographic illustration copies Tom of Finland's stylised eroticism); the Tits T-shirt of 1976 consists of a photo stolen from an American tourist souvenir shirt, and the Destroy 1977 T-shirt comprises a crude nihilistic slogan juxtaposed against a swastika and Maoist badges. Army surplus stores picked up a roaring trade, supplying a generation of punk rockers (and later post industrialists) with cheap, hardwearing, functional clothing. That the anti-uniformity, DIY aesthetic worked for punk rockers is clear by the speed with which other punk groups got the message and produced their own punk designs, rather than procuring ready-mades from Westwood's range; The Clash, for example, in their two-piece suits spray-painted like Jackson Pollock paintings, or their Brigate Rosse T-shirts.

Sadly, but inevitably, as punk rock reached wider audiences a fashionable, off-the-shelf punk clothing range was bound to establish a more uniform expression. Black leather motorbike jackets, leather trousers or tight black denims, and studded bondage belts, are some of the items that became punk fashion accessories; it has been suggested that Sid Vicious is to blame for these particular items becoming so widely worn, being his preferred outfit for live performances, as it had been his punk fan clobber before he joined the Pistols.

With regard to social structures, punk rockers tended (as in most punk concerns) to be more complex than other youth cults, a way of life rather than just fashion. Group dynamics veer towards tribalism, a very robust sense of camaraderie but with emphasis on individual/personal expression. Unlike most gang subcultures, equality between lasses and lads, regardless of sexuality, is broadly taken for granted and racism is frowned upon. Punk rockers first appeared on London's streets amidst a teddy boy/rock'n'roll revivalist fad, leading to frequent aggressive confrontations between the two groups. But retro-teds looked increasingly sad and ridiculous, and soon scurried back to their nice suburban estates. A more problematic and mutating relationship existed between punk rockers and skinheads. There was a mutual respect for shared values, like the championing of working class culture and authenticity of lifestyles confronting social exclusion. But punk politics was firmly entrenched with left-wing and anarchistic causes, particularly anti-racism; sometimes leading to violent street clashes with right-wing orientated skins (reflected in both Britain and American subcultures).

Suburbia (1984)

After her spellbinding and angry first LA punk rockumentary, *The Decline of Western Civilization* (1981), featuring Black Flag, X, The Circle Jerks, and Fear, and capturing the explosive excitement and sustained intensity of their gigs, it was clear that Penelope Spheeris had real punk attitude and street cred... *Suburbia* is the punk-perfect follow-up, a rough'n'raw edged, realist youth-sploitation narrative, employing real runaway and homeless punk youths picked from the streets of Los Angeles. Brutal violence and a tragic end more than compensate for occasional sentimentality. Producer Roger Corman again demonstrates he has his finger on the pulse of transient youth subculture. Made on a low budget, with DIY aesthetic sensibility, the movie captures the savage hypocrisy, gross unfairness and — for many — relentless misery of Reagan-ite America.

The intense excitement of live punk rock gigs (again) becomes the central focus of the unfolding narrative, with blinding performances by West Coast favourites T.S.O.L. and The Vandals; there's also an acting debut for Red Hot Chili Peppers bassist, Flea (as Razzle).

The running time (of ninety-nine minutes) is a little over the usual ninety minute genre threshold, and four or five minutes of extra snipping here and there could have benefited the pacing; also, some subtly positioned backlighting on the natural darkness scenes would not go amiss.

Suburbia is ultimately just a cheap, realist youth-sploitation movie but a particularly fine and well-executed example of the genre. It demonstrates a focused understanding and familiarity with the genre's conventions and skilfully exploits the spectator's expectations. It starts with a clearly defined, blank character vehicle to latch onto — Evan (Bill Coyne) — hastily exemplifies what he must escape (a dysfunctional family home), and provides a motif for his later return (a younger brother he cares for, but cannot help until he proves to himself he can take responsibility). Further, Evan is a young adolescent, ripe for initiation into adulthood. We can assume similar circumstances motivate the rest of the (aptly named) Rejected gang. A series of chance incidents eventuate in offering Evan a particular opportunity, which he takes...

Jokes and amusing moments occur with well-paced regularity, as do outbursts of violence, which occasionally border on shocking. There are also frequent, very well-filmed diegetic music sequences (in tune with *The Decline of Western Civilization*). Outfits, hairstyles, ages, and general attitudes also broadly reflect contemporary aspects of alternative youth culture. The narrative builds to an exciting, climactic showdown in which 'good' briefly appears to triumph, but victory is pyrrhic. Evan is successfully initiated into manhood, but forced to make a sacrifice (his younger brother).

The extra dimension to *Suburbia* is certainly the use of real young punks, living in a similar environment to that depicted. On the whole their acting is very convincing, better than the actors used in many youth-sploitation flicks and upholding the neo-realist tradition. Attention to social realism gives the movie sociological interest, as does the insight into youth motivation. The nasty, comic strip, beer-monster local rednecks (parents) offer a suitable counterpoint reflecting the dominant conservative ideology of the time.

In this instance it's a little churlish to draw attention to its being directed by a woman (aged thirty-four at the time), the punk movement being renowned (as a rule) for taking sexual equality as given, with the minimum of fuss. Gender may cast a shadow over *Suburbia*'s slightly better developed female characters, nudity that is used subtly (but not absent), and more cute male characters, all unusual to this genre but producing a fine film.

In 1987, Spheeris assembled another gang of three New York punk rockers, as *Dudes*. Biscuit, Grant and Milo set off for Hollywood in a clapped-out car, but their tiresome journey gets waylaid by freak events in the Mid Western plains... By which time, sadly, Spheeris has lost her punk touch.

Breaking Glass (1980)

Shabby and silly British punk youth-sploitation movie, directed by Brian Gigson (who also wrote the screenplay); Hazel O'Connor stars as an angst-ridden punk singer on a meteoric rise to stardom, supported by Phil Daniels. The so-called 'punk' soundtrack comprises songs written for the movie, several of which won O'Connor success in the real pop charts. There's even an attempt to get political, with some extras playing Nazi skinheads and smashing up one of O'Connor's shows (pity they didn't destroy the whole film set!).

Other Youth Cultures

An emphasis on personal expression and a broad affinity with preceding youth cultures, along with a wider awareness of alternative art and politics, attributed punk rockers with greater self-awareness than any urban youth movement since the Beatniks. In a sense, punk was the ultimate youth subculture, a truly avant-garde movement prepared, in the first instance, to borrow from and offer homage to previous youth movements, but ultimately to build critiques of these traditions, culminating in auto-critique. Punk's relentless nihilism turned towards itself, questioning its own existence and relationship to wider society. By adopting an alternative, outsider lifestyle, punks forced their own definitions and boundaries into lived experience — enlightenment which turned in on itself and made futile its own existence as a counterculture. Inevitably, punk splintered apart under its own momentum, inspiring the emergence of a cornucopia of smaller, clique youth cults, and affinities to alternative ethnic youth subcultures.

The trans-Atlantic post-punk roots rock scene (inspired by bands like The Cramps and The Gun Club) was another stylised melange of exaggerated, earlier youth styles. For all its nostalgia, it bore only fleeting hints of original American greasers pertaining to the 1950s and 1960s. Goths borrowed from nineteenth century romanticism and the French symbolists, with their emphasis on black clothes, deathly make-up and tiresome obsession with anything morbid. They found musical affinity in the likes of The Cure and Siouxsie and the Banshees, and realising persistent cinematic expression in Tim Burton's movies. The soul boy revival sent formerly mod-ish punk rockers scurrying to boutiques for pleated disco slacks and pressed button-up shirts. They got the message from bands like Talking Heads and Dexy's Midnight Runners that revivals of James Brown and Marvin Gaye were well overdue. Post industrialists are harder to define — more elitist, more outsider, and ultimately a more hardcore punk transition. Stomping boots, grey or khaki utilitarian clothing and shaven-headed machismo suggested more than a hint of Soviet Constructivism, relaxing to sweet melodies from The Fall and Test Dept.

Rude boys are deviant, black youths who formed gangs in Jamaica from the mid 1960s. Having only recently gained independence from Britain and elected a radical socialist government, Jamaica was in a state of flux. Rude boys represented the new, flashy and ostentatious bad boy image, wearing bright and gaudy jackets with big collars, displaying colourful and flowing top-pocket hankies, a prominent medallion on a chunky chain and massive flat-peaked caps. They frequently earned cash from criminal activities, like black market trading, drug dealing or pimping, and many carried guns.

In the same period, there was massive emigration from Jamaica and the West Indies to the UK, encouraged by the British government to meet the demand for cheap manual labour. Around areas like London's Notting Hill, black communities grew and (for the most part) integrated well with white working class neighbourhoods. But the harsh life of drudgery many West Indians found in Britain didn't live up to the promises made by government propaganda. The hardships experienced by many blacks settling in Britain and raising families were directly reflected in the development of reggae music. Reggae also incorporated influences from earlier periods of black history. With their indigenous cultures brutally repressed by slave owners, their histories and cultures were passed on covertly amongst slaves, who were forced to convert as a method of control. But as generations of blacks learned to read and interpret the Bible, the contradictions with their role as slaves became apparent and they adopted their own secret and rebellious interpretations. These eclectic sources converged in Rastafarianism. Rastas believe Bible prophecies had been realised with Haille Selassie's accession to the throne of Ethiopia in 1930, signalling the imminent downfall of 'Babylon' (white colonial power), and the exodus of blacks back to Africa and Zion. Red, green and gold, the colours of the Ethiopian flag, represent the 'roots' of West Indians in Africa. For years, the Rastafarian religion was repressed in Jamaica, but when the Manley government won power in the 1960s, a more sympathetic climate ensued. Rastafarians also ritualistically believe in smoking ganja or 'weed,' wearing the 'dreadlock' (reflecting the lion's mane), and khaki camouflage. By the early 1970s, reggae was becoming the dominant musical expression in Jamaica and spreading among youths in London's West Indian communities. In the latter environment, reggae had a significant impact on young pre-punk rockers, including later members of the Sex Pistols and The Clash, who would promote its popularity among white youth.

The Harder They Come (1972)

The first Jamaican feature film and reggae musical is this sensational and violent youth street crime movie. It's a real shit-kicking little masterpiece. Directed, produced and co-written by Perry Henzell, with a $400,000 budget raised from business proprietors, it's shot to take full advantage of the island's remarkable exterior sunlight and naturalist locations, with stark and gritty realism you can almost smell. It stars reggae singer Jimmy Cliff as Ivanhoe Martin, a country boy moving to the big city (Kingston) after granny snuffs it (based on Rhygin, a real local folk hero and gunman in the 1950s). "You can get it if you really want...tra-la-la-boom-di-boom-di..." He's robbed of all his belongings, can't find work and is forced to live in an old car wreck. Eventually, a nutty fundamentalist preacher employs him as a handyman, but shoves him around and exploits him. Ivan starts dating Elsa (Janet Bartley), the preacher's ward. Preacher discovers he plays his reggae music in the church, so sacks him for it. He catches some twat trying to steal his bike, so slashes up his face and winds up doing time. Back out, he moves into Elsa's pad and persuades a bigwig record producer to record him performing. When the fat recordings boss rips off his music, Ivan's back to rock bottom. Next he tries dealing grass, but his partner sets him up for the local corrupt pigs. A gunfight ensues and Ivan escapes, leaving several dead plods behind. He's wanted and on the run, but still exploited by the record producer, who releases the record to take advantage of the singer's fugitive notoriety. It's a smash hit, but not for Ivan, who's planning his escape from Jamaica on a boat. But Elsa betrays him to the fuzz, forcing Ivan into a dramatic gunfight with the cops.

Cliff also provides a cool reggae soundtrack. It contains one of the nastiest blade-to-face carve-up scenes ever, and a prolonged and stunningly photographed gospel choir sequence in a ramshackle church. The film uses fast-cut jump-cuts and utilises frequent pop art references in shot backgrounds which, along with the plot, sometimes recall Godard's *Breathless*. Three years after its release, the film was banned in Jamaica after the police told the government it was causing imitation crimes. It's shot on super 16mm then blown up to 35mm, and a real one off!

Babylon (1980)

A tough and depressing British flick about a Rasta having a bad day. *Babylon* is set and shot entirely on location in the streets of Brixton. The director, Franco Rosso, is Italian, and there's a reggae soundtrack pulsing throughout. This production began as a TV play commissioned by the BBC, but after several script rewrites, they decided it was too good and should get a theatrical release. Brinsley Forde is a petulant young Rasta, sporting full 'lion-of-Zion' garb, who loses his job, then gets chased and beaten by the filth. At least he's still got his sound system safe in a garage up the road; he can go and calm his nerves with a spliff and bit of dub… Or not. The garage has been busted into and the system is well smashed up! … And it seems he has stabbed the gent responsible with a screwdriver… More gritty realism, shuffling along at a pace, with irony and a sense of humour; this captures Brixton's street life when Rasta subculture was at its peak.

Beyond Street Gangs

In his novel *Fathers and Sons*, the nineteenth century Russian writer, Ivan Turgenev, highlights the growing rift in values between different generations. However far back and deeply rooted in human nature these generation rifts go, Turgenev is warning that the vastly increasing pace of socio-cultural change approaching the twentieth century brings with it generation rifts with far greater violent and disruptive potential than previously experienced. After WWII, the radical shift in socio-economic lifestyles among the majority of people in the developed world brings Turgenev's warning into focus.

Before the war, lifestyles changed little and slowly between parents and their children. Youths wore similar clothes to those of their parents, ate the same food, shared similar cultural interests and expected to do analogous jobs. Following the war, those who had risked their lives and fought for their country demanded a greater stake in the proceeds, more cash and more leisure time. The postwar boom and economic prosperity could afford this, and dramatic social transformation ensued. But the younger generation demanded even more for their newfound disposable incomes and free time; they wanted their own fashions and styles, music and movies. In capitalist societies, the market and culture industry rushed to meet this demand. In the US and Europe during the 1950s, there was a polarisation between young and old generations. Youth adopted new values, clothes and lifestyles, becoming unrecognisable to their parents. Their parents were filled with fear of this monstrous Other: their youth seemed completely out of control. But the generation gap was here to stay, and as subsequent generations became parents themselves, the initial shock was less pronounced; parents better understood the rebellious spirit of youth.

The film industry turned to both portray the new phenomenon and capture the new market with *The Wild One* in 1954. Thus commenced the first cycle of delinquent youth and gang movies, which ran through the 1960s. But these were made by an older generation, tending to lack understanding and preaching stark moral warnings to young rebels. After the watershed of hippies and the flower power generation (a product of that decrepit social anomaly, the nuclear family) failing to bring about the social transformation they promised, and a few notable films like *Jubilee* in the 1970s, the box-office success of *The Warriors* in 1979 sparked off a new cycle of more sociologically enlightened youth gang movies.

Whether re-interpreting recent history, or celebrating the re-emergence of youth anger and contemporary gangs (like *Suburbia*), this new generation of films concentrates on a handful of omnipotent concerns: male bonding and camaraderie, friendship and peer groups, rites of passage and coming-of-age, identity and fashion, group aggressive narcissism and pan-tribalism, social alienation and territorial instincts, and state law and community ethics. These concerns are shared by the following, final films in this section — youth gang films — which do not fit comfortably into the subsections hitherto mentioned.

Over the Edge (1979)

An American delinquent/bad boy youth-sploitation movie, directed by Jonathon Kaplan. *Over the Edge* is low budget, independent production qualities sometimes border on delightful amateurness and naïvety. But its brazen attempts to go for the jugular with cheap sensationalist shock tactics, while maintaining an aura of critical social realism, is rather seductive. If talent spotting beyond the film industry's usual confines ever needs justification, the young Matt Dillon says it all (as Richie) in this, his first movie (Dillon was discovered by scouts at Hommocks School and asked to audition). High school hijinks involving drugs and

Colorado's street-fighting boys, with knives and guns, bring a bit of real excitement to a stultifying suburban existence. When released, the movie generated a bit of tabloid outrage, but the film soon drifted into obscurity. Tim Hunter, who went on to direct *River's Edge*, writes the screenplay.

River's Edge (1987)

The naked strangled body of a teenage girl lies by a river's edge, murdered by her boyfriend, Samson 'John' Tollette (Daniel Roebuck). All her former friends know about the body and the identity of the boy who killed her, but nobody does anything about it… Why?

That's the basic who-dunnit plot premise, but this is a red herring for a why-not-do-it… something, anything (to maximise the exploitation potential of this ruse, neither the murderer's identity nor the knowledge pertaining to the kids is revealed to the spectator at the earliest opportunity, which stinks of Hitchcock). Tim Hunter directs *River's Edge*. It was released to a fanfare of critical acclaim, unusual for a youth-sploitation movie — a genre that mainstream critics tend to ignore unless there's a shocking or controversial angle, for which the film should be banned! But praise in the mainstream press guaranteed commercial success. There are several reasons why it appealed to populist critics: *First*, it refuses to conform to the usual conventions, clichés and expectations associated with the youth-sploitation genre. *Second*, the film explores new, unexpected and intelligent variations, contrasting with popular models. *Third*, it attempts to seriously grapple with contemporary, much misunderstood youth trends in today's real world; the alienation and nihilism felt by youth, the breakdown of loyalty among friends, a lack of commitment to the social and neglect of youth camaraderie (the post-social condition?). Willingness to confront these trends offers an insight into misunderstood youth. *Fourth*, it is very competently made, with attention to shot composition, editing, narrative development, consistently realist believability and cross-genre referencing.

All the adolescents are from fucked-up homes and are left largely to their own devices, in a backwater town where nothing happens. Some of the gang are too drunk, drug-fucked, or busy getting laid, to respond to their friend's murder. There's nothing to hint at any affinity between the kids and Tollette, the murderer, or any desire to protect him. And if the murderer intimidated or threatened any of his victim's friends, it has completely slipped their minds.

In Milpitas, California in 1981, an incident involving analogous events actually occurred. This immediately inspired Neal Jimenez to write the screenplay for *River's Edge*, but it was several years before anyone would finance the project.

Dennis Hopper is superbly cast as Feck, rendering another one of his extraordinary eccentric performance pieces as a mono-legged 1960s hangover and hop-along, who's found his perfect soulmate and sex partner — a rubber inflatable doll. A man amongst boys, he demonstrably prefers hanging out with naughty, drug-taking adolescents. Crispin Glover plays Layne, the petulant leader of the pack, undergoing an existential crisis because he can't decide whether to be neurotic or psychotic. Keanu Reeves, the perfect space-filler whose mere presence improves any movie, here gets his perfect role as Matt (young, dumb and full of cum, same as he ever was). Ione Skye plays Clarissa and Joshua Miller is somebody or other's brother.

Life goes on... Some of the younger kids might be too feral even to be disaffected, don't know who to tell or are waiting for their peers to set an example — rather like *Waiting for Godot* with this bunch. Layne seems to be developing some sort of teenage dementia, so there's a vital lack of leadership and apparently nobody willing or able to replace him. The casual never-say-no-to-drugs attitude and quotidian, disaffected lifestyles adopted by the gang would engender an understandable reluctance to turn to the police. But come on! If that's the rules of your game, then you've also got a contingency group strategy to face off this sort of catastrophe. Or pull together and conspire in one fucking fast. Lack of communication is a gross understatement here and something this gang has developed into a fine art. The eerily alienated planet they inhabit doesn't hint at gang within gang conspiracies, or even much in the way of personal secrets.

Living in a small-minded small town off the beaten track, where folks keep too much to themselves and can't even mind their own business for fear of prying, it's boring and uneventful. At least this is to be assumed in the absence of contrary evidence. Doubtless there are hidden secrets and guilt, but nobody cares anyway. This is the ambience the movie constructs, a place where spite is endemic and the spiteful don't realise they are — they're too bored, imprisoned by ennui. It's an ambience rarely evoked in cinema and less often achieved. Some of those French art types pull it off; Cluzot did it in something and Claude Chabrol made a career out of it. There is no social... and there is no gang, this is post-gang-land and the gang is just kids playing. So how can anything else in their lives be real? Little kids do not do shock well — everything looks fine, like nothing happened, because for kids, nothing did.

Kids (1995)

Director Larry Clark and screenwriter Harmony Karine attempt to get up close to the estranged social dynamics of a gang of young New Yorkers — close enough to spark a wave of media controversy and public debate when the film was released. It highlights the moral confusion and hypocrisy among a group of youths, where friendship seems to be used merely to promote self-interest. Sexual promiscuity in the age of AIDS becomes a depressingly pertinent issue, suggesting that parents and schools are refusing to face up to the way kids behave in the modern age of social fragmentation, so education is failing in its responsibility. Creating its own distinctive cinematic style, *Kids* is simultaneously fascinating, infuriating and worrying. Karine later developed his own mesmerising directorial style, confronting the hopelessness of youth in America's poorest forgotten post-communities, in *Gummo* (1997). Clark returns to analogous themes in *Bully* and *Ken Park* (2002). All are serious cinematic treats!

Fight Club (1999)

The ultimate post-gang street violence movie! With the whole thrust of this book, unequivocally championing the superior qualities and innovation of low budget, independent, exploitation and underground cinema, it's something of a shock to rank a Hollywood movie, with a block-busting budget, up there with the finest. But there are exceptions to every rule, and the rules of *Fight Club* produce a new *Citizen Kane*, punching its way into this millennium. Not only does it go beyond every street gang movie (to date), its exudes punk attitude and street cred, despite its high production values, and absence of spiky haircuts and three-chord riffs. Watching *Fight Club*, you get the feeling that the cat is finally out of the bag — that some dark and dangerous secret, concealed for centuries, is finally and irretrievably exposed. This is pure cinema, a film you can watch again and again, discovering something new and transforming your previous interpretations with each viewing. It's a movie that asks and provokes endless profound questions, but dogmatically refuses to offer the spectator any clear-cut or proscriptive answers. *Fight Club* is a deeply cathartic and subversive viewing experience, which, if you go with it, strips you — and society — to the core, casting every belief into doubt. If any film can possibly change your life, this one will.

Laura Ziskin, a production president at Fox2000 Pictures, augmented the film project after reading the *Fight Club* novel by Chuck Palahniuk. Palahniuk claims his novel is

> based on stories my friends told me and stunts we pulled together... looking for the themes, the topics that brought people together in excited conversation. The longing for fathers... The resentment of lifestyle standards imposed by advertising... The goal... to write a novel based on being with people and listening to them... much of *Fight Club* was written in public, at parties, in bars, at the gym, at work.

But Ziskin was not convinced the novel could be filmed until another production president, Kevin McCormick, read it. He insisted there was a potential movie and was supported by Joshua Donen at Altman Entertainment. The novel was passed around movie executives, but they were divided over its movie potential, until Ross Grason Bell (producer) read it: "What really drew my attention was the underlying theme that you have to break yourself apart to build something new." He was determined it would make a movie and taped a read-through of the book, re-arranging it to be more linear. Jim Uhls was asked to write the screenplay: "It's about numbness and alienation and finding self-empowerment through drastic means." Bell also passed the novel to David Fincher. Fincher, whose previous movies include *Alien^3* and

Se7en, both big budget studio pictures, directs *Fight Club*.

It stars Brad Pitt, perfectly cast as Tyler Durden. As well as being stunningly good looking, Pitt had established his acting credentials, bringing particular presence to rebellious, offbeat and unpredictable characters, and exploiting bisexual appeal. Edward Norton (of *American History X*) also stars, as Jack. Jack's an insomniac and seriously pissed off with his repetitive insurance job, but it pays for his plush apartment and cosy lifestyle. He finds some relief from his anxiety by joining evening therapy groups, alongside strangers with serious problems he doesn't share. Jack has a chance encounter with Tyler Durden, who claims to be a soap salesman, and is immediately intrigued by his eccentric demeanour. They exchange business cards, and soonafter Jack is embroiled in Durden's bizarrely alternative lifestyle, which most significantly involves them fighting each other, and then other people. As the ferocity of the fights grows, an intense male camaraderie develops with homoerotic undertones…

Notes

1 Dick Hebdidge, *Subculture: The Meaning of Style*, London: Methuen & Co, 1979, p. 26.

Lester Bangs, *Psychotic Reactions and Carburetor Dung*, Heinemann: Lon, 1988

Walter Benjamin, *Understanding Brecht*, Verso: Lon, 1977

Ronald Bergan & Robyn Karney, eds, *Foreign Film Guide*, Bloomsbury: Lon, 1988

Luis Buñuel, *My Last Breath*, Fontana: Lon, 1985

William Burroughs, *Exterminator*, Corgi: Lon, 1976

Jayne County with Rupert Smith, *Man Enough To Be A Woman*, Serpent's Tail: Lon, 1995

Michael Coveney, *The World According to Mike Leigh*, Harper Collins: Lon, 1997

Steven Paul Davies, *Sid and Nancy. Love Kills: the Making of Sid & Nancy*, Eye: Screen Press/Momentum Pictures, 2000

Raymond Durgnat, Luis Buñuel, Berkeley: University of California, 1967

Derek Elley, ed, *Variety Movie Guide '97*, Hamlyn: Lon, 1996

Simon Field, ed, various, *Afterimage*, 12 Autumn 1985

Karl & Philip French, *Cult Movies*, Pavilion: Lon, 1999

Christian Fuchs, *Bad Blood*, Creation: Lon, 2002

Dick Hebdidge, *Subculture: The Meaning of Style*, Methuen & Co: Lon, 1979.

Stewart Home, *Cranked Up Really High: Genre Theory And Punk Rock*, Codex: Hove, 1995

Sarah Jacobson, 'The Expose of a Cult Phenomenon' in *Grand Royal Magazine*, No. 6, 1997

Derek Jarman, *Dancing Ledge*, Quartet: Lon, 1984

—, *Kicking The Pricks*, Vintage: Lon, 1996

Stefan Jaworzyn, ed, *Shock Xpress 1*, Titan: Lon, 1991

—, *Shock Xpress 2*, Titan: Lon, 1994

Andrea Juno & V Vale, eds, *ReSearch no: 10 Incredibly Strange Films*, RE/Search: San Francisco, 1986

Chris Kraus & Sylvere Lotringer, *Hatred of Capitalism*, Semiotext(e): NY, 2001

Tom Dewe Mathews, *Censored*, Chatto & Windus: Lon, 1994

Legs McNeil & Gillian McCain, *Please Kill Me: The Uncensored Oral History of Punk*, Grove Press: NY, 1996

Brendan Mullen with Don Bolles & Adam Parfrey, *Lexicon Devil: The Fast Times And Short Life of Darby Crash and the Germs*, Feral House: Los Angeles, 2002

Kim Newman, *Nightmare Movies*, Harmony: NY, 1988

Friedrich Nietzsche, *The Will to Power*, Vintage: NY, 1967

Craig O'Hara, *The Philosophy of Punk*, AK Press: San Francisco, 1999

Danny Peary, ed, *Omni's Screen Flights and Screen Fantasies*, Doubleday & Co: NY, 1984

Hans Richter, *The Struggle for the Film*, Gower: Aldershot, 1986

Penny Rimbaud (aka J J Ratter), *Shibboleth: My Revolting Life*, AK Press: Lon, 1998

Rudy Rucker, RU Sirius & Queen MU, *Mondo: A User's Guide to the New Edge*, Thames & Hudson: Lon, 1992

Jack Sargeant, *Deathtripping: The Cinema of Transgression*, Creation: Lon, 1995

—, *Cinema Contra Cinema*, Fringecore: BVD, 1999

Jon Savage, *England's Dreaming: Sex Pistols and Punk Rock*, Faber & Faber: Lon, 1991

Luda & Jean Schnitzer and Marcel Martin, *Cinema in Revolution*, Farrar, Stravs & Giroux, 1973

Jay Slater, *Eaten Alive*, Plexus: Lon, 2002

Marc Spitz & Brendan Mullen, *We Got The Neutron Bomb: The Untold story of L.A. Punk*, Three Rivers: NY, 2001

Jack Stevenson, *Addicted*, Creation: Lon, 2000

Stephen Thrower, ed, *Eyeball Compendium*, FAB: Godolming, 2003

Parker Tyler, *Underground Film: A Critical History*, Da Capo: NY, 1995

David Thomson, ed, *A Biographical Dictionary of Film*, Andre Deutsch: Lon, 1995

Gee Vaucher, *Crass Art and Other Pre Post-Modernist Monsters*, AK Press: Lon, 1999

John Waters, *Shock Value*, Dell: NY, 1981

Peter Wollen, *Readings and Writings*, Verso: Lon, 1982

Contributors

Chris Barber [w] chrisbarber.eu is a freelance author, editor and copywriter, and graduate in Philosophy with Film Studies. He was involved with various punk bands and underground filmmakers. As a journalist and reviewer he has written extensively on film, travel, true crime and alternative culture, for *QX* magazine, *FilmFour*, *Eyeball*, etc. Also contributed chapters to several books. He now lives between Barcelona and London.

Mark Hejnar co-founded Fast'n'Loud, a punk rock radio show in Chicago in 1983. He directed the award winning videos *Affliction* (1996), *TV Ministry* (1997), *Herd Mentality* (1998) and *Proxy* (2001). He is currently editing a documentary on the late scum rocker GG Allin in his studio in Bangkok, Thailand.

Tessa Hughes-Freeland is a filmmaker and writer. Her films have been screened internationally in museums, alternative spaces and seedy bars. Her articles have appeared in numerous books and magazines such as *Paper Magazine*, *Filmmaker Magazine*, *G.Q.*, *Film Threat* and *The East Village Eye*. She is also the co-founder of The New York Film Festival Downtown.

Richard J. King This ex-Zanti Misfitz/Turnpike Cruisers frontman spent around fifteen years working for the Jettisoundz/Visionary video label and was involved in recording over 200 gigs. He later managed independent movie video label Screen Edge, and has written extensively about music and video. Currently writing sleeve notes and fronting rumblin'-voodoo-punk band RazorDog.

David McGillivray wrote several exploitation films (*House of Whipcord*, *Frightmare*, etc.) in the 1970s. After more than twenty years as Julian Clary's gag-writer, he has recently returned to horror with a series of shorts: *Child Number Four*, *Mrs Davenport's Throat*, *Wednesday*, *In the Place of the Dead* and others.

Born in a condemned hospital on the outskirts of Glasgow in 1966, things just got better for 'human maggot' **Gavin Mitchell**. Who is, despite all of this, "one of the least interesting people you could ever wish to meet" — *Country Life* magazine. Currently in part-time exile and, it's rumoured, in hiding from his pimp.

Neil Palmer is a writer, researcher and musician. Current special interests include, asymmetric culture, literary history, fictive intelligence, rock'n'roll music and how people articulate their sense of the past and the future. Contact [e] palmerneil@hotmail.com

Besides being author of numerous articles, essays, and books on underground film, true crime, fringe cultures, strange behaviour and human folly, **Jack Sargeant** has lectured widely on various subjects ranging from avant-garde cinema to bestiality. In addition he curates film festivals and art shows. Jack currently divides his time between the Northern and Southern hemispheres.

Lance Sinclair is currently a member of The New Wave Hookers. He has contributed to numerous music publications as well as true crime books including *Death Cults: Murder, Mayhem and Mind Control* and *Bad Cop/Bad Cop*.

Stephen Thrower is the author of *Beyond Terror: The Films of Lucio Fulci*, and the editor of *The Eyeball Compendium*. His next book, *Nightmare, USA*, is currently in preparation from FAB Press. The Clash were always shit, and the first This Heat album kicks Johnny Rotten's pimply butt. Tatu forever!

Index of Film Titles